From the *New York Times* bestselling author of *Leaving the World* comes the riveting story of a woman who seemingly has it all, until the man she trusted the most threatens to take it all away.

ABOUT AN HOUR AFTER I MET TONY Hobbs, he saved my life. Thirty-seven-year-old American journalist Sally Goodchild quite literally married her hero. Both foreign correspondents, both on assignment in Cairo, they quickly fell in love and settled into domestic life in London. From the outset, Sally's relationship with Tony and her adopted city was an uneasy one——as she found both to be far more unfamiliar than imagined. But her adjustment problems are soon overshadowed by a troubled pregnancy. When she goes into premature labor, there are doubts whether her child will survive unscathed. And then, out of nowhere, Sally is hit by an appalling postpartum depression——a descent into a temporary, but very personal hell, which even sees her articulating a homicidal thought against her baby. However, when she does manage to extricate herself from this desperate state, she finds herself in a fresh new nightmare, as she discovers that the man she thought knew her better than anyone——loved her more than anyone——now wants to take away the very thing closest to her heart.

A SPECIAL RELATIONSHIP

A NOVEL

DOUGLAS KENNEDY

ATRIA PAPERBACK
New York London Toronto Sydney

ATRIA PASERBACK

A Division of Simon & Schuster, Inc.
1230 Avenue of the Americas
New York, NY 10020

Originally published in Great Britain in 2003 by Hutchinson

First Atria Paperback edition January 2011

ATRIA PAPERBACK and colophon are trademarks of Simon & Schuster, Inc.

For information about special discounts for bulk purchases, please contact Simon & Schuster Special Sales at 1-866-506-1949 or business@simonandschuster.com.

The Simon & Schuster Speakers Bureau can bring authors to your live event. For more information or to book an event, contact the Simon & Schuster Speakers Bureau at 1-866-248-3049 or visit our website at www.simonspeakers.com.

Manufactured in the United States of America

10 9 8 7 6 5 4 3 2 1

Library of Congress Cataloging-in-Publication Data

Kennedy, Douglas, 1955–
    A special relationship / by Douglas Kennedy. — 1st Atria Paperback ed.
        p. cm.
1. Americans—England—Fiction. 2. Man-woman relationships—Fiction. 3. Self-realization in women—Fiction. 4. London (England)—Fiction. I. Title.
    PR6061.E5956S64 2011
    823'.914—dc22
                                        2010031084
ISBN 978-1-4391-9913-8 (pbk)
ISBN 978-1-4391-9915-2 (ebook)

another one for Max and Amelia

In my enormous city it is—night,
as from my sleeping house I go—out,
and people think perhaps I'm a daughter or a wife
but in my mind is one thought only: night.

—ELAINE FEINSTEIN, Insomnia

ONE

ABOUT AN HOUR after I met Tony Hobbs, he saved my life. I know that sounds just a little melodramatic, but it's the truth. Or, at least, as true as anything a journalist will tell you.

I was in Somalia—a country I had never visited until I got a call in Cairo and suddenly found myself dispatched there. It was a Friday afternoon—the Muslim Holy Day. Like most foreign correspondents in the Egyptian capital, I was using the official day of rest to do just that. I was sunning myself beside the pool of the Gezira Club—the former haunt of British officers during the reign of King Farouk, but now the domain of the Cairene beau monde and assorted foreigners who'd been posted to the Egyptian capital. Even though the sun is a constant commodity in Egypt, it is something that most correspondents based there rarely get to see. Especially if, like me, they are bargain basement one-person operations, covering the entire Middle East and all of eastern Africa. Which is why I got that call on that Friday afternoon.

"Is this Sally Goodchild?" asked an American voice I hadn't heard before.

"That's right," I said, sitting upright and holding the cell phone tightly to my ear in an attempt to block out a quartet of babbling Egyptian matrons sitting beside me. "Who's this?"

"Dick Leonard from the paper."

I stood up, grabbing a pad and a pen from my bag. Then I walked to a quiet corner of the veranda. "The paper" was my employer. Also known as the *Boston Post*. And if they were calling me on my cell phone, something was definitely up.

"I'm new on the foreign desk," Leonard said, "and deputizing today for Charlie Geiken. I'm sure you've heard about the flood in Somalia?"

Rule one of journalism: never admit you've been even five minutes out of contact with the world at large. So all I said was, "How many dead?"

"No definitive body count so far, according to CNN. And from all reports, it's making the '97 deluge look like a drizzle."

"Where exactly in Somalia?"

"The Juba River Valley. At least four villages have been submerged. The editor wants somebody there. Can you leave straightaway?"

So that's how I found myself on a flight to Mogadishu, just four hours after receiving the call from Boston. Getting there meant dealing with the eccentricities of Ethiopian Airlines, and changing planes in Addis Ababa, before landing in Mogadishu just after midnight. I stepped out into the humid African night, and tried to find a cab into town. Eventually, a taxi showed up, but the driver drove like a kamikaze pilot, and also took a back road into the city center—a road that was unpaved and also largely deserted. When I asked him why he had chosen to take us off the beaten track, he just laughed. So I pulled out my cell phone and dialed some numbers, and told the desk clerk at the Central Hotel in Mogadishu that he should call the police immediately and inform them that I was being kidnapped by a taxi driver, car license number . . . (and, yes, I did note the cab's license plate before getting into it). Immediately the driver turned all apologetic, veering back to the main road, imploring me not to get him into trouble, and saying, "Really, it was just a shortcut."

"In the middle of the night, when there's no traffic? You really expect me to believe that?"

"Will the police be waiting for me at the hotel?"

"If you get me there, I'll call them off."

He veered back to the main road, and I made it intact to the Central Hotel in Mogadishu—the cab driver still apologizing as I left his car. After four hours' sleep, I managed to make contact with the International Red Cross in Somalia, and talked my way onto one of their helicopters that was heading to the flood zone.

It was just after nine in the morning when the chopper took off from a military airfield outside the city. There were no seats inside. I sat with three other Red Cross staffers on its cold steel floor. The helicopter was elderly and deafening. As it left the ground, it lurched dangerously to the starboard side—and we were all thrown against the thick webbed belts, bolted to the cabin walls, into which we had fastened ourselves before takeoff. Once the pilot regained control and we evened out, the guy seated on the floor opposite me smiled broadly and said, "Well, that was a good start."

Though it was difficult to hear anything over the din of the rotor blades, I did discern that the fellow had an English accent. Then I looked at him more closely and figured that this was no aid worker. It wasn't just the sangfroid when it looked like we might just crash. It wasn't just his blue denim shirt, his blue denim jeans, and his stylish horn-rimmed sunglasses. Nor was it his tanned face—which, coupled with his still-blond hair, lent him a certain weatherbeaten appeal if you liked that perpetually insomniac look. No—what really convinced me that he wasn't Red Cross was the jaded, slightly flirtatious smile he gave me after our near-death experience. At that moment, I knew that he was a journalist.

Just as I saw that he was looking me over, appraising me, and also probably working out that I too wasn't relief worker material. Of course, I was wondering how I was being perceived. I have one of those Emily Dickinson–style New England faces—angular, a little gaunt, with a permanently fair complexion that resists extended contact with the sun. A man who once wanted to marry me—and turn me into exactly the sort of soccer mom I was determined never to become—told me I was "beautiful in an interesting sort of way." After I stopped laughing, this struck me as something out of the "plucky" school of backhanded compliments. He also told me that he admired the way I looked after myself. At least he didn't say I was "wearing well." Still, it is true that my "interesting" face hasn't much in the way of wrinkles or age lines, and my light brown hair (cut sensibly short) isn't yet streaked with gray. So though I may be crowding middle age, I can pass myself off as just over the thirty-year-old frontier.

All these banal thoughts were abruptly interrupted when the helicopter suddenly rolled to the left as the pilot went full throttle and we shot off at speed to a higher altitude. Accompanying this abrupt, convulsive ascent—the G-force of which threw us all against our webbed straps—was the distinctive sound of anti-aircraft fire. Immediately, the Brit was digging into his backpack, pulling out a pair of field glasses. Despite the protestations of one of the Red Cross workers, he unbuckled his straps and maneuvered himself around to peer out one of the porthole windows.

"Looks like someone's trying to kill us," he shouted over the din of the engine. But his voice was calm, if not redolent of amusement.

"Who's 'someone'?" I shouted back.

"Usual militia bastards," he said, his eyes still fastened to the field glasses. "The same charmers who caused such havoc during the last flood."

"But why are they shooting at a Red Cross chopper?" I asked.

"Because they can," he said. "They shoot at anything foreign and moving. It's sport to them."

He turned to the trio of Red Cross medicos strapped in next to me.

"I presume your chap in the cockpit knows what he's doing," he asked. None of them answered him—because they were all white with shock. That's when he flashed me a deeply mischievous smile, making me think: the guy's actually enjoying all this.

I smiled back. That was a point of pride with me—to never show fear under fire. I knew from experience that, in such situations, all you could do was take a very deep breath, remain focused, and hope you got through it. And so I picked a spot on the floor of the cabin and stared at it, all the while silently telling myself: *It will be fine. It will be just . . .*

And then the chopper did another roll and the Brit was tossed away from the window, but managed to latch on to his nearby straps and avoid being hurled across the cabin.

"You okay?" I asked.

Another of his smiles. "I am now," he said.

A further three stomach-churning rolls to the right, followed by one more rapid acceleration, and we seemed to leave the danger zone. Ten nervous minutes followed, then we banked low. I craned my neck, looked out the window, and sucked in my breath. There before me was a submerged landscape—Noah's flood. The water had consumed everything. Houses and livestock floated by. Then I spied the first dead body—face-down in the water, followed by four more bodies, two of which were so small that, even from the air, I was certain they were children.

Everyone in the chopper was now peering out the window, taking in the extent of the calamity. The chopper banked again, pulling away from the nucleus and coming in fast over higher ground. Up in the distance, I could see a cluster of jeeps and military vehicles. Closer inspection showed that we were trying to land amid the chaos of a Somalian Army encampment, with several dozen soldiers milling around the clapped-out military equipment spread across the field. In the near distance, we could see three white jeeps flying the Red Cross flag. There were around fourteen aid workers standing by the jeeps, frantically waving to us. There was a problem, however. A cluster of Somalian soldiers was positioned within a hundred yards of the Red Cross team—and they were simultaneously making beckoning gestures toward us with their arms.

"This should be amusing," the Brit said.

"Not if it's like last time," one of the Red Cross team said.

"What happened last time?" I asked.

"They tried to loot us," he said.

"That happened a lot back in '97 too," the Brit said.

"You were here in '97?" I asked him.

"Oh yes," he said, flashing me another smile. "A delightful spot, Somalia. Especially under water."

We overflew the soldiers and the Red Cross jeeps. But the aid workers on the ground seemed to know the game we were playing, as they jumped into the jeeps, reversed direction, and started racing toward the empty terrain where we were coming down. I glanced over at the Brit. He had his binoculars pressed against the window, that sardonic smile of his growing broader by the nanosecond.

"Looks like there's going to be a little race to meet us," he said.

I peered out my window and saw a dozen Somalian soldiers running in our general direction.

"See what you mean," I shouted back to him as we landed with a bump.

With terra firma beneath us, the Red Cross man next to me was on his feet, yanking up the lever that kept the cabin door in its place. The others headed toward the cargo bay at the rear of the cabin, undoing the webbing that held in the crates of medical supplies and dried food.

"Need a hand?" the Brit asked one of the Red Cross guys.

"We'll be fine," he said. "But you better get moving before the army shows up."

"Where's the nearest village?"

"It *was* about a kilometer due south of here. But it's not there any-more."

"Right," he said. Then he turned to me and asked, "You coming?"

I nodded but then turned back to the Red Cross man and asked, "What are you going to do about the soldiers?"

"What we usually do. Stall them while the pilot radios the Somalian central command—if you can call it that—and orders some officer over here to get them off our backs. But you both better get out of here now. The soldiers really don't see the point of journalists."

"We're gone," I said. "Thanks for the lift."

The Brit and I headed out of the cabin. As soon as we hit the ground, he tapped me on the shoulder and pointed toward the three Red Cross jeeps. Crouching low, we ran in their direction, not looking back until we were behind them. This turned out to be a strategically smart move, as we had managed to dodge the attention of the Somalian soldiers, who had now surrounded the chopper. Four of them had their guns trained on the Red Cross team. One of the soldiers started shouting at the aid workers—but they didn't seem flustered at all, and began the "stalling for time" gambit. Though I couldn't hear much over the din of the rotor motor, it was clear that the Red Cross guys had played this dangerous game before and knew exactly what to do. The Brit nudged me with his elbow.

"See that clump of trees over there," he said, pointing toward a small patch of gum trees around fifty yards from us.

I nodded. After one fast, final glance at the soldiers—now ripping into a case of medical supplies—we made a dash for it. It couldn't have taken more than twenty seconds to cover the fifty yards, but, God, did it seem long. I knew that if the soldiers saw two figures running for cover, their natural reaction would be to shoot us down. When we reached the woods, we ducked behind a tree. Neither of us was winded—but when I looked at the Brit, I caught the briefest flicker of adrenaline-fueled tension in his eyes. Once he realized that I'd glimpsed it, he immediately turned on his sardonic smile.

"Well done," he whispered. "Think you can make it over there with-out getting shot?"

I looked in the direction he was pointing—another meager grove of trees that fronted the now-deluged river. I met his challenging smile. "I never get shot," I said. Then we ran out of the trees, making a manic beeline for the next patch of cover. This run took around a minute—during which time the world went silent, and all I could hear were my feet scything through the high grass. I was genuinely tense. But like that moment in the helicopter when we first came under fire, I tried to concentrate on something abstract like my breathing. The Brit was ahead of me. But as soon as he reached the trees, something brought him to a sudden halt. I stopped in my tracks as I saw him walking backward, his arms held high in the air. Emerging from the trees was a young Somalian soldier. He couldn't have been more than fifteen. His rifle was trained on the Brit, who was quietly attempting to talk his way out of this situation. Suddenly the soldier saw me—and when he turned his gun on me, I made a desperate error of judgment. Instead of immediately acting submissive—coming to a complete halt, putting my hands above my head, and making no sudden movements (as I had been trained to do)—I hit the ground, certain he was going to fire at me. This caused him to roar at me, as he now tried to get me in his sights. Then, suddenly, the Brit tackled him, knocking him to the ground. I was now back on my feet, running toward the scene. The Brit swung a clenched fist, slamming it into the soldier's stomach, knocking the wind out of him. The kid groaned, and the Brit brought his boot down hard on the hand that was clutching the gun. The kid screamed.

"Let go of the gun," the Brit demanded.

"Fuck you," the kid yelled. So the Brit brought his boot down even harder. This time the soldier released the weapon, which the Brit quickly scooped up and had trained on the soldier in a matter of seconds.

"I hate impoliteness," the Brit said, cocking the rifle.

The kid now began to sob, curling up into a fetal position, pleading for his life. I turned to the Brit and said, "You can't . . ."

But he just looked at me and winked. Then, turning back to the child soldier, he said, "Did you hear my friend? She doesn't want me to shoot you."

The kid said nothing. He just curled himself tighter into a ball, crying like the frightened child he was.

"I think you should apologize to her, don't you?" said the Brit. I could see the gun trembling in his hands.

"Sorry, sorry, sorry," the kid said, the words choked with sobs. The Brit looked at me.

"Apology accepted?" he asked. I nodded.

The Brit nodded at me, then turned back to the kid and asked, "How's your hand?"

"Hurts."

"Sorry about that," he said. "You can go now, if you like."

The kid, still trembling, got to his feet. His face was streaked with tears, and there was a damp patch around his crotch where he'd wet himself out of fear. He looked at us with terror in his eyes—still certain he was going to be shot. To his credit, the Brit reached out and put a steadying hand on the soldier's shoulder.

"It's all right," he said quietly. "Nothing's going to happen to you. But you have to promise me one thing: you must not tell anyone in your company that you met us. Will you do that?"

The soldier glanced at the gun still in the Brit's hands and nodded. Many times.

"Good. One final question. Are there any army patrols down river from here?"

"No. Our base got washed away. I got separated from the others."

"How about the village near here?"

"Nothing left of it."

"All the people washed away?"

"Some made it to a hill."

"Where's the hill?"

The soldier pointed toward an overgrown path through the trees.

"How long from here on foot?" he asked.

"Half an hour."

The Brit looked at me and said, "That's our story."

"Sounds good to me," I said, meeting his look.

"Run along now," the Brit said to the soldier.

"My gun . . ."

"Sorry, but I'm keeping it."

"I'll get in big trouble without it."

"Say it was washed away in the flood. And remember: I expect you to keep that promise you made. You never saw us. Understood?"

The kid looked back at the gun, then up again at the Brit.

"I promise."

"Good lad. Now go."

The boy soldier nodded and dashed out of the trees in the general direction of the chopper. When he was out of sight, the Brit shut his eyes, drew in a deep breath, and said, "Fucking hell."

"And so say all of us."

He opened his eyes and looked at me. "You all right?" he said.

"Yeah—but I feel like a complete jerk."

He grinned. "You *were* a complete jerk—but it happens. Especially when you get surprised by a kid with a gun. On which note . . ."

He motioned with his thumb that we should make tracks. Which is exactly what we did—negotiating our way through the thicket of woods, finding the overgrown path, threading our way to the edge of swamped fields. We walked nonstop for fifteen minutes, saying nothing. The Brit led the way. I walked a few steps behind. I watched my companion as we hiked deeper into this submerged terrain. He was very focused on the task of getting us as far away from the soldiers as possible. He was also acutely conscious of any irregular sounds emanating from this open terrain. Twice he stopped and turned back to me, putting his finger to his lips when he thought he heard something. We only started to walk again when he was certain no one was on our tail. I was intrigued by the way he held the soldier's gun. Instead of slinging it over his shoulder, he carried it in his right hand, the barrel pointed downward, the rifle held away from his body. And I knew that he would never have shot that soldier. Because he was so obviously uncomfortable holding a gun.

After around fifteen minutes, he pointed to a couple of large rocks positioned near the river. We sat down but didn't say anything for a moment as we continued to gauge the silence, trying to discern approaching footsteps in the distance. After a moment, he spoke.

"The way I figure it, if that kid had told on us, his comrades would be here by now."

"You certainly scared him into thinking you would kill him."

"He needed scaring. Because he would have shot you without compunction."

"I know. Thank you."

"All part of the service." Then he proffered his hand and said, "Tony Hobbs. Who do you write for?"

"The *Boston Post*."

An amused smile crossed his lips. "Do you really?"

"Yes," I said. "*Really*. We do have foreign correspondents, you know."

"*Really?*" he said, mimicking my accent. "So you're a *foreign correspondent*?"

"*Really*," I said, attempting to mimic his accent.

To his credit, he laughed. And said, "I deserved that."

"Yes. You did."

"So where do you *correspond* from?" he asked.

"Cairo. And let me guess. You write for the *Sun*?"

"The *Chronicle*, actually."

I tried not to appear impressed. "The *Chronicle* actually, *actually*?" I said.

"You give as good as you get."

"It comes with being the correspondent of a smallish newspaper. You have to hold your own with arrogant big boys."

"Oh, you've already decided I'm arrogant?"

"I worked that out two minutes after first seeing you in the chopper. You based in London?"

"Cairo, actually."

"But I know the *Chronicle* guy there. Henry . . ."

"Bartlett. Got sick. Ulcer thing. So they sent for me from Tokyo around ten days ago."

"I used to cover Tokyo. Four years ago."

"Well, I'm obviously following you around."

There was a sound of nearby footsteps. We both tensed. Tony picked up the rifle he had leaned against the rock. Then we heard the steps grow nearer. As we stood up, a young Somalian woman came running down the path, a child in her arms. The woman couldn't have been more than twenty; the baby was no more than two months old. The mother was gaunt, the child chillingly still. As soon as the woman saw us, she began to scream in a dialect that neither of us understood, making wild gesticulations at the gun in Tony's hand. Tony understood immediately. He tossed the gun into the rushing waters of the river—adding it to the flooded debris washing downstream. The gesture seemed to surprise the woman. But as she turned back to me and started pleading with me again, her legs buckled. Tony and I both grabbed her, keeping her upright. I glanced down at her lifeless baby, still held tightly in her arms. I looked up at the Brit. He nodded in the direction of the Red Cross chopper. We each put an arm around her emaciated waist, and began the slow journey back to the clearing where we'd landed earlier.

When we reached it, I was relieved to see that several Somalian Army jeeps had rolled up near the chopper, and the previously marauding troops had been brought under control. We escorted her past the soldiers, and made a beeline for the Red Cross chopper. Two of the aid workers from the flight were still unloading supplies.

"Who's the doctor around here?" I asked. One of the guys looked up, saw the woman and child, and sprang into action, while his colleague politely told us to get lost.

"There's nothing more you can do now."

Nor, it turned out, was there any chance that we'd be allowed back down the path toward that washed-out village—as the Somalian Army had now blocked it off. When I found the head Red Cross medic and told him about the villagers perched on a hill around two kilometers from here, he said (in his crispest Swiss accent), "We know all about it. And we will be sending our helicopter as soon as the army gives us clearance."

"Let us go with you," I said.

"It's not possible. The army will only allow three of our team to fly with them—"

"Tell them we're part of the team," Tony said.

"We need to send medical men."

"Send two," Tony said, "and let one of us—"

But we were interrupted by the arrival of some army officer. He tapped Tony on the shoulder.

"You—papers."

Then he tapped me. "You too."

We handed over our respective passports. "Red Cross papers," he demanded. When Tony started to make up some far-fetched story about leaving them behind, the officer rolled his eyes and said one damning word, "Journalists."

Then he turned to his soldiers and said, "Get them on the next chopper back to Mogadishu."

We returned to the capital under virtual armed guard. When we landed at another military field on the outskirts of the capital, I fully expected us to be taken into custody and arrested. But instead, one of the soldiers on the plane asked me if I had any American dollars.

"Perhaps," I said—and then, taking a chance, asked him if he could arrange a ride for us to the Central Hotel for ten bucks.

"You pay twenty, you get your ride."

He even commandeered a jeep to get us there. En route, Tony and I spoke for the first time since being placed under armed guard.

"Not a lot to write about, is there?" I said.

"I'm sure we'll both manage to squeeze something out of it."

We found two rooms on the same floor and agreed to meet after we'd filed our respective stories. Around two hours later—shortly after I'd dispatched by email seven hundred words on the general disarray in the Juba River Valley, the sight of floating bodies in the river, the infrastructural chaos, and the experience of being fired upon in a Red Cross helicopter by rebel forces—there was a knock at my door.

Tony stood outside, holding a bottle of Scotch and two glasses.

"This looks promising," I said. "Come on in."

He didn't leave again until seven the next morning—when we checked out to catch the early morning flight back to Cairo. From the moment I saw him in the chopper, I knew that we would inevitably fall into bed with each other, should the opportunity arise. Because that's how this game worked. Foreign correspondents rarely had spouses or "significant others"—and most people you met in the field were definitely not the sort you wanted to share a bed with for ten minutes, let alone a night.

But when I woke next to Tony, the thought struck me: *He's actually living where I live.* Which led to what was, for me, a most unusual thought: *And I'd actually like to see him again. In fact, I'd like to see him tonight.*

TWO

I'VE NEVER CONSIDERED myself the sentimental type. On the contrary, I've always recognized in myself a certain cut-and-run attitude when it comes to romance—something my one and only fiancé told me around seven years ago, when I broke it off with him. His name was Richard Pettiford. He was a Boston lawyer—smart, erudite, driven. And I really did like him. The problem was, I also liked my work.

"You're always running away," he said after I told him that I was becoming the *Post*'s correspondent in Tokyo.

"This is a big professional move," I said.

"You said that when you went to Washington."

"That was just a six-month assignment—and I saw you every weekend."

"But it was still running away."

"It was a great opportunity. Like going to Tokyo."

"But I'm a great opportunity."

"You're right," I said. "You are. But so am I. So come to Tokyo with me."

"But I won't make partner if I do that," he said.

"And if I stay, I won't make a very good partner's wife."

"If you really loved me, you'd stay."

I laughed. And said, "Then I guess I don't love you."

Which pretty much ended our two-year liaison there and then—because when you make an admission like that, there's very little comeback. Though I was truly saddened that we couldn't "make a go of it" (to borrow an expression that Richard used just a little too often), I also knew that I couldn't play the suburban role he was offering. Anyway, had I accepted such a part, my passport would now only contain a few holiday stamps from Bermuda and other resort spots, rather than the twenty crammed pages of visas I'd managed to obtain over the years. And I certainly wouldn't have ended up sitting on a flight from Addis Ababa to Cairo, getting pleasantly tipsy with a wholly charming, wholly cynical Brit, with whom I'd just spent the night . . .

"So you've really never been married?" Tony asked me as the seat belt signs were switched off.

"Don't sound so surprised," I said. "I don't swoon easily."

"I'll keep that in mind," he said.

"Foreign correspondents aren't the marrying kind."

"Really? I hadn't noticed."

I laughed, then asked, "And you?"

"You must be joking."

"Never came close?"

"Everyone's come close once. Just like you."

"How do you know I've come close?" I said.

"Because everyone's come close once."

"Didn't you just say that?"

"Touché. And let me guess—you didn't marry the guy because you'd just been offered your first overseas posting . . ."

"My, my—you are perceptive," I said.

"Hardly," he said. "It's just how it always works."

Naturally, he was right. And he was clever enough not to ask me too much about the fellow in question, or any other aspects of my so-called romantic history, or even where I grew up. If anything, the very fact that he didn't press the issue (other than to ascertain that I too had successfully dodged marriage) impressed me. Because it meant that—unlike most other foreign correspondents I had met—he wasn't treating me like some girlie who had been transferred from the Style section to the front line. Nor did he try to impress me with his big city credentials—and the fact that the *Chronicle* of London carried more international clout than the *Boston Post*. If anything, he spoke to me as a professional equal. He wanted to hear about the contacts I'd made in Cairo (as he was new there) and to trade stories about covering Japan. Best of all, he wanted to make me laugh . . . which he did with tremendous ease. As I was quickly discovering, Tony Hobbs wasn't just a great talker; he was also a terrific storyteller.

We talked nonstop all the way back to Cairo. Truth be told, we hadn't stopped talking since we woke up together that morning. There was an immediate ease between us—not just because we had so much professional terrain in common, but also because we seemed to possess a similar worldview: slightly jaded, fiercely independent, with a passionate undercurrent about the business we were both in. We also both acknowledged that foreign corresponding was a kid's game, in which most practitioners were considered way over the hill by the time they reached fifty.

"Which makes me eight years away from the slag heap," Tony said somewhere over Sudan.

"You're that young?" I said. "I really thought you were at least ten years older."

He shot me a cool, amused look. And said, "You're fast."

"I try."

"Oh, you do very well . . . for a provincial reporter."

"Two points," I said, nudging him with my elbow.

"Keeping score, are we?"

"Oh, yes."

I could tell that he was completely comfortable with this sort of banter. He enjoyed repartee—not just for its verbal gamesmanship, but also because it allowed him to retreat from the serious, or anything that might be self-revealing. Every time our in-flight conversation veered toward the personal, he'd quickly switch into banter mode. This didn't disconcert me. After all, we'd just met and were still sizing each other up. But I still noted this diversionary tactic, and wondered if it would hinder me from getting to know the guy—as, much to my surprise, Tony Hobbs was the first man I'd met in about four years whom I wanted to get to know.

Not that I was going to reveal that fact to him. Because (a) that might put him off, and (b) I never chased anyone. So, when we arrived in Cairo, we shared a cab back to Zamalek (the relatively upscale expatriate quarter where just about every foreign correspondent and international business type lived). As it turned out, Tony's place was only two blocks from mine. But he insisted on dropping me off first. As the taxi slowed to a halt in front of my door, he reached into his pocket and handed me his card.

"Here's where to find me," he said.

I pulled out a business card of my own, and scribbled a number on the back of it.

"And here's my home number."

"Thanks," he said, taking it. "So call me, eh?"

"No, you make the first move," I said.

"Old-fashioned, are we?" he said, raising his eyebrows.

"Hardly. But I don't make the first move. All right?"

He leaned over and gave me a very long kiss.

"Fine," he said, then added, "That was fun."

"Yes. It was."

An awkward pause. I gathered up my things.

"See you, I guess," I said.

"Yes," he said with a smile. "See you."

As soon as I was upstairs in my empty, silent apartment, I kicked myself for playing the tough dame. "*No, you make the first move.*" What a profoundly dumb thing to say. Because I knew that guys like Tony Hobbs didn't cross my path every day.

Still, I could now do nothing but put the entire business out of my mind. So I spent the better part of an hour soaking in a bath, then crawled into bed and passed out for nearly ten hours—having hardly slept for the past two nights. I was up just after seven in the morning. I made breakfast. I powered up my laptop. I turned out my weekly "Letter from Cairo," in which I recounted my dizzying flight in a Red Cross helicopter under fire from Somalian militia men. When the phone rang around noon, I jumped for it.

"Hello," Tony said. "This is the first move."

He came by ten minutes later to pick me up for lunch. We never made it to the restaurant. I won't say I dragged him off to my bed—because he came very willingly. Suffice to say, from the moment I opened the door, I was all over him. As he was me.

Much later, in bed, he turned to me and said, "So who's making the second move?"

It would be the stuff of romantic cliché to say that from that moment on we were inseparable. Nonetheless, I do count that afternoon as the official start of us—when we started becoming an essential part of each other's life. What most surprised me was this: it was about the easiest transition imaginable. The arrival of Tony Hobbs into my existence wasn't marked by the usual doubts, questions, worries, let alone the overt romantic extremities associated with a *coup de foudre*. The fact that we were both self-reliant types—used to falling back on our separate resources—meant that we were attuned to each other's independent streak. We also seemed to be amused by each other's national quirks. He would often gently deride a certain American literalness that I do possess—a need to ask questions all the damn time, and analyze situations a little too much. Just as I would express amusement at his incessant need to find the flippant underside to all situations. He also happened to be absolutely fearless when it came to journalistic practice. I saw this firsthand around a month after we first hooked up, when a call came one evening that a busload of German tourists had been machine-gunned by Islamic fundamentalists while visiting the Pyramids at Giza. Immediately, we jumped into my car and headed out in the direction of the Sphinx. When we reached the sight of the Giza massacre, Tony managed to push his way past several Egyptian soldiers to get right up to the blood-splattered bus itself—even though there were fears that the terrorists might have thrown grenades into it before vanishing. The next afternoon, at the news conference following this attack, the Egyptian minister for tourism tried to blame foreign terrorists for the massacre . . . at which point Tony interrupted him, holding up a statement, which had been faxed directly to his office, in which the Cairo Muslim Brotherhood took complete responsibility for the attack. Not only did Tony read out the statement in near-perfect Arabic, he then turned to the minister and asked him, "Now would you mind explaining why you're lying to us?"

Tony was always defensive about one thing: his height . . . though, as I assured him on more than one occasion, his diminutive stature didn't matter a damn to me. On the contrary, I found it rather touching that this highly accomplished and amusingly arrogant man would be so vulnerable about his physical stature. And I came to realize that much of Tony's bravado—his need to ask all the tough questions, his competitiveness for a story, and his reckless self-endangerment—stemmed out of a sense of feeling small. He secretly considered himself inadequate: the perennial outsider with his nose to the window, looking in on a world from which he felt excluded. It took me a while to detect Tony's curious streak of inferiority since it was masked behind such witty superiority. But then I saw him in action one day with a fellow Brit—a correspondent from the *Daily Telegraph* named Wilson. Though only in his mid-thirties, Wilson had already lost much of his hair and had started to develop the sort of overripe fleshiness that made him (in Tony's words) look like a wheel of Camembert that had been left out in the sun. Personally, I didn't mind him—even though his languid vowels and premature jowliness (not to mention the absurd tailored safari jacket he wore all the time with a checked Viyella shirt) gave him a certain cartoonish quality. Though he was perfectly amiable in Wilson's company, Tony couldn't stand him—especially after an encounter we had with him at the Gezira Club. Wilson was sunning himself by the pool. He was stripped to the waist, wearing a pair of plaid Bermuda shorts and suede shoes with socks. It was not a pretty sight. After greeting us, he asked Tony, "Going home for Christmas?"

"Not this year."

"You're a London chap, right?"

"Buckinghamshire, actually."

"Whereabouts?"

"Amersham."

"Ah yes, Amersham. End of the Metropolitan line, isn't it? Drink?"

Tony's face tightened, but Wilson didn't seem to notice. Instead, he called over one of the waiters, ordered three gin and tonics, then excused himself to use the toilet. As soon as he was out of earshot, Tony hissed, "Stupid little prat."

"Easy, Tony . . ." I said, surprised by this uncharacteristic flash of anger.

"'End of the Metropolitan line, isn't it?'" he said, mimicking Wilson's overripe accent. "He had to say that, didn't he? Had to get his little dig in. Had to make the fucking point."

"Hey, all he said was . . ."

"I know what he said. And he meant every bloody word . . ."

"Meant what?"

"You just don't get it."

"I think it's all a little too nuanced for me," I said lightly. "Or maybe I'm just a dumb American who doesn't get England."

"No one gets England."

"Even if you're English?"

"Especially if you're English."

This struck me as something of a half-truth. Because Tony understood England all too well. Just as he also understood (and explained to me) his standing in the social hierarchy. Amersham was deeply dull. Seriously petit bourgeois. He hated it, though his only sibling—a sister he hadn't seen for years—had stayed on, living at home with the parents she could never leave. His dad—now dead, thanks to a lifelong love affair with Benson & Hedges—had worked for the local council in their records office (which he finally ended up running five years before he died). His mom—also dead—worked as a receptionist in a doctor's office, located opposite the modest little suburban semi in which he was raised.

Though Tony was determined to run away from Amersham and never look back, he did go out of his way to please his father by landing a place at York University. But when he graduated (with high honors, as it turned out—though, in typical phlegmatic Tony style, it took him a long time to admit that he received a prized First in English), he decided to dodge the job market for a year or so. Instead, he took off with a couple of friends bound for Kathmandu. But somehow they ended up in Cairo. Within two months, he was working for a dodgy English language newspaper, the *Egyptian Gazette*. After six months of reporting traffic accidents and petty crimes and the usual trivial stuff, he started offering his services back in Britain as a Cairo-based freelancer. Within a year, he was supplying a steady stream of short pieces to the *Chronicle*—and when their Egyptian correspondent was called back to London, the paper offered him the job. From that moment on, he was a *Chronicle* man. With the exception of a brief six-month stint back in London during the mid-eighties (when he threatened to quit if they didn't post him back in the field), Tony managed to drift from one hot spot to another. Of course, for all his talk of frontline action and total professional independence, he still had to bite the corporate bullet and do a couple of stints as a bureau guy in Frankfurt, Tokyo, and Washington, D.C. (a town he actively hated). But despite these few concessions to the prosaic, Tony Hobbs worked very hard at eluding all the potential traps of domesticity and professional life that ensnared most people. Just like me.

"You know, I always end up cutting and running out of these things," I told Tony around a month after we started seeing each other.

"Oh, so that's what this is—a thing."

"You know what I'm saying."

"That I shouldn't get down on one knee and propose—because you're planning to break my heart?"

I laughed and said, "I really am not planning to do that."

"Then your point is . . . what?"

"My point is . . ."

I broke off, feeling profoundly silly.

"You were about to say?" Tony asked, all smiles.

"The point is . . ." I continued, hesitant as hell. "I think I sometimes suffer from 'foot in mouth' disease. And I should never have made such a dumb comment."

"No need to apologize," he said.

"I'm not apologizing," I said, sounding a little cross, then suddenly said, "Actually I am. Because . . ."

God, I really was sounding tongue-tied and awkward. Once again, Tony just continued smiling an amused smile. Then said, "So you're not planning to cut and run?"

"Hardly. Because . . . uh . . . oh, will you listen to me . . ."

"I'm all ears."

"Because . . . I'm so damn happy with you, and the very fact that I feel this way is surprising the hell out of me, because I really haven't felt this way for a long time, and I'm just hoping to hell you feel this way, because I don't want to waste my time on someone who doesn't feel this way, because . . ."

He cut me off by leaning over and kissing me deeply. When he finished, he said, "Does that answer your question?"

"Well . . ."

I suppose actions speak louder than words—but I still wanted to hear him say what I had just said. Then again, if I wasn't very good at outwardly articulating matters of the heart, I'd come to realize that Tony was even more taciturn on such subjects. Which is why I was genuinely surprised when he said, "I'm very pleased you're not cutting and running."

Was that a declaration of love? I certainly hoped so. At that moment, I knew I was in love with him. Just as I also knew that my bumbling admission of happiness was about as far as I'd go in confessing such a major emotional truth. Such admissions have always been difficult for me. Just as they were also difficult for my schoolteacher parents—who couldn't have been more supportive and encouraging when it came to their two children, but who also were deeply buttoned-down and reserved when it came to public displays of affection.

"You know, I can only once remember seeing our parents kiss each other," my older sister Sandy told me shortly after they were killed in an automobile accident. "And they certainly didn't score big points on the tactile front. But that really didn't matter, did it?"

"No," I said. "It didn't at all."

At which point Sandy broke down completely and wept so loudly that her grief sounded something like keening. My own displays of raw public grief were few in the wake of their death. Perhaps because I was too numb from the shock of it all to cry. The year was 1988. I was twenty-one. I had just finished my senior year at Mount Holyoke College—and was due to start a job at the *Boston Post* in a few weeks. I'd just found an apartment with two friends in the Back Bay area of the city. I'd just bought my first car (a beat-up VW Beetle for a thousand bucks), and had just found out that I was going to graduate magna cum laude. My parents couldn't have been more pleased. When they drove up to the college to see me get my degree that weekend, they were in such unusually ebullient form that they actually went to a big post-commencement party on campus. I wanted them to spend the night, but they had to get back to Worcester that evening for some big church event the next day (like many liberal New Englanders, they were serious Unitarians). Just before they got into the car, my father gave me a big uncharacteristic hug and said that he loved me.

Two hours later, while driving south, he nodded off at the wheel on the interstate. The car veered out of control, crashed through the center guard rail, and careened right into the oncoming path of another car—a Ford station wagon. It was carrying a family of five. Two of the occupants—a young mother and her baby son—were killed. So too were my parents.

In the wake of their deaths, Sandy kept expecting me to fall apart (as she was doing constantly). I know that it both upset and worried her that I wasn't succumbing to loud, outward heartbreak (even though anyone who saw me at the time could tell that I was in the throes of major trauma). Then again, Sandy has always been the emotional roller coaster in the family. Just as she's also been the one fixed geographic point in my life—someone to watch over me (as I have watched over her). But we couldn't be more disparate characters. Whereas I was always asserting my independence, Sandy was very much a homebody. She followed my parents into high-school teaching, married a phys ed teacher, moved to the Boston suburbs, and had three children by the time she was thirty. She'd also allowed herself to get a little chunky in the process—to the point where she was crowding one hundred and seventy pounds (not a good look on a woman who only stood five foot three), and seemed to have this predilection for eating all the time. Though I occasionally hinted that she might consider padlocking the refrigerator, I didn't push the point too hard. It wasn't my style to remonstrate with Sandy—she was so vulnerable to all criticism, so heart-on-her-sleeve, and so damn nice.

She's also been the one person with whom I've always been open about everything going on with me—with the exception of the period directly after the deaths of my parents, when I shut down and couldn't be reached by anybody. The new job at the *Post* helped. Though my boss on the city desk didn't expect me to begin work immediately, I insisted on starting at the paper just ten days after my parents were buried. I dived right in. Twelve-hour days were my specialty. I also volunteered for additional assignments, covering every damn story I could—and quickly got a name for myself as a completely reliable workaholic.

Then, around four months into the job, I was on my way home one evening, when I passed by a couple around my parents' age, walking hand-in-hand down Boylston Street. There wasn't anything unusual about this couple. They didn't resemble my mom or dad. They were just an ordinary-looking husband and wife in their mid-fifties, holding hands. Maybe that's what undid me—the fact that, unlike many couples at that stage of a marriage, they seemed pleased to be together . . . just as my parents always seemed pleased to be in each other's company. Whatever the reason, the next thing I knew, I was leaning against a lamppost, crying wildly. I couldn't stop myself, couldn't dodge the desperate wave of grief with which I had finally collided. I didn't move for a long time, clinging to the lamppost for ballast, the depth of my sorrow suddenly fathomless, immeasurable. A cop showed up. He placed his big hand on my shoulder and asked me if I needed help.

"I just want my mommy and daddy," I felt like screaming, reverting back to the six-year-old self we all carry with us, eternally desperate for parental sheltering at life's most fearful moments. Instead, I managed to explain that I was simply coping with a bereavement, and all I needed was a cab home. The cop flagged one down (no easy thing in Boston— but then again, he was a policeman). He helped me into it, telling me (in his own faltering, gruff, kind way) that "cryin' was the only way outta grief." I thanked him, and kept myself in check on the drive back. But when I got to my apartment I fell on my bed, and surrendered once again to grief's wild ride. I couldn't remember how long I spent crying, except that it was suddenly two in the morning, and I was curled up on the bed in a fetal position, completely spent, and hugely grateful that my two roommates had been out that evening. I wanted no one to see me in this condition.

When I woke up early the next morning, my face was still puffy, my eyes still crimson, and every fiber in my body depleted. But the tears didn't start again. I knew I couldn't allow myself another descent into that emotional netherworld. So I put on a mask of stern resolve and went back to work—which is all you can ever do under the circumstances. All accidental deaths are simultaneously absurd and tragic. As I told Tony during the one and only time I recounted this story to him, when you lose the most important people in your life—your parents—through the most random of circumstances, you come to realize pretty damn fast that everything is fragile, that so-called security is nothing more than a thin veneer that can fracture without warning.

"Is that when you decided you wanted to be a war correspondent?" he asked, stroking my face.

"Got me in one."

Actually, it took me a good six years to work my way up from the city desk to features to a brief stint on the editorial page. Then, finally, I received my first temporary posting to Washington. Had Richard found a way to get transferred to Tokyo, I might have married him on the spot.

"It's just you cared for Tokyo a little more," Tony said.

"Hey, if I'd married Richard, I'd be living in some comfortable suburb like Wellesley. I'd probably have two kids, and a Jeep Cherokee, and I'd be writing lifestyle features for the *Post* . . . and it wouldn't be a bad life. But I wouldn't have lived in assorted mad parts of the world, and I wouldn't have had a quarter of the adventures that I've had and got paid for them."

"And you wouldn't have met me," Tony said.

"That's right," I said, kissing him. "I wouldn't have fallen in love with you."

Pause. I was even more dumbfounded than he was by that last remark.

"Now how did that slip out?" I asked.

He leaned over and kissed me deeply.

"I'm glad it did," he said. "Because I feel the same way."

I was astonished to find myself in love . . . and to have that love reciprocated by someone who seemed exactly the sort of man I'd secretly hoped to stumble upon, but really didn't think existed (journalists, by and large, being the wrong side of seedy).

A certain innate caution still made me want to move forward with prudence. Just as I didn't want to think about whether we would last beyond the next week, month, whatever. I sensed this as well about Tony. I couldn't get much out of him about his romantic past—though he did mention that he once came close to marriage ("but it all went wrong . . . and maybe it was best that it did"). I wanted to press him for further details (after all, I had finally told him about Richard), but he quickly sidestepped the matter. I let it drop, figuring that he would eventually get around to telling me the entire story. Or maybe that was me also trying not to push him too hard—because, after two months with Tony Hobbs, I did understand very well that he was somebody who hated being cornered or asked to explain himself.

Neither of us made a point of letting our fellow journos in Cairo know that we had become an item. Not because we feared gossip—but rather because we simply didn't think it was anybody's damn business. So, in public, we still came across as nothing more than professional associates.

Or, at least, that's what I thought. Until Wilson—the fleshy guy from the *Daily Telegraph*—let it be known otherwise. He'd called me up at my office to suggest lunch, saying it was about time that we sat down and had an extended chat. He said this in that slightly pompous style of his—which made it sound like a royal invitation, or that he was doing me a favor by taking me out to the coffee shop in the Semiramis Hotel. As it turned out, he used the lunch to pump me for information about assorted Egyptian government ministers, and to obtain as many of my local contacts as possible. But when he suddenly brought up Tony, I was slightly taken aback . . . because of the care we had taken to keep things out of the public eye. This was the height of naïveté, given that journalists in a place like Cairo always know what their colleagues ate for breakfast. But I still wasn't prepared to hear him ask, "And how is Mr. Hobbs these days?"

I tried to seem unflustered by this question.

"I presume he's fine."

Wilson, sensing my reticence, smiled.

"You presume . . . ?"

"I can't answer for his well-being."

Another of his greasy smiles.

"I see."

"But if you are that interested in his welfare," I said, "you could call his office."

He ignored that comment, and instead said, "Interesting chap, Hobbs."

"In what way?"

"Oh, the fact that he is noted for his legendary recklessness, and his inability to keep his bosses happy."

"I didn't know that."

"It's common enough knowledge back in London that Hobbs is something of a political disaster when it comes to the game of office politics. A real loose cannon—but a highly talented reporter, which is why he's been tolerated for so long."

He looked at me, waiting for a response. I said nothing. He smiled again—deciding that my silence was further evidence of my discomfort (he was right). Then he added, "And I'm sure you're aware that, when it comes to emotional entanglements, he's always been something of a . . . well, how can I put this discreetly? . . . something of a raging bull, I suppose. Runs through women the way . . ."

"Is there some point to this commentary?" I asked lightly.

Now it was his turn to look startled—though he did so in a quasi-theatrical manner.

"I was just making conversation," he said, in mock shock. "And, of course, I was trading gossip. And perhaps the biggest piece of gossip about Mr. Anthony Hobbs is the way that a woman finally broke the chap's heart. Mind you, it's old gossip, but . . ."

He broke off, deliberately letting the story dangle. Like a fool I asked, "Who was the woman?"

That's when Wilson told me about Elaine Plunkett. I listened with uneasy interest—and with growing distaste. Wilson spoke in a low, conspirational tone, even though his surface tone was light, frivolous. This was something I began to notice about a certain type of Brit, especially when faced with an American (or, worse yet, an *American woman*). They considered us so earnest, so ploddingly literal in all our endeavors, that they attempted to upend our serious-mindedness with light-as-a-feather irony, in which nothing they said seemed weighted with importance . . . even though everything they were telling you was consequential.

Certainly, this was Wilson's style—and one that was underscored with a streak of malice. Yet I listened with intent to everything he told me. Because he was talking about Tony—with whom I was in love.

Now, courtesy of Wilson, I was also finding out that another woman—an Irish journalist working in Washington named Elaine Plunkett—had broken Tony's heart. But I didn't feel in any way anguished about this—because I didn't want to play the jealous idiot, musing endlessly about the fact that this Plunkett woman might have been the one who got away . . . or, worse yet, the love of his life. What I did feel was a profound distaste for the game that Wilson was playing—and decided that he deserved to be slapped down. Hard. But I waited for the right moment in his monologue to strike.

". . . of course, after Hobbs burst into tears in front of our chap in Washington . . . do you know Christopher Perkins? Fantastically indiscreet . . . anyway, Hobbs had a bit of a boo-hoo while out boozing with Perkins. The next thing you know, the story was all over London within twenty-four hours. Nobody could believe it. Hard Man Hobbs coming apart because of some woman journo . . ."

"You mean, like me?"

Wilson laughed a hollow laugh but didn't say anything in reply.

"Well, come on—answer the question," I said, my voice loud, amused.

"What question?" Wilson demanded.

"Am I like this Elaine Plunkett woman?"

"How should I know? I mean, I never met her."

"Yes—but I am a woman journo, just like her. And I'm also sleeping with Tony Hobbs, just like her."

Long pause. Wilson tried to look nonplussed. He failed.

"I didn't know . . ." he said.

"Liar," I said, laughing.

The word hit him like an open hand across the face. "What did you just say?"

I favored him with an enormous smile. And said, "I called you a liar. Which is what you are."

"I really think . . ."

"What? That you can play a little head game like that with me and get away with it?"

He shifted his large bottom in his chair and kneaded a handkerchief in his hand.

"I really didn't mean any offense."

"Yes, you did."

His eyes started searching the room for the waiter.

"I really must go."

I leaned over toward him, until my face was about a half-inch away from his. And maintaining my jovial, noncommittal tone, I said, "You know something? You're just like every bully I've ever met. You turn tail and run as soon as you're called out."

He stood up and left but didn't apologize. Englishmen never apologize.

"I'm certain American men aren't exactly apology-prone," Tony said when I made this observation.

"They're better trained than you lot."

"That's because they grow up with all that latent Puritan guilt . . . and the idea that everything has a price."

"Whereas the Brits . . ."

"We think we can get away with it all . . . maybe."

I was tempted to tell him about the conversation with Wilson. But I'd decided that nothing good would come out of him knowing that I was now well informed about Elaine Plunkett. On the contrary, I feared that he might feel exposed . . . or, worse yet, embarrassed (the one emotional state that all Brits fear). Anyway, I didn't want to tell him that hearing the Elaine Plunkett story actually made me love him even more. Because I'd learned that he was just as delicate as the rest of us. And I liked that. His fragility was curiously reassuring, a reminder that he had the capacity to be hurt too.

Two weeks later, I was offered the opportunity to gauge Tony in his home terrain—when, out of the blue, he asked, "Feel like running off to London for a few days?"

He explained that he'd been called back for a meeting at the *Chronicle.* "Nothing sinister—just my annual lunch with the editor," he said casually. "Fancy a couple of days at the Savoy?"

It didn't take any further persuasion. I had been in London only once before. It was during the eighties, prior to my foreign postings—and it was one of those dumb two-week dashes through assorted European capitals, which included four days in London. But I liked what I saw. Mind you, all I saw was assorted monuments and museums and a couple of interesting plays, and a glimpse of the sort of upscale residential life that was lived by those who could afford a Chelsea town house. In other words, my vision of London was selective, to say the least.

Then again, a room at the Savoy doesn't exactly give you a down and dirty vision of London either. On the contrary, I was just a little impressed by the suite we were given overlooking the Thames, and the bottle of champagne waiting for us in an ice bucket.

"Is this how the *Chronicle* usually treats its foreign correspondents?" I asked.

"You must be joking," he said. "But the manager's an old friend. We became chummy when he was running the Intercontinental in Tokyo, so he always fixes me up whenever I'm in town."

"Well, that's a relief," I said.

"What?"

"The fact that you didn't violate one of the cardinal rules of journalism—never pay for anything yourself."

He laughed and pulled me into bed. He poured me a glass of champagne.

"No can do," I said. "On antibiotics."

"Since when?"

"Since yesterday, when I saw the embassy doctor for a strep throat."

"You've got a strep throat?"

I opened my mouth wide. "Go on, peep inside."

"No thanks," he said. "Is that why you weren't drinking on the plane?"

"Booze and antibiotics don't mix."

"You should have told me."

"Why? It's just a strep throat."

"God, you are Ms. Toughie."

"That's me, all right."

"Well, I have to say I am disappointed. Because who the hell am I going to drink with over the next few days?"

Actually, that was something of a rhetorical question, as Tony had plenty of people to drink with over the three days we spent in London. He'd arranged for us to go out every night with assorted journalistic colleagues and friends. Without exception, I liked his choice of cronies. There was Kate Medford—a longtime colleague from the *Chronicle* who now presented the big late afternoon news program on BBC Radio 4, and who hosted a little dinner for us (with her oncologist husband, Roger) at her house in a leafy inner suburb called Chiswick. There was an extremely boozy night out (for Tony anyway) with a fellow journo named Dermot Fahy, who was a columnist on the *Independent* and a great talker. He was also an all-purpose rake who spent much of the evening leering at me, much to Tony's amusement (as he told me afterward, "Dermot does that with every woman," to which I just had to reply, "Well, thanks a lot"). Then there was a former *Telegraph* journo named Robert Matthews who'd made quite a bit of money on his first Robert Ludlum–style thriller. He insisted on taking us for a ridiculously expensive meal at the Ivy, and ordering £60 bottles of wine, and drinking far too much, and briefly regaling us with darkly funny stories about his recent divorce—stories which he told in a brilliant, deadpan, self-mocking style, but which hinted at a terrible private pain.

All of Tony's friends were first-rate conversationalists who liked staying up late and having three glasses of wine too many, and (this impressed the hell out of me) never really talking about themselves. Even though Tony hadn't seen these people in around a year, work was only lightly mentioned ("Haven't been shot by Islamic Jihad yet, Tony?"—that sort of thing), and never at great length. If personal matters did arise—like Robert's divorce—a certain sardonic spin was put on things. Even when Tony gently inquired about Kate's teenage daughter (who, as it turned out, was getting over a near-fatal involvement with anorexia), Kate said, "Well, it's all a bit like what Rossini said about Wagner's operas: there are some splendid quarter-of-an-hours."

Then the matter was dropped.

The intriguing thing about this style of discourse was the way everybody disseminated just enough information to let each other know the state of play in their respective lives—but, inevitably, whenever the talk veered toward the personal, it was swiftly deflected back toward less individual matters. I quickly sensed that to speak at length about anything private in a gathering of more than two people was considered just not done . . . especially in the presence of a stranger like me. Yet I rather liked this conversational style—and the fact that banter was considered a meritorious endeavor. Whenever serious events of the day were broached, they were always undercut by a vein of acerbity and absurdity. No one embraced the kind of earnestness that so often characterized American dinner table debate. Then again, as Tony once told me, the great difference between Yanks and Brits was that Americans believed that life was serious but not hopeless . . . whereas the English believed that life was hopeless but not serious.

Three days of London table chat convinced me of that truth, just as it also convinced me that I could easily hold my own amid such banter. Tony was introducing me to his friends—and seemed delighted that I integrated with them so quickly. Just as I was pleased that he was showing me off. I wanted to show off Tony too—but my only friend in London, Margaret Campbell, was out of town while we were there. While Tony was lunching with the editor, I jumped the tube to Hampstead, and wandered the well-heeled residential backstreets, and spent an hour roaming the Heath, all the while thinking to myself: *this is very pleasant.* Maybe this had something to do with the fact that, after Cairo's ongoing urban madness, London initially came across as a paragon of order and tidiness. Granted, within a day of being there, I was also noticing the litter on the streets, the graffiti, the indigent population who slept outdoors, and the snarling traffic. But these scruffy civic attributes simply struck me as an essential component of metropolitan life.

Then there was the little fact that I was in London with Tony . . . which made the city look even better. Tony himself also admitted the same thing, telling me that, for the first time in years, he actually "got" the idea of London again.

He remained pretty close-lipped about his lunch with the editor—except to say that it went well. But then, two days later, he gave me further details of that meeting. We were an hour into our flight back to Cairo when he turned to me and said, "I need to talk to you about something."

"That sounds serious," I said, putting down the novel I'd been reading.

"It's not serious. Just interesting."

"By which you mean . . . ?"

"Well, I didn't want to mention this while we were in London—because I didn't want to spend our last two days there discussing it."

"Discussing what exactly?"

"Discussing the fact that, during my lunch with the editor, he offered me a new job."

"What kind of new job?"

"Foreign editor of the paper."

This took a moment to sink in.

"Congratulations," I said. "Did you accept it?"

"Of course I didn't accept. Because . . ."

"Yes?"

"Well . . . because I wanted to speak with you first about it."

"Because it means a transfer back to London?"

"That's right."

"Do you want the job?"

"Put it this way: His Lordship was hinting very strongly that I should take it. He was also hinting that, after nearly twenty years in the field, it was time I did a stint at HQ. Of course, I could fight coming back. But I don't think I'd win that one. Anyway, the foreign editorship isn't exactly a demotion . . ."

A pause. I said, "So you are going to take the job?"

"I think I have to. But . . . uhm . . . that doesn't mean I have to come back to London alone."

Another pause as I thought about that last comment. Finally I said, "I have some news too. And I have an admission to make."

He looked at me with care.

"And what's this admission?"

"I'm not on antibiotics. Because I don't have a strep throat. But I still can't drink right now . . . because I happen to be pregnant."

THREE

TONY TOOK THE news well. He didn't shudder or turn gray. There was a moment of stunned surprise, followed by an initial moment or two of reflection. But then he took my hand and squeezed it and said, "This is good news."

"You really think that?"

"Absolutely. And you're certain . . . ?"

"Two pregnancy tests certain," I said.

"You want to keep it?"

"I'm thirty-seven years old, Tony. Which means I've entered the realm of now or never. But just because I might want to keep it doesn't mean you have to be there too. I'd like you to be, of course. However . . ."

He shrugged. "I want to be there," he said.

"You sure?"

"Completely. And I want you to come to London with me."

Now it was my turn to go a little white.

"You all right?" he asked.

"Surprised."

"About . . . ?"

"The course this conversation is taking."

"Are you worried?"

Understatement of the year. Though I had managed to keep my anxiety in the background during our days in London (not to mention the week beforehand, when the first pregnancy test came back positive from my doctor in Cairo), it was still omnipresent. And with good reason. Though part of me was quietly pleased about being pregnant, there was an equally substantial portion of my private self that was terrified by the prospect. Maybe it had something to do with the fact that I never really expected to get pregnant. Though there were the usual hormonal urges, these were inevitably negated by the fact that my happily self-governing life could not incorporate the massive commitment that was motherhood.

So the discovery that I *was* pregnant threw me completely. But people always have the capacity to surprise you. Tony certainly did that. For the rest of the flight to Cairo, he informed me that he thought this pregnancy was a very good thing; that, coupled with his transfer back to London, it was as if fate had intervened to propel us into making some major decisions. This had happened at the right moment. Because we were so right for each other. Though it might be something of an adjustment for both of us to be setting up house together—and for us to be at desk jobs (he was certain I could talk my way into the *Post*'s London bureau)—wasn't it time we finally surrendered to the inevitable and settled down?

"Are you talking marriage here?" I asked him after he finished his little spiel.

He didn't meet my eye but still said, "Well, yes, I, uh, yes, I suppose I am."

I was suddenly in need of a very large vodka, and deeply regretted not being able to touch the stuff.

"I'm going to have to think about all this."

Much to Tony's credit, he let the matter drop. Nor did he, in any way, pressure me over the next week. Then again, that wasn't Tony's style. So, during the first few days after we got back from London, we gave each other some thinking time. Correction: he gave *me* some thinking time. Yes, we spoke on the phone twice a day, and even had an amusing lunch together, during which we never once mentioned the big "elephant in the room" question hanging over us . . . though, at the end of it, I did ask, "Have you given the *Chronicle* your decision?"

"No—I'm still awaiting an update from someone."

He gave me a little smile when he said that. Even though he was under pressure to make a decision, he was still refusing to pressure me. And I could only contrast his low-key approach with that of Richard Pettiford. When he was trying to compel me to marry him, he overstepped the mark on several occasions, eventually treating me (in true lawyerly style) like a reluctant juror who had to be won over to his point of view.

With Tony I didn't even need to respond to his comment about "await-ing an update from someone." He knew that he was asking me to make a big decision, so all I asked him in reply was, "And you still won't be going back for three months?"

"Yes, but the editor does need to know my decision by the end of the week."

And he left it at that.

Besides doing a lot of serious thinking, I also made several key phone calls—the first of which was to Thomas Richardson, the edi-tor-in-chief of the *Post*, and someone with whom I had always had a cordial, if distant, relationship. As an old-school Yankee, he also ap-preciated directness. So when he returned my call, I was completely direct with him, explaining that I was marrying a journalist from the *Chronicle* and was planning to move to England. I also said that the *Post* was my home, and I certainly wanted to stay with the paper, but the fact that I was also pregnant meant that I would eventually need a twelve-week period of maternity leave, commencing about seven months from now.

"You're pregnant?" he said, sounding genuinely surprised.

"It looks that way."

"But that's wonderful news, Sally. And I can completely understand why you want to have the baby in London . . ."

"The thing is, we won't be moving there for three months."

"Well, I'm certain we can work something out at our London bureau. One of our correspondents has been talking about coming back to Bos-ton, so your timing couldn't be better."

There was a part of me that was alarmed about the fact that my boss had so eased my professional passage to London. Now I had no reason not to follow Tony. But when I informed him that my transfer to the London bureau of the *Post* seemed certain, I also said that I was terrified of this huge change in circumstances. Once again, his reply (though predictably flippant) was also reassuring—telling me that it wasn't as if I were going behind the veil. Nor would we be moving to Ulan Bator. And I would have a job. And if we found that we couldn't stand being behind desks in offices . . . well, who's to say that we were indentured to London for the rest of our lives?

"Anyway, we're not the sort of people to become each other's jailers, now are we?" he said.

"Not a chance of that," I said.

"Glad to hear it," he said, with a laugh. "So, I don't suppose it will be the end of the world if we get married in the next few weeks, now will it?"

"Since when did you get so damn romantic?" I asked.

"Since I had a conversation with one of our consular chaps a few days ago."

What this "chap" told Tony was that my passage into Britain—both professionally and personally—would be far more rapidly expedited if we were husband and wife. Whereas I would be facing months of immigration bureaucracy if I chose to remain single. Once again, I was astounded by the rate at which my life was being turned around. Destiny is like that, isn't it? You travel along, thinking that the trajectory of your life will follow a certain course (especially when you're starting to crowd middle age). But then, you meet someone, you allow it to progress, you find yourself tiptoeing across that dangerous terrain called love. Before you know it, you're on a long-distance phone call to your only surviving family member, telling her that not only are you pregnant, but you're also about to . . .

"Get married?" Sandy said, sounding genuinely shocked.

"It's the practical thing to do," I said.

"You mean, like getting pregnant for the first time at thirty-seven?"

"Believe me, that was completely accidental."

"Oh, I believe you. Because you're about the last person I'd expect to get intentionally knocked up. How's Tony taking it?"

"Very well. Better than me, in fact. I mean, he even used the dreaded words 'settling down' and in a positive manner as well."

"Maybe he understands something you still don't get . . ."

"You mean, the fact that we all have to settle down someday?" I said, sounding just ever so slightly sarcastic. Though Sandy had always supported my peripatetic career, she did frequently make noises about the fact that I was heading for a lonely old age, and that if I did dodge the child thing, I would come to regret it in later life. There was something about my freewheelingness that unsettled her. Don't get me wrong—she didn't play the envy card. But part of the reason she was so delighted with my news was that—once I became a mother—we would occupy similar terrain. And I would finally be brought down to earth.

"Now, hang on—I didn't *tell* you to get pregnant, did I?" Sandy asked.

"No—but you've only spent the last ten years asking me when it would happen."

"And now it has. And I'm thrilled for you. And I can't wait to meet Tony."

"Come to Cairo for the wedding next week."

"Next week?" she said, sounding shocked. "Why so fast?"

I explained about wanting to sidestep working and residency permits before we moved to London in just under three months' time.

"God, this is all a little whirlwind."

"Tell me about it."

I knew that Sandy wouldn't be able to make it over for the wedding. Not only did she not have the money or the time, but to her, anything beyond the borders of the United States was Injun country. Which is why, even if she did have the wherewithal to get to Egypt, I'm certain she would have found a way of avoiding the journey. As she openly admitted to me on several occasions: "I'm not like you—I have no interest in *out there*." That was one of the many things I so loved about my sister—she was completely honest about herself. "I'm limited," she once told me, a comment that I found unnecessarily self-lacerating—especially as she was a very smart, very literate woman who managed to keep her life together after her husband walked out on her three years ago.

Within a month of his seismic departure, Sandy had found a job teaching history at a small private school in Medford—and was somehow managing to meet the mortgage and feed the kids at the same time. Which (as I told her) showed far more moxie than ducking in and out of assorted Middle Eastern hellholes. But now I was going to learn all about life on the domestic front—and even on a crackly phone line from Egypt, Sandy quickly sensed my fear.

"You're going to do just fine," she told me. "Better than fine. Great. Anyway, it's not like you're giving up your job, or being sent to Lawrence [perhaps the ugliest town in Massachusetts]. And hey, it's London, right? And after all those war zones you've covered, motherhood won't seem much different."

I did laugh. And I also wondered: *is she telling the truth?*

But the next few weeks didn't allow me much opportunity for extended ruminations about my soon-to-be-changed circumstances. Especially as the Middle East was up to its usual manic tricks. There was a cabinet crisis in Israel, an assassination attempt on a senior Egyptian government minister, and a ferry boat that overturned on the Nile in northern Sudan, killing all 150 passengers aboard. The fact that I was suffering from an extended bout of morning sickness while covering these assorted stories only seemed to accentuate the banality of my condition compared with such major human calamity. So too did the large number of baby books that I had expressed to me by Amazon.com, and which I devoured with the obsessive relish of somebody who had just been told she was about to embark on a complicated voyage and was desperately searching for the right guide to tell her how to get through it. So I'd return home after writing about a local cholera scare in the Nile Delta and start reading up on colic and night feeding and cradle cap, and a range of other new words and terminologies from the child care lexicon.

"You know what I'll miss most about the Middle East?" I told Tony on the night before our wedding. "The fact that it's so damn extreme, so completely deranged."

"Whereas London is going to be nothing but day-to-day stuff?"

"I didn't say that."

"But you are worrying about *that.*"

"A little bit, yes. Aren't you?"

"It *will* be a change."

"Especially as you'll have additional baggage in tow."

"You're not referring to yourself, by any chance?" he asked.

"Hardly."

"Well, I'm happy about the additional baggage."

I kissed him. "Well I'm happy that you're happy . . ."

"It will be an adjustment, but we'll be fine. And, believe me, London has its own peculiar madness."

I remembered that comment six weeks later when we flew north to Heathrow. Courtesy of the *Chronicle,* they were repatriating their new foreign editor and his new wife in business class. Courtesy of the *Chronicle*, we were also being put up for six weeks in a company apartment near the paper's offices in Wapping while we house hunted. Courtesy of the *Chronicle*, all our belongings had been shipped last week from Cairo and would be kept in storage until we found a permanent place to live. And courtesy of the *Chronicle*, a large black Mercedes collected us from the airport and began the slow crawl through evening rush-hour traffic toward central London.

As the car inched along the highway, I reached over and took Tony's hand—noticing, as I still did, the shiny platinum wedding bands adorning our respective left hands, remembering the hilarious civil ceremony at which we were spliced in the Cairo Registry Office—a true madhouse without a roof, and where the official who joined us as husband and wife looked like an Egyptian version of Groucho Marx. Now here we were—only a few short months after that crazy twenty-four hours in Somalia—rolling down the M4 toward . . .

Wapping.

That was something of a surprise, Wapping. The cab had negotiated its way off the highway, and headed south, through red-brick residential areas. These eventually gave way to a jumble of architectural styles: Victorian meets Edwardian meets Warsaw Public Housing meets Cinder Block Mercantile Brutalism. It was late afternoon in early winter. Light was thin. But despite the paucity of natural illumination, my first view of London as a married woman showed me that it was an extended exercise in scenic disorientation, a Chinese menu cityscape, in which there was little visual coherence, and where affluence and deprivation were adjacent neighbors. Of course, I had noticed this hodgepodge aspect of the city on my visit here with Tony. But, like any tourist, I tended to focus on that which was pleasing . . . and like any tourist, I also avoided all of South London. More to the point, I had just been passing through here for a few days—and as I wasn't on assignment, my journalist's antennae had been turned off. But now—*now*—this city was about to become my home. So I had my nose pressed against the glass of the Mercedes, staring out at the wet sidewalks, the overflowing litter bins, the clusters of fast-food shops, the occasional elegant crescent of houses, the large patch of green parkland (Clapham Common, Tony informed me), the slummy tangle of mean streets (Stockwell and Vauxhall), yielding to office buildings, then a spectacular view of the Houses of Parliament, then more office buildings, then more faceless redbrick, then the surprise appearance of Tower Bridge, then a tunnel, and then . . . Wapping.

New bland apartment developments, the occasional old warehouse, a couple of office towers, and a vast squat industrial complex, hidden behind high brick walls and razor wire.

"What's that?" I asked. "The local prison?"

Tony laughed.

"It's where I work."

Around a quarter mile beyond this compound, the driver pulled up in front of a modern building, about eight stories tall. We took the elevator up to the fourth floor. The corridor was papered in an anemic cream paper, with neutral tan carpet on the floor. We came to a wood veneered door. The driver fished out two keys and handed one to each of us.

"You do the honors," Tony said.

I opened the door, and stepped into a small boxy one-bedroom apartment. It was furnished in a generic Holiday Inn style and looked out onto a back alleyway.

"Well," I said, taking it all in, "this will make us find a house fast."

It was my old college friend Margaret Campbell who expedited the house-hunting process. When I called her up prior to my departure from Cairo and explained that, not only was I about to become a full-time London resident, but I was also just married and pregnant to boot, she asked, "Anything else?"

"Thankfully, *no*."

"Well, it will be wonderful to have you here—and, believe me, you will end up liking this town."

"By which you mean . . . ?"

"It's just something of an adjustment, that's all. But hey, come over for lunch as soon as you arrive, and I'll show you the ropes. And I hope you have a lot of cash. Because this place makes Zurich seem cheap and cheerful."

Certainly, Margaret wasn't exactly living in disadvantaged circumstances—she and her family resided in a three-story town house in South Kensington. I phoned her the morning after we arrived in London—

and, true to her word, she invited me over that afternoon. She'd become a little more matronly since I'd last seen her—the sort of woman who now sported a Hermès scarf and wore twin sets. She'd given up a serious executive position with Citibank to play the post-feminist stay-at-home mother, and had ended up in London after her lawyer husband had been transferred here for a two-year stint. But despite this nod to corporate-wife style, she was still the sharp-tongued good friend I had known during my college years.

"I sense this is just a little out of our league," I said, looking around her place.

"Hey, if the firm wasn't footing the sixty grand rent . . ."

"Sixty thousand *pounds*?" I said, genuinely shocked.

"Well, it is South Ken. But hell, in this town, a modest studio in a modest area is going to set you back a thousand pounds a month in rent . . . which is crazy. But that's the price of admission here. Which is why you guys really should think about buying somewhere."

With her two kids off at school all day—and with my job at the *Post* not starting for another month—Margaret decided to take me house hunting. Naturally, Tony was pleased to let me handle this task. He was surprisingly positive about the idea of actually buying a foothold here, especially as all his colleagues at the *Chronicle* kept telling him that he who hesitates in the London property game is lost. But as I quickly discovered, even the most unassuming terraced house at the end of a tube line was exorbitant. Tony still had his £100,000 share from the sale of his parents' place in Amersham. I had the equivalent of another £20,000 courtesy of assorted small savings that I had built up over the past ten years. And Margaret—immediately assuming the role of property advisor—started working the phones and decided that an area called Putney was our destiny. As we drove south in her BMW, she pitched it to me.

"Great housing stock, all the family amenities you need, it's right on the river, and the District Line goes straight to Tower Bridge . . . which makes it perfect for Tony's office. Now there are parts of Putney where you need over one-point-five to get a foot in the door . . ."

"One-point-five *million*?" I asked.

"Not an unusual price in this town."

"Sure, in Kensington or Chelsea. But *Putney*? It's nearly the 'burbs, isn't it?"

"*Inner* 'burbs. But hey, it's only six or seven miles from Hyde Park . . . which is considered no distance at all in this damn sprawl. Anyway, one-point-five is the asking price for a big house in West Putney. Where I'm taking you, it's just south of the Lower Richmond Road. Cute little streets, which go right down to the Thames. And the house may be a little small— just two bedrooms—but there's the possibility of a loft extension . . ."

"Since when did you become a Realtor?" I asked with a laugh.

"Ever since I moved to this town. I tell you, the Brits might be all taciturn and distant when you first meet them—but get them talking about property, and they suddenly can't stop chatting. Especially when it comes to London house prices—which is the major ongoing metropolitan obsession."

"Did it take you a while to fit in here?"

"The worst thing about London is that nobody really fits in. And the best thing about London is that nobody really fits in. Figure that one out, and you'll have a reasonably okay time here. Just as it also takes a while to work out the fact that—even if, like me, you actually like living here—it's best to give off just the slightest whiff of Anglophobia."

"Why's that?"

"Because the Brits are suspicious of anyone who seems to like them."

Intriguingly, however, Margaret didn't play the Anglophobic card with the rather obsequious real estate agent who showed us around the house on Sefton Street in Putney. Every time he tried to gloss over a defect—like the paisley-patterned carpets and the cramped bathroom and the woodchip wallpaper which evidently hid a multitude of plastering sins—she'd break into one of her "You've got to be kidding?" routines, deliberately acting the loud American in an attempt to unsettle him. She succeeded.

"You're really asking four hundred and forty thousand for *this*?"

The real estate agent—in his spread collared pink shirt and his black suit and Liberty tie—smiled weakly.

"Well, Putney has always been very desirable."

"Yeah—but, *gosh*, it's only two bedrooms. And look at the state of this place."

"I do admit that the decor is a little tired."

"Tired? Try archaic. I mean, someone died here, right?"

The agent went all diffident again.

"It is being sold by the grandson of the former occupants."

"What did I tell you?" Margaret said, turning to me. "This place hasn't been touched since the sixties. And I bet it's been on the market . . ."

The agent avoided her gaze.

"Come on, 'fess up," Margaret said.

"A *few* weeks. And I do know the seller would take an offer."

"I bet they would," Margaret said, then turned to me and whispered, "What do you think?"

"Too much work for the price," I whispered. Then I asked the agent, "You don't have anything like this which might just be a little more renovated?"

"Not at the moment. But I will keep your number on file."

I must have heard that same sentence dozens of times over the next ten days. The house-hunting game was terra incognita for me. But Margaret turned out to be a canny guide. Every morning, after she got her kids off to school, she drove us around assorted neighborhoods. She had a nose for the areas that were up-and-coming and those worth dodging. We must have seen close to twenty properties in that first week—and continued to be the bane of every real estate agent that we encountered. "The Ugly Americans," we called ourselves . . . always polite, but asking far too many questions, speaking directly about the flaws we saw, constantly challenging the asking price, and (in the case of Margaret) knowing far more about the complex jigsaw of London property than was expected from Yanks. With pressure on me to find something before I started work, there was a certain "beat the clock" aspect to this search. And so I applied the usual journalistic skills to this task—by which I mean I gained the most comprehensive (yet entirely superficial) knowledge of this subject in the shortest amount of time possible. When Margaret was back home with her kids in the afternoon, I'd jump the underground to check out an area. I researched proximity to hospitals, schools, parks, and all those other "mommy concerns" (as Margaret sardonically called them) which now had to be taken into account.

"This is not my idea of a good time," I told Sandy during a phone call a few days into the house hunt. "Especially as the city's so damn big. I mean, there's no such thing as a simple trip across town. Everything's an expedition here—and I forgot to pack my pith helmet."

"That would make you stand out in the crowd."

"Hardly. This is the melting pot to end all melting pots—which means that no one stands out here. Unlike Boston . . ."

"Oh, listen to the big city girl. I bet Boston's friendlier."

"Of course. Because it's small. Whereas London doesn't need to be friendly . . ."

"Because it's so damn big?"

"Yeah—and also because it's London."

That was the most intriguing thing about London—its aloofness. Perhaps it had something to do with the reticent temperament of the natives. Perhaps it was the fact that the city was so vast, so heterogeneous, so contradictory. Whatever the reason, during my first few weeks in London, I found myself thinking this town was like one of those massive Victorian novels, in which high life and low life endlessly intermingle, and where the narrative always sprawls to such an extent that you never really get to grips with the plot.

"That about gets it right," Margaret said when I articulated this theory to her a few days later. "Nobody's really important here. Because London dwarfs even the biggest egos. Cuts everyone right down to size. Especially since all Brits despise self-importance."

That was another curious contradiction to London life—the way you could mistake English diffidence for arrogance. Every time I opened a newspaper—and read a lurid account of some local minor celebrity enmeshed in some cocaine-and-jailbait scandal—it was very clear to me that this was a society that stamped down very hard on anyone who committed the sin of bumptiousness. At the same time, however, so many of the real estate agents I dealt with comported themselves with a pomposity that belied their generally middle-class origins . . . especially when you questioned the absurd prices they were demanding for inferior properties.

"That's what the market is asking, madam" was the usual disdainful response—a certain haughty emphasis placed on the word *madam*, to make you feel his condescending respect.

"*Condescending respect,*" Margaret said, repeating my phrase out loud as we drove south from her house. "I like it—even though it is a complete oxymoron. Then again, until I lived in London, I'd never been able to discern two contrasting emotions lurking behind one seemingly innocent sentence. The English have a real talent when it comes to saying one thing and meaning the—"

She didn't get to finish that sentence, as a white delivery van pulled out of nowhere and nearly sideswiped us. The van screeched to a halt. The driver—a guy in his twenties with close-cropped hair and bad teeth—came storming out toward us. He radiated aggression.

"The fuck you think you was doing?" he said.

Margaret didn't seem the least bit flustered by his belligerency, let alone his bad grammar.

"Don't you talk that way to me," she said, her voice cool and completely collected.

"Talk how I want to talk, cunt."

"Asshole," she shot back, and pulled the car back out into traffic, leaving the guy standing on the road, gesticulating angrily at her.

"Charming," I said.

"That was an example of a lowly species known as White Van Man," she said. "Indigenous to London—and always spoiling for a fight. Especially if you drive a decent car."

"Your sangfroid was impressive."

"Here's another little piece of advice about living in this town. Never try to fit in, never try to *appease*."

"I'll keep that in mind," I said, then added, "but I really don't think that jerk was saying one thing and meaning another."

We crossed Putney Bridge and turned down the Lower Richmond Road, heading back to Sefton Street—our first port-of-call on this house-hunting marathon. I'd received a call from the agent who'd shown us that first house, informing me that another similar property had just come on the market.

"It's not in the most pleasing decorative order," he admitted on the phone.

"By which you mean *tired*?" I said. He cleared his throat.

"A bit tired, yes. But structurally speaking, it has been considerably modernized. And though the asking price is four-thirty-five, I'm certain they will take an offer."

Without question, the agent was telling the truth about the shabby interior decor. And yes, the house was distinctly cottagey—with two small reception rooms downstairs. But a kitchen extension had been built onto the back—and though all the cabinets and appliances were outdated, I was pretty certain that a ready-made kitchen from somewhere like IKEA could be installed without vast cost. The two bedrooms upstairs were papered in a funeral-home print, with an equally gruesome pink carpet covering the floor. But the agent assured me that there were decent floorboards beneath this polyester veneer (something a surveyor confirmed a week later), and that the woodchip paper in the hallways could be stripped away and replastered. The bathroom had a lurid salmon-pink suite. But at least the central heating was new throughout. Ditto the wiring. There was also substantial space for an attic office. I knew that, once all the decorative horrors were stripped away, it could be made to feel light and airy. For the first time in my transient life, I found myself thinking a surprisingly domesticated thought: this could actually be a home.

Margaret and I said nothing as we toured the house. Once we were outside, however, she turned to me and asked, "So?"

"Bad clothes, good bones," I said. "But the potential is fantastic."

"My feeling exactly. And if they're asking four-thirty-five . . ."

"I'm offering three-eighty-five . . . if Tony gives it the thumbs-up."

Later that night, I spent the better part of my half-hour phone call with Sandy waxing lyrical about the cottage's possibilities and the genuine pleasantness of the neighborhood—especially the towpath fronting the Thames, which was just down the street.

"Good God," she said. "You actually sound housebroken."

"Very funny," I said. "But after all the dismal stuff I've seen, it is a relief to find somewhere that could be actually made livable."

"Especially with all the Martha Stewart plans you've got for it."

"You're really enjoying this, aren't you?"

"Damn right. I never expected to ever hear you sound like someone who subscribes to *Better Homes and Gardens*."

"Believe me, I keep shocking myself. Like I never thought I'd be poring over Dr. Spock as if he were Holy Writ."

"You reach the chapter where he tells you how to flee the country during colic?"

"Yeah—the stuff about false passports is terrific."

"And wait until you experience your first broken night . . ."

"I think I'll hang up now."

"Congrats on the house."

"Well, it's not ours yet. And Tony still has to see it."

"You'll sell it to him."

"Damn right I will. Because I start work again in a few weeks—and I just can't afford, time-wise, another extended house-hunting blitz."

But Tony was so wrapped up in life at the *Chronicle* that he could only make it down to Sefton Street five days later. It was a late Saturday morning and we arrived by tube, crossing Putney Bridge, then turning right into the Lower Richmond Road. Instead of continuing down this thoroughfare, I directed us toward the towpath, following the Thames as it continued snaking eastward. It was Tony's first view of the area by day, and I could tell that he immediately liked the idea of having a river walk virtually on his doorstep. Then I steered him into the green and pleasant expanses of Putney Common, located right beyond our future street. He even approved of the upscale shops and wine bars decorating the Lower Richmond Road. But when we turned into Sefton Street, I saw him take in the considerable number of Jeeps and Land Rovers parked there, signaling that this was one of those areas that has been discovered, and populated, by the professional classes . . . of the sort who looked upon these charming little cottages as family starter homes, to be eventually traded in (as Margaret had informed me) for more capacious residences when the second child arrived and the bigger job came along.

As we toured the area, and seemed to be passing a nonstop procession of baby carriages and strollers and Volvo station wagons with baby seats, we started shooting each other glances of amused disbelief . . . as if to say, "How the hell did we end up playing this game?"

"It's bloody Nappy Valley," Tony finally said with a mordant laugh. "Young families indeed. We're going to seem like geriatrics when we move in."

"Speak for yourself," I said, nudging him.

When we reached the house, and met the agent, and started walking through every room, I watched him taking it all in, trying to gauge his reaction.

"Looks exactly like the house I grew up in," he finally said, then added, "But I'm sure we could improve on that."

I launched into a design-magazine monologue, in which I painted extensive verbal pictures about its great potential once all the postwar tackiness was stripped away.

It was the loft conversion that won him over. Especially after I said that I could probably raid a small stock market fund I had in the States to find the £7000 that would pay for the study he so wanted, to write the books he hoped would liberate him from the newspaper that had clipped his wings.

Or, at least, that's what I sensed Tony was thinking after our first two weeks in London. Maybe it was the shock of doing a desk job after nearly twenty years in the field. Maybe it was the discovery that newspaper life at Wapping was an extended minefield of internal politics. Or maybe it was his reluctant admission that being the foreign editor was, by and large, an "upper-echelon exercise in bureaucracy." Whatever the reason, I did get the distinct feeling that Tony wasn't at all readjusting to this new office-bound life into which he'd been dropped. Any time I raised the issue, he would insist that all was well . . . that he simply had a lot on his mind, and was just trying to find his feet amid such changed circumstances. Or he'd make light of our newfound domesticity. Like when we repaired to a wine bar after viewing the house, and he said, "Look, if the whole thing gets too financially overwhelming, or we just feel too damn trapped by the monthly repayment burden, then to hell with it—we'll cash in our chips and sell the damn thing, and find jobs somewhere cheap and cheerful, like the *Kathmandu Chronicle*."

"Damn right," I said, laughing.

That night, I finally got to show my husband off to my one London friend—as Margaret invited us over for dinner. It started well—with much small talk about our house-to-be, and how we were settling into London. At first, Tony managed great flashes of charm—even though he was tossing back substantial quantities of wine with a deliberate vehemence that I had never seen before. But though I was a little concerned by this display of power drinking, it didn't initially seem to be impeding his ability to amuse, especially when it came to telling tales about his experiences under fire in assorted third world hellholes. And he also kept everyone entertained with his own wry, damning comments on Englishness. In fact, he'd won Margaret over—until the conversation turned political and, *shazam*, he went into an anti-American rant which sent her husband Alexander on the defensive and ended up alienating everyone. On the way home, he turned to me and said, "Well, I think that went *awfully* well, don't you?"

"Why the hell did you do that?" I asked.

Silence. Followed by one of his languid shrugs. Followed by twenty additional minutes of silence as the taxi headed east to Wapping. Followed by more silence as we prepared for bed. Followed by the arrival of breakfast in bed courtesy of Tony the next morning, and a kiss on the head.

"Drafted a little thank-you card to Margaret," he said. "Left it on the kitchen table . . . mail it if you like it . . . okay?"

Then he left for the office.

The card was written in Tony's illegible hieroglyphics but after the second go, I was able to crack the code.

> *Dear Margaret:*
>
> > *Wonderful meeting you. Splendid food. Splendid chat. And tell your husband I did so enjoy our head-to-head on matters political. I do hope it didn't get too heated for all concerned. I plead "in vino stupidus." But what is life without a spirited argument?*
> >
> > *Hope to repay the hospitality soon.*
> >
> > *Yrs . . .*

Naturally, I mailed it. Naturally, Margaret phoned me the next morning when it arrived and said, "May I speak my mind?"

"Go on . . ."

"Well, as far as I'm concerned, his note gives new meaning to the expression 'charming bastard.' But I'm sure I've spoken out of turn."

It didn't bother me. Because Margaret had articulated another emerging truth about Tony—he had a cantankerous underside . . . one that he largely kept hidden from view, but which could make a sudden, unexpected appearance, only to vanish from view again. It might just be a fast, angry comment about a colleague on the paper, or a long exasperated silence if I started going on a little too much about house-hunting matters. Then, a few minutes later, he'd act as if nothing had happened.

"Hey, everyone gets a little moody, right?" Sandy said when I told her about my husband's periodic dark moments. "And when you think of the changes you guys are having to deal with . . ."

"You're right, you're right," I said.

"I mean, it's not like you've discovered he's bipolar."

"Hardly."

"And you're not exactly fighting all the time."

"We rarely fight."

"And he doesn't have fangs or sleep in a coffin?"

"No—but I am keeping a clove of garlic and a crucifix handy under the bed."

"Good marital practice. But hey, from where I sit, it sounds like you're basically not doing too badly for the first couple of months of marriage . . . which is usually the time when you think you've made the worst mistake of your life."

I certainly didn't feel that. I just wished Tony could be a little more articulate about what he was really feeling.

Only I suddenly didn't have enough time on my hands to consider my feelings about our newfangled life together. Because two days after the dinner with Margaret, our offer on the house was accepted. After we paid the deposit, it was I who organized the housing survey, and arranged the mortgage, and found a contractor for the loft and the extensive decorative work, and chose fabrics and colors, and did time at IKEA and Habitat and Heals, and also haggled with plumbers and painters. In between all these nest-building endeavors, I also happened to be dealing with my ever-expanding pregnancy—which, now that the morning sickness was long over, had turned into less of a discomfort than I had expected.

Once again, Margaret had been brilliant when it came to answering my constant spate of questions about the state of being pregnant. She also gave me the lowdown on eventually finding a nanny once my maternity leave was over and I was back at work. And she also explained the workings of the National Health Service, and how to register myself at my local doctor's office in Putney. It turned out to be a group practice, where the receptionist made me fill out assorted forms and then informed me that I had been assigned to a certain Dr. Sheila McCoy.

"You mean I can't choose my own doctor?" I asked the receptionist.

"Course you can. Any doctor in the surgery you like. So if you don't want to see Dr. McCoy . . ."

"I didn't say that. I just don't know if she's the right doctor for me."

"Well, how will you know until you've seen her?" she asked.

I couldn't argue with that logic but, as it turned out, I did like Dr. McCoy—a pleasant, no-nonsense Irish woman in her forties. She saw me a few days later, asked a lot of thorough, no-nonsense questions, and informed me that I would be "assigned" an obstetrician . . . and if I didn't mind crossing the river into Fulham, she was going to place me under the care of a man named Hughes.

"Very senior, very respected, with rooms in Harley Street—and he does his NHS work out of the Mattingly . . . which I think you'll like, as it's one of the newest hospitals in London."

When I mentioned this last comment to Margaret, she laughed.

"That's her way of telling you she doesn't want to horrify you and your need for newness by sending you to one of the grimmer Victorian hospitals around town."

"Why did she think I had a need for newness?"

"Because you're a Yank. And we're supposed to like everything new and shiny. Or, at least, that's what everyone over here thinks. But hey, when it comes to hospitals, give me new and shiny any day."

"I'm not exactly thrilled either about being 'assigned' an obstetrician. Do you think this guy Hughes is some second-rater?"

"Well, your GP told you he has rooms on Harley Street . . ."

"Makes him sound like a slumlord, doesn't it?"

"Tell me about it. I mean, the first time I heard my doctor's office over here referred to as a surgery . . ."

"You thought that's where they operate as well?"

"What can I say? I'm a new, shiny American. But listen, Harley Street is the place for all the big-deal specialists in town. And all those guys do NHS work as well—so you've probably landed yourself a top ob-gyn. Anyway, you're better off having the kid on the NHS. The doctors are the same, and the care's probably better . . . especially if anything goes wrong. Just don't eat the food."

Certainly, there was nothing new or shiny about Mr. Desmond Hughes. When I met him a week later at an office in the Mattingly Hospital, I was immediately struck by his reediness, his beaklike nose, his crisp, practical demeanor, and the fact that, like all British consultants, he was never referred to as Dr. (as I later learned, in this country all surgeons were traditionally called *Mr.*—because, back in less medically advanced times, they weren't considered proper doctors; rather, high-end butchers). Hughes was also a testament to the excellence of British tailoring, as he was dressed in an exquisitely cut chalk-stripe suit, a light-blue shirt with impressive French cuffs, and a black polka-dot tie. Our first consultation was a brisk one. He ordered a scan, he requested blood, he felt around my stomach, he told me that everything seemed "to be going according to plan."

I was a little surprised that he didn't ask me any specific questions about my physical state (beside a general: "Everything seem all right?"). So when we reached the end of this brief consultation, I raised this point. Politely, of course.

"Don't you want to know about my morning sickness?" I asked.

"Are you suffering from it?"

"Not anymore . . ."

He looked at me quizzically.

"Then morning sickness isn't an issue now?"

"But should I be worried that I occasionally feel nauseous?"

"By 'occasionally' you mean . . . ?"

"Two or three times a week."

"But you're never physically sick?"

"No . . . just a hint of nausea."

"Well then, I'd take that to mean that, *periodically*, you feel nauseous."

"Nothing more than that?"

He patted me on the hand. "It's hardly sinister. Your body's going through a bit of a change right now. Anything else troubling you?"

I shook my head, feeling gently (but, oh-so-firmly) chastised.

"Very good then," he said, shutting my file and standing up. "See you again in a few weeks. And . . . uhm . . . you're working, yes?"

"That's right. I'm a journalist."

"That's nice. But you do look a little peaky—so don't overdo it, eh?"

Later that evening, when I related this entire conversation to Tony, he laughed.

"Now you've just discovered two general truths about Harley Street specialists: they hate all questions, and they always patronize you."

Still, Hughes rightly observed one thing: I was tired. This wasn't merely due to the pregnancy, but also to the manifold pressures of trying to find the house, arrange all the building work, and simultaneously feel my way into London. The first four weeks evaporated in a preoccupied blur. Then, my initial month in London was over . . . and I had to start work again.

The *Boston Post*'s office was nothing more than a room in the Reuters building on Fleet Street. My fellow correspondent was a twenty-six-year-old guy named Andrew DeJarnette Hamilton. He signed his copy A. D. Hamilton, and was the sort of aging preppie who somehow managed to lace every conversation with the fact that he'd been to Harvard, and also let it be known that he considered our newspaper to be a mere staging post for his triumphant ascendancy to the *New York Times* or the *Washington Post*. Worse yet, he was one of those determined Anglophiles who'd allowed their vowels to become a little too languid, and who had started to dress in pink Jermyn Street shirts. And he was also the sort of East Coast snot who made the same sort of disdainful noises about my grubby home town of Worcester as that fat little twerp Wilson had done about Tony's suburban place of birth. But given that A. D. Hamilton and I were stuck with each other in a small office, I simply decided to work very hard at ignoring him. At least, we did agree that I would handle most of the sociopolitical stuff, whereas he would corner the market on culture, lifestyle, and any celebrity profiles he could sell to the editor back in Boston. This enabled me to be out of the office on a regular basis—and to start the long, laborious task of making contacts at Westminster, while also attempting to fathom Britain's byzantine social structure. There was also the little problem of language—and the way the wrong choice of words could lead to misconstrued meanings. Because, as Tony was fond of noting, every conversation or social interaction in Britain was underscored by the complexities of class.

I even wrote a short, moderately humorous piece for the paper, entitled "When a Napkin Is Definitely *Not* a Serviette"—in which I explained the loadedness of language on this island. A. D. Hamilton went ballistic when he read the article, accusing me of usurping his territory.

"I'm the cultural chap in our bureau," he said.

"True—but as my piece was about the nuances of class, it was a political piece. And as I am the political *chapette* in this bureau . . ."

"You should check with me in the future before writing something like that."

"You're not the bureau chief, pal."

"But I am the senior correspondent here."

"Oh, please. I have far more seniority on the paper than you do."

"And I have been at this bureau for two years, which means that I have higher rank in London."

"Sorry, but I don't answer to little boys."

After this exchange, A. D. Hamilton and I went out of our ways to avoid each other. This wasn't as difficult as I imagined, because Tony and I had to vacate the company apartment in Wapping and move into Sefton Street. I decided to start filing most of my stories from home, using my advanced pregnancy as an excuse for working from Putney. Not that *chez nous* was the most ideal place to write, as the interior of the house was under construction. The carpets had been pulled up and the floors partially sanded, but they still needed sealing and staining. The living room was being replastered. All the new cabinets and appliances had been installed in the kitchen, but the floor below was chilly concrete. The living room was a catastrophe. Ditto the attic—the conversion of which would now be delayed, as the contractor had been called back to Belfast to deal with his dying mother. At least the decorators had made the nursery their first priority, finishing it during our second week of residency. And thanks to Margaret and Sandy, I had found out which crib and bassinet to buy, not to mention all the other baby paraphernalia. So the stripped pine crib (or "cot" as they called it here) matched well with the pink starry wallpaper—and there was a changing mat and a playpen already in position, ready for use. But no such attention had been lavished on the guest room, which was piled high with boxes. Similarly our own master bathroom lacked a few necessities like wall and floor tiles. And though our bedroom had been painted, we were still waiting for the wardrobes to be fitted, which meant that the room was cluttered with assorted clothes racks.

In other words, the house was a testament to builders' delays and general domestic chaos—and possibly one of the reasons I wasn't seeing much of Tony right now. Mind you, he was fantastically busy—he never seemed to get his pages to bed before eight most evenings—and, in this early phase of his new job, he was also having to stay out late schmoozing with his staff, or work the phones, talking with his assorted correspondents around the planet. But though I accepted his preoccupation with his job, it still bothered me that he dodged any responsibility when it came to dealing with the builders and decorators.

"But you Americans are so much better at threatening people," he said.

I didn't find this comment wildly amusing. But I decided to ignore it, instead saying, "We should get together with some of your friends."

"You're not suggesting having them over, are you?" Tony asked, looking at our half-finished jumble of a kitchen.

"You know, darling—I may be dumb, but I'm not stupid."

"I'm not suggesting you are," he said lightly.

"And I certainly wasn't proposing that we bring them into this disaster area. But it would be nice to see some of the people we met when we came up from Cairo."

Tony shrugged.

"Sure, if you want to."

"Your enthusiasm is spectacular."

"Listen, if you feel like ringing them up, then by all means ring them up."

"But wouldn't it be best if the invitation came from you?"

"The invitation to *what*?"

"To go out and do something. I mean, we live in this amazing cultural capital, right? Best theater in the world. Best classical music. Great art. And we've both been so bound up in work and this damn house that we haven't had a chance to see any of it . . ."

"You really want to go to the theater?" he asked, phrasing the question in such a way that it sounded like I had just suggested joining some wacked-out religious cult.

"Yes, I do."

"Not my thing, actually."

"But might it be Kate and Roger's thing?" I asked, mentioning the couple who had had us over for dinner that first time we were together in London.

"I suppose you could ask them," he said, a little undercurrent of exasperation entering his voice, an undercurrent that had started to make a regular appearance whenever I said something that . . . well, I suppose, *exasperated* him.

But I still called Kate Medford the next day. I got her voicemail, and left a pleasant message, saying how Tony and I were settled in London, how I had become a huge fan of her program on Radio 4, and how we'd both love to see them. It took about four days for her to get back to me. But when she did, she was most friendly—in a rushed sort of way.

"How lovely to hear from you," she said, the crackly line hinting that she was talking to me on her cell phone. "Heard you'd made the move here with Tony."

"And maybe you also heard that we've a baby due in just over three months."

"Yes, the bush telegraph certainly picked up that piece of news. Congratulations—I'm so pleased for you both."

"Thank you."

"And I suppose Tony will eventually adjust to life in Wapping."

This stopped me short. "You've been speaking to Tony?"

"We had lunch last week. Didn't he mention it?"

"My brain's so elsewhere these days," I lied, "what with the job and pregnancy and trying to get the house . . ."

"Ah yes, the house. Putney, I hear."

"That's right."

"Tony Hobbs in Putney. Who would have believed it."

"Roger well?" I asked, changing the subject.

"Desperately busy, as always. And you? Settling in?"

"Getting there. But listen . . . our house is still in no fit state for live-stock, let alone friends . . ."

She laughed. I continued.

"Maybe we could all meet up one night, go to the theater, perhaps . . ."

"The theater?" she said, rolling that one around on her tongue. "I can't remember the last time we did that . . ."

"It was just a suggestion," I said, hating the embarrassed tone creeping into my voice.

"And a lovely one too. It's just we're both so busy right now. But it would be lovely to see you. Perhaps we could do Sunday lunch sometime soon."

"That would be great."

"Well, let me have a chat with Roger and get back to you. Must fly now. So glad you're settling in. Bye."

And our conversation was terminated.

When Tony finally got home that night—well after ten o'clock—I said, "I didn't know you had lunch with Kate Medford last week."

He poured himself a vodka and said, "Yes. I had lunch with Kate last week."

"But why didn't you tell me?"

"Am I supposed to tell you these things?" he asked mildly.

"It's just . . . you knew I was planning to call her to ask about the four of us going out . . ."

"So?"

"But when I mentioned it a few days ago, you acted like you hadn't heard from her since we'd moved to London."

"Did I?" he said, the tone still temperate. After the merest of pauses, he smiled and asked, "So what did Kate say to your idea of an evening at the theater?"

"She suggested Sunday lunch," I said, my voice even, my smile fixed.

"Did she? How nice," he said.

A few days later, I did go to the theater . . . with Margaret. We saw a very well acted, very well directed, and *very long* revival of Ibsen's

Rosmersholm at the National. It was an evening performance—and had come at the end of a day that started with the arrival of plasterers at eight AM, and finished with me filing two stories and just making it across the river right before the curtain went up. The production had received very flattering reviews—which is why I chose it. But about twenty minutes in, I realized I had let myself and Margaret in for an extended three-hour sojourn through some serious Scandinavian gloom. At the intermission, Margaret turned to me and said, "Well, this really is a toe-tapper."

Then, halfway through the second act, I fell fast asleep—only waking with a jolt when the applause came for the curtain call.

"What happened at the end?" I asked Margaret as we left the theater.

"The husband and wife jumped off a bridge and killed themselves."

"*Really*?" I said, genuinely aghast. "Why?"

"Oh, you know—winter in Norway, nothing better to do . . ."

"Thank God I didn't bring Tony. He would have filed for divorce on the spot."

"Not a big Ibsen fan, your husband?"

"Doesn't want anything at all to do with culture. Which is, in my experience, a typical journalist philistine thing. I mean, I suggested going to a play with a couple of friends of his . . ."

Then I recounted my conversation with Tony and my subsequent call from Kate Medford.

"I promise you, she won't get back to you for at least four months," Margaret said when I finished telling her the story. "Then, out of the blue, you'll get this call. She'll sound all friendly, talk about how 'frightfully busy' she's been, and how she'd just love to see you and Tony and the baby, and might you be free for Sunday lunch six weeks from now? And you'll think to yourself: *is this how it works here?* . . . and *is she only doing this because she feels obliged to do this?* And the answer to both questions will be a big resounding *yes.* Because even your good friends here are, to a certain degree, standoffish. Not because they don't want to be around you . . . but because they think they shouldn't be disturbing you, and also because you probably don't really want to hear too much from them. And no matter how much you try to convince them otherwise, that edge of reticence will be there. Because that's how it is here. The English need a year or two to acclimatize to your presence before they decide to be friends. When they are friends, they *are* friends, but they will still keep their distance. Everyone in this country is taught to do that from a very early age."

"None of my neighbors have bothered to introduce themselves."

"They never do."

"And people are so abrupt with each other in shops."

Margaret grinned a big grin.

"Oh, you've noticed that, have you?"

Indeed, I had—particularly in the form of the guy who ran my local news shop. His name was Mr. Noor—and he was always having a bad day. In the weeks that I'd been buying the morning papers at his shop, I'd never known him to ever favor me (or any other customer) with a smile. I had tried many times to force a grin out of him, or to at least engage him in a basic, yet civil conversation. But he had steadfastly refused to budge from his position of ongoing misanthropy. And the journalist in me always wondered what was the root cause of his unpleasantness. A brutal childhood in Lahore? A father who beat him senseless for the slightest infraction? Or maybe it was the sense of dislocation that came with being yanked out of Pakistan and dropped into the chilly dankness of London in the mid-seventies—whereupon he discovered he was a Paki, a wog, a permanent outsider in a society that despised his presence.

Of course, when I once articulated a version of this scenario to Karim—the guy who ran the corner shop next to Mr. Noor's shop—I was greeted with serious laughter.

"The man's never been to Pakistan in his life," Karim told me. "And don't think it's something you've done that's made him treat you the way he does. He does it with everybody. And it's nothing to do with nothing. He's a miserable git, that's all."

Unlike Mr. Noor, Karim always seemed to be having a good day. Even on the bleakest of mornings—when it had been raining nonstop for a week, and the temperature was just above freezing, and everyone was wondering if the sun would ever emerge again—Karim somehow managed to maintain a pleasant public face. Maybe this was something to do with the fact that he and his older brother, Faisal, were already successful businessmen, with two other shops in this corner of South London and plenty of plans afoot for further expansion. And I wondered whether his innate optimism and affability were rooted in the fact that, though a native Brit, he had aspirations—and a curiously American sense of confidence.

But on the morning after my Ibsen night out with Margaret, I didn't need anything from Karim's shop—so my first public contact of the day was with Mr.-Bloody-Noor. As usual, he was in sparkling form. Approaching his cash register with my *Chronicle* and my *Independent* in hand, I said, "And how are you today, Mr. Noor?"

He avoided my eyes, and replied, "One pound ten."

I didn't hand him the money. Instead I looked directly at him and repeated my question, "And how are you today, Mr. Noor?"

"One pound ten," he said, sounding annoyed.

I kept smiling, determined to get a response out of him.

"Are you keeping well, Mr. Noor?"

He just stuck his hand out for the money. I repeated my question again.

"Are you keeping well, Mr. Noor?"

He exhaled loudly.

"I am fine."

I graced him with a very large smile.

"Delighted to hear it."

I handed over my money, and nodded good-bye. Behind me was a woman in her forties, waiting to pay for the *Guardian* she held in her hand. As soon as I left the shop, she caught up with me.

"Well done, you," she said. "He's had that coming to him for years."

She proffered her hand.

"Julia Frank. You live at number twenty-seven, don't you?"

"That's right," I said, and introduced myself.

"Well, I'm just across the road at number thirty-two. Nice to meet you."

I would have lingered, trying to engage her in a chat, if I hadn't been late for an interview with a former IRA man turned novelist, so I simply said, "Drop over sometime." She replied with a pleasant smile . . . which may have been her way of indicating yes, or just another example of the maddening reticence of this city. But the very fact that she stopped to introduce herself (and to compliment me on standing up to Mr. Charm School) kept me buoyed for most of the day.

"So a neighbor *actually* spoke with you?" Sandy said when I called her later that day. "I'm surprised I didn't see a news flash about it on CNN."

"Yeah, it's pretty momentous stuff. And get this—the sun was even out today."

"Good God, what next? Don't tell me somebody smiled at you on the street?"

"Actually, somebody did. It was on the towpath by the river. A man walking his dog."

"What kind of dog?"

"A golden retriever."

"They usually have nice owners."

"I'll take your word for it. But you would not believe how pleasant that path by the river can be. And it's only three minutes from my door. And I know it's not a big damn deal, but while I was strolling by the Thames, I found myself thinking maybe I'm going to find my footing here after all."

That evening, I expressed similar sentiments to Tony after I saw him glancing around the builders' debris amid which we were living.

"Don't despair," I said, "it will all get finished eventually."

"I'm not despairing," he said, sounding forlorn.

"This will be a wonderful house."

"I'm sure it will be."

"Come on, Tony. Things will get better."

"Everything's fine," he said, his voice drained of enthusiasm.

"I wish I could believe you mean that," I said.

"I do mean it."

With that, he drifted off into another room.

But then, at five that morning, I woke up to discover that everything wasn't fine.

Because my body was suddenly playing strange games with me.

And in those first few bewildering moments when the realization hit that something was very wrong, I bumped into an emotion I hadn't encountered for years.

Fear.

FOUR

IT WAS AS if I had been attacked during the night by a battalion of bedbugs. Suddenly, every corner of my skin felt as if it was inflamed by what could only be described as a virulent itch—which no amount of scratching could relieve.

"I don't see any rash," Tony said after he discovered me naked in our bathroom, scraping my skin with my fingernails.

"I'm not making this up," I said angrily, thinking that he was accusing me of falling into some psychosomatic state.

"I'm not saying you are. It's just . . ."

I turned and stared at myself in the mirror. He was right. The only marks on my skin were those made by my frantic clawing.

Tony ran me a hot bath and helped me into it. The scalding water was momentarily agonizing—but once I adjusted to its extreme heat, it had a balming effect. Tony sat down beside the bath, held my hand, and told me another of his amusing war stories—how he contracted head lice while covering some tribal skirmish in Eritrea, and had to get his head shaved by a local village barber.

"The man did it with the dirtiest straight-edge razor imaginable. And, wouldn't you know it, he didn't have the steadiest hand—so by the time he was done, not only was I bald, but I looked like I needed stitches. Even then—having had every last hair scraped away—my head still itched like a bastard. Which is when the barber wrapped my head in a boiling hot towel. Cured the itching immediately—and also gave me first-degree burns."

I ran my fingers through his hair, so pleased to have him sitting here with me, holding my hand, getting me through all this. When I finally emerged from the bath an hour later, the itching was gone. Tony couldn't have been sweeter. He dried me with a towel. He dusted me with baby powder. He put me back to bed. And I did fall fast asleep again, waking with a start at noon—as the itching started over again.

At first, I thought I was still in the middle of some hyperactive dream—like one of those falling nightmares where you know you're plunging into a ravine, until you hit the pillow. Even before I snapped into consciousness, I was certain that another pestilent squad of insects had taken up residency beneath my skin. But the itching had doubled in intensity since last night. I felt sheer unadulterated panic. Dashing into the bathroom, I stripped off my pajama bottom and T-shirt, and checked myself all over for blotchy rashes or any other signs of epidermal inflammation—especially around my bulging belly. Nothing. So I ran another very hot bath and fell into it. Like last night, the scalding water had an immediate salutary effect—scorching my skin into a kind of numbness that deadened the all-pervasive itch.

But as soon as I hauled myself out of the bath an hour later, the itch started again. Now I was genuinely spooked. I rubbed myself down with baby powder. It only intensified the discomfort. So I turned on the taps for another hot bath. Once more I scalded myself, and was consumed by itching as soon as I stepped out of it again.

I threw on a bathrobe. I called Margaret.

"I think I'm going out of my skull," I told her—and then explained the war taking place beneath my skin, and how I was worried it might all be in my mind.

"If you're really itching like that, it can't be psychosomatic," Margaret said.

"But there's nothing showing."

"Maybe you have an internal rash."

"Is there such a thing?"

"I'm no quack—so how the hell do I know. But if I were you, I'd stop being a Christian Scientist about this, and get to a doctor fast."

I heeded Margaret's advice and called the local surgery. But my doctor was booked up for the afternoon, so they found me an appointment with a Dr. Rodgers: a dry-as-dust GP in his late forties, with thinning hair and a chilly bedside manner. He asked me to take off my clothes. He gave my skin a cursory inspection. He told me to get dressed again and gave me his diagnosis: I was probably having a *subclinical* allergic reaction to something I ate. But when I explained that I hadn't eaten anything out of the ordinary for the past few days, he said, "Well, pregnancy always makes the body react in odd ways."

"But the itching is driving me nuts."

"Give it another twenty-four hours."

"Isn't there anything you can prescribe to stop it?"

"If nothing is visible on the skin, not really. Try aspirin—or ibuprofen—if the pain gets too much."

When I related all this to Margaret half an hour later, she became belligerent.

"Typical English quack. Take two aspirin and stiffen your upper lip."

"My usual GP is much better."

"Then get back on the phone and demand to see her. Better yet, insist that she make a house call. They *will* do that, if coerced."

"Maybe he's right. Maybe it is some minor allergic reaction . . ."

"What is this? After just a couple of months in London, you're already adopting a 'grin and bear it' attitude?"

In a way, Margaret was right. I didn't want to whine about my condition—especially as it wasn't my nature to get sick, let alone break out in manic itches. So I tried to busy myself by unpacking several boxes of books, and attempting to read a few back issues of the *New Yorker*. I resisted the temptation to call Tony at the paper and tell him just how bad I was feeling. Eventually I stripped off all my clothes again and started scratching my skin so hard that I actually began to bleed around my shoulders. I took refuge in the bathroom. I let out a scream of sheer, unequivocal frustration and pain as I waited for the bath to fill. After scalding myself for the third time, I finally called Tony at the paper, saying, "I think I'm in real trouble here."

"Then I'm on my way."

He was back within the hour. He found me shivering in the bath, even though the water was still near boiling. He got me dressed. He helped me into the car and drove straight across Wandsworth Bridge, then up the Fulham Road, and parked right opposite the Mattingly Hospital. We were inside the emergency room within moments—and when Tony saw that the waiting room was packed, he had a word with the triage nurse, insisting that, as I was pregnant, I should be seen straightaway.

"I'm afraid you'll have to wait, like everyone else here."

Tony tried to protest, but the nurse was having none of it.

"Sir, please sit down. You can't jump the queue unless . . ."

At that very moment, I supplied the *unless*, as the constant itch suddenly transformed into a major convulsion. Before I knew what was happening, I pitched forward and the world went black.

When I came to, I was stretched out in a steel hospital bed, with several intravenous lines protruding from my arms. I felt insanely groggy— as if I had just emerged from a deep narcotic sleep. For a moment or two, the thought struck me: *where am I?* Until the world came into focus and I found myself in a long ward—one of a dozen or so women, enveloped by tubes, respiratory machines, fetal monitors, and other medical paraphernalia. I managed to focus on the clock situated at the end of the ward: 3:23 PM . . . with a grayish light visible behind the thin hospital curtains. 3:23 PM? Tony and I had arrived at the hospital around eight last night. Could I have been out cold for . . . what? . . . *seventeen hours*?

I managed to summon up enough strength to push the call button by the side of the bed. As I did so, I involuntarily blinked for an instant and was suddenly visited by a huge wave of pain around the upper half of my face. I also became aware of the fact that my nose had been heavily taped. The area around my eyes also felt bruised and battered. I pressed the call button even harder. Eventually, a small Afro-Caribbean nurse arrived at my bedside. When I squinted to read her name tag— *Howe*—my face felt pulverized again.

"Welcome back," she said with a quiet smile.

"What happened?"

The nurse reached for the chart at the end of the bed and read the notes.

"Seems you had a little fainting spell in reception. You're lucky that nose of yours wasn't broken. And you didn't lose any teeth."

"How about the baby?"

A long anxious silence as Nurse Howe scanned the notes again.

"No worries. The baby's fine. But *you* . . . you are a cause for concern."

"In what way?"

"Mr. Hughes, the consultant, will see you on his rounds this evening."

"Will I lose the baby?"

She scanned the chart again, then said, "You're suffering from a high blood pressure disorder. It could be preeclampsia—but we won't know that until we've done some blood work and a urine test."

"Can it jeopardize the pregnancy?"

"It can . . . but we'll try to get it under control. And a lot is going to depend on you. You'd better be prepared to live a very quiet life for the next few weeks."

Great. Just what I needed to hear. A wave of fatigue suddenly rolled over me. Maybe it was the drugs they'd been giving me. Maybe it was a reaction to my seventeen hours of unconsciousness. Or maybe it was a combination of the two, coupled with my newfound high blood pressure. Whatever it was, I suddenly felt devoid of energy. So drained and devitalized that I couldn't even summon the strength to sit myself up. Because I had an urgent, desperate need to pee. But before I could articulate this need—before I could ask for a bedpan or assistance to the nearest toilet—the lower part of my body was suddenly enveloped in a warm, expansive pool of liquid.

"Oh fuck . . . ," I said, my voice loud, desperate.

"It's okay," Nurse Howe said. Reaching for her walkie-talkie, she summoned assistance. Within moments, two large male orderlies were by the bed. One of them had a shaved head and sported an earring; the other was a thin wiry Sikh.

"So sorry, so sorry . . ." I managed to mutter as the two orderlies helped me sit up.

"Don't you worry about it, darling," the shaved head said. "Most natural thing in the world."

"Never happened to me before," I said as they lifted me off the sodden mattress and put me in a wheelchair. My hospital nightgown was stuck against my body.

"First time, really?" Shaved Head asked. "Ain't you had a charmed life. Take my mate here. He pisses his pants all the time, don't you?"

"Don't listen to my colleague," the Sikh said. "He needs to talk rubbish."

"*Colleague?*" Shaved Head said. "Thought I was your mate."

"Not when you accuse me of pants pissing," the Sikh said, starting to wheel me down the ward. Shaved Head walked alongside him, their repartee nonstop.

"That's the problem with you Sikhs—no sense of humor . . ."

"Oh I laugh all the time . . . when something is funny. But not when an oik . . ."

"You callin' me an *oik*?"

"No, I am making a generalization about *oiks*. So, please, try not to take it so personally . . ."

"But if you is making a sweeping general . . ."

"If you *are* making a sweeping generalization . . ." the Sikh said, correcting him.

"Know who my friend . . . sorry, *colleague* . . . thinks he is?" Shaved Head asked me. "Bloody Henry Higgins."

"And why can't the English teach their children how to speak?" the Sikh said.

"Shut it."

It was like listening to an old married couple in the midst of the sort of comic bicker that had been going on, nonstop, for twenty years. But I also realized that they were carrying on this banter for my benefit—to divert me from my humiliation, and stop me feeling like the bad little girl who'd wet herself and was now in a helpless state.

When we reached the bathroom, the two orderlies helped me out of the wheelchair, then positioned me standing up against the sink and waited with me until a nurse arrived. Once she showed up, they took their leave. She was a large cheery woman in her late forties with an accent that hinted at Yorkshire. She gently lifted the drenched nightgown over my head.

"Get you cleaned up in no time," she said, while running a shallow warm bath. There was a mirror over the sink. I looked up and froze. The woman staring at me appeared to be a victim of domestic abuse. Her nose—shrouded in surgical Band-Aids—had swollen to twice its normal size and had turned a slightly purplish color. Both eyes had been blackened, and the areas around the eyelids were also discolored and puffy.

"A nose injury always appears worse than it is," she said, immediately aware of my distress. "And it always clears up very quickly. Give it three, four days, and you'll be back to your beautiful self."

I had to laugh—not simply because I never considered myself beautiful . . . but also because, at the moment, I looked like I belonged in a freak show.

"American, are you?" she asked me.

I nodded.

"Never met an American I didn't like," she said. "Mind you, I've only met two Yanks in my entire life. What you doing living here?"

"My husband's English."

"Aren't you a smart girl," she said with a laugh.

She lowered me into the warm water and gently sponged me down, handing me the washcloth when it came to the area around my crotch. Then she helped me back up, dried me off, and dressed me in a clean nightgown. All the while, she kept up a steady stream of trivial chat. A very English way of dealing with an uncomfortable situation . . . and one that I liked. Because, in her own gruff way, she was actually being gentle with me.

By the time she wheeled me back to the ward, the soggy sheets had been stripped away and replaced with clean linen. As she helped me into bed, she said, "Don't you worry about anything, luv. You're going to be fine."

I surrendered to the cool, starched sheets, relieved to be dry again. Nurse Howe came by, and informed me that a urine sample was needed.

"Been there, done that," I said laughing.

I eased myself out of bed again and into the bathroom, filling a vial with what little pee I still had on reserve. Then, when I was back in bed, another nurse came by and drew a large hypodermic of blood. Nurse Howe returned to tell me that Tony had just called. She'd informed him that Mr. Hughes would be here at eight tonight, and suggested that he try to be at the hospital then.

"Your husband said he'd do his best, and was wondering how you were doing."

"You didn't tell him anything about me wetting the . . ."

"Don't be daft," Nurse Howe said with a small laugh, and then informed me that I shouldn't get too cozy right now, as Mr. Hughes (having been alerted to my condition) had ordered an ultrasound prior to his arrival. Alarm bells began to ring between my ears.

"Then he does believe that the baby's in danger?" I said.

"Thinking that does you no good . . ."

"I have to know if there's a risk that I might mis—"

"There is a risk, if you keep getting yourself in an anxious state. The high blood pressure isn't just due to physiological factors. It's also related to stress. Which is why you fell on your face last night."

"But if I'm just suffering from high blood pressure, why is he ordering an ultrasound?"

"He just wants to rule out . . ."

"Rule out *what*?" I demanded.

"It's normal routine."

This was hardly comforting. All during the ultrasound, I kept staring at the vague outline on the fetal monitor, asking the technician (an Australian woman who couldn't have been more than twenty-three) if she could see if anything was untoward.

"No worries," she said. "You'll be fine."

"But the baby . . . ?"

"There's no need to get yourself so . . ."

But I didn't hear the last part of that sentence, as the itching suddenly started again. Only this time, the area most affected was my midsection and my pelvis . . . exactly where the ultrasound gel had been smeared. Within the space of a minute, the itch was unbearable, and I found myself telling the technician that I needed to scratch my belly.

"Not a problem," she said, removing the large ultrasound wand that she had been applying to my stomach. Immediately, I began to tear at my skin. The technician looked on, wide-eyed.

"Take it slow, eh?" she said.

"I can't. It's driving me crazy."

"But you're going to hurt yourself . . . and the baby."

I pulled my hands away. The itching intensified. I bit so hard on my lip that it nearly bled. I snapped my eyes shut, but they began to sting. Suddenly, my face was awash with tears—the action of shutting my eyes provoking all the bruised muscles around the upper part of my face.

"Are you all right?" the technician asked.

"No."

"Wait here for a sec," she said. "And whatever you do, don't scratch your belly again."

It seemed to take an hour for her to get back to me—though, when I glanced at the clock, only five minutes had elapsed. But by the time the technician returned with Nurse Howe, I was gripping the sides of the bed, on the verge of screaming.

"Tell me . . ." Nurse Howe said. When I explained that I wanted to grate my stomach to pieces—or do anything else to make the itching stop—she examined me, then reached for a phone and issued some orders. She leaned over and clasped my arm.

"Help's on the way."

"What are you going to do?"

"Give you something to stop the itch."

"But say it's all in my head," I said, my voice verging toward mild hysteria.

"You *think* it's in your head?" Nurse Howe asked.

"I don't know."

"If you're scratching like that, it's *not* in your head."

"You sure?"

She smiled and said, "You're not the first pregnant lady to get an itch like this."

An assistant nurse arrived, pushing a tray of medication. She cleaned off the ultrasound gel. Then, using what looked like a sterile paintbrush, she covered my stomach with a pink chalky substance—calamine lotion. It instantly alleviated the itch. Nurse Howe handed me two pills and a small cup of water.

"What are these?" I asked.

"A mild sedative."

"I don't need a sedative."

"I think you do."

"But I don't want to be groggy when my husband gets here."

"This won't make you groggy. It will just calm you down."

"But I *am* calm."

Nurse Howe said nothing. Instead she deposited the two pills in my open palm, and handed me a glass of water. I reluctantly downed the pills and allowed myself to be helped into a wheelchair and transported back to the ward.

Tony arrived just before eight with a few newspapers under his arm and a grim bunch of flowers. The pills had taken full effect—and though Nurse Howe didn't lie about the lack of grogginess, she didn't say anything about the way they deadened all emotional agitation and left me feeling flat, benumbed, muffled . . . but also very aware of the way Tony was trying to mask his disquiet at the state of me.

"Do I look that awful?" I asked quietly as he approached the bed.

"Stop talking rubbish," he said, leaning over to give me a peck on the head.

"You should've seen the other guy," I said, then heard myself laugh a hollow laugh.

"After the way you pitched forward last night, I expected much worse."

"That's comforting to know. Why didn't you call me today?"

"Because, according to the head nurse, you weren't with us until after three."

"But after three . . ."

"Conferences, deadlines, my pages to get out. It's called work."

"You mean, like me? I'm work to you now, right?"

Tony took a deep annoyed breath, a way of informing me that he wasn't enjoying the route this conversation was taking. But despite my flattened drug-induced state, I still continued to play vexed. Because, right now, I felt so completely furious at everything and everyone—most especially, at the diffident man sitting on the edge of my bed, who had gotten me into this mess in the first place by knocking me up. The selfish shit. The little fucker. The . . .

And I thought these pills were supposed to smooth everything right out . . .

"You could ask me if the baby's all right," I said, my voice a paragon of tranquilized calm.

Another of Tony's exasperated intakes of breath. No doubt, he was counting the minutes until he could flee this place and rid himself of me for another night. Then, if his luck held out, I might just fall on my face again tomorrow, and I'd be incarcerated for another couple of days.

"I have been worried about you, you know," he said.

"Of course I know. Because you so radiate worry, Tony."

"Is this what's called 'posttraumatic shock'?"

"Oh, that's right. Try to write me off as Little Ms. Looney Tunes. Rue the day you met me."

"What the hell do they have you on?"

A voice behind Tony said, "Valium, since you asked. And from what I've just overheard, it is not having the desired effect."

Mr. Desmond Hughes stood at the edge of the bed, my chart in his hand, his bifocals resting on the extreme edge of his nose. I asked, "Is the baby all right, doctor?"

Mr. Hughes didn't look up from the chart.

"And a very good evening to you, Mrs. Goodchild. And yes, all seems fine." He turned toward Tony. "You must be Mr. Goodchild."

"Tony Hobbs."

"Oh, right," Hughes said, the only acknowledgment of Tony's name being the slightest of nods. Then he turned back to me and asked, "And how are we feeling tonight? Bit of a ropey twenty-four hours, I gather."

"Tell me about the baby, doctor."

"From what I could see on the ultrasound scans, no damage was done to the baby. Now I gather you were admitted suffering from cholestasis."

"What's that?" I asked.

"Chronic itching. Not uncommon among pregnant women . . . and it often arrives in tandem with preeclampsia, which, as you may know is . . ."

"High blood pressure?"

"Very good . . . though, clinically speaking, we prefer to call it a hypertension disorder. Now the good news is that preeclampsia is often characterized by a high level of uric acid. But your urine sample was relatively normal—which is why I consider you *not* to be suffering from preeclampsia. But your blood pressure is dangerously high. If left unchecked, it can be somewhat treacherous for both the mother and the child. Which is why I am putting you on a beta-blocker to stabilize your blood pressure, as well as an antihistamine called Piriton to relieve the cholestasis. And I would also like you to take five milligrams of Valium three times a day."

"I'm not taking Valium again."

"And why is that?"

"Because I don't like it."

"There are lots of things in life we don't like, Mrs. Goodchild . . . even though they are beneficial . . ."

"You mean, like spinach . . . ?"

Tony coughed another of his nervous coughs. "Uh, Sally . . ."

"What?"

"If Mr. Hughes thinks that Valium will help you . . ."

"Help me?" I said. "All it does is gag me."

"Really?" Mr. Hughes said.

"Very funny," I said.

"I wasn't trying to be amusing, Mrs. Goodchild . . ."

"It's *Ms.* Goodchild," I said. "He's Hobbs, I'm Goodchild."

A quick exchange of looks between Tony and the doctor. *Oh God, why am I acting so weird?*

"So sorry, *Ms.* Goodchild. And, of course, I can't force you to take a substance that you don't want to take. At the same time, however, it is my clinical opinion that it will alleviate a certain degree of stress . . ."

"Whereas it's my *on the spot* opinion that the Valium is doing bad things to my head. So, *no* . . . I'm not touching the stuff again."

"That is your prerogative—but do understand, I do think it is inadvisable."

"Noted," I said quietly.

"But you will take the Piriton?"

I nodded.

"Well, that's something at least," Hughes said. "And we'll continue to treat the cholestasis with calamine lotion."

"Fine," I said again.

"Oh, one final thing," Hughes said. "You must understand that high blood pressure is a most dangerous condition—and one which could cause you to lose the child. Which is why, until you have brought this pregnancy to term, you must essentially put yourself under no physical or emotional strain whatsoever."

"By which you mean . . . ?" I asked.

"By which I mean that you cannot work until after—"

I cut him off.

"*Can't* work? I'm a journalist—*a correspondent.* I've got responsibilities . . ."

"Yes, you do," Hughes said, interrupting me. "Responsibilities to yourself and to your child. But though we will be able to partially treat your condition *chemically*, the fact of the matter is that only complete bed rest will ensure that you stay out of jeopardy. And that is why we'll be keeping you in hospital for the duration . . ."

I stared at him, stunned.

"The duration of my pregnancy?" I asked.

"I'm afraid so."

"But that's nearly three weeks from now. And I can't just give up work . . ."

Tony put a steadying hand on my shoulder, stopping me from saying anything more.

"I'll see you on my rounds tomorrow, Ms. Goodchild," Hughes said. With another quick nod to Tony, he moved on to the next patient.

"I don't believe it," I said.

Tony just shrugged. "We'll deal with it," he said. Then he glanced at his watch and mentioned that he had to get back to the paper now.

"But I thought you'd already put your pages to bed?"

"I never said that. Anyway, while you were unconscious, the Russian deputy prime minister was exposed for his involvement in a kiddie porn ring, and a little war's broken out among rival factions in Sierra Leone . . ."

"You have a man on the scene in Freetown?"

"A stringer. Jenkins. Not bad, for a lightweight. But if the thing blows up into a full-scale war, I think we'll have to send one of our own."

"Yourself, perhaps?"

"In my dreams."

"If you want to go, go. Don't let me stop you."

"I wouldn't, believe me."

His tone was mild, but pointed. It was the first time he'd directly articulated his feelings of entrapment. Or, at least, that's how it came across to me.

"Well, thank you for making that perfectly clear," I said.

"You know what I'm saying here."

"No, actually, I don't."

"I'm the foreign editor—and foreign editors don't dispatch themselves off to cover a pissy little firefight in Sierra Leone. But they do have to go back to the office to get their pages to bed."

"So go then. Don't let me stop you."

"That's the second time you've said that tonight."

He placed his gift of newspapers and wilting flowers on the bedside table. Then he gave me another perfunctory kiss on the forehead.

"I'll be back tomorrow."

"I certainly hope so."

"I'll call you first thing in the morning, and see if I can get over here before work."

But he didn't call me. When I rang the house at eight-thirty, there was no answer. When I rang the paper at nine-thirty, Tony wasn't at his desk. And when I tried his cell phone, I was connected with his voice-mail. So I left a terse message: "I'm sitting here, already bored out of my mind, and I'm just wondering: where the hell are you? And why didn't you answer the phone? Please call me ASAP, as I really would like to know the whereabouts of my husband."

Around two hours later, the bedside phone rang. Tony sounded as neutral as Switzerland.

"Hello," he said. "Sorry I wasn't available earlier."

"You know, I called you at home at eight-thirty this morning and discovered that nobody was home."

"What's today?"

"Wednesday."

"And what do I do every Wednesday?"

I didn't need to furnish him an answer, because he knew that I knew the answer: he had breakfast with the editor of the paper. A breakfast at the Savoy, which always started at nine. Which meant that Tony inevitably left home around eight. *Idiot, idiot, idiot . . . why are you looking for trouble?*

"I'm sorry," I said.

"Not to worry," he said, his tone still so detached, almost uninvolved. "How are you doing?"

"Still feeling like shit. But the itch is under control, thanks to the calamine lotion."

"That's something, I guess. When are visiting hours?"

"Right now would work."

"Well, I'm supposed to be lunching with the chap who skippers the Africa section at the foreign office but I can cancel."

Immediately I wondered: now why didn't he tell me about this lunch yesterday? Maybe he didn't want to let me know, then and there, that he wouldn't be able to visit in the morning. Maybe the lunch was a last-minute thing, given the situation in Sierra Leone. Or maybe . . . oh God, I don't know. That was the growing problem with Tony: *I didn't know*. He seemed to live behind a veil. Or was that just my hypertension fatigue kicking in, not to mention my *cholestasis*, and everything else that was now part and parcel of this wondrous pregnancy? Anyway, I wasn't about to raise the emotional temperature again by kicking up a stink about his inability to get in here immediately. Because I wasn't going anywhere.

"No need," I said. "I'll see you tonight."

"You certain about that?" he asked me.

"I'll phone Margaret, see if she can pay me a visit this afternoon."

"Anything I can bring you?"

"Just pick up something nice at Marks and Spencer's."

"I shouldn't be too late."

"That's good."

Naturally, Margaret was at the hospital within a half hour of my call. She tried not to register shock when she saw me, but didn't succeed.

"I just need to know one thing," she said.

"No—Tony didn't do this to me."

"You don't have to protect him, you know."

"I'm not—*honestly*." Then I told her about my charming little inter-action with Hughes, and how I refused to become a citizen of Valium Nation.

"Damn right you should refuse that stuff," she said, "if it's giving you the heebie-jeebies."

"Trust me to get aggressive on Valium."

"How did Tony handle all this?"

"In a very English, very phlegmatic kind of way. Meanwhile, I'm quietly beginning to panic . . . not just at the thought of three weeks' enforced bed rest in here, but also the realization that the paper isn't going to like the fact that I'm out of action."

"Surely the *Post* can't let you go?"

"Want to put money on that? They're financially strapped like every damn newspaper these days. Rumor has it that management has been thinking about cutting back on their foreign bureaus. And I'm certain that, with me out of the picture for the next few months, they'll evict me without a moment's thought."

"But surely they'll have to give you some sort of a settlement?"

"Not if I'm in London."

"You're jumping to conclusions."

"No—I'm just being my usual Yankee realist self. Just as I also know that, between the mortgage and all the renovations, spare cash is going to be scarce."

"Well then, let me do something to make your life in hospital a little easier. Let me pay for a private room in here for the next couple of weeks."

"You're allowed to upgrade to a private room?"

"I did when I had my kids on the NHS. It's not even that expensive. Around forty pounds a night tops."

"That's still a lot of money over three weeks."

"Let me worry about that. The point is: you need to be as stress-free as possible right now . . . and being in a room on your own will certainly aid the process."

"True—but say my pride doesn't like the idea of accepting charity from you?"

"It's not charity. It's a gift. A gift before I kiss this city good-bye."

This stopped me short. "What are you talking about?" I asked.

"We're being transferred back to New York. Alexander only heard the news yesterday."

"When exactly?" I asked.

"Two weeks. There's been a big shake-up at the firm and Alexander's been made the senior partner heading up the litigation department. And since it's mid-term at school, they're shipping us all back in one go."

I now felt anxious. Margaret was my one friend in London.

"Shit," I said.

"That's about the right word for it," she said. "Because as much as I complain about London, I know I'm going to miss it as soon as we're ensconced back in the 'burbs, and I turn into some soccer mom, and start to hate every other WASP I meet in Chappaqua, and keep wondering why everyone looks the same."

"Can't Alexander ask to stay on longer?"

"Not a chance. What the firm wants, the firm gets. Believe me, three weeks from now I am going to *so* envy you. Even though this town may be completely maddening, it's always interesting."

By the time Tony arrived at the hospital that evening, I had been transferred into a perfectly pleasant private room. But when my husband asked me how the upgrade came about—and I told him of Margaret's largesse—his reaction was both abrupt and negative.

"And why the hell is she doing that?"

"It's a gift. To me."

"What did you do, plead poverty with her?" he asked.

I stared at him, wide-eyed.

"Tony, there's no need for . . ."

"Well, did you?"

"Do you really think I would do something like that?"

"Well, she obviously felt so sorry for you that . . ."

"Like I said: *it's a gift*. Her very kind way of helping me out . . ."

"We're not accepting it."

"But why?"

"Because I'm not accepting charity from some rich American—"

"This is not *charity*. She's my friend and—"

"I'll pay for it."

"Tony, the bill is already settled. So what's the big deal?"

Silence. I knew what the big deal was: Tony's pride. Not that he was going to admit such a thing. Except to say, "I just wished you'd talked this over with me."

"Well, I didn't hear from you all day—and until I was moved in here, where there's a phone by the bed, it was a little hard to get up to make calls. Especially when I've been ordered to hardly move."

"How are you doing?"

"The itch is a little better. And there is a lot to be said for being out of that godforsaken ward."

A pause. Tony evaded my gaze.

"How long did Margaret pay for the room?"

"Three weeks."

"Well, I'll cover anything after that."

"Fine," I said quietly, dodging the temptation to add, "Whatever makes *you* happy, Tony." Instead I pointed to the Marks and Spencer bag in his hand and asked, "Dinner, I hope?"

Tony stayed an hour that night—long enough to watch me gobble down the sandwich and salad he brought me. He also informed me that he'd called A. D. Hamilton at the *Post* to explain that I had been rushed to hospital last night.

"I bet he sounded disconsolate," I said.

"Well, he didn't exactly radiate enormous concern . . ."

"You didn't say anything about how I'd be out of commission for the next few weeks?" I asked.

"I'm not that dim."

"I'm going to have to call the editor myself."

"Give yourself a couple of days to feel a little better. You're shattered."

"You're right. I am. And all I want right now is to fall asleep for the next three weeks, then wake up and discover that I'm no longer pregnant."

"You'll be fine," he said.

"Sure—once I stop looking like a battered wife."

"No one would believe the 'battered wife' thing anyway."

"Why's that?"

"Because you're bigger than me."

I managed a laugh, noting my husband's ability to divert me with humor whenever we veered into argumentative terrain, or when he sensed that I was becoming overly exercised about something. But though I was concerned about plenty right now, I was also too tired to start a recitation of everything that was worrying me—from my physical state, to the fear I had of losing the child, to how the *Post* would react to my extended medical absence, not to mention such trivial domestic details as the state of our half-finished house. Instead, a wave of exhaustion seized me—and I told Tony that I'd best surrender to sleep. He gave me a somewhat perfunctory kiss on the head and said he'd drop by tomorrow morning before work.

"Grab every book you can find," I said. "It's going to be a long three weeks in here."

Then I passed out for ten straight hours, waking just after dawn with that mixture of drowsy exultation and sheer amazement that I had slept so long. I got up. I wandered into the en suite bathroom. I glanced at the mangled face in the mirror. I felt something close to despair. I had a pee. The itching started again. I returned to my bed and called the nurse. She arrived and helped me pull up my nightgown, then painted my stomach with calamine lotion. I dropped two tabs of Piriton, and asked the nurse if it was possible to have a cup of tea and a slice or two of toast.

"No problem," she said, heading off.

As I waited for breakfast to arrive, I stared out the window. No rain— but at 6:03 AM, it was still pitch black. I suddenly found myself thinking how, try as we might, we never really have much control over the trajectory of our lives. We can delude ourselves into believing that we're the master captain, steering the course of our destiny . . . but the randomness of everything inevitably pushes us into places and situations where we never expect to find ourselves.

Like this one.

Tony arrived at nine that morning, bearing the morning papers, three books, and my laptop computer. We only had twenty minutes together, as he was rushing to get to the paper. Still, he was pleasant in a pressed-for-time way and happily made no further mention of our little disagreement about the private room business yesterday. He sat on the edge of the bed and took my hand. He asked all the right questions about how I was feeling. He seemed pleased to see me. And when I implored him to keep the pressure on the builders and the decorators (as the last thing I wanted was to walk back into a construction site with a baby in my arms), he assured me that he would make certain they were all kept on task.

When he left, I felt a decided twinge of jealousy. He was heading out into the workaday world, whereas I had been barred from doing anything productive. Complete bed rest. No physical activity whatsoever. Nothing stressful to send my blood pressure into higher stratospheric levels. For the first time in my adult life, I had been confined to quarters. And I was already bored with my incarceration.

Still, I did have one crucial piece of business to get out of the way. So later that morning, I wrote an email to Thomas Richardson, the editor of the *Post,* explaining my medical situation and how I would be out of action until the arrival of the baby. I also assured him that this was all due to circumstances beyond my control, that I would be back on the job as soon as my maternity leave was over, and that as someone who had spent all of her professional life chasing stories, I wasn't taking very well to being corralled in a hospital room.

I read through the email several times, making certain I had struck the right tone, emphasizing the fact that I wanted to return to work ASAP. I also enclosed the phone number of the hospital, in case he'd like to speak with me. After I dispatched this, I punched out a short message to Sandy, explaining that Murphy's Law had just been invoked on my pregnancy and detailing the fun-filled events of the past forty-eight hours. I also gave her the number at the Mattingly. "All phone calls gratefully accepted," I wrote, "especially as I have been sentenced to three weeks *in bed*."

I pressed send. Three hours later, the phone rang and I found my sister on the other end of it.

"Good God," Sandy said, "you really do know how to have a complicated life."

"Believe me, this wasn't deliberate."

"And you've also lost your famous sense of humor."

"Now I wonder how that happened."

"But don't mess around with this. Preeclampsia is serious stuff."

"It's *borderline* preeclampsia."

"It's still pretty dangerous. So you'd better stop playing Action Girl for the first time in your life, and listen to what the doctor tells you. How's Tony handling it?"

"Not badly."

"Do I detect a note of uncertainty in your voice?"

"Perhaps. Then again, he is very busy."

"By which you mean . . . ?"

"Nothing, nothing. I'm probably just overly sensitive to everything right now."

"Try to take things easy, eh?"

"There's not a lot else I can do."

Later that afternoon, I received a call from Thomas Richardson's secretary. She explained that he was away on business in New York for the next few days. But she had read him my email and he wanted me to know of his concern about my condition, and that I shouldn't think about anything right now except getting better. When I asked if I could speak to Mr. Richardson personally after his return, she paused for a moment and said, "I'm certain he'll be in touch."

That comment bothered me all day. Later that evening, during Tony's visit, I asked him if he detected anything sinister behind her response. He said, "You mean, why didn't she come straight out and say: 'I know he wants to fire you'?"

"Something like that, yes."

"Because he probably *isn't* planning to fire you."

"But it was the way she said, *'I'm certain he'll be in touch.'* She made it sound so damn ominous."

"Didn't she also tell you that Richardson said you shouldn't think about anything else right now?"

"Yes, but . . ."

"Well, he's right. You shouldn't think about all that. Because it won't do you any good, and also because, even if something sinister is going on, there's nothing you can do about it."

That was the truth of the matter. I could do absolutely nothing right now, except lie in bed and wait for the child to arrive. It was the most curious, absurd sensation—being shut away and forced to do nothing. I had spent my entire working life filling just about every hour of every day, never allowing myself extended periods of good old-fashioned downtime, let alone a week or two of sheer unadulterated sloth. I always had to be active, always had to be accomplishing something—my workaholism underscored by a fear of slowing down, of losing momentum. It wasn't as if this desire to keep on the move was rooted in some psychobabbly need to *dodge self-examination* or *run away from the real me.* I just liked being busy. I thrived on a sense of purpose—of having a shape and an objective to the day.

But now, time had suddenly ballooned. Removed from all professional and domestic demands, each day in hospital seemed far too roomy for my liking. There were no deadlines to make, no appointments to keep. Instead, the first week crept into the next. There was a steady stream of books to read. I could catch up on four months of back issues of the *New Yorker*. And I quickly became addicted to Radios 3 and 4, listening avidly to programs that grappled with obscure gardening questions, or presented a witty and informed discussion of every available version of Shostakovich's Eleventh Symphony. There was a daily phone call from Sandy. Margaret—bless her—managed to make it down to the hospital four times a week. And Tony did come to see me every evening. His post-work arrival was one of the highlights of my otherwise prosaic hospital day. He'd always try to spend an hour—but often had to dash back to the office or head off for some professional dinner thing. If he didn't seem otherwise preoccupied, he was amusing and reasonably affectionate. I knew that the guy was under a lot of pressure at the paper. And I knew that getting from Wapping to Fulham chewed up an hour of his time. And though he wouldn't articulate this fact, I sensed that he was silently wondering what the hell he had landed himself in—how, in less than a year, his once autonomous life as a foreign correspondent had been transformed into one brimming with the same sort of workaday and domestic concerns that characterized most people's lives. But he wanted this, *right*? He was the one who made all the convincing arguments about coming to London and setting up house together. And after my initial doubts, I fully embraced those arguments. Because I wanted to.

But now . . .

Now I still wanted all that. But I also wanted a sense of engagement from my husband—of shared mutual concerns. Yet any time I asked him if something was worrying him, he would do what he'd always do: assure me that *"Everything's fine."* And then he'd change the subject.

Still, when Tony was on form, he was the best company around. Until we had to talk about something domestic and serious. Like my situation with the *Boston Post*.

Around ten days after sending that initial email to Thomas Richardson, I was growing increasingly concerned that he had yet to call me—even though Margaret and Sandy both assured me that he didn't want to disturb my convalescence.

"Why don't you just concentrate on feeling better," Sandy told me.

"But I *am* feeling better," I said, telling the truth. Not only had the itching finally vanished, but I was regaining my equilibrium (and without the help of Valium). More tellingly, the beta-blockers were doing their job, as my blood pressure had gradually decreased—to the point where, by the end of the second week, it was only marginally above normal levels. This pleased Hughes enormously. When he saw me on his biweekly rounds—and glimpsed the new blood pressure levels on my chart—he told me that I seemed to be making "splendid progress."

"You obviously have willed yourself better," he said.

"I think it's called all-American bloody-mindedness," I said, a comment that elicited the smallest of laughs from Hughes.

"Whatever it is, your recovery is remarkable."

"So you think that the pregnancy is no longer in the danger zone?"

"Now I didn't exactly say that, did I? The fact remains that we now know that you are prone to hypertension. So we must be vigilant especially as you're due so soon. And you must try to avoid any undue stress."

"I'm doing my best."

But then, two days later, Richardson called me.

"We're all deeply concerned about your condition . . ." he said, starting off with his usual paternalistic patter.

"Well, all going well, I should be back on the job in six months tops—and that's including the three months of maternity leave."

There was a pause on the transatlantic phone line and I knew I was doomed.

"I'm afraid we've been forced to make a few changes in our overseas bureaus—our finance people have been insisting on some belt tightening. Which is why we've decided to turn London into a single-correspondent bureau. And since your health has put you out of the picture . . ."

"But, as I said, I *will* be back within six months."

"A.D. *is* the senior correspondent in the bureau. More to the point, he *is* on the job now . . ."

And I was absolutely certain that A.D. had been plotting my downfall ever since I phoned in sick.

"Does this mean you're firing me, Mr. Richardson?" I asked.

"Sally, *please*. We're the *Post*, not some heartless multinational. We take care of our own. We'll be paying you full salary for the next three months. Then if you want to rejoin us, a position will be made available to you."

"In London?"

Another edgy transatlantic pause.

"As I said, the London bureau will now be staffed by only one correspondent."

"Which means if I want a job, I'll have to come back to Boston?"

"That's right."

"But you know that's impossible for me right now. I mean, I'm only married a few months, and as I am having a baby . . ."

"Sally, I do understand your situation. But you have to understand mine. It was your decision to move to London—and we accommodated that decision. Now you need to take an extended period of health leave, and not only are we willing to pay you in full for three months, but also guarantee you a job when you can work again. The fact that the job won't be in London . . . well, all I can say is: circumstances change."

I ended the call politely, thanking him for the three months' pay, and saying that I'd have to think about his offer—even though we both knew that there was no way I'd be accepting it. Which, in turn, meant that I had just been let go by my employer of the last sixteen years.

Tony was pleased to hear that, at least, I'd be able to help with the mortgage for the next few months. But I quietly worried about how, after my *Post* money stopped, we'd be able to manage all our manifold expenses on one income.

"We'll work it out" was his less-than-reassuring reply.

Margaret also told me to stop worrying about the money problem.

"Given the number of newspapers in this town, I'm sure you can eventually find some freelance work. But only when it becomes necessary. Tony's right—you *do* have three months' grace. Right now, you should only be thinking about getting through the next week. You're going to have enough to cope with once the baby arrives. On which note, I don't suppose I could interest you in a cleaner? Her name's Cha, she's been with us for the entire time we've been in London, she's completely brilliant at what she does, and is now looking for additional work. So . . ."

"Give me her number and I'll talk it over with Tony. I'll also need to review the domestic budget before . . ."

"Let me pay for her."

"No way. After arranging the private room for me you're making me feel like a 'Help the Needy' case."

"Hey, I'm a sucker for good causes."

"I can't accept it."

"Well, you're going to have to. Because it's my going-away gift to you. Six months of Cha, twice a week. And there's nothing you can do about it."

"Six months? You're crazy."

"Nah—just rich," she said with a laugh.

"I'm embarrassed."

"That's dumb."

"I'll have to talk it over with Tony."

"He doesn't have to know that it's a gift."

"I prefer being straight with him. Especially about something like this. I mean, he wasn't exactly pleased to learn that you paid for the private room."

"Well, in my experience, 'being straight' is never the shrewdest marital strategy . . . especially when the male ego is involved."

"Whether he accepts the gift or not, you've been the best friend imaginable. And you shouldn't be leaving."

"This is the problem of being a corporate wife. Those who pay you the big bucks also dictate where you live. I think it's what's called a Faustian bargain."

"You're my one pal here."

"As I told you, that will change . . . eventually. And hey, I'll always be at the end of a phone line if you need an ear to scream into . . . though, given that it's me who'll be drowning in the vanilla confines of Westchester County, it's you who'll be receiving the hysterical transatlantic phone calls."

She left town two days later. That evening, I finally got up the nerve to inform Tony about Margaret's good-bye gift.

"You cannot be serious," he said, sounding annoyed.

"Like I said, it was her idea."

"I wish I could believe that."

"Do you actually think I'd do something as tacky as talking her into giving us a cleaner for six months?"

"It's just a little coincidental, especially after . . ."

"I know, I know—she paid for this damn room. And you can't stand the idea of somebody actually making my life a little easier by . . ."

"That's not the point—and you know it."

"Then what *is* the point, Tony?"

"We can well afford to pay for a bloody cleaner, that's all."

"You don't think Margaret *knows* that? This was merely a gift. And *yes*, it was a far too generous one—which is why I said I wouldn't accept it until I talked it over with you. Because I had a little suspicion that you'd react exactly like this."

Pause. He avoided my angry gaze.

"What's the cleaner's name?" he asked.

I handed him the piece of paper on which Margaret had written Cha's name and her contact number.

"I'll call her and arrange for her to start next week. At our expense."

I said nothing. Eventually he spoke again. "The editor would like me to go to the Hague tomorrow. Just a fast overnight trip to do a piece about the war crimes tribunal. I know you're due any moment. But it's just the Hague. Can be back here in an hour, if need be."

"Sure," I said tonelessly. "Go."

"Thanks."

Then he changed the subject and told me a rather entertaining story about a colleague at the paper who'd been caught fiddling his expenses. I fought the temptation to show my amusement, as I was still smarting after our little exchange . . . and didn't like the fact that, once again, Tony was up to his usual "mollify her with humor" tricks. When I didn't respond to the story, he said, "What's with the indignant face?"

"Tony, what do you expect?"

"I don't follow you . . ."

"Oh come on, that fight we just had . . ."

"That wasn't a fight. That was just an exchange of views. Anyway, it's ancient history now."

"I just can't bounce back the way . . ."

He leaned over and kissed me.

"I'll call you from the Hague tomorrow. And remember—I'm on the cell phone if . . ."

After he left, I must have spent the better part of an hour replaying our little spat in my head, taking apart the argument, piece by piece. Like some postmodernist literary critic, I was trying to excavate all the *subtextual implications* of the fight—and wondering what its ultimate meaning might be. Granted, on one level, this dispute had again been rooted in Tony's vanity. But what I couldn't get out of my brain was the larger, implicit realization that I had married someone with whom I didn't share a common language. Oh, we both spoke English. But this wasn't simply a case of mere Anglo-American tonal differences. This was something more profound, more unsettling—the worry that we would never find a common emotional ground between us; that we would always be strangers, thrown in together under accidental circumstances.

"Who knows anyone?" Sandy said to me during our phone call that evening. But when I admitted that I was beginning to find Tony increasingly hard to fathom, she said, "Well, look at me. I always considered Dean to be a nice, stable, slightly dull guy. But I bought into his decent dullness because I thought: *at least I'll be able to count on him. He'll always be there for me.* And when I met him, that was exactly what I was looking for. What happens? After ten years of staid decency and three kids, he decides he hates everything about our staid secure suburban life. So he meets the Nature Girl of his dreams—a fucking park ranger in Maine—and runs off to live with her in some cabin in Baxter State Park. If he now sees the kids four times a year, it's an event. So, hey, at least you realize you're already dealing with a difficult guy. Which, from where I sit, is something of an advantage. But I'm telling you stuff you already know."

Maybe she was right. Maybe I just needed to let everything settle down, and enter the realm of *acceptance* and other optimistic clichés. As in *look on the bright side, forget your troubles, keep your chin up . . .* that sort of dumb, sanguine thing.

Over and over again, I repeated these Pollyanna-ish mantras. Over and over again, I kept trying to put on a happy face. Until fatigue finally forced me to turn off the light. As I drifted off into a thinly veneered sleep, one strange thought kept rattling around my brain: *I am nowhere.*

Then another thought seized me: *Why is everything so soggy?*

At that moment, I jolted back into consciousness. In the initial few seconds afterward, I absently thought: *so that's what they call a wet dream.* Then I squinted in the direction of the window and noticed that it was light outside. I glanced at the bedside clock and saw that it read 6:48 AM. Then an earlier thought replayed itself in my head.

Why is everything so soggy?

I sat up, suddenly very awake. I frantically pulled off the comforter. The bed was completely drenched.

My waters had broken.

FIVE

I DIDN'T PANIC. I didn't succumb to trepidation or startled surprise. I just reached for the call button. Then I picked up the phone and dialed Tony's cell phone. It was busy, so I phoned his direct line at the paper and left a fast message on his voicemail.

"Hi, it's me," I said, still sounding calm. "It's happening . . . so please get yourself to the Mattingly as soon as you get back to London. This is definitely it."

As I put down the receiver, a midwife showed up. She took one look at the sodden bedclothes and reached for the phone. Two orderlies arrived shortly thereafter. They raised the sides of my bed, unlocked its wheels, and pushed me out of the room, negotiating a variety of corridors before landing me in the maternity ward. En route, I began to feel an ever-magnifying spasm. By the time the doors swung behind me, the pain had intensified to such an extent that I felt as if some alien were gripping my innards with his knobbly fist, determined to show me new frontiers in agony. A midwife was on the scene immediately—a diminutive woman of Asian origin. She grabbed a packet of surgical gloves from a nearby cart, ripped them open, pulled them on, and informed me that she was going to do a quick inspection of my cervix. Though I'm certain she was attempting to be as gentle as possible, her gloved fingers still felt like highly sharpened claws. I reacted accordingly.

"You are experiencing severe discomfort, yes?" she asked.

I nodded.

"I will have a doctor see you as soon as . . ."

"Is the baby all right?"

"I'm sure everything is . . ."

There was another maniacal spasm. I reacted loudly, then asked, "Can I have an epidural now?"

"Until the doctor has examined . . ."

"*Please* . . ."

She patted my shoulder and said, "I'll see what I can do."

But ten godawful minutes passed until she returned with a porter . . . by which time I felt so tortured that I would have signed a document admitting to be the cause of everything from the French Revolution to global warming.

"Where have you been?" I asked, my voice raw and loud.

"Calm yourself, please," she said. "We had three other women waiting before you for ultrasound."

"I don't want ultrasound. I want an epidural."

But I was whisked straightaway into the ultrasound suite, where my belly was coated with gel and two large pads applied to the surface of the skin. A large fleshy man in a white jacket came into the room. Beneath the jacket he was wearing a checked Viyella shirt and a knit tie. His feet were shod with green wellington boots. Take away the white jacket and he could have passed for a member of the rural squirearchy. Except for the fact that the boots were splattered with blood.

"I'm Mr. Kerr," he said crisply. "I'm covering for Mr. Hughes today. In a spot of bother, are we?"

But suddenly he was interrupted by the ultrasound technician who said that sentence you never want to hear a medical technician say to a doctor, "I think you should see this, sir."

Mr. Kerr looked at the screen, his eyes grew momentarily wide, then he turned away and calmly sprang into action. He spoke rapidly to a nurse— and, much to my horror, I heard him utter the words: "Baby resuscitator."

"What is going on?" I asked.

Mr. Kerr approached me and said, "I need to examine you right now. This might be a bit uncomfortable."

He inserted his fingers into me and began to press and probe. I was about to demand information about what the hell was going on, but another rush of pain made me scream with extremity.

"I'll have the anesthetist here in a jiffy," Mr. Kerr said. "Because we need to perform an emergency caesarean."

Before I could react to that, he explained that the ultrasound had shown that the umbilical cord might be around the baby's neck.

"Will the baby die?" I said, interrupting him.

"The fetal monitor is showing a steady heartbeat. However, we need to move fast, because . . ."

But he didn't get to finish that sentence, as the doors swung open and two orderlies with carts came rushing in. The first was pulled up next to me. Then a small Indian woman in a white coat arrived and walked over to the bed. "I'm Dr. Chatterjee, the anesthetist," she said. "Relief is on the way."

She swabbed the top of my left hand with a cotton ball. "Little prick now," she said, as she inserted a needle into the top of my hand. "Now start counting backward from ten."

I did as instructed, muttering "Ten, nine, eig . . ."

And then the world went black.

It's strange, being chemically removed from life for a spell. You don't dream under anesthetic, nor are you even notionally aware of the passage of time. You've entered the realm of nothingness, where all thoughts, fears, worries cannot invade your psyche. Unlike that easily permeable state called sleep, you're being kept in suspended chemical animation. Which—after the agonizing trauma of the past hour—suited me just fine.

Until I woke up.

It took me a moment or two to realize where I was—especially as my first view of the world was a pair of glowing fluorescent tubes, lodged above me. My eyes were half-glued together, making everything seem bleary, obscure. More tellingly, my head was shrouded in a freakish fog—which made all voices seem leaden, oppressive, and also left me wondering (for the first few minutes of consciousness) where the hell I was. Gradually, the jigsaw pieces began to fall into place: hospital, ward, bed, sore head, sore body, baby . . .

"Nurse!" I yelled, scrambling for the button by the side of the bed. As I did so, I realized that I had tubes coming out of both arms, while the lower half of my body was still numb.

"Nurse!"

After a few moments, a dainty Afro-Caribbean woman arrived by my bedside.

"Welcome back," she said.

"My baby?"

"A boy. Eight pounds, two ounces. Congratulations."

"Can I see him now?"

"He's in the intensive care unit. It's just a routine thing, after a complicated delivery."

"I *want* to see him. Now." And then I added, "Please."

The nurse looked at me carefully.

"I'll see what I can do."

She returned a few minutes later.

"Mr. Kerr is coming to see you."

"Do I get to see my baby?"

"Talk to Mr. Kerr."

He arrived just then. Same white jacket, same shirt, same wellington boots—only this time bloodier than before . . . no doubt, thanks to me.

"How are you feeling now?"

"Tell me about my son?"

"Quite a straightforward caesarean . . . and the cord around his neck wasn't as tight as I feared. So, all in all . . ."

"Then why is he in intensive care?"

"Standard postoperative care—especially for a newborn after a difficult delivery. We did have to immediately ventilate him after birth . . ."

"Ventilate?"

"Give him oxygen. He did arrive a little floppy, though he responded well to the ventilation . . ."

"So the cord around the neck might have caused brain damage?"

"As I said before, I was pleased to discover that the cord hadn't wound itself firmly around your son's neck. But we've already run an ultrasound to make certain there was no blood on the brain . . ."

"Was there?"

"No, it was completely negative. More to the point, his Apgar scores were completely normal."

"His what?" I asked.

"Apgar is a sort of checklist we run on every newborn child, gauging things like their pulse, reflexes, respiration, and overall appearance. As I said, your son easily scored within the normal range. And in a day or so, we will run an EEG and an MRI, just to make certain that everything in the neurological department is working properly. But, at this point, I would try not to worry about such things."

Oh please . . .

"I need to see him."

"Of course. But you do realize that his initial appearance may upset you. Pediatric ICUs are not the easiest of places, after all."

"I'll handle that."

"All right then. But do understand, you will have to take things very easy for the next week or so. You've just had a major operation."

He turned and started walking away. But then he wheeled back and said, "Oh, by the way—congratulations. Any sign of the father yet?"

"Didn't he ring the hospital?" I asked the nurse.

"Not that I've heard," she said. "But I'll check with my colleagues. And if you write down his number, I'll call him again."

I looked at the clock on the wall. Six-fifteen.

"Couldn't I try to call him?" I asked.

But as I said this, two orderlies showed up, wheelchair in tow. This one was custom-built to accommodate a patient who was wired to assorted drips, as it featured a frame from which plasma and saline bottles could be suspended.

"Let me phone him for you," the nurse said. "These fellows are going to need the chair back soon. Isn't that right?"

"Always big demand for our best wheelchairs," one of the orderlies said, adding, "Come on, luv. Let's bring you up to see your baby."

The nurse handed me a pad and a pen. I scribbled down Tony's work number, his cell, and our home phone. She promised me she'd leave messages on all three numbers if she couldn't reach him directly. Then the orderlies went to work on moving me from the bed to the chair. I had expected to have been unplugged from my varying tubes—and then forced to endure having the lines reinserted into my veins. But the guys—both of whom looked like members of a wrestling tag team— couldn't have been more dexterous when it came to lifting me off the bed and into the chair, while simultaneously keeping me attached to my assorted tubes. As soon as I was seated, a combination of exhaustion and postoperative shock seized me. My head swam, the world became vertiginous, my stomach convulsed. But after an attack of the dry heaves, all I was left with was a foul taste in my mouth and runny eyes.

The nurse used a large cotton pad to clean up my face.

"You sure you want to do this right now?" she asked me.

I nodded. The nurse shrugged and motioned for the guys to take me on my way.

They pushed me through the maternity ward, passing half a dozen women, all with babies by their bedsides in little adjacent cribs. Then we entered a long corridor until we reached a service elevator. When the door opened, I saw that we had company—an elderly woman on a gurney, wired for sound to sundry monitors and intravenous bags, her breathing a near-death rattle. Our eyes met for a moment—and I could see her panic, her terror. All I could think was: a life ending, a life beginning. If, that is, my son was going to pull through.

The elevator rose two floors. The doors opened, and we were directly in front of a set of double doors, by which was a sign: *Pediatric ICU*. The chattier of the two orderlies leaned over and whispered in my ear, "If I was you, luv, I'd keep my eyes down until we get up alongside your baby. Take it from me, it can be a bit distressing in there."

I followed his advice, and gazed downward as we crept through the ward. Though I wasn't looking upward, what struck me immediately was the pervasive deep blue light of the ICU (as I later learned, it was to aid those babies suffering from jaundice). Then there was the absence of all human voices . . . the only sound provided by the electronic beeps of medical equipment, the steady metronomic rhythm a reassuring reminder of a small functioning heart.

After around a minute, the chair stopped. By this point, my eyes were tightly shut. But then, the chatty orderly touched me gently on my shoulder and said, "We're here, luv."

A part of me wanted to keep my eyes closed, and demand to be turned around and brought back to my own room. Because I wondered if I would be able to bear what I saw. But I knew I had to see him—no matter how upsetting his condition might be. So I raised my head. I took a deep breath. I opened my eyes. And . . .

There he was.

I knew he would be in an incubator—which meant that he seemed dwarfed by the Plexiglas sarcophagus in which he had been placed. And I knew that there would be wires and tubes. But what shocked me was the sight of an entire network of wires and tubes running from every corner of his body—including two plastic ducts that had been pressed into his nostrils, and an oxygen meter running from his belly button. He looked alien, almost otherworldly—and so desperately assailable. But another terrible thought hit me: *could that really be my son?* They say that you should be swamped by unconditional love the moment you first see your child . . . and that *the bonding process* should begin immediately. But how could I bond with this minuscule stranger, currently looking like a horrific medical experiment?

The moment such awful thoughts crossed my mind, I felt a deep abiding shame—an immediate appalling realization that, perhaps, I was incapable of maternal love. But in that same nanosecond, another voice crept into my brain, telling me to calm down.

"You're suffering from postoperative trauma," this rational, mollifying voice informed me. *"Your child might be gravely unwell, you've been pumped full of chemicals, you've lost significant quantities of blood . . . so everything is naturally skewed. It's called shock—and the worst shock of all is seeing your newborn baby in such a distressing state. So you're entitled to feel as if the world is upside down. Because, in fact, it is."*

So I tried to calm myself down—and look again at my son, and await that torrent of attachment to wash over me. But staring into the incubator, all I felt was fear. Sheer terror—not just about whether he had suffered brain damage, but whether I would be able to cope with all this. I wanted to cry for him—and for myself. I also wanted to flee the room.

The talkative orderly seemed to sense this, as he gently touched my shoulder and whispered, "Let's get you back to your bed, luv."

I managed to nod—and then found myself choking back a sob.

They brought me back down to the room. They gently lifted me back into bed, and reset my assorted bags above me. There was a mirror on the dressing table. I picked it up. My face was the color of ash. I tried to move my facial muscles, but found them immobile—as if they had seized up, or remained under the spell of the anesthetics that were still coursing through my bloodstream. I looked like one of those people you see in news footage who have managed to walk away from a bomb blast—their faces paralyzed into countenances of expressionless shock. I put down the mirror. I sank back down against the hard, starchy hospital pillow. I found myself thinking: *this is like free-fall . . . I'm tumbling into a void, but I'm too astray to care.*

Then, out of nowhere, I started to cry. The crying had an almost animalistic rage to it—loud, vituperative, and unnervingly hollow. The nurse who came running must have thought I was reacting to the state of my baby—and riding the usual post-caesarean roller coaster. But the fact of the matter was: I didn't know what I was crying about. Because I couldn't feel anything. My emotional world had gone numb. But I still needed to scream.

"All right, all right," the nurse said, taking me by both hands. "I'm sure it was a bit of a shock, seeing your baby . . ."

But I drowned her out by howling even louder . . . even though it hadn't been my intention to lose it like this. I didn't really know what I was doing—except crying for crying's sake. And not being able to stop myself.

"Sally . . . *Sally* . . ."

I ignored the nurse, pushing away her hands, curling up into a fetal position, clutching a pillow next to my face, and biting it in an attempt to stifle the howls. But though the pillow muffled the sound, it didn't end the crying. The nurse put a steadying hand on my shoulder, using her free hand to speak into the walkie-talkie she usually kept strapped to her belt. When she finished, she said, "Just hold on—help should be here in a moment."

The help was another nurse, pushing a cart laden down with medical paraphernalia. She was accompanied by the doctor on duty. The nurse who had been keeping the bedside watch spoke quickly to her colleagues. The doctor picked up my chart, scanned it, spoke to the nurses again, then left. After a moment, I felt a hand raising the left sleeve of my nightgown, as the first nurse said, "The doctor thinks this might help you relax a bit, Sally."

I didn't say anything—because I was still biting the pillow. But then came the sharp jab of a needle, followed by a warming sensation cascading through my veins.

Then the plug was pulled, and the lights went out.

When I returned to terra firma, I didn't suffer the same convulsive shock that accompanied my reawakening after the delivery. No, this was a slower fade-in—accompanied by a Sahara-dry mouth and the sort of mental murk that made me wonder if I had woken up in a land of cotton wool. The first thing I noticed was a small decanter of water by the side of the bed. I lifted it and drained it in around ten seconds. Then I felt a huge urgent need to pee. But my scars and my tubes were restricting my movements, so I reached for the button and summoned the nurse.

Only this time it was a different nurse—a thin, beaky woman in her mid-forties with an Ulster accent and a manner that could be kindly described as severe. Her nameplate read: *Dowling*.

"Yes?" she asked.

"I need to go to the bathroom."

"How badly?"

"Very badly."

She heaved a small, but telling sigh of distaste, reached under the bed, pulled out a white tin enamel bedpan, and said, "Lift up your bottom."

I tried to do as instructed, but couldn't even summon the strength for this simple task.

"I think you're going to have to help me."

Another small, disgruntled sigh. She pulled back the bedclothes. She inserted her hand under my bottom and forced it upward, then pulled back my nightgown and shoved the bedpan underneath me.

"All right," she said, "get on with it."

But it was impossible to "get on with it" in my current position—as I felt like someone who had been put into a kinky sexual posture. Anyway, who the hell can pee lying down?

"You have to help me up," I said.

"You're a lot of work, aren't you?" she said.

I wanted to shout something back at her, but the fog was too pervasive to permit me to engage in an argument. Also, I couldn't hold my bladder for much longer.

"All right then," she said wearily, gripping my shoulder and pushing me upward. She braced me in that position as I finally let go. The urine felt warm beneath me, and possessed a chemical stench that was so strong the nurse immediately wrinkled her nose in disgust.

"What've you been drinking?" she said, without the slightest hint of irony.

But then a voice behind her asked, "Do you always talk to patients like that?"

Tony.

I could see him looking me over—taking in not just my awkward astride-a-bedpan position, but also my anemic complexion, shell-shocked eyes, and general distraught condition. He gave me a small half-smile and a quick nod of the head, but then turned his attention back to the nurse. Like any petty tyrant, she was suddenly defensive and cowed when caught in the act.

"Really, I meant no offense."

"Yes you did," he said, making a point of staring long and hard at her nameplate. "I saw how rough you were with her."

The woman's face fell. She turned to me and said, "I'm really sorry. I'm having a bad day, and I didn't mean to take it out on . . ."

Tony cut her off.

"Just remove the bedpan and leave us."

She did as ordered, then gently lowered me back against the pillows, and tucked the blankets in.

"Can I get you anything now?" she asked nervously.

"No—but I would like the name of your supervisor," Tony said.

She hurried off, looking genuinely scared.

"So how did you enjoy the play, Mrs. Lincoln?" he asked me. He kissed me on the head. "And how's our boy doing?"

"Poorly," I said.

"That's not what they told me last night."

"You were here last night?"

"Yes—while you were sleeping. The nurse said you'd been . . ."

"A little unstable, perhaps? Or maybe she said something really English and understated. Like, 'your wife's gone totally ga-ga.'"

"Is that what you think, Sally?"

"Oh, don't give me that fucking rational tone-of-voice, *Anthony*."

I could see him tense—not just because of my illogical temper, but also because I was now suddenly crying.

"Would you like me to come back later?" he asked quietly.

I shook my head. I took a deep breath. I managed to curb the tears. I said, "So you *were* here last night?"

"That's right. I arrived just before eleven—direct from the airport. And I went straight up to see you. But they told me—"

"—that I'd been sedated for excessive crying?"

"—that you'd been having a hard time of it, so they'd given you something to help you sleep."

"So you were here at eleven?"

"That's what I said before. Twice in fact."

"But why weren't you here before then?"

"Because I was in the bloody Hague, as you bloody well know. Now can we talk about more important things . . . like Jack."

"Who's Jack?"

He looked at me, wide-eyed.

"Our son."

"I didn't realize he'd been given a name yet."

"We talked about this four months ago."

"No, we didn't."

"That weekend in Brighton, when we were walking along the promenade . . ."

I suddenly remembered the conversation. We'd gone down to Brighton for a "get-away-from-it-all weekend" (Tony's words), during which it rained nonstop and Tony got hit with mild food poisoning after eating some suspect oysters in some overpriced seafood joint, and I kept thinking that this seaside town was an intriguing mixture of the chic and the tatty—which was probably why the English liked it so much. But before Tony started regurgitating his guts out in our freebie suite at the Grand, we did take a brief, soggy walk along the seafront, during which he mentioned that Jack would be a fine name if the baby turned out to be a boy. To which I said (and I remember this precisely): "Yeah, Jack's not bad at all."

But that wasn't meant to be interpreted as tacit approval for the name Jack.

"All I said was—"

"—that you liked the name Jack. Which I took as your approval. Sorry."

"Doesn't matter. I mean, it's not like it's legal and binding as yet."

Tony shifted uneasily on the edge of the bed.

"Well, as a matter of fact . . ."

"What?"

"I went down to Chelsea town hall this morning and got the forms to register him. Jack Edward Hobbs . . . Edward for my father, of course."

I looked at him, appalled.

"You had no right. No fucking right . . ."

"Keep your voice down."

"Don't tell me to keep my voice down when you . . ."

"Can't we get back to the subject of Jack?"

"He's *not* Jack. *Understand?* I refuse to let him be called Jack . . ."

"Sally, his name's not legal until you cosign the registration form. So will you please . . . ?"

"What? Be reasonable? Act like a stiff-upper-lip anal Brit when my son is upstairs, dying . . ."

"He is not dying."

"He *is* dying—and I don't care. You get that? I *don't* care."

At which point I fell back against the pillows, pulled the covers over my head, and fell into another of my extended crying jags. Like yesterday's crying jag, it was punctuated by a dreadful hollowness. A nurse was on the scene within moments. I could hear a lot of rapid-fire whispering . . . and phrases like, *"we've seen this sort of thing before," "often happens after a difficult delivery," "poor thing must be under such terrible strain,"* and (worst of all) *"she'll be right as rain in a few days."*

Though the covers were over my head, I retreated back to my fetal position, once again biting deeply into the pillow in an attempt to stifle my screams. Like last night, I also didn't struggle when I felt a firm hand hold my shoulder while someone else turned back the bedclothes, rolled up my sleeve, and pricked my arm with a hypodermic.

Only this time, I didn't get dispatched to never-never land. No, this time I seemed to be placed in a state of otherworldly immobility. I felt as if I were suspended directly above this room, looking down on the comings and goings of patients and medical staff. I had the benign disinterest of an accidental tourist who had somehow managed to end up in this curious *quartier*, and would certainly prefer to be elsewhere, but had imbibed so much cheap French fizz that she was paralytically incapable of knowing the time of day, and so she was perfectly happy to keep floating overhead. Neither sleeping nor fully conscious . . . just *there*.

I remained in this narcotic, blissed-out state until the following morning—when hard shafts of sunlight streaked through the windows, and my brain was as shadowy as a film noir, and I felt curiously rested, even though I didn't know if I had slept.

In fact, for the first ten seconds of consciousness, I luxuriated in that state of nowheresville, where there is no such thing as a past or a present . . . let alone a future.

Then the world crashed in on me. I scrambled for the call bell. The same tight-faced Northern Irish nurse was on duty—only now, after Tony's dressing-down, she was sweetness itself.

"Good morning there, Ms. Goodchild. You seemed to be sleeping awfully well. And have you seen what's arrived while you were sleeping?"

It took a moment or so for my eyes to focus on the three large floral arrangements that adorned various corners of the room. The nurse gathered up the gift cards and handed them to me. One bouquet from the editor of the *Chronicle*. One from Tony's team on the foreign pages. One from Margaret and Alexander.

"They're beautiful, aren't they?" Nurse Dowling said.

I stared at the arrangements, having absolutely no opinion about them whatsoever. They were flowers, that's all.

"Could I get you a cup of tea now?" Nurse Dowling asked. "Perhaps a little breakfast?"

"Any idea how my son is doing?"

"I don't honestly know, but I could find out straightaway for you."

"That would be very kind. And if I could . . . uh . . ."

Nurse Dowling knew exactly what I was talking about. Approaching the bed, she removed the bedpan from the cabinet in the side table, helped me straddle it, and removed it after I filled it with yet another half gallon of malodorous urine.

"God, what a stink," I said as Nurse Dowling settled me back on the pillows.

"The drugs do that," she said. "But once you're off them, you'll lose that bad smell. How do the stitches feel today?"

"The pain's still there."

"That'll take at least a week to go away. Meantime, why don't I bring you a basin of water, so you can freshen up and brush your teeth?"

Talk about five-star service. I thanked the nurse, and asked her again if she could find out how Jack was doing.

"Oh, you've already chosen a name for him," she said.

"Yes," I said. "Jack Edward."

"Good strong name," she said. "And I'll be right back with the tea and any news of Jack."

Jack. Jack. Jack.

Suddenly I felt the worst wave of shame imaginable.

"He is dying—and I don't care. You get that? I don't care."

How could I have said that? Had I so completely lost it that I *actually* expressed indifference about whether or not my son lived? Instead of making excuses for myself—telling myself it was all postoperative stress, and an out-of-body reaction to all the drugs they'd been pumping into me—I immediately began to engage in a serious course of self-flagellation. I was unfit to be a mother, a wife, a member of the human race. I had jettisoned all that was important to me—my newborn child and my husband—through one deranged outbreak of rage. I deserved everything bad that would now happen to me.

But, most of all, yesterday's bizarre, out-of-kilter rage had vanished. All I could now think was: *I need to be with Jack.*

Nurse Dowling returned with a breakfast tray and some news.

"I gather your little one's doing just fine. They're really pleased with the progress he's making, and he can probably be moved out of ICU in a couple of days."

"Can I see him this morning?"

"No problem."

I picked at my breakfast—largely because whatever appetite I had was tempered by an equally urgent need to speak with Tony. I wanted to utter a vast *mea culpa* for my insane behavior yesterday, to beg his forgiveness, and also tell him that he and Jack were the best things that had ever happened to me. And, of course, I'd sign the registration document naming him Jack Edward. Because . . . because . . . be . . .

Oh fuck, not this . . .

The crying had started again. Another extended bout of loud, insufferable keening. *Come on, knock it off,* I told myself. But as I quickly discovered, this was an absurd idea because I fell apart once more. Only this time I was cognizant enough of this sudden breakdown to be genuinely spooked by it. Especially as I worried that the medical staff might start writing me off as mentally askew and worthy of more intensive chemical treatment. So I stuffed the pillow back into my mouth, clutched it against me like a life preserver, and started counting backward from one hundred inside my head, telling myself that I had to have myself under control by the time I reached zero. But during this countdown, I could feel my voice growing louder and louder—even though I wasn't speaking at all. The strain against my eyes became intolerable. There was such compression behind them that I was certain they'd explode out of my head at any moment. But just when I thought I was about to let go entirely, Nurse Dowling showed up accompanied by the orderly. I felt her hand against my shoulder, calling my name, asking me what was wrong. When I couldn't answer, I heard her turn to the orderly and mention something about getting the head nurse. At which point I had just reached the number thirty-nine, and suddenly heard myself shout, *"Thirty-nine!"*

This threw everybody—most especially Nurse Dowling, who looked at me wide-eyed, as if I had completely abandoned all reason. Which was very close to the truth.

"What's happened?" she asked.

I didn't know the answer to that question—so all I said was, "Bad dream."

"But you were awake."

"No," I lied. "I fell asleep again."

"Are you sure you're okay?" she asked.

"Absolutely," I said, touching my very wet face and attempting to wipe away the remnants of all that crying. "Just a little nightmare."

The head nurse arrived at my bedside just in time to hear that last comment. She was a formidable Afro-Caribbean woman in her early forties—and I could tell that she wasn't buying a word of it.

"Perhaps you need another sedative, Sally."

"I am completely fine," I said, my voice nervous. Because the last thing I wanted right now was a further trip into an opiated never-never. Which is why it was critical that I bring myself under control.

"I'd like to believe that," the head nurse said, "but your chart shows that you've already had two such incidents. Which, I must tell you, is not at all unusual after a physically traumatic delivery. But it is a cause for concern. And if it persists . . ."

"It won't persist," I said, sounding very definitive.

"Sally, I am not at all trying to threaten you. Rather, I just want to point out that you have a legitimate medical problem which we will treat if . . ."

"Like I said—it was just a little nightmare. I promise it won't happen again. I really, *really* do promise."

A quick glance between the head nurse and Nurse Dowling.

The head nurse shrugged. "All right," she said, "we'll forgo medication right now. But if you have another incident . . ."

"I *won't* be having another incident."

My voice had jumped an edgy octave or two. Another telling glance between the head nurse and Nurse Dowling. *Defuse the situation, defuse it now.*

"But I would desperately like to see my son, Jack," I said, my voice back in reasonable territory.

"That should be possible after Mr. Hughes comes by on his rounds this morning."

"I have to wait until then?"

"It's just another hour or so . . ."

"Oh come on . . ." I said, my voice going loud again. When I saw another telling glance between the head nurse and Nurse Dowling, I knew that I should cut my losses and wait the hour.

"I'm sorry, I'm sorry," I said, a little too rapidly. "You're right, of course. I'll wait until Mr. Hughes shows up."

"Good," the head nurse said, looking me straight in the eye. "And you mustn't worry too much about what's going on right now. You've been through a great deal."

She smiled and touched my arm, then left. Nurse Dowling said, "Anything else I can get you?"

"If you could just hand me the phone, please."

She brought it over to the bed, then left. I dialed home. I received no answer . . . which bothered me just a little, as it was only eight-thirty in the morning, and Tony was a notoriously late sleeper. Then I called his cell phone and got him immediately. I was relieved to hear him in traffic.

"I'm sorry," I said. "I'm so damn sorry about . . ."

"It's all right, Sally," Tony said.

"No—it's not. What I said yesterday . . ."

"Meant nothing."

"I was horrible."

"You were in shock. It happens."

"It still doesn't excuse what I said about Jack . . ."

A telling pause. "So you like the name now?"

"Yes, I do. And I like you too. More than I can say."

"Now there's no need to go all soppy on me. What's the latest word on our boy?"

"I won't know anything until Hughes does his rounds. When will you be in?"

"Around tea time."

"Tony . . ."

"I have pages to get out . . ."

"And you also have a deputy. Surely the editor was most sympathetic . . ."

"Did you get his flowers?"

"Yes—and a bouquet from Margaret too. You called her?"

"Well, she is your best friend."

"Thank you."

"And I also spoke with Sandy. Explained that it had been a complicated delivery, that you were a bit under the weather, and told her it was best if she didn't ring you for a few days. Naturally, she's phoned me three times since then to see how you're doing."

"What did you tell her?"

"That you were making steady progress."

Sandy being Sandy, I was certain that she didn't believe a word of his reassurances—and was now frantically worried about my condition. She knew damn well that if she couldn't talk to me, something rather serious was going on. But I was grateful to Tony for keeping her at bay. Much as I adored my sister, I didn't want her to hear how fragile I was right now.

"That was the right thing to tell her," I said.

"Listen, I have to run now," Tony said. "I'll try to be in by early evening, all right?"

"Fine," I said, even though I didn't mean it—as I really wanted him at my bedside right now for some necessary emotional support.

But who in their right mind would want to be with me at the moment? I had turned into a crazy woman, who'd lost all sense of proportion, and spat bile every time she opened her mouth. No wonder Tony wanted to dodge me.

For the next hour, I sat and stared upward at the ceiling. One thought kept obsessing my head: *Jack, brain damaged?* I couldn't even conceive of what motherhood was going to be like if that was the case. How would we cope? What fathomless, inexhaustible hell would await us?

Mr. Hughes arrived promptly at ten. He was accompanied by the head nurse. As always, he wore a beautifully cut pinstripe suit, a spread-collar pink shirt, and a black polka-dot tie. He deported himself like a cardinal visiting a poor parish. He nodded hello but said nothing until he had perused the notes hanging on the bedstead clipboard.

"So, Mrs. . . ."

He glanced back at the clipboard.

". . . Goodchild. Not the most pleasant few days I'd imagine?"

"How is my son?"

Hughes cleared his throat. He hated being interrupted. And he showed his displeasure by staring down at the chart while speaking with me.

"I've just been looking in on him at ICU. All vital signs are good. And I spoke to the attending pediatrician, Dr. Reynolds. He told me that an EEG performed this morning indicated no neurological disturbance. But, of course, to make certain that everything is functioning properly, an MRI will be conducted around lunchtime today. He should have results by evening time—and I know he'll want to see you then."

"Do you think that brain damage did occur?"

"Mrs. Goodchild . . . though I can fully understand your worry—

what mother wouldn't be worried under the circumstances?—I am simply not in a position to speculate about such matters. Because that is Dr. Reynolds's territory."

"But do you think that the EEG results . . . ?"

"Yes, they do give one cause for optimism. Now, would you mind if I looked at Mr. Kerr's handiwork?"

The head nurse drew the curtains around my bed, and helped me raise my nightgown and lower my underwear. Then she pulled away the bandages. I hadn't seen my wounds since the delivery, and they shocked me: a criss-crossing sequence of railroad tracks, bold in their delineation and barbaric in execution.

Though I was trying my best to stifle all emotion, I couldn't help but emit a small sharp cry. Mr. Hughes favored me with an avuncular smile, and said, "I know it looks pretty grim right now—a real war wound—but once the stitches are removed, I promise you that your husband won't have anything to complain about."

I wanted to say, *To hell with my husband. It's me who's going to have to live with the disfigurement.* But I kept my mouth shut. I couldn't afford to deepen my problems.

"Now I gather you've been having a bit of, uh, shall we say, emotional disquiet."

"Yes—but it's over with."

"Even though you had to be sedated yesterday?"

"But that was yesterday. I'm just fine now."

The head nurse leaned over and whispered something in Hughes's ear. He pursed his lips, then turned back to me and said, "According to the staff here, you had a bit of a turn this morning."

"It was nothing."

"You know, there's absolutely no shame in going a little wonky after giving birth. Quite commonplace, actually, given that one's hormones are just a little all over the place. And I do think that a course of antidepressants . . ."

"I need nothing, doctor—except to see my son."

"Yes, yes—I do understand. And I'm sure nurse here can arrange to have you brought upstairs once we're done. Oh—and you do know that you will be with us for at least another six to seven days. We want to make certain you're right as rain before sending you out into the world again."

He scribbled some notes onto my chart, spoke quickly to the head nurse, then turned back to me with a farewell nod.

"Good day, Mrs. Goodchild—and try not to worry."

That's easy for you to say, pal.

A half hour later—after having my surgical dressings changed—I was up in pediatric ICU. Once again, I followed the advice of that benevolent porter and I kept my eyes firmly focused on the linoleum as I was wheeled in. When I finally looked up, the sight of Jack made my eyes sting. Not that there was any change in his condition. He was still enveloped in medical tubes, still dwarfed by the Plexiglas incubator. Only now I had a desperate need to hold him, to cradle him. Just as I had a despondent fear that I might just lose him. Or that he would have to go through life with a terrible mental disability. Suddenly, I knew that whatever happened to him—whatever horrors were revealed by the MRI—I'd handle it. Or, at least, I'd deal with it—the way you deal with life's most unexpected, fiendish cards. But, oh God, how I didn't want that to come to pass; how I'd do anything now to make certain he was going to be all right . . . and how I knew just how powerless I was to change anything now. What had happened *happened*. We were now nothing more than fortune's fools—and hostages to whatever came our way.

I started to weep again. This time, however, I didn't feel the undertow of emotional hollowness that had so characterized the past few days. This time, I simply wept for Jack—and for what might become of him.

The orderly kept his distance while I cried. But after a minute or so, he approached me with a box of Kleenex and said, "It might be best if we head back now."

And he returned me to my room.

"Good news," Nurse Dowling said after I was helped back into bed. "Mr. Hughes says you can come off those nasty drips—so it looks like you're tube free. First steps toward freedom, eh? How's the little one doing?"

"I don't know," I said quietly.

"I'm sure he's going to be just fine," she said, her sing-song platitudinous voice now sounding like fingernails on a blackboard. "Now what can I get you for lunch?"

But I refused all food, refused a rental television, refused the offer of a sponge bath. All I wanted was to be left alone—to lie in bed with the blankets pulled up to my chin, shutting out the cacophony of the world.

That's how I passed my day—counting down the hours until Tony finally arrived and the pediatrician presented us with the *empirical* proof of our son's condition. I was conscious but purposely detached from everything around me. Or, at least, I thought it was a deliberate detachment on my part. But, at times, I really did feel as if an occupying power had taken up residence in my brain, encouraging me to push away the world and all its complexities.

Then it was six o'clock. Much to my surprise, Tony showed up exactly when he said he would, bearing a bouquet of flowers and a nervousness which I found immediately endearing.

"Were you sleeping?" he asked, sitting down on the edge of the bed and kissing my forehead.

"A facsimile of sleep," I said, forcing myself to sit up.

"How are you faring?"

"Oh, you know—Day of the Living Dead."

"Any news from upstairs?"

I shook my head. And said, "You look tense."

Tony just smiled a stiff smile and lapsed into silence. Because there was nothing to say until the pediatrician made his appearance. Or perhaps anything we did say would have sounded irrelevant and empty. Our shared anxiety was so palpable that saying nothing was the smartest option.

Fortunately, this silence only lasted a minute or so, as a new nurse came by and said that Dr. Reynolds would like to see us in a consulting room by the MRI suite on the fifth floor. Tony and I exchanged a nervous glance. Requesting us to meet him in a private consulting room could only mean bad news.

Once again I was helped into a wheelchair. Only this time Tony pushed me. We reached the elevator. We traveled up three stories. We headed down a long corridor. We passed the suite of rooms marked MRI and were escorted into a small consulting room, with nothing more than a desk, three chairs, and a light box for x-rays. The porter left us. Tony pulled over a chair next to my wheelchair and did something he'd not done before: he took my hand. Oh, we had held hands on occasion—by which I mean two or three times maximum. This was different. Tony was trying to be supportive—and, in doing so, he was letting me know just how scared he was.

After a moment, Dr. Reynolds came in, carrying a folder and a large oversize manila envelope. He was a tall, soft-spoken man in his late thirties. I tried to read his face—the way a person on trial tries to read the face of the foreman before the verdict is delivered. But he was giving nothing away.

"Sorry to have kept you both . . ." he said, opening the envelope, clipping the MRI film to the light box, and illuminating it. "How are you feeling, Ms. Goodchild?"

"Not bad," I said quietly.

"Glad to hear it," he said, favoring me with a sympathetic smile that let it be known he was aware of my recent follies.

"How's our son, doctor?" Tony asked.

"Yes, I was just about to come to that. Now . . . this is a picture of your son's brain," he said, pointing to the MRI film . . . which, to my untutored eye, looked like the cross-section of a mushroom. "And after consultation both with the pediatric neurologist and the radiologist, we've all reached the same conclusion: this is a perfectly normal infant brain. Which, in turn, means that, based on this MRI—and the recent EEG—we *sense* that there has been no brain damage."

Tony squeezed my hand tightly, and didn't seem to mind that it was a cold and clammy hand. It was only then that I realized I had my head bowed and my eyes tightly closed, like someone expecting a body blow. I opened them and asked, "You just said that you *sense* there's been no brain damage. Doesn't the MRI offer conclusive evidence?"

Another sympathetic smile from Reynolds.

"The brain is a mysterious organism. And after a traumatic birth—in which there was initially a question about whether the brain was denied oxygen—you cannot be completely one hundred percent definitive that there was no damage. Having said that, however, all clinical evidence points to a positive outcome . . ."

"So there is something to worry about," I said, getting agitated.

"If I were you, I'd move forward optimistically."

"But you're *not* me, doctor. And because you're more than hinting that our son has been brain damaged—"

Tony cut me off.

"Sally, that is *not* what the doctor said."

"I *heard* what he said. And what he said is that there is a chance our son was denied oxygen to the brain and is therefore . . ."

"Ms. Goodchild, *please*," Reynolds said, his voice calm and still commiserative. "Though I can fully appreciate your concerns, they are—with respect—somewhat overblown. As I said before, I really do think you have nothing to worry about."

"How can you say that . . . *how* . . . when you yourself admit that you can't be one hundred percent certain that—"

Again, Tony intervened.

"That's enough, Sally."

"Don't tell me—"

"Enough."

His vehement tone silenced me. And I suddenly felt appalled—both at the illogicality of my rant and at the irrational anger I had shown this very decent and patient doctor.

"Dr. Reynolds, I am so sorry . . ."

He raised his hand.

"There's nothing to apologize about, Ms. Goodchild. I do understand just how difficult things have been. And I'll be back here tomorrow if you have any further questions."

Then he wished us a good evening and left. As soon as he was out of the room, Tony looked at me for a very long time. Then he asked, "Would you mind telling me what the hell that was all about?"

I looked away. And said, "I don't know."

SIX

AS PROMISED, THEY kept me in the hospital for another five days. During this time, I was allowed constant visits with Jack in pediatric ICU. They had decided to keep him "under continued observation" in the unit for a few more days.

"Do understand," Dr. Reynolds said, "there's nothing at all sinister about this. We're just erring on the side of caution."

Did he really expect me to believe that? Still, I said nothing. Because I knew it was best if I *tried* to say nothing.

At times, I found myself observing Jack as if he were a strange, hyper-real piece of modern sculpture—an infant medical still life, enshrouded by tubes, on permanent display in a big plastic case. Or I was reminded of that famous eight-hour Andy Warhol film—*Empire*—which was one long static shot of the Empire State Building. Watching Jack was the same. He'd lie there, motionless, rarely moving a muscle (though, from time to time, there'd be the tiniest flex of his hand). And I'd find myself projecting all sorts of stuff onto him. Such as: how I hoped he'd like the bouncy chair I'd bought for him. Whether his diapers would be as disgusting as I imagined. Would he go for Warner Brothers cartoons or Disney (*please may he be a smartass Bugs Bunny kid*). And would his acne be as horrible as mine had been when I was thirteen . . . ?

All right, I was getting way ahead of myself. But an infant is like a *tabula rasa*, upon which an entire story will be written. And now, staring at Jack in that Plexiglas bowl, all I could think was: he might not have a life . . . or one that is substantially diminished, and all because of the way his body moved a few wrong inches in the womb. Something over which neither of us had any control—but which could completely change everything that happened to both of us from now on. Even if Reynolds was right—and Jack had managed to walk away unscathed from this accident—would this early brush with catastrophe so haunt me that I'd become one of those fiendishly overprotective mothers who would worry every time her ten-year-old negotiated a flight of stairs? Or would I become so convinced that doom was lurking right around the corner that I'd never really rest easy again, and would live life now with an omnipresent sense of dread?

The ICU duty nurse was now at my side—a young woman in her early twenties. Irish. Exceptionally calm.

"He's a beauty," she said, looking in on him. "Do you want to hold him?"

"Sure," I said tentatively.

She unhooked a few of his tubes, then lifted him up and placed him in my arms. I attempted to cradle him—but still found myself worried about unsettling all the medical paraphernalia attached to him . . . even though the nurse assured me that I wouldn't be disturbing anything vital. But though I pasted a caring smile on my face, I knew I was wearing a mask. Because, like the last time, I couldn't muster a single maternal feeling toward this baby. All I wanted to do was hand him back again.

"You're grand," the nurse said when I lifted him up toward her. "No hurry."

I reluctantly cradled him again. And asked, "Is he really doing all right?"

"Just grand."

"But you're sure that he didn't suffer any damage during birth?"

"Hasn't Dr. Reynolds spoken to you about this?"

Oh, yes he had—and oh, what an idiot I had made of myself. Just as I was making an idiot of myself right now—asking the same damn questions again. Voicing the same obsessive worries . . . while simultaneously being unable to hold him.

"Dr. Reynolds said he *sensed* there was no brain damage."

"Well, there you go then," she said, relieving me of Jack. "Unlike a lot of the babies in here, there's no doubt that your fella's going to be fine."

I held on to that prognosis—using it as a sort of mantra whenever I felt myself getting shaky (which, truth be told, was very often), or fatalistic, or edging into borderline despair. I knew I needed to show a positive, improved face to the world—because I was now being watched for any signs of disarray . . . especially by my husband and by Mr. Hughes.

Both men dropped by to see me regularly. Hughes would show up on his morning rounds. He would spend a good ten minutes looking me over, inspecting my war wounds, studying my chart, and briskly interrogating me about my mental well-being, while casting the occasional sidelong glance at the head nurse to make certain that I wasn't fabricating my improved personal state.

"Sleeping well, then?" he asked me on the third day after Jack's birth.

"Six hours last night."

He wrote this down, then looked at the nurse for verification. She supplied it with a rapid nod of the head. He asked, "And the, uh, episodes of emotional discomfort—these have lessened?"

"I haven't cried in days."

"Glad to hear it. Nor should you, because your boy is on the way to a complete recovery. As you are. Two more nights here and we can send you home."

"With my son?"

"You'll have to speak with Dr. Reynolds about that. That's his domain. Now, anything else we need to speak about?"

"My breasts . . ." I said in a semi-whisper.

"What about them?" he asked.

"Well, they've become a bit . . . hard."

"Haven't you been expressing milk since the birth?" he asked.

"Of course. But in the last forty-eight hours, they've started feeling rock solid."

In truth, they felt as if they had been filled with fast-drying reinforced concrete.

"That's a perfectly common postpartum syndrome," Hughes said, still not looking up from my chart. "The milk ducts tend to constrict, and the breasts begin to feel somewhat leaden . . ."

He cleared his throat, then added, "Or, at least, that's what I've been told."

The head nurse masked a smile.

"However," Hughes continued, "there is a way of ameliorating the condition. You'll show Mrs. Goodchild what to do, won't you, nurse?"

The head nurse nodded.

"And it's very good to hear that you are in such improved form, Mrs. Goodchild."

It's Ms., buster. But, of course, I didn't articulate this sentiment, for fear of sending up warning flags yet again. Especially as I was determined to walk out of here the day after tomorrow in a chemical-free state. So I simply smiled at Mr. Hughes and said, "I really feel like I'm on the mend."

But when Tony arrived that night, I was on the verge of screaming. This had nothing to do with my fragile emotional state—rather, with the instrument of torture that was currently attached to my left breast. It looked like a clear aerosol can with a hornlike aperture at one end and a reservoir at the bottom. It was attached to an electric power pack. Once turned on, it acted like a vacuum cleaner, sucking all the milk out of the breast.

I had been using this charming device ever since Jack's birth—as they needed my milk to give to Jack up in pediatric ICU. Initially, extracting milk via this vacuum was only moderately uncomfortable. But then my breasts grew hard, and suddenly the breast pump became my nemesis. When I first used it to unblock a milk duct I let out a howl, which made the head nurse cross with me.

"What seems to be the problem?" she asked me, sounding decidedly peevish.

"It hurts like fuck," I shouted, then immediately cursed myself for roaring without thinking. So I collected myself and said in a suitably contrite voice, "I'm so sorry."

The nurse ignored my apology, and instead took the pump and repositioned it on my right breast. Then, placing her spare hand on my left shoulder, she turned on the juice. Within ten seconds, the pain was outrageous—and I bit down hard against my lip, shutting my eyes tightly.

"Steady on," the nurse said. "The thing is to build up enough pressure so that the milk duct has no choice but to clear."

This took another dreadful minute—during which time the solidified breast felt as if it was being squeezed with vindictive force. *Don't scream, don't scream*, I kept telling myself. But each pressurizing squeeze of the horn made such self-restraint increasingly improbable—until, suddenly, there was this rupture-like spurt, and I could feel a warm liquid enveloping the nipple.

"There we are," the head nurse said, sounding pleased with herself. "One unblocked breast. Now you'll need to let it keep pumping for a good ten minutes to completely clear the ducts of milk . . . and then you can start on the other one."

Tony walked in when I was working on the left breast—and in the final throes of pain meltdown. This tit appeared to be twice as blocked as its counterpart—and having started the extraction process, I knew I couldn't stop, as the leaden feeling intensified fourfold, to the point where it was just as unbearable as this torture-by-suction. Tony's eyes grew immediately wide when he found me gripping the mattress with one hand, while using the other to clutch the dreaded breast pump. My face was screwed up into (judging from my husband's shocked expression) a mask of near-dementia.

"What on earth are you doing?" he asked.

"Shut up," I said, sensing that, any moment . . .

I let out a little cry, as the duct cleared and watery liquid came jetting forth. Tony said nothing. He just watched me as I continued to drain out the breast. When I was finished, I dropped the pump into a bowl on the bedside table, closed up my dressing gown, put my head in my hands, and thanked God, Allah, the Angel Moroni, *whomever*, that my stint on the rack was over (or, at least, for today anyway—as the head nurse warned me that I'd have to repeat this charming bit of plumbing several times a day if I wanted to keep my milk ducts cleared).

"You okay now?" Tony asked, sitting down on the bed.

"I have been better," I said, then explained exactly why I had been engaged in such a masochistic endeavor.

"Lucky you," Tony said. "How's our chap?"

I gave him an update on my visit this morning, and then told him that I was still waiting to hear from Reynolds this evening about when he'd be moved out of pediatric ICU.

"The nurse hinted to me it could be as early as tomorrow—as they really think he's doing just fine. Anyway, they want to discharge me in two days' time—so you might have us both at home before you know it."

"Oh . . . great," Tony said.

"Hey—thanks for the enthusiastic response," I said.

"I am pleased, *really*. It's just—I only heard today that the editor wanted me to pop over to Geneva later on in the week. Some UN conference on . . ."

"Forget it," I said.

"Of course, now that I know you're coming home . . ."

"That's right—you'll just have to get someone else to cover for you."

"No problem," Tony said quickly. Which was a relief—because I had never told Tony before that he couldn't do something (having both agreed from the start that we'd keep the word *no* out of our domestic vocabulary . . . within reason, of course). But I certainly wasn't spending my first night home from hospital by myself with Jack. Though my husband seemed a little thrown by my vehemence, he slipped into reassurance mode.

"I'll call His Lordship tonight, tell him it's out of the question. And I promise you a great homecoming meal, courtesy of Marks and Spencer. But the champagne will come from elsewhere."

"Like Tesco?"

He laughed. "Very witty," he said. "But, then again, you can't drink, can you?"

"I think I'll manage a glass."

We looked in on Jack that night. He was sleeping soundly and seemed content. And the nurse on duty told us that Dr. Reynolds had okayed his move to my room tomorrow morning—a prospect that terrified me. Because he would be my responsibility now.

But the next morning, I was paid a visit by Dr. Reynolds in my room.

"Now I don't want to upset you," he began, "but it seems that Jack has developed jaundice."

"He *what?*"

"It's a common postpartum condition that affects almost fifty percent of all newborn babies—and it usually clears up in ten days."

"But how did he get it?"

"Well, to give you the proper textbook definition: jaundice occurs when there is a breakdown of red blood cells and you get a buildup of a yellow pigment called bilirubin."

"But what causes this buildup of . . . what was it again?"

"Bilirubin. Generally, it comes from breast milk."

"You mean, *I* have made him jaundiced?"

"Ms. Goodchild . . ."

"What you're telling me is that I've poisoned him."

That dangerous edge had crept into my voice—and though I was aware of its ominous presence, there was nothing I could do to curb it. Because I really didn't understand what it was doing here in the first place.

Dr. Reynolds spoke slowly and with great care.

"Ms. Goodchild, you simply must not blame yourself. Because there's nothing you could have done to prevent this, and also because—as I said before—it is such a typical ailment in new babies."

"Can jaundice be dangerous?"

"Only if the levels of bilirubin get too high."

"Then what happens?"

I could see Dr. Reynolds shift uncomfortably from one foot to the other.

"Then," he finally said, "it can prove toxic to the brain. *But*—and I must emphasize this—such levels are extremely rare. And so far, your son is not showing any signs of . . ."

But I wasn't listening to him anymore. Instead, another voice had taken up residency inside my head. A voice that kept repeating, *"You've poisoned him . . . and now he's going to be even more brain damaged. And there's no one to blame but you . . ."*

"Ms. Goodchild?"

I looked up and could see Dr. Reynolds eyeing me with concern.

"Are you all right?"

"What?"

"I seemed to have lost you for a moment."

"I'm . . . all right," I said.

"Did you hear what I said—about not holding yourself accountable for your son's jaundice?"

"Yes, I heard."

"And it will clear up in around ten days. During that time, we will have to keep him in the ICU. But, once again, there's nothing particularly ominous about that—it's just standard procedure for any newborn with jaundice. Is that understood?"

I nodded.

"Would you like to go up and see him?"

"All right," I said—but my voice sounded flat, devoid of emotion. Once again, I could see Reynolds studying me with concern.

The blue light of the ICU masked the yellowish tint that now characterized Jack's skin. Nor could I discern the discoloration around my son's pupils which Reynolds told me was another feature of jaundice. But it didn't matter that I couldn't see the actual physical evidence of his illness. I knew how sick he was. And I knew that, despite Reynolds's protestations, it *was* my fault.

Afterward, I called Tony at work and broke the news to him. When I mentioned that Jack had become jaundiced because of my breast milk, my husband said, "Are you sure that you weren't a Catholic in another life? Because you certainly love to wallow in guilt."

"I am not wallowing in guilt. I am simply *admitting* the truth of the matter: his illness is my doing."

"Sally, you're talking rubbish."

"Don't accuse me of . . ."

"It's jaundice, not AIDS. And if the doctor says that it will clear up in a few days . . ."

"You're not listening to me," I shouted.

"That's because you're being preposterous."

By the time Tony arrived at the hospital that night, I had managed to pull myself out of my self-flagellation jag—and immediately apologized to him for shouting on the phone.

"Don't worry about it," he said tersely.

We went up to the ICU together. Again, the blue fluorescent tubes cast the ward in a spectral light and also bleached out the yellowed pigment of our son's skin. When Tony asked the attending nurse just how bad the jaundice was, she reassured us that his was a very standard case and that (as Reynolds had told me) it would be cleared up in a matter of days.

"So there's nothing to worry about?" Tony asked, giving his question a certain for-my-benefit pointedness.

"He should make a full recovery, with no lasting side effects," the nurse said.

"See?" Tony said, patting my arm. "All is well."

I nodded in agreement—even though I didn't believe it. I knew the truth. Just as that nurse knew the truth. After all, she didn't say he *will* make a full recovery; she used the conditional verb *should*. Because she wasn't at all certain that Jack would get better and she knew that my milk had poisoned him.

But I wouldn't dare articulate any of this right now. No way was I going to open my big mouth and blurt out the reality of the situation. Especially given that everyone was now watching me for signs of stress and strain.

For the next thirty-six hours, I maintained this calm-and-collected front, showing a sane, rational face to the doctors and nurses of the Mattingly, visiting Jack several times a day at the ICU, and always nodding in agreement when they kept feeding me optimistic falsehoods about his progress.

Then, as expected, I was given the all-clear to go home. It was something of a wrench to leave Jack behind in the ICU—but I was glad for his sake that he was still sequestered from me, in a place where I could do him no harm. And every time a strange rational voice inside my brain admonished me for beating myself up over Jack's illness, another more forceful, prosecutorial voice reminded me just how culpable I was.

Getting out of the hospital was, therefore, something of a relief. Especially as Tony not only had dinner waiting for me when I came home, but (as promised) he'd also hired Margaret's cleaner, Cha, to give the place a thorough going-over . . . which meant that it now looked like a moderately tidy building site. And yes, he did have a bottle of Laurent-Perrier in the fridge. But when he handed me a glass, all I could think was: *this is not exactly a triumphant homecoming, now, is it?*

Still, I clinked my glass against his and downed the French fizz in one long gulp. Tony immediately refilled it.

"You're thirsty," he said.

"I think it's called needing a drink."

"And so say all of us."

I drained my glass again.

"I'm glad I bought two bottles," Tony said, topping me up once more. "You okay?"

I didn't feel that question needed answering. Just as I decided to side-step my usual overexplanation of how I was feeling—because it was so damn obvious what was wrong here: I had come home from the hospital after having a baby, but without the baby . . . even though I knew that Jack was better off without me.

"Nice bit of domestic news today," Tony said. "The builders were in—"

"You could have fooled me."

"Anyway, the foreman—what's his name? . . . Northern Irish guy . . . Collins, right? . . . he was asking for you. And when I mentioned you'd had the baby, but he was in intensive care . . . well, Jesus, you should have seen the Catholic guilt kick in. Said he'd get a full crew in the next few days, and try to have all the work done within a fortnight."

"It's good to know that a potentially brain-damaged baby can finally get a builder to . . ."

"Stop it," Tony said quietly, pouring me yet another glass.

"Have I already drunk the last one?"

"Looks that way. Shall I get dinner on?"

"Let me guess. Curry vindaloo?"

"Close. Chicken tikka masala."

"Even though you know I can't stand Indian."

"If you can't stand Indian, you've come to the wrong country."

"Yes," I said. "I have done just that."

Tony got one of those uncomfortable looks on his face again.

"I'll get things under way in the kitchen."

"And I'll go unblock a milk duct."

Oh, God, we were off to a great start. To make things even merrier, both my breasts were now feeling like reinforced concrete again. So I retreated to the bathroom, and stared at the half-finished cabinets and untiled floors as I powered up the torture pump and screamed only three times until the right nipple finally spouted milk. However, the left breast seemed more pliable now. After five minutes of electrically induced suction, it burst forth. Then I staggered up off the toilet seat, dumped the pump in the sink, walked into the nursery, sat down in the wicker chair, and found myself staring blankly at the empty crib. That's when I felt myself reverting back into sinking mode, the same feeling that hit me right after the birth, and had now decided to pay me a second call. It was as if this brightly colored room had become a cube, in which I was trapped as it headed on a downward trajectory. And the cube was simultaneously diminishing in size—to the point where all I could do was brace both legs and both feet against all four walls, in an attempt to stop it from crushing me.

"What the hell are you doing?"

Tony's voice stopped my free-fall—and also yanked me back to the here and now. The cube had become a room again. I was no longer plummeting, but I was certainly in an awkward and damnably embarrassing position, crouched against a wall, with my hands gripping the floorboards.

"Sally, are you all right?"

I didn't know how to answer that question—because I still wasn't certain where I was. So I said nothing, and let Tony help me back to my feet, and into the chair. He looked at me with that unspoken mixture of anxiety and contempt which seemed to characterize his reaction to my now-frequent moments of distress.

Only this time, the distress was short-lived. As soon as he had me seated back in the chair, it vanished—and I felt functioning again.

"Dinner ready?" I asked.

"Sally, what were you doing on the floor?"

"I don't know, really. Little fainting spell, I think."

"But you looked like you were trying to claw your way out of the room."

"That's what I get for drinking three glasses of champagne on an empty womb."

I found this witticism hugely funny—and suddenly couldn't stop laughing. Once again, Tony just stared at me and said nothing.

"Oh, come on, Tony," I said. "You've got to give me an A plus for bad taste."

"Maybe you shouldn't drink anything more tonight."

"With bloody Indian food? You must be joking."

Only we weren't eating chicken tikka masala (that was Tony's idea of a joke); rather, a wonderfully high carbohydrate spaghetti alla carbonara, with lots of freshly grated Parmesan cheese, and a big green salad, and a loaf of buttery garlic bread, and a decent bottle of Chianti Classico, all courtesy of Marks and Spencer.

It was pure comfort food. Days of hospital muck had left me suddenly ravenous. I ate like a hostage on his first full night of freedom. Only I didn't feel free of anything. Rather, the food was simply acting as a momentary diversion against . . .

What? I thought I'd rid myself of all the furies that had seized hold of me. But now . . . what the hell was that bad piece of surrealism in Jack's room? Maybe Tony was right: throwing back copious amounts of champagne after a long stretch of sobriety probably wreaked havoc with my equilibrium. And the sight of Jack's empty crib simply sent me over the edge.

"You seem to be nursing that glass of wine," Tony said.

"After that performance on the floor, I thought I'd better turn Mormon for the night. I'm sorry."

He shrugged.

"Not to worry," he said in a flat tone of voice that wasn't reassuring.

"Thank you for this beautiful dinner," I said.

"Ready-made food isn't exactly beautiful."

"Still, it was very thoughtful of you."

Another of his shrugs. We fell silent. Then, "I'm scared, Tony."

"That's not surprising. You've been through a lot."

"It's not just that. It's whether Jack will turn out . . ."

He cut me off.

"You heard what the nurse said yesterday. All vital signs are good. The MRI showed nothing. His brain waves are registering as normal. So, in fact, there's little to worry about."

"But Dr. Reynolds wasn't definitive about that . . ."

"Sally . . ."

"And I'm absolutely certain that Reynolds is trying to cushion us from the possibility that Jack has brain damage. I mean, he's a very straightforward, decent man, Reynolds—especially after that uppity prick, Hughes—but he's also like every damn doctor. As far as he's concerned, we're his problem . . . but only up until that point when Jack is discharged from the Mattingly. So, naturally, he'll keep as much from us as he can."

"Please stop sounding like one of those batty conspiracy theorists . . ."

"This is not some fucking conspiracy theory, Tony. This is our son, who is now entering his second week in intensive care . . ."

"And who everyone says will be just fine. Do I have to keep repeating that over and over? Have you lost all reason?"

"You're saying I'm crazy?"

"I'm saying, you're being irrational . . ."

"I have a *right* to be irrational. Because . . ."

But then, out of nowhere, I applied the emotional brakes. I was shouting. Suddenly, like somebody changing rooms, I found myself back in far more sensible surroundings, truly appalled (yet again) by such a temperamental overload, let alone the way it had just abruptly ended. This wasn't like anger's normal aftermath—where, once the exchange of words was over, I'd fume for a bit and then, when it was clear that Tony wasn't going to apologize (something he seemed genetically incapable of doing), I'd take it upon myself to sue for peace. No, this was . . . well, *strange* was the only word to describe it. Especially as the anger just fell off me. One moment, I was in full throttle fury. The next . . .

"I think I need to lie down."

Tony gave me another of his long, nonplussed looks.

"Right," he finally said. "Want me to help you back to bed?"

I haven't been in bloody bed since I've come back home, Tony . . . or hadn't you noticed?

"No, I'll manage," I said.

I got up, and left the kitchen, and went to the bedroom, and changed into my pajamas, and fell into bed, and pulled the blankets up over my head, and waited for sleep to come.

But it didn't arrive. On the contrary, I was shockingly wide awake, despite a deep, painful fatigue. But my mind was in high-octane overdrive—ricocheting from thought to thought, worry to worry. Entire horrendous scenarios played themselves out in my head—the last of which involved Jack, aged three, curled up, ball-like in an armchair, unable to focus on me, or his general surroundings, or the world at large, while some hyper-rational, hyper-calm social worker said in a hyper-rational tone of voice, "I really do think that you and your husband must consider some sort of 'managed care' environment for your son. A place where his needs can be attended to twenty-four hours a day."

But then, this catatonic child sprang up from the chair, and abruptly commenced the most extreme temper tantrum imaginable—screaming nonsyllabic sounds, upturning a side table, and knocking out of his way everything that strayed into his path as he charged across the living room, before falling into the bathroom and smashing the mirror with his fist. As I struggled to calm him down—and get a towel wrapped around his now hemorrhaging hand—I caught brief sight of myself in the shattered glass: aged beyond recognition in the three short years since Jack's birth; the perma-crescent-moons beneath my eyes and the cleaved lines giving a clear indication of my so-called quality of life since my poor brain-damaged boy had been born.

However, my moment of exhausted self-pity was quickly over—as he began to slam his head against the sink. And—

"Tony!"

No answer. But, then again, why would there be—as I was in bed and the door was shut. I glanced at the clock: 2:05. How did that happen? I hadn't been asleep, had I? I turned over. Tony wasn't next to me in bed. All the lights in the room were still on. Immediately I was out of bed and in the corridor. But before I headed downstairs to see if he was up, watching a late-night movie, I saw the light on the still uncarpeted stairs leading up to his office.

The attic conversion had been finished while I had been in the hospital, and Tony had evidently expended considerable effort on putting it together. His fitted bookshelves were now stacked with his extensive library. Another wall was filled with CDs. He had a small stereo system and a shortwave radio in easy reach of the large stylish desk that he chose with me at the Conran Shop. There was a new Dell computer center stage on the desk, and a new orthopedic Herman Miller chair, upon which Tony was now sitting, staring intently at a word-filled screen.

"This is impressive," I said, looking around.

"Glad you like it."

I wanted to mention something about how it might have been nice if he'd concentrated his energies on unpacking the more shared corners of the house . . . but thought it wise to hold my tongue. It had been getting me into enough trouble recently.

"What time is it?" he asked absently.

"Just a little after two."

"Couldn't sleep?"

"Something like that. You too?"

"Been working since you went off to bed."

"On what? Something for the paper?"

"The novel, actually."

"Really?" I said, sounding pleased. Because Tony had been threatening to start his first foray into fiction when I met him in Cairo. At the time he intimated that if he ever got transferred back to dreaded, prosaic London, he was finally going to try to write the Graham Greene–esque novel that had been rattling around his head for the past few years.

There was a part of me that always wondered if Tony had the long-term discipline that was required for this prolonged task. Like so many journos who'd done time in the field, he loved the manic hunt for a story, and the hurried, frenetic rush to file copy by the necessary deadline. But could he actually retreat to a little room, day in, day out, to incrementally push a narrative along—as he once bragged to me that two hours was about the longest time he'd ever spent writing a story?

Yet here he was, in the middle of the night, working. I was both impressed and pleasantly surprised.

"That's great news," I said.

Tony shrugged. "It might turn out to be crap."

"It might turn out to be good."

Another shrug.

"How far are you into it?" I asked.

"Just a few thousand words."

"And . . . ?"

"Like I said, I haven't a clue if it's up to anything."

"But you will keep writing it?"

"Yeah—until my nerve fails me. Or when I decide it's beyond useless."

I came over to him and put my hand on his shoulder.

"I won't let you stop."

"That a promise?" he asked, finally looking up at me.

"Yes. It is. And listen . . ."

"Yes?"

"I'm sorry about before."

He turned back to the screen.

"I'm sure you'll feel better in the morning . . . if you can stop worrying."

But when I woke at seven that morning, Tony wasn't next to me in bed. Rather, I found him asleep on the new pull-out sofa in his study, a small pile of printed pages stacked up by the computer. When I brought him a cup of tea a few hours later, my first question was, "How late did you work?"

"Only till three," he said, sounding half awake.

"You could have come down and shared the bed."

"Didn't want to wake you."

But the next night, he did the same thing. I'd just come back from the hospital—my second visit of the day to Jack. It was nine o'clock—and I was slightly aggrieved to find Tony already at work in his office, as he had told me he couldn't make it to the hospital this evening, because of yet another international crisis (something in Mozambique, I think) that was keeping him.

"Anyway, it's not as if Jack will be missing me," he said when he phoned me that afternoon at home.

"But I'd like it if you were with me."

"And I'd like it too. But . . ."

"I know, I know—work is work. And who cares if your son . . ."

"Let's not start that," he said sharply.

"Fine, fine," I said, sounding truly touchy now. "Have it your way. I'll see you at home."

So finding him in his office that evening really did peeve me.

"I thought you said you'd be working late at the paper."

"We got the pages to bed earlier than expected."

"Well, thanks a lot for rushing over to the Mattingly to see your son."

"I only got in fifteen minutes ago."

"And went straight to work on your novel?"

"That's right."

"You really expect me to believe that?"

"I was inspired," he said, without the faintest trace of irony.

"I suppose you'll now want dinner?"

"No—I grabbed something at the office. Anyway, what I really want to do is work on, if that's okay."

"Don't you want to know how Jack is?"

"I do know that. I called the hospital around six, and got a full update from the ICU nurse. But, I suppose, you know that already."

I wanted to scream. Instead, I just turned on my heel and left. After throwing something together in the kitchen, and washing it back with a single glass of wine (I wasn't risking another descent into weirdness), I poured Tony a glass and brought it back up to his office.

"Oh, ta," he said, looking up from the screen.

"How's it going?" I asked.

"Good, good," he said in a tone that indicated that I was interrupting his flow.

"Want to watch the *Ten O'Clock News*?"

"Better keep on with this."

Two hours later, I stuck my head back in his office.

"I'm going to bed now," I said.

"Fine."

"You coming?"

"Be down in a moment."

But when I turned the bedside light off fifteen minutes later, he hadn't joined me. And when I came to at eight the next morning, the space next to me was empty.

So, once again, I climbed the stairs to his office—only to find him under the duvet on his sofa bed.

This time, however, I didn't bring him a cup of tea. Nor did I wake him. But when he staggered downstairs around ten, looking harassed, the first thing he said to me was, "Why the hell did you let me sleep in?"

"Well, since we now seem to be living separate lives, I don't have to be your alarm clock."

"I spend two nights on the sofa, and you're already talking about separate lives."

"I'm just wondering if you're trying to tell me something. Or if this is some passive-aggressive—"

"*Passive-aggressive*. For fuck's sake, I was just working late. On the novel—which *you* so want me to write. So what's the problem?"

"I'm just . . ."

"Insanely insecure."

I didn't know what to say to that. Except, "Perhaps."

"Well, you shouldn't be. And I will be at the hospital tonight. And I will share our bed. All right?"

True to his word, Tony did show up at the Mattingly around eight that evening. He was half an hour late, but I decided not to make a big deal of it. I had already spent the better part of an hour making eye contact with my son. He seemed to be watching me watching him—and for the first time in weeks, I actually found myself smiling.

"Look at this," I said as Tony walked down the ward toward us. He crouched down beside us and looked at his son.

"I told you he would be all right," he said.

Yes, you did. But why do you have to remind me of that now?

"He really sees us," I said, deciding it was not the moment to respond to Tony's comment.

"I suppose he does." He waved briefly in his direction. "Hello there. We are your parents, you poor bugger."

"He'll be just fine. Because we'll make sure of that."

"Your mother's an all-American optimist," Tony said to Jack. Our son just peered out at us, no doubt wondering where he was, and what was this thing called life.

That night, Tony did get into bed with me, and read Graham Greene's *The Honorary Consul*, and kissed me good night. Though sex was still definitely out of the physical question, a cuddle would have been nice. But, then again, a casual cuddle (or, at least, one without the follow-through of sex) was never Tony's style. When I woke the next morning . . . true to form, I found him upstairs, sprawled out on his sofa bed, more pages piled up by the computer.

"You seem to be having very productive nights," I said.

"It's a good time to work," he said.

"And it also gives you the excuse not to sleep with me."

"I did last night."

"For how long?"

"Does that really matter? You *were* asleep, after all."

"As soon as I was conked out, you went upstairs."

"Yes, that's right. But I did come to bed with you as requested, didn't I?"

"I suppose so," I said, realizing I had nowhere to go in this argument.

"And the novel is getting written."

"That's nice."

"So what's the problem?"

"There is no problem, Tony."

But I also knew that my husband was shrewdly ensuring that, when Jack came home, he'd be able to sidestep all the broken, sleepless nights by using his novel as an excuse . . . and the sofa bed in his office as his refuge.

Once again, however, I feared raising this point, as I could see that every time I said something contrary, he'd sigh heavily and make me feel like the nag I never wanted to be. And he had let my little free-fall episode come and go without major comment. Just as he'd also been admirably Teflon-like when I was riding the hormonal roller coaster in the hospital. So, to keep the domestic peace (especially given Jack's imminent arrival home), I thought it best not to push this point. *Grin and bear it:* the great marital bromide.

But I decided to sidestep all such negative thoughts by using the next few days to get the house into some sort of reasonable shape before our son filled every imaginable space. Fortunately, the foreman and his team were outside our front door at eight the next morning, ready to start work (Tony must have really played on their guilt—or simply stopped paying them). And Collins—the Northern Irish boss of the crew—was solicitousness itself, asking me with great concern about my "wee one," telling me he was "sorry for my troubles," but that, "God willing, the wee fella will be just grand." He also assured me that he and his boys would be able to finish all the large-scale work within a week.

"Now don't you worry about a thing, except your wee fella. We'll get the job done for you."

I was genuinely touched by such kindness—especially in the light of the fact that he had been such a completely irresponsible pain prior to this, never true to his word, always messing us about, always acting as if he was doing us a favor. Suddenly, his inherent decency had emerged. Though I could have cynically written it off as him caving into emotional blackmail, I couldn't help but think that he was probably like every builder—playing the middle from both ends, taking on far more jobs than he could handle, and never letting the right hand know what the left hand was doing. But there's something about a child in danger that brings out the grace in almost all of us . . . unless, like Tony, you build up a wall against all panic, all doubt, all sense of life's random inequities.

Once again, I sensed that this emotional *cordon sanitaire* was Tony's way of coping with his own undercurrent of worry. As elliptical as he could be, I still knew him well enough by now to see through his veneer of diffidence. And though I was truly pleased that he was getting on with the novel, I also realized that it was a defense mechanism—a distancing device, in which he could push me and the potential problem that was Jack to one side.

"No doubt, it will only be a matter of time before he starts working out ways to get transferred back to Cairo—alone," Sandy said when she called me that morning.

"He's just quietly freaking," I said.

"Yeah—responsibility is such a bitch."

"Look, everyone has their own way of dealing with a crisis."

"Which, in Tony's case, means play ostrich."

Of course, this hadn't been my first phone conversation with my sister since I'd been rushed to hospital. Ever since I had come home, we'd spoken two to three times a day. Naturally, Sandy was horrified by my news.

"If that deadbeat ex-husband of mine hadn't just taken off for a monthlong hike with his outdoorsy paramour, I'd be over in London like a speeding bullet. But there's no one else to look after the kids, and the bastard's hiking without a cell phone, so he's completely out of contact."

True to form, however, she did not react with horror to the big question mark hovering over Jack. Instead, she worked the phones, calling every obstetrician and pediatrician she knew in the Boston area, demanding information and second opinions, and all those other *"some-*

thing must be done!" attempts to ameliorate a crisis that we love to practice in the States.

"I really think it's going to turn out all right," I told Sandy in an attempt to get her off the subject of my contrary husband. "More importantly, they're moving Jack today out of pediatric ICU."

"Well, that's something. Because according to my friend Maureen's husband—"

And it would turn out that Maureen's husband was a certain Dr. Flett, who happened to be the head of pediatric neurology at Mass General—and he had said that . . .

"—if the baby is responding to normal stimuli after seven days the signs are pretty good."

"That's exactly what the doctors here told me," I said.

"Yes," Sandy said, "but they're not the head of pediatric neurology at one of the leading hospitals in America."

"The doctors here really have been terrific," I said.

"Well, if I had a couple of million in the bank, I'd fly you and Jack over here by MedEvac today."

"Nice thought—but this isn't exactly Uganda."

"I'm yet to be convinced of that. Are you better today?"

"I'm fine," I said carefully. Though I had mentioned my initial postpartum dive to Sandy, I didn't go into great detail . . . especially as I didn't want to unsettle her further, and also because I was pretty certain that my brief emotional downturn had been nothing more than that. But Sandy, per usual, wasn't buying my calmness.

"I've got this other friend—Alison Kepler—she's the chief nurse in the postpartum division of Brigham and Women's Hospital . . ."

"Jesus, Sandy," I said, interrupting her. "Half of Boston must know about Jack's birth . . ."

"Big deal. The thing is, I'm getting you the best proxy medical advice imaginable. And Alison told me that postpartum depression can come in a couple of waves."

"But I'm *not* having a postpartum depression," I said, sounding exasperated.

"How can you be certain? Don't you know that most depressed people don't know they're depressed?"

"Because I find myself getting so damn pissed off with Tony, that's how. And don't you know that most depressed people are unable to get really pissed off at their husband . . . or their sister?"

"How can you be pissed off at me?"

How can you so lack a sense of humor? I felt like screaming at her. But that was how my wonderful, humorless sister saw the world: in an intensely logical, *what you say is what you mean* sort of way. Which is why she would never—repeat, *never*—survive in London.

But in the first few days out of the hospital, I was certain that I was beyond the mere surviving stage of postpartum shock. Perhaps this had something to do with Jack's liberation from pediatric ICU. On Wednesday, I arrived for my morning visit at ten-thirty—only to be met by the usual morning nurse, who said, "Good news. Jack's jaundice has totally cleared up—and we've moved him to the normal baby ward."

"You sure he's free of everything?" I asked.

"Believe me," she said, "we wouldn't release him from here unless we were certain all is well."

"Sorry, sorry," I said. "I've just turned into a perpetual worrier."

"Welcome to parenthood."

The baby ward was two floors down. The nurse phoned ahead to inform them that I was the actual mother of Jack Hobbs ("We can't be too careful these days"). When I arrived there, the head nurse on duty was waiting.

"You're Jack's mum?" she asked.

I nodded.

"Your timing's perfect," she said. "He needs to be fed."

It was extraordinary to see him free from all the medical apparatus that had mummified him for the past ten days. Before he looked so desperately vulnerable. Now his face had shaken off that drugged look of shock that had possessed him during the first few days of his life. And though Sandy (through her platoon of experts) had reassured me that he'd have no received memories of these early medical traumas, I couldn't help but feel more guilt. Guilt that I had done something wrong during my pregnancy—even though I couldn't exactly pinpoint what that was.

And suddenly, that reproving voice inside my head started repeating, over and over again, *"You brought this on yourself. You did it to him. Because you really didn't want him . . ."*

Shut up!

I found myself shuddering and gripping the sides of Jack's crib. The nurse on duty studied me with concern. She was in her mid-twenties, large, dumpy—but someone who immediately exuded decency.

"Are you all right?" she asked.

"Just a little tired, that's all," I said, noticing her name tag: *McGuire*.

"Wait until you get him home," she said with an easy laugh. But instead of getting annoyed at this innocently flippant comment, I managed a smile—because I didn't want anyone to know the manic distress that was encircling me at the moment.

"Ready to take him?" the nurse asked.

No, I am not ready. I'm not ready for any of this. Because I can't cope. Because . . .

"Sure," I said, my smile tight.

She reached in, and gingerly gathered him up. He was very docile until he was put into my arms. At which point, he instantly began to cry. It wasn't a loud cry, but it was certainly persistent—like someone who felt instantly uncomfortable with the hands now holding him. And that admonishing voice inside my head told me, *"Well, of course he's crying. Because he knows it was you who did him harm."*

"Is he your first?" the nurse asked.

"Yes," I said, wondering if my nervousness was showing.

"Don't worry about the crying then. Believe me, he'll get to like it within a day."

Why are you trying to humor me? It's so clear that Jack knows I meant him harm, knows I really was trying to hurt him, knows I'm incapable of being a mother. Which is why he can't stand this first physical contact with me. He knows.

"Can I get you a chair?" the nurse asked me.

"That would be good," I said, as my legs were suddenly feeling rubbery.

She found a straight-back plastic chair. I sat down, cradling Jack. He kept roaring—a true cry from someone who was terrified by the company they were now keeping.

"Maybe if you tried feeding him . . ." the nurse suggested. "He's due a feed."

"I've been having problems extracting milk," I said.

"Well, he'll clear that problem up straightaway," she said with another of her amiable laughs that was supposed to put me at my ease, but just made me feel even more self-conscious. So, cradling the still-screaming Jack with one arm, I tried to lift my T-shirt and bra with my spare hand. But Jack's cries made me hyper-nervous, with the result that every time I attempted to yank up my shirt, I seemed to be losing my grip on him. Which made him even more disconcerted.

"Let me take him there for a moment while you sort yourself out," the nurse said.

I'm not going to sort myself out. Because I can't sort myself out.

"Thank you," I said. As soon as she relieved me of Jack, he stopped crying. I pulled up my T-shirt and freed my right breast from the nursing bra I was wearing. My hands were sweaty. I felt desperately tense—in part, because my milk ducts had been blocked again over the past few days. But also because I was holding my child and all I felt was terror.

You're not fit for this . . . you can't do this . . .

Once the breast was exposed, the nurse returned Jack to me. His reaction to my touch was almost Pavlovian: *cry when you feel Mommy's hands.* And cry he did. Profusely. Until his lips touched my nipple, at which point he started making the greedy suckling noises of someone who was desperately hungry.

"There he goes," the nurse said, nodding approvingly as he clamped his gums around my nipple and began to suck hard. Immediately, it felt as if a clothespin had been applied to my breast. Though his mouth may have been toothless, his gums were steel-reinforced. And he clamped down so hard my initial reaction was a muffled, surprised scream.

"You all right there?" the nurse asked, still trying to be all smiles—even though, with each passing moment, I was certain that she was writing me off as inadequate and completely unsuited for maternal duties.

"His gums are just a little . . ."

But I didn't get to finish the sentence as he bit down so hard that I actually shrieked. Worse yet, the pain had been so sudden, so intense, that I inadvertently yanked him off my breast—which sent him back into screaming mode.

"Oh, God, sorry, sorry, sorry," I said.

The nurse remained calm. She immediately collected Jack from me, settling him down moments after she had him in her arms. I sat there, my breast exposed and aching, feeling useless, stupid, and desperately guilty.

"Is he all right?" I asked, my voice thick with shock.

"Just got a little fright, that's all," she said. "As did you."

"I really didn't mean to . . ."

"You're grand, really. Happens all the time. Especially if you're having a little problem with the milk flow. Now hang on there a sec—I think I know how we can sort this problem out."

Using her free hand, she reached for a phone. Around a minute later, another nurse arrived with the dreaded breast pump.

"Ever use one of these things before?" Nurse McGuire asked.

"I'm afraid so."

"Off you go then," she said, handing it to me.

Once again, the pain was appalling—but, at least this time, short-lived. After a minute of vigorous pumping, the dam burst—and though I now had tears streaming down my face the relief was enormous too.

"You right now?" the nurse asked, all cheerful and no-nonsense.

I nodded. She handed Jack back to me. God, how he hated my touch. I moved him quickly to the now-leaking nipple. He was reluctant to go near it again, but when his lips tasted the milk, he was clamped onto it like a vise, sucking madly. I flinched at the renewed pain—but forced myself to stay silent. I didn't want to put on another show for this exceedingly tolerant nurse. But she sensed my distress.

"Hurts a bit, does it?" she asked.

"I'm afraid so."

"You're not the first mother who's said that. But you'll get used to it."

God, why was she so damn nice? Especially when I didn't deserve it. I mean, I'd read all the damn books and magazine articles, extolling the life-enhancing pleasures of breast-feeding: the way it *cements* the relationship between mother and child, and fosters the deepest of maternal instincts. *Breast is best* ran the theme of all these pro-suckling diatribes—and they were quick to denounce nonbelievers as wantonly selfish, uncaring, and inadequate. All of which I felt right now. Because the one thing nobody ever told me about breast-feeding was: *it hurts so fucking much.*

"Well, of course it hurts," Sandy said when I phoned her around noon that day. "Hell, I used to dread every moment of it."

"Really?" I said, grabbing onto this revelation.

"Believe me, it didn't give me a big motherly buzz."

I knew she was lying—for my benefit. Because I was often in and out of Sandy's house in the months right after the birth of her first son. And she didn't display the slightest sign of discomfort while breast-feeding. On the contrary, she was so damn adept at this business that I once saw her ironing a shirt while simultaneously suckling her son.

"It's just a bit of a shock at first, that's all," she said. "When are you going back to the hospital?"

"Tonight," I said, hearing the dread in my voice.

"I bet he's beautiful," she said. "Do you have a digital camera?"

"Uh, no."

"Well, get one and you can start emailing me photos."

"Right," I said, my voice so flat that Sandy immediately said, "Sally . . . tell me."

"Tell you what?"

"Tell me what's going on?"

"Nothing's going on."

"You don't sound good."

"Just a bad day, that's all."

"Are you sure about that?"

"Yes," I lied. Because the truth was . . .

What?

I had no damn idea what the truth here was. Except that I *didn't* want to go back to the hospital that night. As soon as I hung up the phone, I escaped from the workmen who were everywhere in the house, and took refuge in Tony's study. I sank into his desk chair and stared at the pile of manuscript pages stacked facedown to the left of his computer keyboard. There was the large black Moleskine notebook, underneath a circular pen holder. I always knew that Tony was an inveterate keeper of diaries. I found this out the first night we slept together at his shambolic Cairo flat—when I woke up around three to take a pee and discovered him in the living room, scribbling in a black-bound book.

"So what do I rate—a five, an eight?" I asked him, standing nude in the doorway.

"That's private," he said, shutting the book and recapping his pen. "Just like everything in this book."

The tone was pleasant—but coolly firm. I took the hint and never asked him about his notebook again . . . even though, over the coming months, I'd often see him writing away in it. Someone once said anyone who kept a journal was a bit like a dog going back to sniff his own vomit. But to me, anyone who chronicled their day-to-day life—and, simultaneously, their deeply personal reactions to those closest to them—ultimately wanted it to be read. Which is why—I surmised—Tony had casually left his Moleskin notebook on top of his desk. Because though he knew I respected his privacy, to the point of never coming into his study, I couldn't help but wonder if he wasn't also playing a subtle *passive-aggressive* game with me, silently saying: *There it is . . . go on, open it if you dare.*

Then again, he might have just left it there by accident . . . which meant that all my psychobabbly thoughts about his alleged tactical behavior were further examples of my heightened fragility.

I was feeling pretty damn fragile right now. So fragile that—as tempted as I was to open the notebook and learn whatever horrible truth was contained inside ("*We are a terrible match,*" "*Why is she so bloody literal about everything?*" "*I have constructed a prison of my own making.*" I really was having inventive flights of paranoid fancy)—I knew that I would be venturing into territories best sidestepped. Anyway, who in their right mind really wants to know the private thoughts of their spouse?

So I pulled my hand away from the notebook, and also resisted the temptation to read a few manuscript pages and see whether Tony was playing Graham Greene or Jeffrey Archer. Instead, I simply unfolded the sofa bed, opened the wicker box where Tony kept the duvet and pillows, made the bed, pulled down the shade on the dormer window, turned the phone to voicemail, took off my jeans, and got under the covers.

Even though there was an excessive amount of hammering and sanding on the lower floors, I was asleep within minutes—a fast, blacked-out tumble into oblivion.

Then I heard a familiar voice.

"What are you doing here?"

It took a moment or two to work out where I was. Or to adjust to the fact that it was now night, and the room had just been illuminated by the big floor lamp that stood to the right of the desk, and that my husband was standing in the doorway, looking at me with concern.

"Tony?" I asked, my voice thick with sleep.

"The hospital has been trying to reach you . . ."

Now I was completely awake.

"They *what*?"

"Jack had a minor setback this afternoon. The jaundice returned."

Now I was on my feet, grabbing for my clothes.

"Let's go," I said, pulling on my jeans. Tony put a steadying hand on my arm.

"I've been there already. It's okay now. They were worried at first that it might be a serious relapse. But the blood tests showed only a very minor overload of bilirubin, so there's nothing to worry about. However, they did move him back to pediatric ICU . . ."

I shrugged off Tony's hand.

"Tell me in the car."

"We're not going . . ."

"Don't tell me we're not going. He's my . . ."

"We're not going," Tony said, holding my arm with more vehemence.

"If you're not going, I'm . . ."

"Will you listen?" he said, his voice suddenly raised. "It's nearly midnight."

"What?" I said, sounding genuinely shocked.

"It's seven minutes to twelve."

"Bullshit."

"You've been asleep all day."

"That can't have happened."

"Well, the hospital has been trying to ring you at home since three this afternoon."

Oh, no . . .

"And I must have left you ten messages on your cell . . ."

"Why didn't you try the builders?"

"Because I didn't have their bloody cell number, that's why."

"I was taking a nap after seeing Jack this morning."

"A twelve-hour nap?"

"I'm sorry . . ."

I gently shook off his grip and finished getting dressed.

"I'm still going over there," I said.

He blocked my path toward the door. "That's not a good idea right now. Especially after . . ."

"After *what?*" I demanded. But I already sensed the answer to that question.

"Especially after the difficulties you had this morning."

That bitch, Nurse McGuire. She told on me.

"It was just a feeding problem, that's all."

"So I gather—but one of the nurses on duty said you nearly yanked Jack off your breast."

"It was a momentary thing. He hurt me."

"Well, I'm sure he didn't mean to."

"I'm not saying that. Anyway, it wasn't as if I threw him across the room. I just had a bit of a shock."

"Must have been quite a shock if the nurse reported it to her superior."

I sat down on the bed. I put my head in my hands. I really did feel like grabbing my passport, running to the airport, and catching the first plane Stateside.

You can't do this . . . you're a maternal disaster area . . .

Then another calm and lucid voice entered my head, repeating, over and over again, a soothing mantra: *You don't care . . . You don't care . . . You really don't care.*

Why should a catastrophe of a mother like me care about her child? Anyway, even if I did care, *they* (the doctors, the nurses, my husband) all knew the truth about me. They had the evidence. And they saw just how . . .

How *what?*

How . . . I wasn't understanding any of this.

How . . . one moment, I was wracked with grief and guilt for what had befallen Jack . . . the next, I couldn't give a damn.

Because I'm unfit. That's right, U-N-F-I-T. Like that old country-and-western song about D-I-V-O-R . . .

"Sally?"

I looked up and saw Tony staring at me in that quizzical, peeved way of his.

"You really should go to bed," he said.

"I've just slept twelve hours."

"Well, that was your decision."

"No—that was *my body's* decision. Because my body's noticed something which you definitely haven't noticed . . . the fact that I am completely run down after a little physical exertion called 'having a baby.' Which, I know, in your book, is just about up there with stubbing your toe . . ."

Tony gave me a thin smile and started stripping the sofa bed.

"Think I'll go to work now," he said. "No need to wait up for me."

"I'm not going back to sleep."

"That's your call. Now if you'll excuse me . . ."

"You don't care what's going on, do you?"

"Excuse me, but who ran to the hospital this evening when our son's mother turned off all the phones and put herself out of touch with the world?"

His comment caught me like a slap across the face—especially as he said it in an ultra-detached voice.

"That is so unfair," I said, my voice a near-whisper. Tony just smiled.

"Of course you'd think that," he said. "Because the truth is usually most unfair."

Then he sat down in his desk chair, swiveled it away from me, and said, "Now if you'll excuse me . . ."

"Fuck you."

But he ignored that comment, and instead said, "If you do feel like making me a cup of tea, that would be most welcome."

I responded to this comment by storming out of his office, slamming the door behind me.

Marching downstairs, my initial reaction was to fly out the door, jump into a taxi, tell the driver to floor it to the Mattingly, march straight into pediatric ICU, demand to see Jack immediately, and also demand that they find that Irish stool pigeon, so I could confront that Ms. Holier-Than-Thou with the lies she'd peddled about me. And then . . .

I would be bound and gagged and dispatched to the nearest rubber room.

I started to pace the floor. And when I say pace, I *mean* pace. As in a manic back-forth motion: *here-there, here-there, here-there*. Only when the thought struck me—*look at you, treading up and down the room like a laboratory animal on amphetamines*—did I force myself to sit down. At which point I had a bad attack of the chills. An arctic wind had blown down Sefton Street and had somehow penetrated the very fabric of my house, leaving me convinced that the floorboards were rotting, rising damp was prevalent, and this entire shit heap investment, this mean little example of domestic Victoriana, was going to be blown off its dirt foundations, leaving us destitute and in the street.

But then, the climate changed. The mercury soared eighty degrees. I'd left mid-January in the Canadian Rockies and was now somewhere in the tropics. Aruba, baby. Forget the frostbite. *We're having a heat wave, a tropical heat wave.* Like one hundred and ten in the shade, with ninety-six percent humidity. Suddenly, I was sweating. So drenched in perspiration that I had to strip off all my clothes.

Which is exactly what I did—not noticing that our front curtains were open and someone was getting out of a black cab parked right outside, and the driver was gawking at me, wide-eyed, and I felt like turning full-frontal toward him, and showing off my caesarean scar. Instead, some intrinsic modesty took over and I made a dash upstairs for the bathroom, and turned on the cold tap full-blast, and jumped under the downpour (thank God, I'd insisted on an American power shower), and then . . .

What are you doing?

I turned off the water. I leaned my head against the tiled wall. I felt another stab of panic—because I was so completely adrift and out of control. What was scaring me most was the realization that there seemed to be no logical progression to these strange, manic interludes. I had become an emotional pinball, bouncing wildly off every object in my path. In the midst of these mood swings, there would be moments of extreme, painful clarity—like the one I was negotiating right now, where I felt like beating my skull against the wall and repeating over and over again, *What are you doing?*

To which I could only answer: *I really don't know. Because I don't even know how things operate within me anymore.*

Oh, listen to yourself. Little Miss Self-Pity. A mild postpartum dip in your equilibrium—something any sensible, balanced person could handle—and you cleave in two. Tony's right to treat you as some sort of silly recalcitrant. Because you're making an idiot of yourself. Worse yet, you keep going down this manic road, and questions will start being raised about your sanity. So get a grip, eh? And while you're at it, go make your husband a cup of tea.

I followed the advice of this hyper-censorious internal counselor—and stepped out of the shower, determined to put everything right. As I dressed and dried my hair, I told myself that, from this moment on, calm lucidity would prevail. I would go to the hospital tomorrow morning and apologize for not showing up today. I would seek out Nurse McGuire, and let her know that I perfectly understood her concerns about my mental well-being yesterday, but would then demonstrate that I was in control by breast-feeding Jack with uncomplaining aplomb. And on the domestic front, I'd soothe all of Tony's concerns by going Stepfordish for a while, and playacting the perfect wife.

So, not only did I make my husband a cup of tea, but I also arranged a large plateful of his favorite cookies and found a bottle of Laphroaig (his malt whisky of preference). Then I negotiated the stairs, nearly losing my balance (courtesy of far too many items on the tray) on at least two occasions. When I reached his office door, it was closed. I used my foot to knock.

"Tony," I said.

He didn't answer—even though I could hear low-volume music coming from within.

"Tony, please—I've got your cup of tea . . ."

The door opened. He looked at the laden tray.

"What's this?"

"Sustenance for your literary endeavors. And an apology."

"Right," he said with a nod. Then, relieving me of the tray, he said, "Think I'd better get back to the desk."

"Going well?"

"I suppose so. Don't wait up." And he closed the door.

Don't wait up.

Typical. So *bloody* typical. Pissing on my parade, per usual. And while I was trying to be so good.

Stop it. Stop it. He's working, after all. And you did have that little "set-to" (to be bloody English about it) just before, which you can't expect him to get over in ten minutes . . . even if he did make that shitty comment about . . .

Enough. Tony's right. You really should just go to bed. The only problem is: having just been asleep for the past twelve hours . . .

All right, all right. Stay busy. Do something to make the hours pass.

That's how I ended up unpacking just about every box and crate still strewn around the house. The entire process took around six hours and I had to work around what remained of the builders' mess. By the time I was finished, dawn light was just making a tentative appearance—and I had the weary but satisfied buzz that comes from finishing a major domestic chore that had been naggingly unfinished for months. Walking around the house—now nearing a state of actual livability—I felt a curious sanguinity. There was finally a sense of space and proportion and (most of all) order.

Order was something I truly craved right now.

I ran a bath. I sat soaking in the tub for nearly an hour. I told myself: *You see . . . a little displacement activity, and the gods of balance and equilibrium land comfortably on your shoulders. Everything's going to be fine now.*

So fine that, after I got dressed, I felt fully energized—even though I hadn't been to bed all night. I peeped in on Tony in his office. He was crashed out on his sofa . . . but I did notice a stack of new pages on the ever-growing manuscript pile. So I tiptoed over to his desk, made certain his radio alarm was set for nine AM, then scribbled a fast note:

> *Off to the hospital to see our boy. Hope you like the clean-up job on the house. Dinner tonight on me at the restaurant of your choice? I await your reply.*
>
> *Love you . . .*

I signed my name, hoping that he'd respond favorably to the idea of the sort of pleasant nights out we used to have in Cairo. With Jack due home within days, this would be our last chance to roll out of the house unencumbered.

I went downstairs. I checked my watch. Just after seven AM I opened the front door and noticed that someone on the far side of the road was in the middle of building work, with an empty Dumpster out front for assorted debris. I glanced back at the stack of empty cardboard boxes and now-broken-down packing crates, and thought: this would save a trip to the dump. I also remembered how everyone on the street emptied their attics into our Dumpster during the first stage of our renovations. So I decided that there would be few objections if a few items from my house ended up intermingling with my neighbor's debris.

However, as I was in the process of dumping the second lot of boxes into this large bin, a house door opened and a man in his mid-forties came out. He was dressed in a dark gray suit.

"You know, that is *our* skip," he said, his voice full of tempered indignation. Immediately I became apologetic.

"Sorry, I just thought that, as it was kind of empty . . ."

"You really should ask permission before tossing things into other people's skips."

"But I just thought . . ."

"Now I'd appreciate it if you'd remove all your rubbish—"

However, he was interrupted by a voice that said, "Oh for God's sake, will you listen to yourself."

The gent looked a little startled. Then he became immediately sheepish, as he found himself staring at a woman in her late forties—blond, big boned, with a heavily lined face (blondes always start to fracture after the rubicon of forty is crossed), but still striking. Equally eye-catching was the very large Labrador she had by her side. She had been walking by us when she heard our exchange. I recognized her immediately: she was the woman who had spoken to me approvingly in the shop after I forced Mr. Noor to be polite to me. And I could tell from the reaction of the Suit that he was distinctly uneasy in her presence. He avoided her accusatory gaze and said, "I was simply making a point."

"And what point was that?"

"I really do think this is between myself and—"

"When I was having my new kitchen put in last year, and there was a skip out front, who filled it up one night with half the contents of his loft?"

The Suit now looked appalled—because he had been publicly embarrassed. From my few short months in England I knew that embarrassment was considered the most fearsome of personal calamities—and to be avoided at all costs. But whereas in America, the guy would have countered by saying something politic like, "Mind your own effing business," here he suddenly went all pale and diminished, and could only mutter, "Like I said: I was just trying to make a point."

To which my Good Samaritan with the Labrador gave him a cold, knowing smile, and said, "Of course you were." Then she turned back to me and asked, "Need a hand with the rest of the boxes?"

"I'll be fine. But I . . ."

"Nice to see you again, Sally," she said, proffering her hand. "It *is* Sally, right?"

I nodded. "Julia?"

"Well done."

The gent cleared his throat, as if to announce his departure. Then he turned tail and hurried back into his house.

"Twit," Julia said under her breath after he was gone. "No wonder his wife walked out last month."

"I didn't know . . ."

She shrugged. "Just another domestic drama—like we've all had. And, by the way, I heard you're a new mother. Wonderful news. I would have dropped over with a little something, but I've been away most of the last two months in Italy with my son Charlie."

"How old is he?"

"Fourteen. And what did you have—a boy or a child?"

"A boy," I said, laughing. "Jack."

"Congratulations. How's life without sleep?"

"Well . . . he's not home yet."

Then I explained, in the briefest way possible, what had befallen him.

"Good God," she said quietly. "You've really had a ghastly time of it."

"Him more than me."

"But are you all right?"

"Yes and no. Sometimes I can't really tell."

"Got time for a cup of tea?"

"I'd love to—but I really need to be at the hospital early this morning."

"Completely understood," she said. "Anyway, drop by whenever. And do throw as much rubbish in that fool's skip as you like."

With a pleasant smile, she ended our little encounter.

I followed her instructions, and threw all the remaining empty boxes into the skip, along with four brimming bags of builders' debris. Then I walked to the tube, thinking: "I actually have a friendly neighbor."

At the hospital, I was on my ultra-best behavior. And I was hugely relieved to discover that Jack's return to pediatric ICU had been a brief one, as he was back on the normal baby ward. The usual head nurse was there as well—eyeing me up carefully, the way one does with anyone who's been labeled "a loose cannon."

But I gave her a big smile and said, "Is Nurse McGuire around? I think I owe her an apology for being so extreme yesterday."

Immediately the head nurse relaxed. Acts of contrition usually do that.

"I'm afraid she's off on a week's holiday—but when she's back, I'll tell her what you said."

"And I am sorry I didn't make it last night. It's just . . . well, to be honest about it, I was so tired I simply passed out."

"Don't worry about it. Every mother is exhausted after giving birth. And the good news is: that little relapse last night was nothing more than that. In fact, you might be able to bring him home as early as tomorrow."

I was all smiles. "That is great news."

"Are you up for feeding him now? He's definitely hungry."

Doing my best to disguise my unease, I nodded, keeping the fixed smile on my face. The head nurse motioned for me to follow her. We walked down the ward to Jack's crib. He was lying on his side, crying loudly. I tensed—wondering if he'd really start bawling when I picked him up. But I tried to mask this by saying, "He sounds really hungry."

The head nurse smiled back. Then there was an awkward moment, where I stood by the crib, not knowing if I should pick him up, or if the nurse was going to hand him to me. Looking rather warily at me again, the nurse motioned for me to take him. My hands were sweaty as I reached in. And yes, his squeals did amplify as I lifted him.

Keep your nerve, keep your nerve, I told myself. *And, for God's sake, don't look fearful.*

I pulled Jack close to me, rocking him gently. His crying redoubled. I quickly settled down into the hard straightback chair by the crib, opened my shirt, released my left breast from the nursing bra, squeezed the area around the nipple in an effort to expend a little milk, but felt nothing but solidified concrete.

Don't think about it, just get him on the breast and hope that you don't start screaming. Nurse is studying your every move.

I gently directed Jack's head toward the nipple. When he found it he began to suck ravenously. I shut my eyes as the pain hit. But then his voraciousness suddenly paid off—as his vacuumlike suction cleared the ducts and milk poured forth. It didn't matter that his steel-trapped gums were squeezing the hell out of the nipple, or that my level of discomfort was rising by the minute. He was eating.

"Are you in a bit of pain there?" the head nurse asked.

"Nothing that can't be managed," I said.

This was the correct response, as the nurse nodded approvingly and said, "I'll leave you to it."

As soon as she was out of sight, I leaned over and whispered into Jack's ear, "Thanks."

After ten minutes, I transferred Jack to the other nipple—and, once again, his vacuum of a mouth cleared all obstructions within moments and milk flowed freely.

Of course, I've read the usual pop psychology stuff about how physical blockages can lead to psychological blockages. But though I used to be skeptical of this kind of body-mind linkage, I have to admit that when I left the hospital that morning, I felt as if I had finally rid myself of the gloomy impasse in which I had lived since Jack's birth.

"Well, God bless my nephew's suction," Sandy said when I called her around nine AM her time to tell her that, finally, I had been able to feed my son without the use of a dreaded breast pump. But when I said that I was now feeling almost blissed-out, she said, "Great to hear it—but don't get yourself into a state if you suddenly slip back into the dumps again. Once Jack comes home you're going to be dealing with broken nights—when three hours of uninterrupted sleep will seem like a total triumph."

"But I haven't been to bed all night, and I feel totally terrific."

"Why didn't you get to bed last night?"

"Because I was asleep all day yesterday."

"I don't like the sound of that."

"Really, it was the best thing that could have happened to me. I needed to shut down for a while. And now, I feel as if my equilibrium is back to normal, and I've really got things back into proportion, and I'm feeling genuinely at one with things."

Long pause. I said, "You still there, Sandy?"

"Oh, I'm here. But I'm also wondering if you've suddenly turned into a Moonie."

"Thanks a lot."

"Well, what the hell do you expect when you start saying garbage like 'I'm at one with things.'"

"But I am."

"You now have me very worried."

That was typical Sandy—even more literal than I was when it came to judging other people's moods. But I knew I was all right—though when I returned home that morning from the hospital, there was a note waiting for me from Tony, saying:

> *Invitation Declined With Regret. US Deputy Secretary of*
> *State in town tonight. Just received last-minute invitation*
> *for dinner at the Embassy. Will make it up to you.*

Great, just great. But after last night's stupidity, I wasn't going to call him up and hector him for turning down my invitation. Instead, I'd put a positive spin on this situation. Rather than fall into bed now for a nap, I'd force my way through the day on no sleep, then go by the hospital around seven and would be back home in bed by ten—tired out enough to sleep straight through the night without interruption.

Come morning, I'd be back on a normal schedule—and ready to bring my son home.

Of course, by the time I reached the Mattingly that night, I had been up for twenty straight hours, and was starting to veer into numb-with-fatigue territory. The evening feeding session at the hospital went on longer than expected—as Mr. Hughes made a surprise visit to the baby ward. He was showing a group of his students around this corner of the hospital—and when he saw me feeding Jack, his led his entourage over toward me. I had my son at my breast—and turned my wince into a look of maternal contentment as he approached us.

"Bonding well, are we?" he asked.

"No problems," I said, all smiley.

"And judging from the way your boy is absorbed in the task at hand, all is flowing well?"

"Everything is working just fine."

"Splendid, splendid. Mind if I give the little chap a quick look over?"

Jack was not pleased to be disengaged from his source of food. As he kicked up, I quickly tucked my breast back into my shirt—especially as one of the male medical students with Hughes seemed particularly interested in my now bloated nipple. But judging from the critical way he was eyeing it, his interest was definitely more clinical than sexual. Meanwhile, all the other students were crowding around the crib. He started explaining in highly technical language about Jack's complicated delivery, and how he had to be ventilated after birth. He then explained about how I was suffering from high blood pressure throughout my pregnancy . . . to the point where he wondered whether it was best to deliver the child prematurely— as high blood pressure can prove hazardous to the mother's health.

"You never told me that," I said.

Suddenly, all eyes were upon me. Hughes gave me a frown. He didn't like to be interrupted in mid-discourse—especially by some pesky American.

"Something the matter, Mrs. Goodchild?" he asked.

"You never told me you were considering a premature delivery."

"That's because your high blood pressure condition wasn't pre-eclampsic . . . and because it did eventually stabilize. But, truth be told, when you were first admitted with high blood pressure, you were a borderline case for an emergency caesarean . . ."

"Well, thanks for the information, even if it is a little after the fact. I mean, if there was a danger to me and my baby, shouldn't I have been given that emergency caesarean option at the time?"

"Curiously enough, it is always better for the child if it is carried to full term. And curiously enough, Mrs. Goodchild, we are rather up-to-date on modern obstetric practice on this side of the pond . . . which means that we did do what was medically best for you and your son. More to the point, just a fortnight or so after a most complex and perilous delivery, your son appears to be flourishing. Good evening, Mrs. Goodchild."

And he moved on to the next crib.

Brilliant. Well done. Bra-fucking-vo. I'm surprised the State Department hasn't headhunted you for your diplomatic skills.

I put my hands against both sides of the crib, and lowered my head, wondering if all eyes were upon me, and if I should try to rectify things with an apology. But when I looked back up with the intention of saying something, Hughes and company were engrossed in another patient. Anyway, I had been put in my place, cut down to size, *embarrassed*.

I gripped the edge of the crib even tighter—and felt myself get very shaky again: a downward swoop which, out of nowhere, transported me to a vertiginous place positioned right over a deep, gaping chasm.

"Baby needs feeding again, I'm afraid," said a voice to my right. It was the nurse on duty—a severe, stocky woman who had been hovering in the vicinity while Hughes gave me a dressing-down, and (judging from the look she was giving me right now) thoroughly approved of his criticisms. Especially as Jack was still crying wildly, and I was just standing there, looking spacey.

"Sorry, sorry," I said as I picked up Jack, settled down again in the straight-back chair, and reattached him to my left nipple. Thankfully, he had the milk duct opened within seconds.

"Now I spoke with Dr. Reynolds earlier today—and he feels that your son is ready to be discharged. So you can collect him tomorrow morning if that doesn't present any problems."

I avoided her gaze.

"None at all."

"Very good then."

Ten minutes later, having settled Jack back in his crib, I was in a cab rolling down the Fulham Road, crying like an idiot. The driver—a young fellow, lean and tough looking—kept glancing at me in his rearview mirror, not exactly pleased that he had this blubbering woman in the back of his cab, but still torn between asking me what was wrong and not wanting to interfere. Anyway, I've never been one of those tell-all types who confide in strangers. But yet again, I was the architect of my own mess-up . . . and was also wildly overreacting to Hughes's disparagement of me.

By the time we reached Putney, I did finally manage to get myself under a degree of control. But when I paid off the driver, he deliberately avoided looking at me.

I walked into the empty house and bolted upstairs to the bedroom. I threw off my clothes, put on a T-shirt, and climbed into bed. I pulled the covers over my head. I blocked out everything.

When I jolted awake again at eight the next morning, I was so pleasantly groggy from such an unbroken period of unconsciousness that it took a moment or so to realize: *I've actually slept.*

Tony had assured me that he would take the morning off to drive me to the hospital to collect Jack. But when I shuffled down to the kitchen, I found a Post-it on top of a couple of crumpled bank notes.

> *Emergency at the paper. Here's $50 for a cab there and back.*
> *Will try to get home ASAP this evening.*
> *T xxx*

I grabbed the phone. I punched in the number of Tony's direct line. I got his voicemail. So I phoned his cell.

"Can't talk right now," he said.

"I don't care what *emergency* you have on your hands. You're meeting me at the hospital, understand?"

"I can't talk."

Then he hung up.

Immediately I rang back. He had obviously turned off his phone after our last conversation, as I was put through directly to his voicemail.

"How dare you—*how fucking dare you*—pull this. You get your sorry English ass over to the hospital, or I am not going to be responsible for what happens next. Do you get that?"

I hung up, my heart pounding, my head full of righteous indignation and genuine upset. More tellingly, I hated the way I sounded on the phone. I also hated the extremity of my reaction, and the way I shifted from serenity to rage in a matter of a few moments. But . . . I'm sorry . . . he just couldn't stand me up on this one. Not on the first trip home with our newborn son.

But he did. Because I didn't hear from him for the rest of the morning. Anyway, I didn't have time to think about this latest example of Tony's complete indifference, as I needed to be at the hospital on time or further darken my reputation as a harpy. So I ducked into the shower, and slapped some makeup on my face, and was at the Mattingly by eleven AM.

"Is your husband with you this morning?" the head nurse asked, eyeing me over, evidently wondering just what my emotional temperature might be this morning.

"I'm afraid he had a crisis at work."

"I see. And how do you plan to get your son home?"

I hoisted up the carrier, which in my crazy rush to get out of the house I had managed to remember to bring.

"And you did bring some clothes for him?"

Oh please, I'm not a total deadbeat.

"Of course," I said politely.

"Very well then."

Jack still reacted with upset when I touched him. And he didn't enjoy my diaper-changing technique—which was supervised by the head nurse, just to make certain that I was doing it properly.

It was also a struggle to get him into his onesie. He also hated being strapped into the carrier.

"I presume your local health visitor will be calling on you tomorrow," she said.

"I don't know—I haven't heard from anyone yet."

"Well, no doubt, she will be visiting you very soon—so if you have any postpartum questions, she's the person to ask . . ."

In other words: if you're making a total mess of things, help will be on its way . . .

"Thank you for that. In fact, thank you for everything."

"I hope he makes you very happy," she said.

One of the nurses helped me downstairs with the carrier. She also got one of the porters to call me a cab. On the way back to Putney, the driver spent most of his time on his cell phone, and seemed genuinely oblivious to the fact that I had a newborn in the back of his cab. But when he swerved to dodge an oncoming white minivan, he rolled down his window and shouted, "Stupid cunt! Don't you know I've got a little baby in the back?"

When we reached Sefton Street, the driver got out of the car and helped me with Jack to the front door.

"Where's your husband then?" he asked after I settled the fare.

"At the office."

"Guess someone has to earn the dosh," he said.

It was so strange entering my empty house with this tiny creature. Like all of life's bigger passages, you expect a sense of profundity to accompany the occasion. And like all of life's bigger passages, the event itself is a complete letdown. I opened the door. I picked up the carrier. I brought Jack inside. I closed the door behind me. End of story. And, once again, all I could think was: this might have been an occasion if my husband was here.

Jack had fallen asleep during the cab ride, so I hoisted him upstairs to the nursery and unfastened the straps. Exercising the utmost care, I lifted him gently into his crib. He pulled his arms tight against himself as I covered him with the little quilt that Sandy had sent me. He didn't stir. I sat down in the wicker chair opposite the crib, my head splitting from the ongoing aftereffects of the night before. I looked at my son. I waited to feel rapture, delight, maternal concern, and vulnerability—all those damn emotions that every writer of every motherhood guide promises you will inhabit in the days after your child's birth. But all I felt was a profound, terrible hollowness—and a sense that, bar the fact that this child had been literally cut out of me, I had no further connection with him.

A ringing phone snapped me out of this desperate, vacant reverie. I was hoping it was Tony—sounding contrite and suitably humble. Or

Sandy—with whom I could have bitched at length about my detached, taciturn husband. Instead, I received a call from a woman with a decidedly London accent who introduced herself as Jane Sanjay, and said that she was my health visitor. Her tone was surprising—breezy, pleasant, *I'm here to help*. And she wondered if she might drop by and see me this afternoon.

"Is there any reason why you need to see me right away?" I asked.

She laughed. "Don't panic—I'm not the baby police."

"But what did they tell you at the hospital?"

More laughter. "Honestly nothing. We don't talk to the hospitals anyway—unless there's something seriously wrong. And you don't sound like the sort of person with whom there's anything wrong."

Don't let the American accent fool you. I really don't know what the hell I'm doing.

"So," she asked, "might I come by in an hour or so?"

Jane Sanjay was around thirty with an easy smile and an unfussy manner. Having expected a real social worker type, I was rather taken aback to see this quietly attractive Anglo-Indian woman, decked out in black leggings and electric silver Nikes. Her face-to-face manner echoed her phone style—and she put me immediately at ease, making all the right jolly noises about Jack, asking me a bit about how an American ended up in London (and sounding highly impressed when she learned about my Egyptian stint with the *Boston Post*), and questioning me gently about my general postpartum state. Part of me wanted to put on a happy face and tell her that everything was just hunky-dory—out of fear of looking like the height of incompetence. But who doesn't want to take another person into their confidence—especially someone who, though in an official capacity, seems to have a sympathetic ear? So after running through what she described as a standard checklist of baby care concerns—his feeding and sleep patterns, how often I was having to change his diapers (or nappies, to use the local parlance), and how to deal with standard infant complaints like colic and diaper rash—she then asked me (in her breezy way) how I was bearing up. And when I answered with a hesitant shrug, she said, "Like I said on the phone, I'm not the baby police. And everyone who has a baby always gets regular visits from a health visitor. So really, Sally, you mustn't think that I'm snooping here."

"But *they* have told you something, haven't they?" I asked.

"Who is *they*?"

"The people at the Mattingly."

"Honestly, no. But did something happen there that I should know about?"

"Nothing specific. I just think . . . uh . . ." I hesitated for a moment, then said, "Well, put it this way: I don't think they liked my style there. Perhaps because I was a little overwrought."

"So what?" she said with a smile. "You had a terribly difficult delivery, and then your child was in an intensive care unit for an extended period of time. So you had a perfect right to feel distraught."

"But I did manage to get up the nose of the consultant."

"Between you and me . . . that's his problem. Anyway, like I said on the phone, I heard nothing from the hospital—and, believe me, had they been worried about you, I would have heard."

"Well, that's good news, I guess."

"So, if you do want to tell me anything . . ."

A pause. Instinctually, I started rocking the little baby seat in which Jack was currently sleeping. Then I said, "I guess I've been feeling a little up-and-down since his arrival."

"Nothing uncommon about that."

"And, of course, I'm sure things will be different now that he's finally home with us. But . . . uh . . . well, up to this point . . ."

I broke off, wondering how the hell to phrase what I was about to say. To her credit, Jane Sanjay didn't jump in, prodding me to finish the sentence. Instead, she said nothing, and waited for me to pick up the thread of conversation.

"Let me ask you something directly," I finally said.

"Of course," she said.

"Is it unusual to feel as if you're not exactly . . . *bonding* . . . with your child straightaway?"

"Unusual? You must be joking. In fact, just about every other new mum I see ends up asking me the same question. Because everyone expects that they're going to instantly bond with their baby. Or, at least, that's what they read in all the baby books. Whereas the truth is usually a little more complex than that—and it can take a considerable amount of time to adjust to this new creature in your life. So, *really*, it's nothing to sweat, eh?"

But that night, there was plenty to sweat. To begin with, Jack woke up around ten PM and then refused to stop crying for the next five hours. To heighten the awfulness of this nonstop bawling, both of my breasts became blocked again—and despite Jack's vacuum-like jaws (and repeated uses of the dreaded breast pump), milk refused to flow. So I rushed into the kitchen and frantically spooned several scoops of formula powder into a bottle, then poured in the specified amount of water, shook it up, popped it into the microwave, nearly burned my hand on the heated bottle, pulled a rubber nipple out of the sterilizer, attached it to the bottle, raced back to the nursery, where Jack was now wailing, picked him up, sat him on my knee, and plugged him into the bottle. But after three or four slurps of the formula, he suddenly became ill and vomited up milk all over me. Then the screaming really started.

"Oh, Jesus, Jack," I said, watching regurgitated formula dribble down my T-shirt. At which point, I heard Tony's voice behind me, saying, "Don't blame him."

"I'm not blaming him," I said. "I just don't like being covered in puke."

"What do you expect, giving him a bottle? He needs your milk, *not . . .*"

"Who the hell are you, Dr. Spock?"

"Any fool knows that."

"My tits are blocked again."

"Then unblock them."

"And why don't you fuck off back to your aerie?"

"With pleasure," he said, slamming the door behind him.

Tony had never slammed a door behind him before. And he did it with such force that it not only startled me, but also scared Jack. His crying redoubled in response to the loud bang. I suddenly had this absolute, immediate urge to punch out a window with my fist. Instead, I stripped off my vomit-drenched shirt, pulled up my bra, and—picking up Jack from the crib—attached him to the right nipple. As he sucked and sucked, I felt as if my head was about to implode—the pain from the obstructed breast suddenly feeling minor compared to the amplifying pressure cooker between my ears. And when—out of nowhere—the breast unclogged and Jack began to greedily feed, my reaction wasn't one of relief. Rather, I entered a strange new terrain . . . a place I'd never ventured before. A realm called hysteria.

Or, at least, that's what it felt like to me. Incessant sobbing, accentuated by a mounting internal scream. It was a most peculiar sensation, this silent wail. It was as if I had retreated into a corner of my skull, from which I could hear myself—at a distant remove—crying. But gradually, these external tears were overwhelmed by a huge lunatic screech. When this howl reached such a magnitude that it threatened to deafen me, I had no choice but to pull Jack off my breast, lay him down in his crib, and negotiate the corridor toward our bedroom. Whereupon I fell onto the bed, grabbed a pillow, and used it to baffle my ears.

Curiously, this seemed to have a salutary effect. Within seconds, the internal howling stopped. So too did my sobbing. But in its place came silence. Or what, at first, seemed like silence . . . but then, out of nowhere, turned out to be the absence of sound. It was as if both eardrums had been perforated and now I was hearing nothing, which was something of a relief, as I could no longer take the wail between my ears. So I lay there for what seemed to be only a few moments, luxuriating in this newfound deafness. Until the door flew open and Tony came in, looking surprisingly agitated. Initially, I couldn't hear what he was saying (even though I had removed the pillow from around my ears). But then, out of nowhere, my hearing snapped back into life. One moment, Tony was silent pantomime, the next, his voice came crashing into my ears. And underscoring his angry tone was the nearby sound of Jack crying.

"—don't understand how the hell you can just lie there when your son's—" Tony said, this sentence crashing into my ears.

"Sorry, sorry, sorry," I said, jumping to my feet and brushing past him. When I reached the nursery, I retrieved Jack from the crib and had him back on my left nipple within seconds. Fortunately, the milk flowed immediately—and Jack's cries were temporarily silenced. We all stop crying when we get what we want . . . for a moment or two anyway.

I leaned back in the wicker chair as he fed away. I shut my eyes, I willed myself back into the realm of deafness. Instead, I heard Tony's voice. It was back in his usual modulated range.

"What happened there?"

I opened my eyes. I sounded peculiarly calm.

"What happened *where*?" I asked.

"You on the bed—with the pillow 'round your head. Remember?"

"My ears . . ."

"Your ears?"

"Yeah—earache or something. Couldn't take it . . . the earache, that is. Just a momentary thing. Just . . ."

I shut my eyes again, unable to stand the sound of my own jerky train of thought.

"Should I call the doctor?"

My eyes jumped open again.

"No need," I said, suddenly sounding lucid. Anything but some doctor—looking warily at my fragile state, and adding to (what I imagined was) an ever-growing file about my maternal incompetence.

"I really do think . . ."

"Everything's fine now," I said, cutting him off. "It was just a little temporary distress."

Temporary distress. How bloody English of me.

Tony studied me carefully, saying nothing

"You ever get a flash earache?" I asked. "Hurts like a bastard. And then . . . bam, it's gone."

"If you say so," he said, sounding unconvinced.

"Sorry I shouted at you."

"*Comme d'habitude,*" he said. "Mind if I go back to work?"

"No problem."

"I'm upstairs if you need me."

And he left.

Comme d'habitude. You bastard. Spending a derisory half hour with me and your new son (on the first day he's home) before retreating to your sanctum sanctorum. And then getting all affronted when I get just a little peeved by your little lecture about Mother's Milk versus Formula. (How the hell did he know that? Some article on the Chronicle's *women's pages, no doubt—which*

Tony probably glanced at for around fifteen seconds.) No doubt, once Jack started crying again, my husband would plead the need for sleep (because somebody has to earn the money around here) and head for the silent comfort of his office sofa bed, leaving me to walk the floors for the night.

Which is exactly what happened. To make things even more maddening, I encouraged Tony to sleep elsewhere. Because by the time he came downstairs again—it was sometime after one AM—Jack was back in bawling mode, the thirty minute feed being his sole respite from a long evening's cry. So when Tony found me in the living room with Jack, occasionally stealing a glance at the television, while simultaneously trying to rock him to sleep, I tried to play nice.

"Poor you," Tony said. "How long has he been going on like that?"

"Too long."

"Anything I can do?"

"Get some sleep. You need it."

"You sure about that?"

"This can't go on all night. He's going to have to pass out eventually."

Eventually was the operative word here—as Jack did not settle down again until 3:17 AM exactly (I was watching BBC News 24 at the time—which always has the precise time in one corner of the screen). By this time, not only were both breasts unblocked, but had been wrung dry by his persistent feeding. After five hours of tears, he burped a milk-saturated burp, and passed right out.

I couldn't believe my luck—and swiftly got him upstairs into his crib, then stripped off my grungy clothes, took a very hot shower, and crawled into bed, expecting sleep to hit me like a sucker punch.

But nothing happened. I stared up at the ceiling, willing myself to pass out. No sale. I reached for a book from the pile of reading matter by the bed. I tried to read a couple of pages of *Portrait of a Lady* (well, I was an American in Europe, after all). But even Henry James's dense, lugubrious style didn't put me to sleep. So I got up and made myself a cup of chamomile tea, and looked in on Jack (still conked out), and washed down two aspirins, and got back into bed, and tried to negotiate the further adventures of Isabel Archer, and waited for sleep to arrive, and . . .

Suddenly, it was crowding five AM, and I was reaching the point in the novel where Isabel was about to ruin her life by marrying that malignant nobody, Gilbert Osmond, and I kept thinking that Edith Wharton did this sort of thing far more smartly in *The House of Mirth* and, God, didn't James write long sentences, and if he couldn't put me to sleep, nobody could, and . . .

Jack began to cry again. I put down the book. I went into the nursery. I removed his dirty diaper. I cleaned his dirty bottom. I dressed him in a clean diaper. I picked him up. I sat down in the wicker chair. I lifted up my T-shirt. He attached himself to my left nipple. I winced in anticipation of the forthcoming pain. And . . .

Miracle of miracles—a no-problem flow of milk.

"Well, that's good news," Jane Sanjay said when she dropped by late that afternoon to check on my progress. "How many feeds now without a blockage?"

"I've just done the third of the day."

"Houston, it looks like we've got full flow," she said.

I laughed, but then added, "Now, if I can just get some sleep."

"Was he up all night?"

"No—just me."

"Well, hopefully it's a one-off bad night. But you seem to be holding up pretty well under the circumstances. Better than I would, believe me."

"You've no kids."

"Hey, do I look crazy?"

However, by two the next morning, I was seriously beginning to wonder if I was veering into craziness. Tony had been out all evening at some foreign correspondents' dinner, and rolled in drunk around two AM—to find me slumped in front of the television, with Jack on my lap, crying his eyes out, unable to settle down, and completely satiated from an extended one-hour feed.

"Still up?" Tony asked, attempting to focus his eyes on us.

"Not by choice. Still standing?"

"Just about. You know what a journo's night out is like."

"Yeah—I vaguely remember."

"Want me to do anything?"

"How 'bout hitting me over the head with a club?"

"Sorry—a little too caveman for my taste. Cup of tea?"

"Chamomile, please. Not that it'll do any good."

I was right—it didn't do any good. Because Tony never got around to making the cup of tea. He went into our bedroom to use the bathroom, then somehow managed to end up crashed out across the bed, fully clothed, out for the count. Had I wanted to sleep, this would have presented a problem—as there was no way I was going to get him to budge from his cross-bed sprawl. But I had no need of a bed—because, once again, I couldn't turn off my brain . . . even though Jack finally turned off his at three that morning.

"Two nights without sleep?" Jane Sanjay said the next afternoon. "This is worrying—especially as your son seems to be conking out for around four hours a night . . . which, I know, isn't exactly a lot of sleep time for you, but is certainly better than *no* sleep. What do you think's going on?"

"I haven't a damn clue—except that my brain is more than a little hyperactive right now."

"Well, this motherhood thing is never easy to absorb. Has your husband been helping with some of the all-night duties?"

"He's been a little busy on the work front," I said, not wanting to start complaining to a stranger about Tony's disinterest in most baby matters.

"Could you maybe consider a night nurse for a couple of days, just to allow you to crash for a bit? Lack of sleep is seriously bad news."

"Tell me about it. But I'm sure I'll collapse tonight—without fail."

But I didn't fall asleep. And it wasn't Jack's fault. On the contrary, the little gent went down around ten and didn't stir until four the next morning. This miraculous six-hour window should have been filled with deep comatose sleep. Instead I spent it drinking endless mugs of herbal tea and stewing for an hour in a steaming bath (laced with assorted chill-out aromatherapy oils), and watching one of those endlessly talkative Eric Rohmer movies on Film4 (only the French can mix flirtation with liberal quotations from Pascal), and starting to read Dreiser's *Sister Carrie* (all right, I'm a glutton for punishment), and doing my best not to disturb my sleeping husband who was spending a rare night in our bed

(I sensed he was in the mood for sex, but passed out from "night-after-hangover exhaustion" before anything could happen).

Ten-ten. Eleven-eleven. Twelve-twelve. One-one. Two-two. Three-three . . .

It became a game with me, trying to glance at my watch right at the specific moment when the time was denoted by the same two numbers. A thoroughly dumb game, only worth playing if you're in the sort of advanced exhausted state that comes with three straight nights without sleep.

And then, before I could glimpse four-four, Jack was awake, and the new day had begun.

"How'd you sleep?" Tony asked me when he finally emerged from bed that morning at nine.

"Five hours," I lied.

"That's something, I suppose," he said.

"Yeah—I feel a lot better."

Jane Sanjay told me she wouldn't be coming in today—but gave me her cell number, just in case I needed to talk. But I didn't need to talk. I needed to sleep. But I couldn't sleep, because Jack was awake all day. And our shared routine was repeated over and over again.

Into the nursery. Remove his dirty diaper. Clean his dirty bottom. Dress him in a clean diaper. Pick him up. Sit down in the wicker chair. Lift up T-shirt. Offer nipple. And then . . .

By the time he finished sucking me dry at three that afternoon, my vision was starting to blur. Seventy-two hours of nonstop consciousness did that. It also played games with my depth perception, and made me feel as if I was Gulliver in the land of Brobdingnag—where even a dining chair suddenly looked as tall as a church steeple.

However, I could put up with the strange recalibration of domestic furniture. Just as I could also handle a woolly feeling behind the eyes, and the fact that everything was slightly distended and fuzzy.

What I couldn't cope with was the feeling of calamity that was seizing me—a deep dark trough of despondency that I was finding hard to resist. Especially since—as I peered straight down into this trench—the hopelessness of my situation took hold. I wasn't just a useless mother and wife, but someone who was also in a no-exit situation from which there was no escape. A life sentence of domestic and maternal drudgery, with a man who clearly didn't love me.

Then, as I mused even further on my total despair, Jack began to cry again. I rocked him, I walked him up and down the hallway, I offered him a pacifier, my withered nipple, a clean diaper, more rocking, a walk down the street in his buggy, a return to his crib, thirty straight minutes of more bloody rocking in his bloody rocking chair . . .

When we had reached hour three of this uninterrupted crying jag, I sensed that I was heading for a rapid crash landing—where the idea of tossing myself out of a second-floor window suddenly seemed infinitely preferable to another single minute of my son's bloody yelping.

Then I remember reaching for the phone and punching in Tony's office number and getting his secretary on the line. She said he was in a meeting. I said it was an emergency. She said he was in with the editor. I said, I don't give a shit, it's an emergency. Well, she said, can I tell him what it's about?

"Yes," I said, sounding most calm. "Tell him if he's not home in the next sixty minutes, I'm going to kill our son."

SEVEN

I DIDN'T WAIT FOR Tony to return the call. Because—after five straight hours of nonstop bellowing—Jack had suddenly exhausted himself into sleep. So, once I settled him down in the nursery, I unplugged the phone next to my bed. Then I threw off my clothes, crawled under the duvet, and finally surrendered to exhaustion.

Suddenly it was one in the morning and Jack was crying again. It took a moment or two to snap back into consciousness and work out that I had been asleep for more than nine hours. But that realization was superseded by another more urgent consideration—how in the hell could my son have slept so long without a diaper change, let alone food?

Guilt is the most motivating force in life—and one that can get you instantly to ignore the most impossible of hangovers, or lurch out of hours of sleep in a nanosecond. Dashing into the nursery, I quickly discovered that, yes, Jack did need a diaper change—but that, courtesy of the empty bottle I saw left on top of a chest of drawers, he had been fed sometime earlier. The sight of the bottle threw me, because the only time I had ever offered Jack this breast substitute, he'd utterly rejected it. But now . . .

"So you didn't kill him after all."

Tony was standing in the door frame, looking at me with an exhausted middle-of-the-night wariness. I didn't meet his stare. I simply picked Jack up and brought him over to the changing mat, and started to unfasten his diaper.

"I'm sorry," I finally said, around the same time I was wiping Jack's bum free of milky shit.

"You had my secretary rather upset," Tony said. "She actually hauled me out of the meeting with the editor, saying it was a family emergency.

Thankfully she had the common sense to say nothing more in front of His Lordship—but once I was outside his office, she informed me what you told her and then asked me if I wanted to call the police."

I shut my eyes and hung my head, and felt something approaching acute shame.

"Tony, I didn't know what I was saying . . ."

"Yes, I did sense that. Still, I thought it best to make certain that you hadn't taken the infanticide option, so I called home. When you didn't answer . . . well, I must admit that, for a moment or two, I actually did wonder if you had gone totally ballistic and done something irretrievably insane. So I thought it worth coming home. And when I walked in the door, there you both were, conked out. So I unplugged the baby alarm in his room, to let you sleep on."

"You should have woken me."

"You haven't been sleeping . . ."

"I told you I slept five hours last night," I said.

"And I knew you were lying straightaway."

Silence.

"You know, I'd never dream of hurting Jack . . ."

"I certainly hope not."

"Oh Jesus, Tony . . . don't make me feel worse than I do."

He just shrugged, then said, "Jack will take a bottle, you know. Or, at least, he took it from me."

"Well done," I said, not knowing what else to say. "And you changed him as well?"

"So it seems. Sorry to have plugged the baby alarm back in. But once he was settled down, I thought I'd get back upstairs to the book . . ."

"No need to apologize. I should be up anyway."

"You sure you're all right?"

Except for an appalling case of guilt, I was just fine.

"I'm so sorry."

Tony just shrugged. "You've said that already."

I finished changing the diaper. I closed up Jack's onesie. I picked him up, settled us both down in the wicker chair, lifted my T-shirt, and felt him clamp down hard on my nipple. I let out a small sigh of relief when the milk started flowing immediately.

"Oh, one other thing," Tony said. "I took the liberty of making an appointment for you with the GP, tomorrow afternoon at two."

"Why?" I said, though I already knew the answer to that question.

"Well, if you're not sleeping . . ."

"I'm sure it's just a passing phase."

"Best to get it seen to, don't you think? And I've also phoned a company called Annie's Nannies—someone in the office recommended them—about getting you some help."

"I don't need help. I'm fine. Anyway, a nanny's going to cost us lots."

"Let me worry about that."

I said nothing. Tony pointed his thumb in the direction of his office. "Mind if I . . . ?"

"Work away," I said.

As soon as he was gone, I pressed my head down against Jack and started to cry. But this teary episode was short-lived—as Jack reacted unfavorably to my shuddering body and showed his displeasure by biting down even harder on my breast: a corrective measure that let it be known that I should stay on task.

So I applied the emotional brakes, and sat there in silent shame, wondering how I could have said such a thing—and feeling, for the first time since his birth, this overwhelming need to protect Jack and ensure that he came to no harm.

But as soon as I thought that, another unsettling rumination hit me: *do I need to protect him against myself?*

I didn't sleep for the rest of the night. Nor did I find time for a nap in the morning, as Jack was wide awake. So by the time Jack and I reached the doctor's office that afternoon, exhaustion was beginning to settle in on me again—something that my GP diagnosed immediately.

Fortunately, my doctor of choice—McCoy—was on duty, as I don't think I could have managed that dry little prig who saw me the last time. Immediately, Dr. McCoy was pleasantly solicitous—and spent several minutes looking Jack over. She already knew everything about his difficult arrival. This made me instantly wonder if word had filtered back from the hospital that I had been such a drama queen while I'd been at the Mattingly. Then she turned her attention to me—and sensed that something was wrong.

"Is he keeping you up at night?" she asked.

"It's me who's keeping me up at night," I said, then explained my irregular sleep patterns over the past few days.

"You *must* sleep," she said. "It's crucial for your well-being, and for your baby. So what I'd like to propose is a mild sedative that should help knock you out, should the sleeplessness return. One important question: have you also been feeling a bit depressed or down?"

I shook my head.

"You sure about that?" she asked. "Because it's not at all unusual to suffer from such things when you're unable to sleep. In fact, I'd call it rather commonplace."

"Honestly, all I need is a couple of nights of decent sleep . . ."

"Well, these pills should help you. One small but important thing to remember—after you've taken one of the sedatives, you mustn't breast-feed for at least eight hours, as the drug will be in your system."

"No worries about that," I said.

"And if the sleeplessness continues—or if you are starting to feel a little low—you really must come back to see me immediately. This is nothing to play around with."

Heading home, I knew that she knew. Just as I knew that Tony had undoubtedly told her about my threat against Jack. No doubt, Dr. McCoy had now filed me away under "At Risk" as Hughes had obviously spoken with her about my assorted contretemps in the hospital. So she could tell I was lying. Just as Tony knew that I was lying about my ability to sleep the previous night. Just as everyone was now convinced that I was a diabolically inappropriate mother who couldn't handle even the simplest of maternal tasks. Because . . .

Oh God, it's starting again . . .

I slowly depressed the brake. I gripped the steering wheel. I felt myself beginning to seize up—that sense of diminution that made me feel as if everything had the potential to overwhelm me. Including the jerk in the Mercedes behind me. He leaned on his car horn in an attempt to get me moving.

He succeeded, as I released the brake and inched forward. But his blasts of the horn also managed to waken Jack—who continued to cry while I was getting my prescription filled at the pharmacy. He was still

crying when we arrived home, and he continued to do so for the balance of the afternoon. I checked him thoroughly, making certain that
he wasn't suffering from diaper rash, gum infections, malnutrition,
lockjaw, the bubonic plague, or any other horrors I could conjure up
in my mind. I also offered him my ever-ready nipples—and two hours
after he sucked me dry, switched him to bottled formula with no complaints.

Until, that is, he came off the bottle and started to roar again. In
desperation, I picked up the phone and called Sandy. She immediately
heard his sizable wail.

"Now that's what I call a set of lungs," she said. "How's it going?"

"Beyond bad"—and I told her everything, with the exception of the
threat I made against Jack. I couldn't admit such a desperate error of
judgment to anyone . . . even to the sister to whom I always confided
everything.

"Well," she said, "sounds like completely standard operating baby
bullshit to me. And the nonstop crying could be colic—which certainly
drove my guys ga-ga when they were infants, and also sent me bonkers.
So I hear where you're coming from. But it will pass."

"You mean, like a gallstone?"

That night, Jack managed to cease his tragic aria just around the time
that Tony walked in—smelling of six gin and tonics too many, and suddenly interested in having sex with me for the first time in . . .

Well, it had been so long since we'd had sex that I had actually forgotten just how badly Tony performed when drunk.

By which I mean, foreplay involved slobbering on my neck, popping
the buttons on my jeans, shoving his hand into my pants, and fingering
me as if he was stubbing out a cigarette in an ashtray (which, as it turned
out, just happened to contain my clitoris). Then, after this impressive
display of anti-erotic crotch grab, he pulled down his suit pants and
briefs, and shoved himself into me, coming in less than a minute . . .
after which he rolled off me and mumbled some vaguely incoherent
apology about having a "hair trigger" when drunk (so that's what they
call it). Then he disappeared into the bathroom . . . at which point the
thought struck me: this was not the romantic sexual reunion I had been
hoping for.

I was well out of the bedroom by the time Tony emerged from the toilet, phoning up our local home delivery pizza joint, as our cupboards were particularly bare right now. When he staggered downstairs, he uncorked a bottle of red wine, poured out two glasses, and downed his in two long drafts. Then he burped and said, "So how was your day?"

"Wonderful," I said. "I've ordered you a pepperoni with extra cheese. Does that work?"

"What more could a man ask for?"

"Any reason why you're so drunk?"

"Sometimes you just have to . . ."

"Get drunk?"

"You read my mind."

"That's because I know you so well, dear."

"Oh, do you now?" he said, suddenly a little too loud.

"I was being ironic."

"No, you weren't. You were being critical."

"Let's stop this right now."

"But it's fun. And long overdue."

"You mean, like the shitty sex we've—sorry, *you've*—just had?"

And I left the room.

No, I didn't throw myself on the bed, crying irrationally. Nor did I lock myself in the bathroom. Nor did I pick up the phone and moan down the line to Sandy. Instead, I retreated to the nursery and positioned myself in the wicker chair, and stared ahead, and found myself very quickly returning to the despondency zone I had entered two nights earlier. Only this time my brain wasn't flooded with forlorn thoughts about the hopelessness of everything. This time, there was simply a large silent void—a sense of free-floating vacuity, in which nothing mattered, nothing counted. The world had been rendered flat. I was about to totter off the edge. And I didn't give a fuck.

Nor did I move when I heard the front doorbell ring. Nor did I respond when, around five minutes later, I heard a knock on the door, followed by Tony's slurred voice, informing me that my pizza was downstairs.

Time suddenly had no meaning for me. I was simply cognizant of sitting in a chair, staring ahead. Yes, I knew that there was a child asleep on the other side of the room. Yes, I knew that said child happened to be my son. But beyond that . . .

Nothing.

Some time later, I stood up and walked into the bathroom. After peeing, I went downstairs. I sat on the sofa. I turned on the television. The screen flickered into life. I stared at it, noting that it was BBC News 24. I also noted that the time was 1:08 and that there was a pizza box on the coffee table by the sofa. But beyond that . . .

I curled up on the sofa. I looked ahead. I was aware of the moving images. I could also smell the pizza. I needed to eat. Because I hadn't eaten anything since . . .

Yesterday? The day before?

Didn't matter.

Then Jack started crying. Suddenly I was all action. Manic action. Cursing myself for my listlessness, my little catatonic escapade. *Go, go, go*—I told myself. *Get on with it. You now know the drill by heart:*

Into the nursery. Remove his dirty diaper. Clean his dirty bottom. Dress him in a clean diaper. Pick him up. Sit down in the wicker chair. Lift T-shirt. Offer nipple. And then . . .

After the feed, he passed right out. I staggered to my bedroom and found the bed empty (Tony—surprise, surprise—having taken his pizza and his impending hangover up to his office). I curled up on top of the duvet, and . . .

Nothing.

An hour, two hours, three . . .

My bladder called again—the one thing that would get me out of the near-fetal position into which I had entwined myself. In the bathroom, as I sat on the toilet, I saw the bottle of sleeping pills on the shelf above the sink. The key to the real emptiness I craved.

When I reached the sink, I resisted the temptation to start ingesting the bottle, five pills at a time, ten big gulps, ensuring permanent oblivion. It's not that the idea of everlasting sleep didn't appeal to me—it's just that I was too damn tired to do anything about it. So I popped three pills (one above the recommended dose . . . but I wanted the extra knock-out assistance) and got back into bed, and . . .

The baby alarm went off. This time, however, I didn't rise and shine. No, this time my head felt as if it had been filled with a sticky, glutinous substance that made all my actions seem molasses-slow and fuzzy. But, yet again, I followed the drill:

Into the nursery. Remove his dirty diaper. Clean his dirty bottom. Dress him in a clean diaper. Pick him up. Sit down in the wicker chair. Lift T-shirt. Offer nipple. And then . . .

Back to bed. Back to sleep. Instantaneous sleep. Which seemed to stretch on indefinitely. Until . . .

Tony was shaking me with considerable, anxious force, telling me to get up.

But I didn't want to get up. Because getting up would mean facing into the day/night/whatever it was. Getting up would mean regarding the disaster that was my life. Getting up would . . .

"It's Jack," Tony said, sounding scared. "He seems to be unconscious."

"What?"

"He won't wake up. And his eyes—"

I was on my feet, even though everything was still a chemically induced blur. Though I must have made the journey from my bedroom to the nursery twenty times a day, now it suddenly seemed like a labyrinth, strewn with heavy objects that I kept bumping into. When I reached Jack's crib, it took several moments for my eyes to snap into focus. But when they did, I felt as if someone had just kicked me in the stomach. Because Jack appeared to be catatonic.

As I picked him up, he went all floppy—his limbs splaying like a rag doll, his head lolling, his eyes unfocused, blank. I pulled him toward me and shouted his name. No response. I fought off the urge to shake him. I brought my face to his and could feel his faint breath, which was a relief. Then I turned to Tony and told him to call an ambulance.

They arrived within five minutes. The paramedics took over. We rode in the back of the ambulance with Jack. We roared through the streets, heading further south. Jack had been attached to a heart monitor, and my eyes roamed between his tiny body (strapped down to a gurney) and the steady beat being registered on the monitor. The paramedic in charge kept throwing questions at us: any convulsions or seizures or episodes of breathlessness or previous catatonic incidents?

Nothing, nothing, nothing.

And then we were at a hospital called St. Martin's. There were two doctors waiting for us in the ambulance bay. The paramedic spoke with them. Jack was wheeled directly into a consulting room, filled with medical hardware. A woman doctor in her mid-twenties was in charge. Calm, efficient, immediately registering our fear. As she checked all vital signs, she too ran through the same checklist that the previous paramedic had used, and then asked if he was on any specific medication.

At which point, I felt something close to horror. Because I knew what the next question would be.

"Are you yourself on any medication?" she asked me.

"Yes," I said.

"What kind exactly?"

I told her.

"And might you have breast-fed your son before the stipulated eight hours?"

I could feel Tony's stare on me. Had somebody handed me a gun right now, I would have happily blown away the top of my head.

"Jack woke me up out of a heavy sleep," I said, "and I was so fogged, I didn't think . . ."

"Oh, for God's sake," Tony said. "Where is your brain?"

The doctor slightly touched Tony's sleeve, a hint that he should stop. Then she said, "Believe me, it happens all the time. Especially with very tired new mothers."

"But will he be all right?" Tony asked.

"What time did you take the pills?" the doctor asked me.

"Don't know."

"What do you mean, you don't know?" Tony said, the anger now showing.

"Middle of the night, I think."

"You *think*?" Tony said.

"May I handle this, please?" the doctor asked, then turned, put her hand on my arm, and addressed me directly.

"Now you mustn't get upset about what's happened."

"I've killed him," I heard myself saying.

"No, you have *not*," she said, her voice firm. "Now tell me—"

"I threatened to kill him, now—"

She gripped my arm tightly.

"Just please tell me . . . you took the pills around, what, five, six this morning?"

"I suppose . . ."

"And then he woke you up and you fed him . . . ?"

"Don't know . . . but it was still dark."

"That's good. And who found him in this state?"

"Me," Tony said, "around nine this morning."

"Which was probably around three to four hours after you fed him?"

"I guess so."

She turned to the nurse and spoke in a low voice, issuing instructions.

"Is he going to be all right?" Tony asked.

"I think so. I've asked the nurse to put your son on a saline drip to keep him hydrated—and we'll also keep him on a heart monitor, just to be absolutely sure that everything is fine. But, from my experience of this situation, the baby simply has to sleep the medicine off."

"But will there be any long-term damage?" Tony asked.

"I doubt it. The fact is, the dosage of the drug he received in the breast milk was so nominal that . . ."

That was the moment that my knees gave way and I hung on to the side of the gurney containing Jack like a passenger on a sinking cruise liner, not wanting to abandon ship, but also not knowing what the hell to do.

"Are you all right?" the doctor asked me.

How many times in the last few weeks had I heard that damn question?

"I just need to . . ."

A nurse helped me into a chair, and asked me if I'd like a glass of water. I nodded. Then I put my head between my legs and started to gag. But all that came up was watery spew.

"Oh, Jesus," Tony said as I continued to heave.

"Would you mind waiting outside?" the doctor asked him. After he left, the nurse cleaned me up and then helped me to a gurney opposite the one on which Jack was still strapped. I sat on the edge of it, my legs dangling down the side.

"When did you last eat?" the doctor asked me.

"Don't know. A couple of days ago, I think."

"And how long have you been feeling depressed?"

"I'm not depressed."

"If you can't remember when you last ate . . ."

"Just tired, that's all."

"That's another sign of depression."

"I am *not* . . ."

But I heard myself being cut off. By myself. But without deciding to cut myself off. The doctor said, "And if you've been on sleeping pills, you obviously haven't been . . ."

"I tried to kill him."

"No, you didn't."

"I should die."

"That's another sign of depression."

"Leave me alone."

I put my face in my hands.

"Have you ever suffered from depression before?"

I shook my head.

"And this is your first child?"

I nodded.

"All right then . . . I'm going to admit you."

I said nothing. Because I was otherwise engaged—pushing the palm of my hands against my eyes, in an attempt to black out everything.

"Did you hear what I said?" the doctor asked, her tone still calm, considerate. "You seem to be showing pronounced signs of postpartum depression—and under the circumstances, I think it wise to admit you for observation."

My palms pressed down even harder against my eyes.

"And you must understand that what you are going through is not uncommon. In fact, postpartum depression is . . ."

But I rolled over onto the gurney and started to baffle my ears with a pillow. The doctor touched my arm, as if to say "Understood," then I heard her mention something about going outside to have a word with my husband. I was left alone in the observation room with Jack. But I couldn't bear to look at him. Because I couldn't bear what I had done to him.

A few minutes later, the doctor returned.

"I've spoken to your husband. He's been informed of my diagnosis, and agrees that you should be kept in. He also understands that it's hospital policy to admit the mother and child together . . . which will also allow us, in the short term, to make certain that there are no side effects from Jack's mild . . ."

She stopped herself from using a clinical term, like *overdose*.

"Anyway, your husband said he had to dash off to work. But he will be back tonight . . ."

I pulled the pillow back over my ears again. The doctor saw this and stopped her monologue. Instead, she picked up a phone and made a fast call. Then, after hanging up, she came back to me and said, "It's going to be all right. And you will get through this."

That was the last time I saw her, as two orderlies arrived and flipped up the brakes on Jack's gurney, and wheeled him off. As he disappeared out the door, a nurse came in and said, "Don't worry—you'll be following him in a moment."

But I wasn't worried. Because I was feeling nothing. Just an all-purpose general numbness, a sense that, once again, nothing mattered because nothing mattered.

The orderlies returned for me around ten minutes later. They strapped me down (but not too tightly), then wheeled me down a long corridor until we reached a freight elevator. En route, everything seemed gray, badly lit, scruffy. And there was a prevalent toxic smell—an intermingling of disinfectant and fetid rubbish. But then the elevator doors opened. I was pushed inside, and we rode upward. The doors opened again, and I was pushed forward down another long, gray corridor until we reached a set of fortified doors, with wire mesh covering the glass on both sides and a coded lock to the right of the door. A sign above the lock contained two words: *Psychiatric Unit.*

One of the orderlies punched in a code, there was a telltale click, and I was pushed inside, the doors closing behind me with a decisive thud.

Another long corridor. From my side-view position, I could see that, along this hallway, all the doors were made of steel and had been fitted with outside throw bolts. On and on we went—until we turned right and passed a small ward with regular doors. Beyond this was another series of doors—none of them with the formidable locks or fortifications I'd seen earlier. Just before one of these doors, we stopped. Then an orderly opened it and I was pushed inside.

I was in a room—around twelve feet by twelve, with a window (barred), a television bracketed to the wall, and two hospital beds. Both were empty, but judging from assorted personal debris on the small locker beside one of them, I already had a roommate. A nurse came into the room. She was in her late forties—thin, beaklike features, old-style horn-rimmed glasses, a carefully modulated voice.

"Sally?"

I didn't answer. I just continued to stare ahead—even though I was still taking everything in.

"Sally?"

I looked at her name tag: *Shaw*.

"George Bernard?" I suddenly said. The nurse peered at me carefully. "Sorry?"

"George Bernard . . . *Shaw*," I said, and then fell into a serious torrent of laughter. The nurse gave me an even smile.

"It's Amanda Shaw actually."

This struck me as the funniest thing I ever heard—and my laughter redoubled. Nurse Shaw said nothing—and, in fact, let me laugh like an idiot until I was spent.

"All right now?" she asked.

I returned to my balled-up posture on the bed. She nodded to one of the orderlies, who unfastened the straps that had been placed around me.

"Now if you wouldn't mind, Sally, these gentlemen need the bed, so . . ."

I lay motionless.

"All I'd like you to do is sit up and we'll take care of the rest."

I didn't react.

"Sally, I'm going to ask you again. Will you please sit up, or should these gentlemen give you assistance?"

A pause. I could discern the threat lurking behind her even-tempered voice. I sat up.

"Good, very good," Nurse Shaw said. "Now do you think you could get down off the bed?"

I hesitated. Nurse Shaw tilted her head slightly, and the two orderlies were on either side of me. One of them whispered, "Come on, luv"— his voice uncomfortable, almost a little beseeching. I let them help me down, and onto the bed. Then, without a word, they returned to the gurney and steered it out of the room.

"Right then," Nurse Shaw said. "Let me explain a few things about the unit . . ."

The unit.

"First of all, your baby is in the ward around ten paces down the corridor from here. So, you can have complete access to him whenever you want, twenty-four hours a day. And you can also bring him in here with you . . . though we do prefer if he sleeps in the ward, as it will allow you to get some much-needed rest."

And it will allow you to keep him out of my clutches . . .

"Now, the next thing that's important to realize is that you're not a prisoner here. Because, unlike some individuals in the unit, you haven't been sectioned . . ."

Sectioned rhymes with dissection . . .

"So if you want to go for a walk, or leave the unit for whatever reason, there's no problem whatsoever. All we ask is that you inform the head nurse on duty that you're leaving . . ."

Because the front door's barred at all times . . . and also because we don't want some ga-ga dame like yourself running off with the baby . . . especially since you want to do him so much harm.

"Any questions?"

I shook my head.

"Fine. Now you'll find a hospital nightgown in the locker by the bed, so if you wouldn't mind changing into that, I'll see to it that your clothes are given a good wash."

Because I spewed up all over them.

"And then, I gather it's been a while since you've eaten, so I'll have some food sent up straightaway. But before all that, would you like to check in on your son?"

Long pause. Finally, I shook my head. Nurse Shaw was reasonableness itself.

"No problem whatsoever. But do remember—to see him, all you have to do is ring the call bell by the side of the bed."

But why would he want to see me? Especially after I poisoned him. No wonder he always cried around me. From the start, he could sense my antipathy toward him.

"Oh, one final thing: the unit psychiatrist, Dr. Rodale, will be in to see you in about two hours. All right?"

I can't wait.

"Well then, that's everything covered. So I'll leave you to get changed, and then I'll have one of my colleagues come back with lunch very shortly."

Nurse Shaw left. I lay on the bed, not moving. Time went by. Nurse Shaw returned.

"Need some help changing, Sally?"

I sat up and started stripping off my clothes.

"That's good," Nurse Shaw said, and left.

The hospital nightgown stank of bleach and felt scratchy against the skin. I rolled up my street clothes into a big ball and shoved them into the locker. Then I crawled in between the equally scratchy sheets, and shut my eyes, and hoped for sleep. Instead, the door opened. A plumpish young nurse in her early twenties came in, *Patterson* on her name tag.

"G'day."

Australian.

"You all right?"

I said nothing.

"No worries. Lunch here."

She was having a one-way conversation with a catatonic. But there was nothing I could do about it. I'd entered yet another facet of this strange landscape—in which mere speech suddenly seemed impossible, or somehow beyond my grasp.

The nurse placed the lunch tray on the sliding table positioned next to the bed. She eased it over. I lay there and did nothing. The nurse smiled at me, hoping to get a response.

"Cat got your tongue? Tongue got your cat?"

I shut my eyes.

"All right, all right—it was a dumb joke," she said. "But you've still got to eat. I mean, your roommate stopped eating for more than five days. And then . . ."

She cut herself off, as if she was about to reveal something she didn't want me to hear. Or, at least, not yet.

"But you're going to tuck into this lunch, aren't you? Or, at least, have a drink of something."

I reached out for the tray. I took the glass of water. I brought it to my mouth. I drank a little while still in a prone position, which meant that some of the water ran down my face and onto the bedclothes. Then I put the glass back on the tray.

"Atta girl," the nurse said. "Now how about a little tucker?"

I wanted to smile at the use of bush jargon in a South London hospital. But I couldn't do a damn miserable thing except lie there, feeling like a general all-purpose idiot.

"Tell you what. Why don't I just leave lunch here and come back in half an hour, eh? But, please, do yourself a favor and munch on something."

But how can I eat when I can't eat? Don't you see that? Doesn't that make completely logical sense to you?

Half an hour later, she was back. And she didn't like the sight of the untouched lunch tray.

"Oh come on," she said, still sounding chirpy as hell. "You've got to want something in your turn, don't you?"

No. I want nothing. Because I want to shrivel. Like a prune. Do everyone a huge service and disappear from view. Permanently.

She sat down on the bed and squeezed my arm.

"I know this is all really crap—and that you're in one of those 'circumstances beyond your control' things. But a word of warning—the doc is coming by to see you in about an hour. And she takes a really dim view of postpartum anorexia, eh? If you don't believe me, talk to your roomie when they bring her back from the operating room. So do yourself a favor—and at least take a bloody bite out of the apple before the doc shows up."

But to bite an apple I have to bite an apple. Get it?

The doctor was a woman in her late forties. Very tall, very plain, with mid-length brown hair sensibly cut, wearing a sensible suit under her white hospital coat, with sensible bifocals on the end of her nose. Everything about her exuded high rationality—and a take-no-crap view of things. She immediately worried me.

"Ms. Goodchild—*Sally*—I'm Dr. Rodale, the unit's psychiatrist."

She proffered her hand.

But to take your hand I have to take your hand.

She smiled tightly at my inability to make the necessary social gesture.

"Right then," she said, pulling up a chair next to my bed, then reaching into her briefcase for a clipboard and a pen. "Let's try to make a start . . ."

It was she who made a start—asking me to verify my age, whether this was my first child, my first experience of depression, and/or the first time I had ever gone silent like this. She also had gathered—from looking at Jack's chart—that his had been a traumatic delivery, and was wondering if this had impacted on my mental health . . . blah, blah, blah, blah, blah, blah, blah, blah . . .

Now what was interesting to me about Dr. Rodale's one-way interrogation was the briskness of her inquiry, and the way she plowed on even when I refused to answer her. And it struck me that—though she may have been a shrink—she wasn't of the touchy-feely *let's talk to your inner child* school of psychotherapy. No, she was simply after the necessary information to work out the sort of treatment I needed.

There was a problem, however—I wasn't responding to her questions. Something she picked up rather quickly.

"Now Sally," she finally said after getting nowhere on the answer front, "I am well aware that you *can* hear me and that you recognize your surroundings, your situation, and the effect you are having on others. Which means that your refusal to talk must be regarded as psychosomatic in nature."

A tight smile.

"However, if you do feel that you simply cannot talk at the moment, so be it. Do understand, though, that in order for me to render a proper diagnosis—and prescribe an appropriate course of treatment—you *will* have to answer my questions. So, shall we start over again?"

I said nothing. She reiterated her checklist of questions. Halfway through her list, I shifted position in the bed and turned away from her, showing her my back. I kept my back to her. She stood up and brought her chair around to the other side of the bed.

"There now, we can see each other again."

I flipped over and showed her my back again. Dr. Rodale exhaled a long, weary breath.

"All you are doing, Ms. Goodchild, is impeding the speed of your recovery—and increasing the amount of time you will be spending with us. However, once again, I cannot force you to answer my simple medical questions. The choice is yours. For the moment, anyway. Just as you can decide whether or not to eat. But, as you well know, you cannot live without food. So if you continue to refuse food, that choice may well be taken care of for you.

"However, I do see from your notes that your GP prescribed a mild sedative to help you sleep. I am going to ask the nurse to administer the same dose to you this evening. And when I return to see you again tomorrow, I do hope we will be able to make better progress than today. Good afternoon."

Around five minutes after she left, the doors swung open and I met my roommate. Actually I didn't meet her—as she was in a state of postoperative coma. Or, at least, I presumed she was suffering from postoperative *something*—as she was brought in on a gurney, and had a large bandage wrapped around her skull. Though I was still lying prone on my bed, I could see that she was a black woman around my age. Nurse Patterson helped the orderlies get the gurney into position. Once they left, she read her chart, checked her pulse, and rearranged her bedclothes. Then, seeing me staring at her, she said, "Her name's Agnes. Her little boy, Charlie, is in the ward with your guy. You'll probably have a bit to talk about when she comes 'round—because she's been through what you're going through. In fact, she's *still* going through it—which is a real shame, but there you are. There's no rhyme or reason to the dance you're dancing. It's just a matter of bringing it under control before it dances you right into serious physical trouble—which is what happened with poor Agnes here. But hey, let her tell you all about it. Very bright woman, our Agnes—a senior civil servant. But hey, that's the thing about illness—it doesn't give a hoot who you are, right?"

She came over and sat down on my bed again. I so wished she wouldn't do that.

"And while we're on the subject of bad things happening to good people—don't you love that expression?—I'm going to let you in on a little secret: you did not make the best impression with the doc. And she is definitely the sort of doctor with whom you want to cooperate, if you take my meaning. Very old school. Very into the old chain of command, and knowing what's best for you—which, I hate to say it, she probably does. Because whatever about her manner—which does get up a lot of people's noses—she does know exactly how to snap girls like you out of this mess. Only—take it from me—the road out of here is about five times shorter and easier if you help us to help you . . . and, yeah, sorry for the dumb cliché. So, come on, let's try a little food again."

Hey, don't you think I want to help you out here? The problem is what the problem is, which is the fact that there is a problem which presents a problem when it comes to addressing said problem because the problem is . . .

She pulled over the table, and cut off a bit of sandwich for me and brought it to the vicinity of my mouth.

"Just a couple of fast bites, nothing to it . . ."

Listen, I know you mean well, but . . . no, I'm not going to get into it again.

"Apple? Glass of milk? Couple of our best choice cookies? Nothing take your fancy?"

Just silence.

"Well, how about we get you out of the bed and take you in to see Jack. He's probably due a feed by now . . ."

This really made me react, as I suddenly clutched the pillow to myself and buried my face in it.

"Looks like I just put my big foot in it," Nurse Patterson said. "But hey, the baby needs to eat too, right?"

Her beeper went off. She glanced at it.

"That's me accounted for. Catch you later. And if you need any-thing, just buzz."

I needed nothing—and certainly not the arrival, an hour later, of Tony. He was bearing a copy of that day's *Chronicle* and a festive bag of Liquorice Allsorts. As he leaned down to kiss me, I saw his watch: 5:12 PM. Guilt must have egged him on to visit so early—a good three hours before he put his pages to bed.

"How's it going?" he asked me.

I said nothing.

"Brought you . . ."

He placed his gifts on the bedside locker, then looked for a chair, wondering whether to sit down or not. He decided to stand. He also decided to focus his attention slightly away from me—since my sickly, catatonic state so obviously disturbed him.

"I've just been in to see Jack. Good news—he's awake again, and from what the nurse told me, he gobbled down two bottles he was so damn hungry. Which, she said, is a good sign that he's completely back to normal."

Because he's out of my tender loving care.

"Anyway, the nurse also said that you can visit him . . ."

Stop it, stop it, stop it. I don't want your kindness. I don't deserve it.

I pulled the pillow over my head.

"She also said you'd been doing a bit of this too."

I pulled the pillow around my ears.

"If you want me to leave, I will."

I didn't move. Finally he said, "I hope you're better."

I heard him leave. I removed the pillow. And then I heard a voice opposite me.

"Who are you?"

It was my roommate, Agnes. She was sitting up in bed, looking un-focused and fogged-in. But hey, I wasn't exactly one to brag about my lucidity right now.

"You here yesterday? Don't remember . . . You were here, right? But maybe . . ."

She broke off, looking confused—as if she couldn't hold on to this jangled train of thought.

"Agnes—that's me. You always put a pillow over your head like that? Agnes . . . you got that?"

Yeah—and I'm glad to see I'm not the only resident of Planet Weird.

"Agnes. As in *Agnes*. A-G-N-E . . ."

Nurse Patterson came in here.

"She's a woman of few words, our Sally," she said.

"Sally?" Agnes asked.

"That's what I said. S-A-L-L-Y. And she's not really talking much today. But we'd all like it if you kept trying—'cause sooner or later, we've got to hear that American accent of hers."

Agnes blinked several times, trying to filter this information.

"Why's she American?" she asked.

"*Why?*" Nurse Patterson asked with a laugh. "Because I imagine she was born there, that's why. And she's got a little baby boy, just like you."

"He's called Charlie?" Agnes asked.

"No—your son's called Charlie . . ."

"I know, I know. I just thought . . ."

She interrupted herself again, sounding lost.

"Jack," Nurse Patterson said. "He's called Jack."

"And I'm . . . I'm . . ."

"A little scrambled, that's all," Nurse Patterson said. "Just like last time. But, I promise you, by tomorrow morning you'll be all-clear again. Now what do you want for tea?"

Agnes shook her head.

"Ah now, we're not going down that road again," Nurse Patterson said. "Especially since that's what got you . . ."

"Oatmeal," Agnes said. "I'll eat oatmeal."

"And oatmeal you shall have. And what do you fancy, Sally?"

I did my now-usual silent routine.

"This is not doing you any good, Sal."

She approached me with a glass of water and another small cup.

"Now I'm not going to force food down your throat, but I am going to have to ask that you take these pills. Which are exactly the same pills you were taking last night . . ."

And which allowed me to poison my son.

She rattled the plastic pill cup by my ear.

"Come on now, doctor's orders and all that. And the payoff is: you get to sleep through the night. Oh—and as your husband may have mentioned, Jack is up and about, and ordering us all around. So . . ."

She shook the pills again.

"Please, Sal. Don't make me . . ."

She didn't finish that sentence. Because she didn't need to. I sat up. I took the pills. Then I forced myself onto my feet and shuffled into the adjoining bathroom, Nurse Patterson loudly congratulating me for getting up. Once inside, I avoided looking at myself in the mirror. Instead, I just emptied my bladder and returned to bed, and pulled the bedclothes over me, and waited for the pills to kick in.

Then it was morning. My head was somewhere high up in a vaporous stratospheric zone. When I began to work out the *where am I?* question, I noticed that there was a needle in my arm, and an intravenous bag suspended above me. My roommate was absent. There was a new nurse on duty who was positioning another delectable repast in front of me. She was short and Scottish.

"Good sleep?"

I responded by getting to my feet, taking hold of the stand with my bag, and pushing it toward the bathroom.

"Need some help there?" the nurse asked.

No, I'm a fully fledged veteran of assorted hospital drips.

In the bathroom, I peed, then went to the sink to wash my hands and splash water on my face. That's when I saw the nightmare that was myself. My face puffy, my eyes streaked with red, my hair matted, my . . .

Oh, forget it.

I walked back into the room. The nurse helped me back into bed, repositioning the drip bag to my left. "Now there's oatmeal, and toast, and some fried eggs, and some good strong builders' tea—"

I turned away. The nurse continued talking.

"—and after breakfast, I'm sure you'll want to go visit your baby. So what do you want to start with first?"

I ate nothing. The nurse tried to interest me in a slice of toast. I turned away.

"Okay so," she said. "But I know that Dr. Rodale will not be pleased."

She left the breakfast by the bed. Agnes came back into the room. She was a tall, elegant woman—despite the shell-shocked exhaustion and her slightly tentative gait.

"You were here yesterday, right?" she asked, getting back into bed. "The American, right? Or are you someone new? My memory . . ."

Another of her fractured sentences. She peered at me quizzically.

"Why don't you talk? Baby got your tongue?"

She laughed hysterically. And I thought: *Got it in one, sweetheart.*

Then, abruptly, the laughter ceased.

"You've got to eat," she said. "It'll get you into trouble if you don't. I mean, big trouble. I know it. Because I had it. And you don't want it. *You don't want it.*"

Then she lapsed into silence again.

"You are American, aren't you?"

She put her hands over her face.

"Sorry, sorry, sorry. I don't mean to keep repeating myself. But . . ."

And then she went quiet again.

Dr. Rodale showed up around three that afternoon. My untouched lunch was by the bed. She glanced at it, then turned her eyes to my chart. *What's up, doc?*

"And how are you today, Sally?"

I stared at the wall. Dr. Rodale's lips twitched, then she made a note or two on my chart.

"Right . . . I see that you refused dinner last night, as well as breakfast and lunch today. Once again, this is your prerogative—but do understand that we are keeping you on a drip. And within the next day or two, we will have to make a decision about how to assist you out of your current state. I also gather you had a trouble-free night. Sleep well?"

No response.

"No side effects from the sedatives . . . bar the usual slight grogginess on waking?"

No response.

"And I see, as well, that despite several offers, you've shown no interest in seeing your son, Jack. Which, of course, is not an uncommon facet of your condition—though one which also cannot be doing either you or your child much good. Now, if you like, we do have a resident psychotherapist who can speak with you about the emotional issues you're facing. But in order for her to perform her function, you must be able to speak. Which puts us all in something of a Catch-22 situation, wouldn't you agree? So, can you please try to talk to me now?"

No response.

"I cannot emphasize how difficult you're making things for us . . . and ultimately for yourself."

No response.

"Very well then. We'll talk again tomorrow."

Then she turned her attention to Agnes. From her cowed response to this approaching figure, it was clear that Dr. Rodale genuinely scared her.

"And how are we feeling today, Agnes? Appetite back?"

"I'm eating."

"No aftereffects this time?"

"My memory . . ."

"That's just short-term. Within another twenty-four hours, you'll be back to normal."

"Is that the last one?"

Dr. Rodale did not look up from her chart.

"We'll see."

I pulled the covers over my head. Because I now knew—or, at least, I think I knew—the sort of treatment Agnes had been undergoing.

But though I understood that I had to talk and eat . . . well, it was that old bit of tortured logic all over again: *to talk I have to talk . . . to eat I have to eat*. Which, right now, was impossible. Because though I instinctively knew how to talk and/or eat, it was as if I had lost the ability to carry out these two functions. My operating system was down—and try as I wanted to, I could not trigger the mechanism that would get me to open my mouth. And though I felt a certain rising panic, it was overshadowed by a desperate inertia. I just didn't care enough about anything anymore.

Tony arrived at eight that night. He had obviously been briefed by Nurse Patterson—now back on duty—because he eyed the untouched dinner tray with unease, and sat down on the bed, and looked at me with a mixture of hopelessness and distaste and worry (yes, my complex husband had the singular ability to radiate all three moods at the same time, with just a few minor facial contractions). He didn't kiss me or touch my hand—and, once again, he had a hard time looking at me straight on. But he did say "Hello." When that got him nowhere, he then said, "Jack is good."

And then, "They're genuinely worried about you not eating or talking."

And then, "Okay . . . I'll go now."

Is that his way of saying "I know when I'm not wanted"?

Agnes's husband (or partner or significant other or whoever he was) showed up that night. He surprised me. I'd envisaged some elegant, muscular Jamaican—well-dressed, exuding confident swagger and easy charm, and every other cliché about Afro-Caribbeans you care to mention. As it turned out, he was a quiet, reserved white guy in his late thirties, dressed in a standard-issue gray suit, blue shirt, dull tie; slightly hesitant in manner and careful about his comportment in this situation. But what was also abundantly clear was that he adored Agnes—and was also genuinely unsettled by her present situation. He sat next to her, holding her hand, talking in a low, reassuring voice, even making her laugh on one occasion. You can never fathom other couples, can you? Never work out the spark of attraction in two such opposites, let alone the complex ties that bind, and whether they are robust enough to survive a crisis like . . . well, like this one.

What a gray little man he was—and how I so suddenly envied her such predictability, such ongoing stability (while well knowing that appearances are always deceptive). When Nurse Patterson arrived during the visit with my sleeping pills, I took them at once, without prompting. Because I didn't want to watch this happy scene anymore.

Once again, the sedatives did their wondrous chemical work and I slept for a massive eleven hours, waking up just after six-fifteen the next morning. God, how fogged in I felt. Because these pills didn't really induce sleep. Rather, they clubbed you over the head and left you stupefied. It took me a good twenty minutes to find the equilibrium necessary to stand up and pull myself (and my IV stand) to the bathroom.

The day followed a similar pattern to the previous days. The Scottish nurse offered me breakfast. I remained silent. Agnes tried to engage me in conversation. I remained silent (even though I was pleased to see that a degree of mental clarity was coming back to her). She went off to play with her son, Charlie. I squandered the morning staring at the ceiling, and wondering why I was squandering the morning like this, and also having no energy to do anything but squander the morning like this.

Then it was lunchtime—and I didn't eat lunch, except courtesy of the tube in my arm. Then it was three PM, and Dr. Rodale walked in. Like actors in a bad play, we knew our prosaic lines by heart. Or, at least, she knew her lines, whereas I simply had to maintain my weak, silent stance. The interview went according to form . . . with the good doctor making her usual noises about the increasing gravity of my situation, and then finally saying, "I will be calling your husband at his office this afternoon to discuss your situation and the options open to us."

Tony arrived around eight that evening. This time he did kiss me on the cheek. He did pull up a chair close to me. He did take my hand. And said, "You have got to start eating."

I just looked at the wall.

"Your doctor—Rodale, isn't it?—she called me at the paper and said, if you didn't start consuming solid food, she wanted to consider ECT. As in electroconvulsive therapy. As in shock treatment. She said it was the best way to bring you out of whatever place you are right now—but she'd need my consent to do it."

Silence. He wasn't looking at me again.

"I don't want to give my consent. But I also don't want to see you continue in this state. So—" He leaned forward. "I'd snap out of this if I were you."

I turned away.

"Sally, *please* . . ."

I pulled the covers back over my head. *Oh why do I pull infantile stuff like this?* Suddenly, he pulled the covers off me. Looking me straight on, he hissed, "Don't force my hand."

Then he left. And I found myself thinking, *He'll sign the papers in a New York minute. And then I can assume my new role as Electro-Girl. Juice me up, Scotty . . .*

After he was gone, Agnes got out of bed and walked over to where I lay. Her gait was still hesitant. So too the focus of her eyes. But she sounded lucid.

"It's Sally, right?"

I didn't answer.

"Well, listen up, American. My husband didn't want to sign the papers either. I mean, he begged me for a week to try to come 'round and eat something and act like I knew where I was. But I didn't. And when I kept tearing the feeding tube out of me . . . well, it left them with no choice. The night before they began the therapy, my husband sat by me and started crying, pleading with me for one last time to eat something, anything. But . . ."

Pause.

". . . the next morning, I pulled the tube out again. And that evening, they started the ECT."

Pause.

"Just had my fifth yesterday. Guess it's doing some good, 'cause I'm eating again, and I'm able to play again a bit with Charlie. But . . ."

Pause.

". . . they say you only suffer short-term memory loss. But that's not what I've been suffering. Kind of more like an entire section of my brain's been wiped. And I keep trying to find it—keep rooting around for it. But . . ."

Pause.

". . . know what I think? I think all that electricity ends up frying it right out of you. Burns it to a crisp. The doctor keeps saying, once the treatment's over, it'll all come back again. But I don't believe her. Not for a moment. 'Cause—"

Pause.

"Listen to me. You can avoid this. You can. Just one mouthful of food, eh? Just one. Here . . ."

She pulled over the table, on which sat the untouched dinner tray of food. She reached for a bread roll and pulled off a piece of it.

". . . just a piece of bread. I'll even butter it for you."

She did just that. And put it next to my face. I turned away. She used her spare hand to pull my head back.

"Come on, you can do this."

I turned away again. She forced me back. I turned away. Suddenly she put the roll directly against my mouth. I turned away. She yanked me back, her grip tight now. This time, she forced the bread against my teeth. Which is when I snapped, and brushed it away, and spat in her face. Without stopping to think, she suddenly backhanded me across my face. The shock was ferocious. So too was the pain. And I heard myself shouting, "Nurse!"

Nurse Patterson came into the room.

"So . . . you can talk after all."

Of course, I retreated into silence for the rest of the night. Of course, I didn't touch the dinner tray. Of course, I took my knockout pills like a good girl, and then waited for sleep to club me. But when I woke the next morning . . . no, I wouldn't say that the fog had lifted, or that I was suddenly feeling reborn, rejuvenated, or at one with myself and the world. On the contrary, I still suffered from post-sedative fuzz and a general feeling of all-purpose toxicity, combined with a strange weariness . . . even after another eleven hours of unconsciousness. But, for the first time in days, I actually felt hungry. And when the Scottish nurse brought in the breakfast tray, I mumbled two words, "Thank you."

This made her look up at me, a little startled, but rather pleased as well.

"You're most welcome. Think you can eat?"

I nodded. She helped me sit up and rolled the table over the bed, and set up the tray, even opening the paper napkin for me, like a waiter in a restaurant.

"Could you drink some tea, perhaps?" she said.

I nodded again.

"I'll be right back."

Eating was not an easy process after nearly a week. But I did manage to ingest half a bowl of porridge. It was slow going—and, once or twice, I felt distinctly queasy. But I kept at it. Because I knew I had to.

The nurse poured me a cup of tea and looked on as I ate, beaming. I realized that, to her, any patient who turned a corner was a success story.

"Don't worry about finishing everything," she said. "You're doing grand."

Halfway through breakfast, Agnes stirred awake. Like me, she too was on heavy knockout pills, so it also took her a moment or two to work out where she was, and what she was doing here. But then, gradually, the world came into focus again—and she caught sight of me hovering over the breakfast tray, fork in hand.

To her credit, she said nothing. She just gave me a small nod, then got up and went to the bathroom. When she came back, she came over to my bed and said, "Sorry about last night."

"It's okay," I said, just about getting the word out.

"How did breakfast go down?"

I shrugged.

"That's how I felt too—first time I ate after . . . Then again, the food's such crap around here . . ."

I managed a little smile.

What I found difficult, though, was the actual act of talking. I could get a word or two out, but then something seized my larynx, refusing to let go.

"Don't sweat it," Agnes said when she saw me struggling. "It takes time to come back."

When lunch arrived, I managed to eat half a chicken leg and the white goo that they passed off as mashed potatoes, and a portion of overcooked carrots that had a decidedly plastic texture. But it was important that I make a good show of my lunch—because Dr. Rodale was due in shortly—and I wanted to be absolutely certain that my rediscovered appetite was noted for the record.

She certainly walked into our room with newfound pleasantness.

"I've just heard your good news, Sally," she said. "Breakfast *and* lunch. Most reassuring. And I gather you've even managed to articulate a word or two. Do you think you can speak a bit now?"

"I'll try," I said, the words taking some time to form.

"No rush," she said, clipboard and pen at the ready. "But it would be most helpful to know . . ."

And she ran through the entire checklist again. My answers were largely brief—and I seemed to be using words of one syllable. But with her coaxing, I was able to answer all her questions—and, courtesy of my cooperativeness, I seemed to have brought her around to my side. Because when she was finished, she congratulated me on "a job well done" and emphasized how her previous tough tone was a way of breaking through the barriers that had been constructed in my head, courtesy of my postpartum depression.

"Of course, the road ahead is by no means certain—and it must be negotiated with prudence. For example, do you feel ready to see Jack yet?"

I shook my head.

"Perfectly understandable," she said, "and under the circumstances, probably sensible. You should see him when you feel ready to see him— which, we hope, will not be too far off."

She then explained that what I was going through was undoubtedly horrible for me, but by no means unique. Now that I had started to place my feet back on terra firma, it was possible to treat my condition largely through the use of antidepressants. With any luck, I should start to see some significant improvement within six weeks.

Six weeks? In here?

Dr. Rodale saw the shocked look on my face.

"I know that sounds like a horrible length of time—but, believe me, I've seen depressions that, in their most virulent phase, have dragged on for months. And the good news is: if you start responding well to the antidepressants, we will be able to send you home as soon as you're judged fit to go home."

You mean, when I'm no longer a danger to myself and my baby?

But as soon as that thought crossed my head, another one cut in: *Knock it off now.*

"You look like you want to ask me something," she said. "Any questions?"

"No," I said—and the sound of my voice brought another pleased look to her face.

"No questions at all?"

"I'm fine," I lied.

EIGHT

T HE DOCTOR WAS right. Just as there is no such thing as a free lunch, so there is no instant cure for depression—no fizzy Alka-Seltzer evaporation of the black swamp into which you've plunged. Rather, it's a slow, piecemeal progression back to terra firma (whatever that is), with frequent manic diversions en route, just to make certain that you're not getting too damn cocky about the rapidity of your recovery.

Still, Dr. Rodale often reminded me that I was free to leave of my own accord whenever I wished. Not that she actively encouraged me to flee the coop. Rather, I sensed that she was legally obliged to keep informing me of my freedom of movement. She also felt professionally obliged to tell me that, for my own sake, I really should stick it out in the unit until (as she so inclusively put it) "we all feel comfortable about your return to the home front."

The home front. As in: the place of quotidian tranquility to which you return after bloody combat on the battlefield . . . though when did my London home front ever resemble a serene refuge?

Still, Tony decided to play the role of the dutiful, caring spouse—and even expressed contrition for his anger toward me when I was still in coma land.

"You know, I was just articulating a desperate frustration . . . and worry," he said the evening after I started eating again. "And it was also an attempt to help you . . . uh . . ."

Snap out of it?

"Anyway, it's good to have you back. The alternative would have been . . . frightful."

But electrifying . . .

"Been to see Jack yet?" he asked.

196

I shook my head.

"No rush, none at all," he said. "The doctor told me it's going to take a little . . . uh . . . time, and the two of you could be in here for some weeks . . ."

Tony did his best to mask his glee at such a respite from *la vie conjugale*, not to mention the broken nights of early babyhood (not that he'd had much experience of Jack's sleep terrorism, courtesy of his office aerie).

"I've informed the editor about your . . . uh . . . condition, and he's been most sympathetic. Told me to take as much time off as we needed."

To sit by my bed and hold my hand and keep me company? I don't think so.

But Tony proved me wrong on that one. Day in, day out, he showed up at the hospital and spent at least an hour with me, always bringing me a collection of that day's newspapers—and, as I started to become more compos mentis, a steady supply of novels and back issues of the *New Yorker*. He even went out and splurged on a Discman with an FM radio and a very fancy pair of Bose headphones, which had a little power pack that helped block out all external noise. And he gradually brought in around twenty or so CDs from home. Much to my surprise, he showed an appreciation of my musical taste. Lots of baroque concerti grossi by Handel and Corelli. My prized 1955 recording of Glenn Gould playing Bach's *Goldberg Variations*. Ella Fitzgerald's sublime collaborations with Louis Armstrong. And Bill Evans's famous *Sunday at the Village Vanguard* disc—which, ever since I'd heard it in college, always struck me as the height of sophisticated cool . . . and did even more so now from my confined vantage point of a South London hospital.

The music became a touchstone for me—a way of measuring my gradual return to some sort of sentient state. But I was also aware of something that Dr. Rodale told me: "At first, you'll possibly wonder if the antidepressants are doing anything. It takes a little time to bite—and it never works the same way with everybody."

She warned me about possible side effects—and before there was any sense of the drug biting, there was no doubt that its chemical byproducts were playing games with my system. First came a desert-like dryness in my mouth, spreading rapidly to my throat and eventually (and most disturbingly) to my eyes.

"We'll get you some liquid tears to keep the eyes hydrated," Dr. Rodale said. "Meanwhile, keep drinking two liters of water per day."

Then there was a kind of nausea—in which my stomach began to
heave, but nothing followed.

"This should settle down—but you *must* keep eating."

Food was Dr. Rodale's big obsession—making me wonder if she'd
spent a lot of time treating anorexics (or had herself been one). I suppose
she had a point—because, according to Nurse Patterson, refusal to eat
was a common postpartum syndrome, and one that tended to exacer-
bate the depression, for a lot of obvious physiological reasons.

"When you don't eat," she said, "you become even more susceptible
to the downward curve."

I was eating again—but my progress back to something approaching
an appetite was slow, due in part to the horrendous slop they served at
the hospital. So Tony began to do a Marks and Spencer's run for me
every day, picking up sandwiches and salads, and even conferring with
the nurses about what I should be eating.

Once again, his solicitousness surprised and pleased me. Of course,
I knew he'd never articulate why he was suddenly being thoughtful and
considerate.

"Does it matter what his motivations are?" Ellen Cartwright asked
me. "The important thing is: Tony is showing concern. And don't you
think that's a good thing?"

Ellen Cartwright was the unit's resident therapist. Dr. Rodale pushed
pills, Ellen got you in touch with your inner idiot. But like everyone I'd
met so far at the hospital, she was a serious pragmatist—and someone
who also adopted a very English point of view about the messiness of
life: there's a great deal to be said about muddling through.

Ellen favored long, capacious skirts and big, baggy linen shirts. She
was in her early fifties—and from her style, her long gray hair, and her
taste in Subcontinent bangles, I sensed that there was a touch of the
subculture veteran about her. But when it came to dealing with the
complexities of my condition, she was reassuringly practical.

"You've switched countries, you've put your career on hold, you've
become a mother, while all the time trying to adjust to married life
with a man about whom you're frequently uncertain . . . and that's

before we factor in the fact that the birth of your child was a difficult experience for yourself and for him. Now, when you add up all that, can you really sit there and tell me you think you're making too big a deal about all this?"

"I just feel so . . . I don't know . . . *inadequate*."

"In what way?"

"Every way."

If our conversations had a general theme, it was this long-standing feeling of inadequacy—the perennial worry of the perennial B student (which I was throughout high school and college) who never felt she was achieving her potential . . . who was always just about "all right" at everything, but could never excel. And it didn't matter that I had done time on a major newspaper, or had been a foreign correspondent, or had the reputation for being very confident on the professional front. In private, the doubts always loomed—and I kept wondering when I'd eventually be found out.

"But you never were 'found out,'" Ellen Cartwright said, "because you were obviously very good at what you did."

"You're just trying to make me feel better about myself."

"Actually, you're right—I am trying to do that. You should feel positive about such accomplishments. I mean, the way you talk about the *Boston Post*, you make it sound like you were hired to work the till in some supermarket. Can't you see what you've already accomplished?"

"What I see," I said, "is someone who threatened the life of her child."

How I wanted to see things differently. But during the first two weeks on antidepressants, I still felt sheer, absolute terror about even just looking in on Jack. I articulated this fear on a regular basis both to Ellen and to Dr. Rodale. And when Tony danced around this question all I could say was, "I just can't see him yet."

After two or three times, Tony had the good sense to stop asking me that question—because it was so obvious that I couldn't handle it. He didn't even mention visiting Jack—though I knew that he poked his head into the children's ward every night that he came to see me.

But Dr. Rodale remained as direct as ever—and seemed to be using my inability to see Jack like my initial inability to eat: a benchmark hurdle that, once crossed, would indicate a further return to stability . . . not to mention a sign that the antidepressants were finally kicking in.

Certainly, I was beginning to feel a gradual undercurrent of . . . *what*? Calmness? Not exactly—as I could still suffer from episodes of extreme anxiety. Chemically induced bliss? Hardly—as I often had to lock myself up in the bathroom to sob uncontrollably. And as for the amelioration of guilt . . .

"So far, I would call your progress steady and encouraging," Dr. Rodale said as I entered week three of the antidepressants. "You're eating, your moods seem steady, you're doing positive things like reading and listening to music . . ."

Yes, but appearances can be deceptive. Because every morning, when I finally climbed out of my drug-induced coma, the realization of where I was (and the reasons that had brought me here) came crashing in on me with desperate ferocity. It took the next dose of antidepressants and a long private hour with Glenn Gould on my Discman to force me into a false sense of quietude.

From the outset of my admission to hospital, Sandy was phoning constantly—initially monitoring my progress (as I found out later) by talking to the nurses. She also spoke a few times with Tony. He managed to talk her out of coming to London after my admission to St. Martin's, correctly telling her that I was in no fit condition for visitors. Then, when I was back in the land of the moderately functional, I told her that it wasn't the best moment for a transatlantic visit, hinting that I really didn't want her to see me in my current condition. The fact that her eldest son had just broken his wrist in a bicycle accident kept her on the other side of the pond . . . to my intense relief. But we still spoke daily. We agreed on a specific hour (four PM in London/eleven AM in Boston—when she had a half-hour break from her morning teaching load), and she'd call a pay phone in a visitors' room down the hall from where I was. As it was outside visitors' hours, it was always empty. Both Ellen and Dr. Rodale considered it an important part of my recovery to maintain close contact with family—so the phone was considered mine for that half-hour period every afternoon.

At first, Sandy sounded like she herself needed a course of antidepressants—or so said Tony, who actually called her in Boston to break the news about my hospital incarceration. Even when I finally started to speak with her, her anxiety was apparent and, *comme d'habitude*, she had spoken to every possible leading expert on postpartum depression in the Greater Boston area. Not only that, she'd also made contact with some heavyweight professor of pharmacology at Harvard Med, who gave her the low-down on my antidepressant load ("It is absolutely the right dosage for you"). And she also established telephone contact with Dr. Rodale ("Well, you are my only sister," she said, when I expressed a certain wariness about such interference), who she also thought sounded like good news.

"Oh, she is," I said in one of our early phone calls. "As long as you obey her every command."

"Well, at least you didn't get sent down for shock treatment—which, I've found out, is a last-ditch solution over here."

"They use it here too," I said, thinking about poor scrambled Agnes.

"Hey, that doctor's gotten you back to some sort of equilibrium."

"I wouldn't go that far."

"Believe me, from the stories I've heard—"

But I didn't want to hear such stories. I just wanted to be out of here.

"You're going to have to let them be the judge of that," Sandy said, surprising me with her "the English doctors know right" stance. "You're still fragile. I can hear it."

Then, just to underscore the fragility of everything, word came back about Agnes. It was nearly three weeks since she'd checked herself out, and I'd had a variety of roommates since then—all short-term internees, and all of whom I treated with polite diffidence, using my Discman and assorted reading matter to keep my distance. I was also allowed to take a walk in the hospital grounds whenever I wanted to—so, once a day, I'd put on the street clothes that Tony had brought me and spend fifteen minutes walking around the inner courtyard of the hospital. It wasn't exactly the most aesthetically pleasing of spots—as it was a concrete quadrangle, with a patch of green in the middle, around which the hospital staff smoked cigarettes. While I made my daily circle around this grubby enclosure, I always found myself thinking how easy it would be for me to escape—even though I was here of my own alleged free will. In fact, I believed that Dr. Rodale encouraged me to take this quotidian walk to enforce the fact that I wasn't a prisoner, and also to get me to accept the reasons I'd ended up here. Because I'm certain that Ellen informed her of the escape fantasy I articulated regularly during several sessions.

"So what's this 'escape fantasy'?" Ellen asked me when I first brought it up.

"It's simple, really," I said. "I get dressed and go out for my walk around the courtyard. Instead, I leave the hospital and head for the nearest taxi stand. I arrive back at our house. I pack a bag. I grab my passport. I jump the tube to Heathrow. I buy a ticket on the first plane to Boston, New York, Washington, even Philadelphia—anywhere on the East Coast . . ."

"And when you get off the plane in America . . . ?"

I shrugged.

Ellen gave me a commiserative smile.

"We all have dreams of leaving," she said.

"Even you?"

"Everybody. But what you must try to remember at all times is that you have an illness. Depression isn't a punishment for being a bad little girl. Nor is it a sign of personal weakness. It is *an illness*—and one from which you will be eventually released. But this is a very serious condition with which you are grappling. So serious that . . ."

She hesitated for a moment, then said, "Dr. Rodale and I debated whether or not to tell you what I'm about to tell you . . . but we decided you should hear it from us rather than from anyone around the unit. You remember Agnes Shale who shared the room with you when you first arrived?"

"Has something happened?"

"I'm afraid so. Agnes jumped under an underground train last week and was killed."

I shut my eyes and said nothing.

"According to her husband, she'd been doing fine for the first week or so. But then, she stopped taking the antidepressants—because, I gather, they weren't agreeing with her. The sleeplessness started again. But her husband assured us that she was bonding well with her son—and, outwardly anyway, seemed to be coping well with things. Until . . ."

She reached over and took a sip from a glass of water on the table by her chair.

"Now I want to be absolutely clear about something," she said. "And it's something that you yourself need to understand. Agnes's suicide cannot be conclusively tied to the fact that she checked herself out of hospital before anyone here believed she was ready to leave. Depression is always an atypical illness—by which I mean that it can never be empirically tracked or second-guessed. So, do believe me, I am not trying to put a *'See what happens if you don't listen to us'* spin on this story. All I want to emphasize is that we all have to be very vigilant about your condition—because it is still a brittle one. But, given time, you will get better."

Sandy concurred with this point of view when I recounted what happened to Agnes during our telephone call that afternoon.

"Your therapist is right. You definitely don't want to surrender to regression."

Surrender to regression? My dear sister had been reading far too many self-help books again.

But I did realize that Ellen had been right to tell me the story—that it had a sobering effect, making me prudent about the status of my equilibrium and the slow tempo of recuperation.

So I kept taking the antidepressants, and I kept talking three times a week to Ellen, and I kept talking to Sandy (who kept threatening to jump on a plane and visit me—but was far too financially strapped to do so). And when Tony had to skip a few visits because of the usual global crises, I was perfectly sanguine. By the end of week four, the crying fits that marked most days had stopped. When I weighed myself I saw that I had regained half the fifteen pounds I'd lost (and that was enough!). Dr. Rodale let me give up the sleeping pills, because I was making it through the night without interruption. Every so often—whenever I felt myself edging toward that black fathomless swamp—I seemed able to skirt the edge and reroute myself back to more stable terrain. The urge to plunge into this morass was still present, but there now seemed to be a safety mechanism in place—a fragile fail-safe that kept me away from the precipice . . . for the moment anyway.

Then, a few days into week five, I woke up one morning and took my pills and ate my breakfast and announced to the nurse on duty that I would like to see Jack. There was no sudden lifting of the cloud that made me make this decision; no rays of sunlight streaming through the previously fogged windows of my brain. Nor did I have a massive born-again revelation about the wonders of motherhood.

I just wanted to see him.

The nurse didn't slap me on the back and say, "Great news . . . and about bloody time too, thank God." She just nodded for me to follow her.

The baby ward had a heavily reinforced steel door, with a substantial lock—a sensible precaution in a psychiatric unit. The nurse punched in a code, then pulled the door open. There were only four babies in residence. Jack was in the first crib. I took a deep steadying breath and looked in.

He'd grown, of course—by a half-foot at least. But what struck me so forcibly—so wonderfully, in fact—was the way he had lost that initial premature, postdelivery amorphous quality, and was now such a distinctive little guy. He was also fast asleep—and though I initially hesitated about picking him up, the nurse gave me an encouraging nod. So, with extreme care, I reached for him and brought him up next to me. Instead of crying, he snuggled his head against mine. I kissed him and smelled that powderlike new-baby smell, which was still prevalent all these weeks after his birth. I held him for a very long time.

That evening, I asked Nurse Patterson if Jack could be moved into my room. When Tony arrived that evening, he was genuinely taken aback to see me bottle-feeding Jack.

"Well then . . ." Tony said.

"Yes," I said. "Well then indeed."

Word spread fast about my reunion with Jack. Dr. Rodale was all smiles the next afternoon, informing me that "this was very welcome news indeed," while cautioning me that I still needed to approach each day with a degree of circumspection, and with the understanding that nothing was straightforward when it came to the skewed landscape of depression.

Ellen, meanwhile, tried to get me to concentrate on one salient point. "Jack will never remember a thing about this entire time."

"Lucky for him," I said.

"And I think that once you are fully recovered, you will begin to forgive yourself—even though, from where I sit, there's nothing to forgive."

They kept me in for another two weeks. It passed quickly—especially as I was now spending my entire waking day with Jack. They moved him to the baby ward every night (as Dr. Rodale insisted that I get solid uninterrupted sleep), but brought him back as soon as I was up in the morning—which meant that when he stirred out of sleep, I was there to change and feed him. Just as he was also by my side until I went to bed at night. I even started to bring him out on my daily walk around the hospital courtyard. With the exception of sleep, the only time that I relinquished his company was during my thrice-weekly sessions with Ellen.

"The general feeling is that you're just about ready to go home," she said at the start of week seven. "The question is: do you think yourself ready?"

I shrugged. "I have to leave here sometime."

"Have you talked with your husband about perhaps having some help at home with Jack?"

Actually, it had been Tony himself who had brought up this issue—reminding me that, before I'd entered the hospital, he'd found out the name of a child-care agency in Battersea called Annie's Nannies, and perhaps I'd like to now give them a ring. Though I told Ellen that I would be definitely investigating this possibility, there was also a part of me that felt I should try to make a go of looking after Jack myself—that bringing a nanny in would be another indication of my domestic ineptitude . . . especially as I wasn't working right now, and Jack was still at that stage where he was sleeping for much of the day. So I wrote a note to our cleaner Cha, asking her if she might be able to come in three additional mornings per week and keep an eye on Jack, thereby giving me a short respite from Baby Land. Tony liked this plan—especially as it was going to be around a third the cost of a full-time nanny. Ellen, however, was skeptical.

"If you can afford it, you really should consider constant help," she said. "You're still not completely out of the woods yet . . ."

"I'm doing fine," I said.

"Without question. Your progress has been tremendous. But surely, you can afford a month or two of full-time nannying, just until you're at a stage where—"

But when I argued that I could easily handle my son—especially as he was still at the nonmobile stage of development—she said, "I sense you're still feeling guilty, aren't you? And still thinking that you have to prove to the world that you are a competent mother."

I shrugged but didn't say anything.

"As I've been telling you since the start of our sessions together, there's absolutely nothing wrong with admitting that you can't cope with certain situations . . ."

"But I am coping now."

"And no one's trying to contradict that. But you're also in the controlled environment of a hospital—where all meals are provided, somebody changes the bedclothes, and prepares the formula for Jack, and looks after him at night while you sleep . . ."

"Well, the cleaner will be able to do most of that for me—with the exception of the nights. And if he starts ruining my sleep again, I can always nap while she's on duty."

"All right, that may be so—but I still get the feeling that there's a certain remorse about—"

"Did Agnes feel terribly guilty about . . . ?"

She looked at me carefully.

"About what?"

"About failing her son and her husband."

"I can't talk about another patient. But . . . do you think about Agnes often?"

"All the time."

"Did you become close while you were sharing the room?"

"Hardly—since I was so out of it. But . . . of course I think about her a lot. Because . . ."

I faltered. So Ellen asked, "Because you wonder if you'll end up under an underground train yourself?"

"Yes," I said. "That's exactly what I wonder."

"All I will say is what I said to you before," Ellen said. "Agnes left before any of the hospital staff felt she was ready to leave. You, on the other hand, are leaving with our medical approval. Because we feel you're ready to get on with life again."

"You mean, this isn't life?"

For the first time since we started our sessions, I actually managed to make my therapist laugh.

But before they sent me back to "life," there was an extended question-and-answer session with Dr. Rodale, whose primary concern was getting the ongoing pharmacological load just right. So she wanted to know every detail about my current sleep patterns, my diet, my mood swings, my sense of calm, my sense of unease, my sense of ease with Jack, my sense of ease with Tony.

"Oh, I'm certain my husband will revert to type as soon as I'm home . . . now that I seem to be back in the rational world."

"So that submerging feeling you often described to me . . . what was the term you used again . . . ?"

"The black swamp."

"Yes. The black swamp. Do you often feel yourself drawn back there?"

"Only when the previous dose of antidepressants is starting to wear off."

She nodded—and informed me that she wanted to ever so slightly increase the dosage to ward off those lapses.

"Does this mean I'm going to be on antidepressants for the foreseeable future?" I asked.

"It looks that way. But if they help you cope . . ."

Ah yes, so this was what I had become: a woman who needed help coping . . .

Still, Dr. Rodale finished our session by saying that she was genuinely delighted with my recovery.

"Yours is the sort of story that helps counterbalance . . ."

Stories like Agnes's?

Then she told me that I could leave anytime I was ready to leave.

And so, the next morning, Tony showed up with the car around ten. Nurse Patterson was off-duty, but I'd thanked her the night before. I also thanked Ellen and Dr. Rodale, having agreed to see Dr. Rodale in two weeks to discuss my ongoing relationship with antidepressants. Ellen offered me the chance to continue our sessions. I took her number and said I'd think about it. When I mentioned Ellen's offer to Tony, he said, "Well, if you need to pay someone to tell them what a bad husband I am, go right ahead."

As usual, this comment was delivered in a sardonic tone. But I sensed there was also a hint of guilt behind it.

Still, his comment did have the effect of transferring whatever guilt he felt onto me—and certainly didn't make me want to stretch the family finances any further by doling out £70 an hour to a therapist. My condition had stabilized, after all. The drugs were working. And if I needed to talk my dumb head off, there was always Sandy at the end of a transatlantic phone line. I was going to be just fine.

But within five days of my homecoming, Tony reverted to type.

All credit to Jack: he behaved like the perfect gentleman during his first days in Putney. He slept for five solid hours at a go. He slurped down five bottles. He didn't complain about the service, or the newness of his bedding, or the strange surroundings. Tony seemed reasonably content in his company, just as he also did low-key solicitous things like sterilizing and preparing several bottles, and even changing his diaper on two occasions. No, he didn't take the night shift when Jack woke at three AM . . . but he did insist that I grab a nap the next afternoon while he kept an eye on the boy.

But then, after those first few days, he had to go back to the paper—and his return to work also marked the beginning of a distancing process. He started to come in late—nine, ten, even eleven. Then, one night, he called me from the Groucho Club around one-fifteen in the morning, telling me that a dinner with some *Chronicle* colleagues was running just a little late.

"Fine, no problem," I said. "And the way Jack is going tonight, I'll probably be up when you get home."

When he rolled in at five, I certainly was still wide awake—balancing Jack on my lap, trying to negotiate him through a particularly bad dose of colic, watching CNN. Tony was drunk. Seriously drunk. And not pleasant.

"What are you, my mother?" he asked, staring at me with unfocused eyes and equally unfocused contempt.

"I was just up with Jack," I said, maintaining a low, subdued tone of voice.

"Well, I am not your fucking child," he said, the words slurring. "And I don't . . . *don't* . . . like the idea of being . . . I mean, the fucking nerve of you, waiting up for me, like I'm some truant . . ."

"Tony," I said quietly. "Go to bed."

"Don't you tell me . . ."

"Go to bed."

He looked at me, his eyes blinking with dim bemusement. Then he turned and staggered upstairs. Shortly thereafter, Jack finally conked out. I took him to the nursery, and then went to my room. My husband had fallen facedown on our bed, covering the entire span of it with his rumpled body. I threw a blanket over him, and unplugged the baby alarm, and brought it with me as I climbed the stairs to Tony's study, and pulled open the sofa bed, and found the duvet, and climbed under it, and fell asleep.

Then there was light in my eyes, and Tony was by my side, proffering a cup of coffee. Even though it took a few moments for my eyes to come into proper focus, I could see that he looked terrible . . . and terribly guilty.

"I think I owe you a very large apology," he said.

"You were drunk," I said, sounding absurdly benign.

"I was beastly."

"Thank you for the coffee," I said, smiling sweetly.

One of the more intriguing aspects of Life on Antidepressants was the way it eventually whittled away all rough edges, all potential sharp emotional corners, and left you feeling curiously placid about much of the shit that life can throw at you. The doctor was right—its effects were cumulative. Though I was already registering its increasing efficacy while I was still in hospital, its tranquilizing benefits were only really beginning to kick in now that I was back on the proverbial home front. What struck me most forcibly was how the antidepressants had softened so much of my natural contrariness, my instinctive need to talk back when challenged. It's not as if I had suddenly become programmed into robotic, hubby-worshiping complacency. Rather, I felt like I'd been dispatched to a torpid, tropical place where the general rule of behavioral thumb was: *who cares?* I was no longer in South London; I was beached on some super-laid-back, ganja-hazed island where all of life's vicissitudes were greeted with a stoned shrug.

All right, maybe I'm exaggerating a bit here—but the fact is, the antidepressants numbed that part of the brain in which anger and resentment lurked. Had Tony rolled in drunk and turned nasty on me in the past, I certainly wouldn't have forgiven him after one mumbled, hungover apology. But now, I accepted the cup of coffee, the clumsy kiss on the head, and the nervous tone of contrition.

It wasn't just the drugs that made me so *ego te absolvo*. There was a deep part of me that was terrified of becoming combative—fearing that it would send out warning signals about my mental stability. Anyway, considering the extremity of my own conduct in the days leading up to my hospitalization, I had to cut Tony some slack here . . . and let him adjust to having us around again. In turn, he spent the next two weeks being ultra-polite—if a little preoccupied. No, there were no further five-in-the-morning boozing sessions, but he was frequently held up at the paper until nine or ten several nights a week, and—of course—the novel was still flowing (or so he said). Which meant that, around midnight most evenings, he'd excuse himself and vanish upstairs.

I didn't complain. I just traveled down the antidepressant path of least resistance. When he wanted to share our bed (around twice a week) and have sex with me, I was pleased. When he "needed" to stay out late at the *Chronicle* and/or hide upstairs, I accepted it. I was just grateful that we had silently negotiated a degree of familial stability between us and that my own stability was holding up.

Another curious thing about the slow progression out of depression: you begin to crave routine. And dealing with a baby is certainly bound up in the metronomic regularity of feeds, diaper changes, the usual gaseous postbottle discomfort, rocking him to sleep, being close at hand at all times, coping with colic, coping with another feed, another diaper change, the usual gaseous postbottle . . .

More tellingly I was now so enjoying my son. Gone was the terrible fear that I couldn't handle the basics of motherhood, let alone that terrifying postpartum fear that I would do him harm. On the contrary, I now delighted in his company—reveling in the way his hand closed around my finger, the way he nuzzled his head against mine as I held him, the fact that it was so wonderfully easy to make him laugh.

"Sounds like you guys really are an item now," Sandy said to me after I mentioned the sheer pleasure I was getting from Jack's company.

"He's a terrific kid," I said.

"It's great to hear you so up. You must be relieved."

"Just a little," I said with a laugh.

As I wasn't exactly on the lookout for great intellectual or professional stimulation right now—and also seriously wanted to keep everything on a profoundly even keel—I accepted this circumscribed domestic routine with a certain degree of relief. Cha the cleaner was on hand from nine until midday every morning—and she proved herself to be highly capable with Jack. She kept him happy while I caught up with sleep or took myself off for a walk down the towpath. She organized his clothes, dealt with all the paraphernalia of babyhood, and gave me a necessary three-hour respite from motherhood . . . which I was then happy to resume.

One morning, sitting in Coffee Republic on the High Street, nursing a latte, looking at all the other moms with strollers around me, staring out at the monocultural blandness of Putney's main thoroughfare, the thought struck me: *this is my life now.*

And the New England stoic in me reasoned: you have managed to survive a major tumble into deep deranged muck. You've come through—shakily, but you are functioning. You seem to have achieved an entente cordiale *with your husband. You have your son—with whom you are now fully engaged. Eventually, you will find your way back to the workaday world. But for now . . .*

This is my life.

And it could be far worse—or marked by real misfortune.

Like my poor sister Sandy. She rang me late the next night in a state of convulsive shock. Her ex-husband, Dean, had been killed earlier that day in a climbing accident on Mount Katahdin in northern Maine. A trail guide, he'd been leading a group across a particularly treacherous corner of the mountain known as the Knife Edge, because it was just that: a thin finger of terra firma spanning a deep gorge. Dean must have traversed it several dozen times and was an experienced mountaineer. But earlier that morning a wind blew up and sent him right over the edge. They found his body a few hours later—his neck snapped like a twig, his head caved in. Instantaneous death, they figured.

"He probably never knew what hit him," Sandy said.

I thought: given that he'd fallen nearly a thousand feet, he must have been aware of what was going to hit him—that, verily, his life was about to end. But I didn't say this to her.

"Dumb bastard," Sandy said, crying. "I always warned him about that damn mountain. You know, we climbed it on our honeymoon . . ."

I did remember—and always thought what a strange thing to do to celebrate a new marriage. But Dean was always outdoorsy, and Sandy was madly in love with him at the time, and love will make you do completely out-of-character things like climb a mountain, even though Sandy was the type who preferred avoiding stairs whenever possible.

"You know what really gets me: that one time we went up Katahdin together, I kept doing this big song-and-dance when we reached the Knife Edge about how I couldn't cross it; that it was just too terrifying for me, and I'd end up stranded in the middle of the trail. Know what Dean said? 'I'll never leave you stranded anywhere.' And, of course, I believed him."

She started to cry again—telling me her three boys were taking the news hard, and that Dean's new girlfriend was distraught. I'd never met the woman—but I always disliked her, because of her role as the happy homewrecker. Now, however, all I could feel was desperate pity for her—especially as she was at the back of the climbing group when the accident happened and saw him go over.

And there was Sandy—now weeping uncontrollably over the death of a man whom, just a few weeks earlier, she was referring to as "that scumbag ex-husband of mine." But that's the nature of a divorce, isn't it? You find yourself loathing that person around whom your world once centered. Sometimes you cannot help but wonder if the reason you now despise him is because you still so desperately love him.

Sandy said that the funeral would be in three days' time. Immediately, I said, "I'll be there." She argued that I was in no fit state to cross the Atlantic, that she had the three boys to support her. But I knew that three kids under the age of twelve were going to need support of their own during this horrendous time. So I said, "I think I can do this." And I told her I'd get back to her within a few hours.

Tony was exceptionally sympathetic when I informed him of the news. He virtually insisted that I go—offering to get his secretary to

book the ticket to Boston for me, while also suggesting that I call Annie's Nannies to see if they could find full-time round-the-clock help for
four or five days.

"But won't that cost us a fortune?" I asked.

"It's a family emergency," he said.

But before I called the nanny agency, I phoned Dr. Rodale—and was
fortunate enough to catch her during office hours at her private office on
Wimpole Street. She'd seen me for a fast consultation at the hospital just
last week, and seemed genuinely pleased with my progress. Not pleased
enough to lower my dosage of antidepressants, but confident enough
about my current stability to okay me to travel the Atlantic.

That day, Cha was in working—and when I mentioned that I would
be out of the country for seventy-two hours and was having to find a
full-time nanny, she told me she'd do the job for £100 a day, all in. I
hired her on the spot. That afternoon, we moved one of the single beds
I'd bought for the guest room into the nursery, so Cha could sleep next
to Jack. When I told Tony of this arrangement, he seemed pleased with
it . . . especially as it also meant not having to pay agency fees, let alone
bringing a stranger into the house. Nor did I have to indulge in the
usual paranoid fantasies about a husband left alone in a house with a
nanny—as I thought that, even at his most drunken, there's no way that
he would make a pass at a fifty-five-year-old Thai house cleaner.

Having received the medical all-clear and organized child care, I
found myself two days later on a Virgin flight to Boston. When I got
to the airport, I received something of a surprise—as it turned out that
Tony had booked me into their better class of seat called premium economy. As soon as I checked in, I rang him at the office and said, "Are you
insane . . . and I mean that in the nicest possible way?"

"Aren't you pleased?"

"Of course, I'm pleased. I'm just desperately worried about the cost."

"It wasn't too bad, really. Just three hundred more than the usual
economy fare."

"But that's still a lot of money."

"You're still recovering from a tough business . . . and you need to
be in reasonable shape to deal with the next few days. Sandy is going to
need a lot of support."

"I'm so grateful," I said.

"Don't be. It's the least I . . ."

I couldn't tell if he'd been pulled away from the phone, or had suddenly gone quiet on me.

"Tony, you still there?" I asked.

"Sorry, sorry, got . . ."

Another odd pause. My cell phone was obviously playing up again.

"Listen, I've got to go," he said.

"You okay?"

"Fine, fine . . . just being hauled into conference, that's all."

"Look after our great guy," I said.

"Have no fear. Travel well. Call me tonight when you land."

"I will."

"Love you," he said.

Some hours later, halfway over the Atlantic, it struck me that that was the first time Tony had told me he loved me since . . .

Well, I couldn't really remember the last time he said that.

The next three days were a nightmare. My sister was a wreck. My three nephews were in various stages of incomprehension and grief. The funeral turned into a territorial exercise, with Sandy, the children, and myself on one side of the church, and Dean's family sitting on the opposite side with Jeannie (his new love), her people, and a lot of tanned, muscular types who looked like they were members of the Sierra Club (the flag of this organization covering Dean's casket). Though Dean's parents spent a little time after the funeral with their three grandchildren, everyone studiously avoided Sandy and her younger sister with the glassy jet-lagged/antidepressant-fueled eyes. The entire day was an ordeal—made around five times worse by the fact that, courtesy of my antidepressants, I was forbidden to touch even the most minimal mouthful of alcohol. And God, this was one of those times when I really could have used a drink. I could not get over the internecine pettiness into which families descend . . . even after something as traumatic as an accidental death. Surely, Dean's demise pointed up the most salient fact of temporal existence: that everything is so desperately momentary. Yet we spend so much of our time here in endless conflict with others that we lose sight of the ephemeralness of life. Or is it because we so recognize the evanescent, fugitive nature of all endeavor that we try to give it meaning through conflict? Are we that fatuous, that preposterous?

When we got back to Sandy's house that evening, the children were so drained and exhausted that they fell into their beds and straight to sleep. At which point Sandy sat down on the sofa next to me and fell apart. I held her as she sobbed into my shoulder. She cried for nearly a quarter hour without interruption. When she finally subsided, she dried her eyes and said, "That asshole broke my heart."

We sat up late that night, talking, talking. She'd received a call the day before from Dean's lawyer, informing her that everything in his estate (which wasn't much—bar a life insurance policy worth around $250,000) had been left to his girlfriend. Which, in turn, meant that Sandy's already sizable financial problems were even more severe—as Dean's small $750 per month child support contribution was an important component of the household budget. I didn't know what to say, except that I wished I myself were well-heeled enough to give her a monthly check for that amount.

"You've got enough crap on your plate," she said.

At which point—as if on cue—Tony rang from London. I glanced at my watch. Seven PM in Boston, midnight in London. Much to my immense relief, all he wanted to do was see how I was doing, and to report that all was well with Jack. We'd spoken the previous nights—and on each occasion, Tony expressed genuine concern about Sandy's welfare, and also quizzed me on my own mental state. This time, he also gave me an update on Cha ("She's handling everything just fine—even if she never smiles"), and wanted to know everything about the funeral. His tone was easy, receptive. As he took down the details of my return flight ("I'll have a car pick you up at Heathrow"), he mentioned that he was doing a fast day trip to Paris tomorrow morning. Some G7 foreign ministers thing. But not to worry—Cha had been briefed, he'd be back on the last Eurostar train tomorrow night, ready to greet me when I walked in the next morning.

When the call ended, Sandy said, "You guys seem to be in a good place."

"Yes—it's amazing the effect antidepressants can have on a rocky marriage."

"It's not just the drugs that pulled you through all this. You should also give yourself a little credit."

"For what? Coming completely unstuck, and ending up in a psychiatric unit?"

"You had an illness . . ."

"So they keep telling me."

"And you're through the worst of it now."

"So they keep telling me."

"And Tony's behaving himself."

"I think we've established a kind of armistice between us."

"Sounds better than a lot of marriages I know."

"Like you and Dean?"

"We were doing fine . . . or, at least, that's what I thought. Until he heeded the call of the wild."

"Maybe he . . ."

"What? Hated the fact that I'd gotten fat and dumpy?"

"Stop that."

"But it's the truth."

"No, the truth here is that Dean probably just needed a bit of drama in his life."

She looked at me quizzically.

"Drama? I don't follow."

"He might have been perfectly content with you and the boys. But then this woman came along and . . ."

"Yeah?"

"Maybe he saw an opportunity for drama, that's all. A new life out in the woods. Very romantic—until you realize that leading groups of tourists up and down the same mountain also gets boring. And 'boring' is the one thing in life we most fear . . . more so than death, I think. Because it accentuates the uselessness of everything. Which is why you should never underestimate the human need for drama—it makes us believe we're all starring in this wide-screen epic of our own making, rather than getting bogged down in the usual day-to-day stuff."

Sandy looked at me carefully.

"What was the name of those antidepressants you're on?"

I certainly popped the specified two capsules when I woke the next morning. Then I called home. No answer in London—making me speculate that Cha must have taken Jack out for a walk in his stroller. So I called Tony on his cell, just to say a quick hello, but received his voicemail.

"Know you're in Paris," I said, "but I simply wanted to say a quick bonjour and tell you that I am so looking forward to getting home and seeing you guys."

I spent the afternoon in a shopping mall with Sandy, buying a few baby clothes and even splurging on a Banana Republic leather jacket for Tony. I popped two more antidepressants at lunchtime, and dropped the final two tablets right after saying good-bye to my sister at Logan Airport—in which she became teary about yet again dispatching her sister to alien terrain.

"You'll pull through this," I told her. "Because you have to."

Before I boarded the flight, I went to a phone and called the house in London, hoping to touch base with Cha before she went to sleep (or, for that matter, if she was still up, walking the floors with Jack). But there was no answer. I glanced at my watch: 7:15 in Boston, just after midnight in London. She was evidently having an easy night of it with the boy, and had already gone to sleep.

Which is exactly what I did after settling down into my large premium economy seat, silently thanking Tony for such a spontaneous act of generosity. When we were airborne, I screwed in a pair of earplugs, blacked out the world with an eyeshade, and let the tautness of the last few days give way to exhausted sleep.

Then we were in London—and as Tony said, there was a minicab driver waiting for me at the arrivals gate. We'd been shoved across the Atlantic at *allegro con molto* speed, and had therefore arrived forty minutes ahead of schedule. Which meant we were cruising down the M4 at 6:45 AM—and I was resisting the temptation to ring home on my cell phone, for fear of waking Tony or Cha.

We made Putney in record time—a mere half hour from the airport. The driver helped me to the front door with my bag. I took out my key and unlocked it, opening it as quietly as possible. I stepped inside. And immediately knew that something was astray. The front hallway had been stripped of a collection of framed historical photographs of Old Cairo that Tony had brought back from Egypt.

Maybe he'd decided to put them elsewhere in the house . . .

But then, as I headed up the stairs toward the nursery, I glanced sideways into the living room. This stopped me dead. Almost all the bookshelves had been emptied, along with Tony's extensive collection of CDs, and the fancy overpriced stereo he'd treated himself to shortly after we moved in.

We'd been burgled.

I ran up the stairs, shouting for Tony. I threw open the nursery door. Nothing . . . by which, I mean: no crib, no playpen, no toys, no baby carrier, no Jack. I stood in the middle of the empty room—divested of all its furniture, all its toys, and every bit of clothing I'd bought for him.

I blinked in shock. This wasn't a burglary.

Then I dashed upstairs to Tony's study. It had been completely stripped bare. I rushed down to our bedroom and flung open the wardrobe. All his clothes were gone, but mine were still there. And when I charged into the bathroom, all that I found in the medicine cabinet were my toiletries.

I reeled back into the bedroom. I sat down. I told myself: *this isn't making sense . . . this simply isn't logical. My husband and my son have vanished.*

NINE

I T TOOK ME several minutes to force myself up off the bed. I had no idea where this story was going. All I knew was: I had just walked into a nightmare.

The kitchen. It was the one room in the house I'd yet to check. I stood up. I went downstairs—and immediately saw that the sterilizer, all baby bottles, and the high chair we'd bought were gone. So too was the entire stock of formula, diapers, baby wipes, and all other infant paraphernalia.

I couldn't fathom it. Someone had come along and expunged every trace of Tony and Jack from the house. No sign of them remained whatsoever.

I grabbed the phone and punched in the number of Tony's cell phone. I was instantly connected with his voicemail. My voice was decidedly shaky as I spoke. "Tony, it's me. I'm home. And I must know what's going on. Now. Please. *Now.*"

Then I rang his office—on the wild off-chance that he might be in at seven-something in the morning. Again I was connected to his voicemail. Again I left the same message.

Then I rang Cha. No voicemail this time. Just a computer-generated voice informing me that the cell phone I was ringing had been switched off.

I leaned against the kitchen counter. I didn't know what to do next.

The front doorbell rang. I ran toward it, hoping against hope that Tony was outside with Jack in his arms. Instead, I found myself facing a large beefy guy in his late twenties. He was in a tight, ill-fitting suit, a white shirt open at the collar, a tie dappled by food stains. He had no neck—just a straight roll of fat from his chin to his collarbone. He radiated greasy menace.

"Sally Goodchild?" he asked.

"Yes, that's me," I said.

"Got something for you," he said, opening his briefcase.

"What?"

"I'm serving you with papers," he said, all but shoving a large document in my hand.

"Papers? What sort of papers?"

"An *ex parte* court order, luv," he said, thrusting a large envelope into my hand.

Job done, he turned and left.

I tore open the envelope and read. It was an order given by the Honorable Mr. Justice Thompson, yesterday at the High Court of Justice. I read it once, I read it twice. It didn't make sense. Because what it stated was that, after an *ex parte* hearing in front of Mr. Justice Thompson the court had granted Anthony Hobbs of 42 Albert Bridge Road, London SW11, *ex parte* interim custody of his son, Jack Hobbs, until a further order was given.

I ran down the street until I caught up with the process server, getting into his parked car.

"You've got to explain this to me," I said.

"Not my job, luv," he said.

"Please," I said. "I need to know . . ."

"Get yourself a solicitor, luv. He'll know what to do."

He drove off.

I went back to the house. I sat down at the kitchen table. I tried to reread the court order again. Three sentences into it, I dropped it, clasped my arms around me, and felt the sort of deep chill that sparked off a low-level internal tremor.

This can't be happening . . . this can't be . . .

I stood up. I looked at the clock on the wall. Seven fifty-seven. I grabbed the phone. I tried Tony again. His voicemail answered again. I said, "Tony—I don't know what sort of game you're playing here . . . but you have to talk to me now."

The court has granted Anthony Hobbs of 42 Albert Bridge Road, London SW11 . . .

I got to my feet. I opened the kitchen cabinet and reached into the bowl where all car and extra house keys were kept. The car keys were gone. Which meant that he had taken the car along with . . .

A wave of terror seized me.

After an ex parte *hearing in front of Mr. Justice Thompson . . .*

Why did he need a hearing? What was he arguing? What did I do that merited . . . ?

I reached again for the phone and called the local minicab company. They had a car at my front door in five minutes. I gave the driver the address: 42 Albert Bridge Road, SW11.

We headed right into rush-hour traffic. The driver was a recent arrival in England. He had yet to master the A-to-Z atlas of city streets, and his battered C-reg Volvo was in need of a new set of shocks. But he kept humming contentedly to himself as we sat, becalmed, in eight AM gridlock. He also lost his way twice—but seemed genuinely concerned by my ever-growing agitation in the backseat.

"It's okay," he said. "I get you there."

But it took nearly an hour to negotiate the two-mile crawl to Albert Bridge Road. When we arrived, some instinct told me to ask him to wait for a moment while I got out of the cab and negotiated the ten steps up an imposing three-story-over-basement Victorian town house. I used the brass door knocker to announce my arrival, whacking it frantically. After a moment, it was opened by a diminutive, olive-skinned woman with tired eyes and a Hispanic accent.

"Yes?" she asked, looking at me warily.

Peering over her shoulder, I got a glimpse of the entrance foyer. Very minimalist. Very sleek. Very architect designed. Very expensive.

"Who lives here?"

"Miss Dexter."

"Anyone else?"

"She has a friend."

"What's his name?"

"Mr. Tony."

"And does Mr. Tony have a little boy?"

"A *beautiful* little boy," she said, actually smiling.

"Are they here now?"

"They've gone away."

"Where?"

"The country."

"Whereabouts?"

"I don't know. Miss Dexter has a place in the country."

"Do you have a phone number, an address?"

"I can't give . . ."

She began to shut the door. I put my foot in its way.

"I'm the little boy's mother. I just need to know . . ."

"I can't," she said.

"Please help me here."

"You have to go."

"Just a phone number. I'm—"

The word "desperate" was on my lips, but I couldn't get it out, as I found myself overwhelmed by despair and shock. The housekeeper looked at me with alarm.

"*Please*," I whispered.

She glanced around nervously, as if somebody could be watching us, then said, "They went to his office."

"When?"

"Half an hour ago. They had to stop there before they went to the country."

I touched the top of her hand.

"Thank you."

I walked quickly back to the cab.

"Can you get me to Wapping now?"

En route, I tried to process the limited information I'd received. The woman was named Dexter. She obviously had money—not just for that big Albert Bridge Road pile, but also for a country place. And the fact that my husband was referred to as Mr. Tony meant . . .

What? That he'd been around and about this house since . . . ?

After an ex parte *hearing in front of Mr. Justice Thompson* . . .

I reached for my phone, about to try Tony's cell phone again. But then I stopped myself, thinking that if he knew I was on my way to the *Chronicle*, he'd have a chance to run interference or . . .

What is he doing? What?

"Get yourself a solicitor, luv. He'll know what to do."

But I knew no solicitors in London. I really knew no one here. No one at all I could call now and say . . .

No, this was all too absurd. This was some horrible prank, some fantastical misunderstanding that had ballooned into . . .

And he was so friendly on the phone when I was back in Boston. Before then, he couldn't have been more considerate when Sandy's ex fell off the mountain. *Go, darling, go . . . and here's a better class of air ticket to make your journey more comfortable. Because while you're out of town . . .*

Stop it, stop it—you sound like one of those demented conspiracy theorists.

We approached the Wapping gates. I paid the driver £30 and then approached the security cordon—a place Tony always referred to as Checkpoint Charlie. But instead of the Stasi on duty, I found myself face-to-face with a uniformed guard at a little visitors' booth.

"Can I help you?" he asked.

"I'm here to see my husband," I said.

"Which paper does he work for?"

"The *Chronicle*. Tony Hobbs—the foreign editor."

"Oh right, him. And you're his missus?"

I nodded. As he rang a number, he asked me to take a seat. He spoke into the phone, explained who I was, and then heard something from the person on the other end that made him cast a sideways glance at me, as if I was potential trouble. After he hung up, he turned to me and said, "Someone will be out here in a moment."

"*Someone*?" I said, standing up. "Didn't you speak with my husband?"

"Someone will explain . . ."

"Explain *what*?"

"She'll be here shortly," the guard said.

"Who is *she*?"

The guard looked a little alarmed by my raised voice. But instead of saying anything, he just turned away from me and busied himself with paperwork.

So I sat down in one of the plastic waiting room chairs, clutching myself tightly. A minute or so later, Judith Crandall walked in. She was Tony's secretary—a woman in her late fifties who had been working for the foreign desk since she joined the paper thirty years earlier. "The original *Chronicle* lifer," as Tony called her (takes one to know one)—and someone who knew where all the bodies were buried. She was also a rabid chain smoker, and had a lit cigarette in hand as she approached me. Her face looked grim, uneasy.

"Hello, Sally," she said.

"What's going on?" I said, my voice loud again.

She sat down in the chair next to mine and pulled it toward me, so we were huddling together conspiratorially.

"Tony resigned from the paper yesterday," she said.

This took a moment to register.

"You're lying," I said.

She took a deep drag off her cigarette.

"I wish I was."

"Why?"

"You'll have to ask him."

"But he's here, isn't he?"

"He was here—until about fifteen minutes ago."

"You're lying. He's *here*. With Jack."

She stubbed out her cigarette and immediately lit up another one.

"I am not lying," she said in a low, conspiratorial whisper. "He left fifteen minutes ago."

"With my son?"

"He was on his own. He showed up with his car and cleared his desk. Then he came over to a few of us and said good-bye and left."

"Did he give you any forwarding address?"

"Albert Bridge Road in Battersea."

"Same address that was in the court order . . ."

She said nothing, but looked away—which is when I knew that she was aware of everything that had happened.

"Who's this other woman?" I asked.

"I don't know."

"You do know," I said.

"He didn't talk about her."

"Please . . ."

"I'm serious."

"Liar," I shouted.

The guard stepped off from behind his desk and approached me.

"I'm going to have to ask you to leave now."

"Sally," Judith said, taking me by the hand, "this is doing no good."

"He took my child. You know that. He's disappeared with my son. And now I'm not leaving. Because I know you're hiding him. *I know it.*"

That last sentence came out as a shriek—causing Judith and the guard to blanch. He recovered quickly, however, and said, "I'm saying this just once: you leave now of your own accord, or I will be forced to escort you off the premises myself. And if you fight us, I will have no choice but to call the police."

Judith was about to reach for my hand but thought better of it.

"Please, Sally, don't make him do that."

"You know everything, don't you?" I said, my voice a near-whisper. "You know who this Dexter woman is, and how long he's been seeing her, and why he's taken out an order barring me from . . ."

I started to weep. Judith and the guard backed away. I dropped into the chair, sobbing wildly. The guard was going to make a move toward me, but Judith stopped him, whispering something in his ear. Instead she crouched down beside me and said, "You need help. Can I call someone for you?"

"Oh, is that what he told you . . . that I'd gone completely ga-ga and *needed help*?"

My angry voice prompted the guard to approach me again.

"I'll go," I said.

I stormed out of the security booth without looking back.

I found myself on a road called the Highway, staggering in the direction of Tower Bridge, but not really knowing where I was headed. A high, long wall ran the southern length of the Highway. After around twenty paces, I slumped against it—unable to move any further. Though I was still standing on my feet, I could feel myself plummeting: that same descending swoop I so associated with the initial stages of my postpartum disaster. Only this time, it was accentuated by the realization that my husband had vanished with my son—and had obtained a court order to bar me from seeing him.

Here, finally, was legal confirmation of what the world already knew:

I was a disaster as a mother. Here, finally, was proof that I should do everyone a favor and walk the quarter mile to Tower Bridge, and climb over one of the railings and—

"Ma'am, are you all right?"

It was a constable—walking his beat and finding me slumped against the wall. Looking—

Well, I must have been looking pretty damn desperate for a big-city policeman to take notice of a lone woman holding up a wall.

"Ma'am . . . ?"

"Yeah, fine."

"You don't sound fine."

"I'm . . . uh . . ."

"Do you know where you are now?"

I nodded.

"Where then, please?"

"London."

"Yes, but where exactly?"

"Wapping."

"You're North American?"

I nodded again.

"Visiting London?"

"No—live here."

"And you don't need help right now?"

"Just . . . upset . . . private thing . . . uh . . . a taxi."

"You'd like a taxi?"

"Please."

"Going where?"

"My house."

"And where's that exactly?"

I told him. Saying Putney immediately identified me as a proper resident—because what American tourist ever ventured to that south-western corner of the city?

"You sure you just want to go home?"

"Yes. Home. Can I go now?"

"No one's stopping you, ma'am. Could I get you a cab?"

"Please."

He raised his hand. A taxi stopped within seconds. I thanked the constable, climbed in, gave the driver my address, then slumped across the backseat.

I was back home by ten. The silence of the house was huge. I glanced at the court order on the table, the stripped shelves, the bare nursery. I walked into the bathroom and popped two antidepressants. I lay down on the bed. I shut my eyes, opening them a moment later out of some strange hope that I would suddenly find myself back in my restored former life. But instead, I found myself dominated by one sole horrifying realization:

They've taken Jack away from me.

I reached for the bedside phone. I dialed Tony's cell. Again, the voicemail came on. Again I left a message.

But I knew that he didn't have to call me. He had his court order, good for two weeks. He'd gone away, with no forwarding phone number, bar his cell phone—on which he could use his voicemail to screen all calls and dodge the possibility of talking with me. He had it all thought out.

But why had he resigned his job? The *Chronicle* was the one great constant in his life—and a place from which he would loathe being permanently separated.

I put down the phone. I picked it up—and tried Cha again. This time I got lucky. She answered on the third ring. But when she heard my voice, she was immediately nervous.

"I cannot talk," she said in her tentative English.

"Why not? What did they tell you?"

A hesitant pause. Then, "They told me I am not working for you again."

"When did they move everything out?"

"Two days ago. They also brought a nanny to be with the baby."

A nanny? What nanny?

"When you say 'they,' you mean my husband and . . ."

Another hesitant pause.

"Tell me, Cha."

"I don't know her name. A woman."

"Was her name Dexter?"

"I didn't know her name."

"How old was she?"

"I don't know."

"What did she look like?"

"I don't know."

"Cha . . ."

"I have to go now."

"Could you somehow come over this morning? I really need to—"

"They told me I don't work for you anymore."

"That's my decision, not theirs. And I want you to keep working here."

"I can't."

"Why not?"

"They paid me . . ."

"Paid you to do what?"

"Paid me to stop working for you."

"But . . . I don't understand . . ."

"They said I shouldn't talk to you . . ."

"Cha, you've got to explain . . ."

"I have to go back to work."

The line went dead. I hit redial, and was immediately connected with a recording, informing me that the cell phone I had been speaking to had been switched off.

"They paid me . . ."

"Paid you to do what?"

"Paid me to stop working for you."

"But . . . I don't understand . . ."

I didn't understand anything. Because everything right now was beyond comprehension.

The doorbell rang. I raced downstairs. But when I answered it, I found myself facing a blond, smug-looking man in a black suit, dark blue shirt, a smart floral tie.

"Are you a lawyer?" I asked.

He laughed a bemused laugh, while also eyeing me warily.

"Graham Drabble from Playfair Estate Agents in Putney. We're here to measure up the house . . ."

"What are you talking about?"

"You are Mrs. Hobbs, right?"

"My name is Sally Goodchild."

"Well, I was instructed by a Mr. Hobbs . . ."

"My husband. And what did he 'instruct' you to do?"

"Sell your house."

"Well, he didn't tell me," I said, and shut the door.

He's selling the house? But he can't do that, can he?

While there was one part of my brain that simply wanted to crawl upstairs into bed, pull the covers over my head, and embrace hysterical denial, another more dominant voice overrode such fatalistic logic, insisting: *get a lawyer now.*

But I hadn't a clue about London lawyers, or the English legal system, or *ex parte* orders. A year in this city—and I hadn't made a single real friend. Except for Margaret. But she was another Yank. And now she was back Stateside with her lawyer husband . . .

Margaret.

Not thinking, I dialed her number in New York. It rang and rang. Finally, Margaret answered—sounding groggy and half-awake.

"Oh, God," I said, "I've woken you up."

"That's . . . uh . . . okay, I think . . ."

"Listen, I'll call back . . ."

"Sally?" she said, finally working out who I was.

"I'm really sorry about . . ."

"What's wrong?"

"I didn't mean to bother you so early."

"What's wrong?"

I told her everything, trying not to break down en route. When I was finished, she sounded genuinely shocked.

"That's crazy."

"I wish it was . . ."

"But . . . he gave you no intimation before you went to the States that he was planning this?"

"Nothing. In fact, while I was in hospital, he was actually supportive."

"And this woman . . ."

"I don't know who she is. Except that she lives in a very big house on a very desirable road opposite Battersea Park, and she has a place in the country, not to mention the current company of my husband and child."

"He can't just snatch your child like that."

"Well, there's a court order . . ."

"But what was his rationalization?"

"As he's completely gone to ground, I can't ask him. But the bastard's trying to sell the house from under me."

"But it's in both your names, right?"

"Of course it's in both our names. But as I haven't a clue how the law works here . . ."

"Alexander's in Chicago on business right now. I'll wait an hour until he's up, then give him a call and try to find out the name of a good attorney in London. Meantime, you hang in there, hon."

She called back two hours later.

"First of all, Alexander's horrified about what's happened—and he's certain . . . *certain* . . . that you will be able to negotiate some sort of deal . . ."

"Negotiate? *Negotiate*? There's nothing to *negotiate* here. Jack's my son. And I . . ."

"Sally, hon, *easy*. We're both on your side here."

"I'm sorry, sorry . . . it's just . . ."

"No need to explain. What's happened is outrageous. But Alexander's found an excellent firm in London—Lawrence and Lambert. He doesn't know anybody there personally—but he said that they come highly recommended. And, of course, you can use Alexander's name when you call them. Meanwhile, I'm always here whenever you just need to talk."

As soon as I finished the call, I phoned Lawrence and Lambert. The receptionist was very brusque.

"Is there a party you wish to speak with directly?"

"That's the thing—another lawyer recommended that I get in touch with you . . ."

"But he didn't give you the name of someone here?"

"Uh no . . ."

"Well, if I don't have a name . . ."

"I need to speak with someone who deals with family law . . ."

"We have five attorneys here who deal with family law."

"Well . . . could you put me through to one of them, please?"

I was put on hold. Then, after a moment, a young woman answered. Her accent was seriously Essex.

"Virginia Ricks's office."

"Uh . . . does Miss Ricks do family law?"

"Who is this?"

I told her my name and explained how I had been recommended by Alexander Campbell.

"And Mr. Campbell knows Ms. Ricks, does he?"

"I don't think so."

"Well, Ms. Ricks is tied up most of the day in court . . ."

"It is rather urgent."

"What's your name again?"

I told her—and gave her both my home and cell numbers.

Once I was off the phone, I had to face up to a very large question: what should I do next?

The answer was: nothing. There was absolutely nothing that I could do right now. Nor did I have anyone to turn to here. Nor did I know the whereabouts of Tony and Jack. Nor—

I suddenly decided to take a gamble that, maybe, the entire country house story was just that—*a story*. So I called the minicab company, and asked them to send another car around. This time, the driver knew the way. Traffic had marginally lightened, so we made it in just fifteen minutes. Once again, I banged heavily with the big brass knocker. The housekeeper was deeply unhappy to see me.

"I told you, they are not here."

"I just want to make certain . . ."

I pushed past her into the house. The housekeeper yelled after me. I went from room to room, shouting my son's name. The house was large with high minimalist decor, good art, sleek modern furniture. I dashed up a flight of steps, and poked my head into a large master bedroom, then headed down a corridor, stopping dead when I saw . . .

A nursery.

Not just any nursery. It was identical to the one we had at home. The same wallpaper. The same crib and wardrobe and chest of drawers. The same revolving night light that played a lullaby as it turned. The same colorful mobile suspended above the crib. It was as if his room had been picked up and transposed completely to this house. And it made me realize the extent of the planning that had gone into this operation.

The housekeeper came rushing in, furious, unnerved.

"You leave now, or I call the police."

"I'm leaving," I said.

I'd asked the driver to wait for me outside.

"I'd like to go back to Putney now."

Halfway there, however, I realized that I had run off without any cash.

"I need to stop at a cash machine, please," I said.

We pulled up in front of a NatWest machine on West Hill—possibly the ugliest section of road in South London. I fed in my card, hit the numbers, and was greeted with the following message on the screen:

> This account has been closed. Please contact your local
> branch should you have any further queries.

Instantly I refed the card into the machine and pressed the necessary numbers, and once again read:

> This account has been closed. Please contact your local
> branch should you have any further queries.

Account closed? He couldn't have . . .

I rifled through my wallet until I found an AmEx card that I held jointly with Tony. I fed it into the machine. I punched in the PIN. I read:

> Card No Longer Valid.

No, no, *no*. I saw the driver glance at me with concern. I checked my purse. My net liquid worth was £8.40—and the round-trip fare was bound to be at least £20. I tried my own account, into which my *Boston Post* salary used to be paid. It had been largely depleted over the last few months, since I was no longer employed by the *Post*. Whatever remaining funds were left over from the paper's final payout to me had been transferred to our joint account—to help cover the mortgage and also pay for some of the final renovations to the house. But I was still hoping that there might be a little cash left in it—so I punched in the PIN requesting £200. The screen message read:

Insufficient Funds.

I tried £100. The message read:

Insufficient Funds.

I tried £50. Bingo. Five ten-pound notes came sliding out toward me. My new liquid worth was £58.40.

Actually, it was £36.40 by the time I paid off the driver.

Back at the house, I rang the bank. The customer service representative confirmed that the joint account I held with Tony had been closed down two days ago. Ditto our shared Visa card—though the good news was that the outstanding balance of £4,882.31 had been paid off. How kind of him.

"What about any outstanding funds in the joint account?" I asked. "Where did they end up?"

"There were no outstanding funds. On the contrary, there was an overdraft of £2,420.18 . . . but it's also been cleared."

"Let me ask you something: don't you need the written permission of both parties to close down a bank account?"

"But the account was always in Mr. Hobbs's name. He just added you as an adjunct signatory ten months ago."

An adjunct signatory. It said it all.

I tried to reason all this through. Tony quits his job. Jack's nursery is exactly replicated in the house of that Dexter woman. And our bank accounts are both closed, after debts of around £7,300 are paid off.

What the hell was going on here?

"Don't you get it?" Sandy said after I called her and horrified her with a detailed account of my London homecoming. "He's met some rich bitch. And the way he's set the whole thing up makes it pretty damn clear that he wanted you to find out about the whole setup straight away. I mean, he could have used your own address in the court order. Why didn't he?"

"I don't know."

"Maybe because he wanted you to know immediately about his new life. I mean, imagine if he had just disappeared with Jack, without letting you have his new address. You'd have the cops on his tail. This way . . . you know exactly what's happened . . ."

"But not *why* it's happened."

"To hell with *why*. He's taken Jack. You've got to get him back. But the first thing you've got to do is find a lawyer."

"I'm waiting for someone to call me back."

"How are you going to pay for it?"

"Remember the bonds Mom and Dad left each of us?"

"Mine were cashed in long ago."

"Well, I'm about to do the same. They should be worth around ten thousand dollars now."

"That's something, I guess."

"But if I don't have any other income . . ."

"One thing at a time. Get on to the lawyer. Now."

"Right," I said, suddenly feeling exhausted.

"More important, do you have some friends in town who can look after you?"

"Sure," I lied. "I've left a couple of messages."

"Bullshit," she said. And then her voice cracked. "Jesus, Sally—this is horrible."

"Yes," I said. "It is."

"And I wish I could jump on a plane right now . . ."

"You've got enough to cope with."

"You won't do anything stupid . . ."

"Not yet."

"Now you have me scared."

"Don't be."

But the truth was: I had me scared too.

I called back Virginia Ricks at three that afternoon. I was connected to her voicemail. I left a message. I called back at five PM. This time, I was connected to her secretary again.

"Like I told you before," she said, "she's out at court all day."

"But it is urgent. Genuinely *urgent*. And I desperately need . . ."

I broke off, covered the mouthpiece with my hand, and started to sob. When I was finally able to speak again, I discovered that the line was dead.

I called back. Now I found myself on voicemail again.

"It is absolutely imperative that you get Ms. Ricks to call me back as soon as possible."

But I received no further calls for the rest of the day. Or night. Except for Sandy who rang at six PM London time and then again at ten PM to check up on me.

"No news at all?" she asked.

"I've been waiting by the phone all night. For what, I don't know."

"You did try Tony's cell phone again?"

"Only about five more times. It's locked onto voicemail. Which means it's pointless continuing. He's screening all his calls."

"But you'll still keep trying?"

"What other option do I have?"

"You should go to sleep."

"It's an idea, yeah."

I took two sleeping tablets with my end-of-the-day dose of antidepressants. Around three that morning, I jerked awake—and the silence of the house seemed cavernous. I walked into the empty nursery. I could hear the voice of Ellen Cartwright—the hospital therapist—telling me over and over again, *It's not your fault . . . it's not your fault.*

But I knew better. I was the architect of my own disaster. I had nobody to blame but myself. And now . . .

Now I was desperate for a friendly, reassuring voice. So, at eight that morning, I rang the private number that Ellen gave me, "in case of any emergency," as she said at the time. Well, this definitely qualified as an emergency, which meant I hoped she'd be sympathetic about the earliness of the call.

But I didn't speak to Ellen—instead I got her answering machine, which informed me that she was on annual leave and would be back three weeks from now.

Three weeks. I couldn't last three weeks.

I made myself some tea. I ran a bath. But I was terrified of getting into the bath, out of fear that Tony would ring and I wouldn't hear the call. And the phone was on the far side of the bedroom—well away from the bath, which meant that it might take me a good seven rings before I reached it, by which time I would have missed the call, and then . . .

All right, this was completely manic logic—*I could find an extension cord and move the phone closer to the bath, right?*—but I couldn't latch on to any sort of logic just now. I was in the deepest trouble imaginable—and the same damn question kept replaying itself inside my head: *what can I do now?*

Once again, the answer was: *nothing . . . until the lawyer calls.*

Which she finally did around nine-thirty that morning. From her cell phone, stuck somewhere in traffic. Her voice was crisply cadenced, upper-class.

"Sally Goodchild? Ginny Ricks here. My secretary said you called yesterday. Something urgent, yes?"

"Yes, my husband's vanished with our son."

"Vanished? Really?"

"Well, not exactly vanished. While I was out of the country, he got a court order giving him custody of my baby . . ."

"You know," she said, cutting me off, "this is probably best discussed face-to-face. How are you fixed at the end of the week . . . say Friday around four PM?"

"But that's two days from now."

"Best I can do, I'm afraid. Lots of divorcing couples right now. So Friday it is then, yes?"

"Sure."

"You know where to find us?"

And she gave me an address in Chancery Lane.

When Margaret called me that afternoon for a transatlantic update, I mentioned that I had managed to get an appointment with someone from Lawrence and Lambert.

"Well, that's a start."

"But she can't see me for two days, and . . . I don't know . . . maybe I'm prejudging her on the basis of one fast phone call, but her tone was so damn supercilious."

"They're all a bit like that," she said.

"Alexander doesn't know of anybody else over here?"

"I can ask him again, but by the time I get back to you it will be to-morrow, and by the time you call the firm and get an appointment . . ."

"All right, point taken."

"Don't you have some friends there who can point you toward some lawyer they know?"

Here was that question again: *don't you have friends in London?* The long answer to which was: *I arrived here pregnant. A few months later, I ended up being confined to quarters with high blood pressure. Since then . . . well, let's not go through that happy scenario again. So, no—I've found no toehold here whatsoever. And it's all my own fault.*

"No—I really don't know many people around town."

"Hey, don't beat yourself up over that," she said. "It took me more than a year to meet anyone in London. It's that kind of a town."

"I'm desperate to see Jack," I said.

More than desperate. It was an actual physical ache.

"I can't even begin to imagine . . ."

"Don't say it . . ."

The next forty-eight hours were hell. I tried to stay busy. I cleaned the house. Twice. I called my old bank in Boston, asked them to cash in my bonds, and wire the entire amount over to me. I took my antidepressants with metronomic regularity—and often wondered if this pharmacological compound was keeping me in check; if, without it, I would have already descended into complete mania. Somehow I was managing to push my way through the day. I even called back Tony's secretary and apologized for the scene at Wapping the previous day.

"There's absolutely no need for an apology," Judith Crandall said. "I understand completely."

"But do you understand why Tony quit?"

A silence. Then, "Sally . . . it's not that I am unduly loyal to Tony, it's just . . . I don't think it's my business to involve myself in your business."

"But Tony told you about my . . . illness . . . didn't he?"

"Yes, he did mention that you had been . . . unwell."

"So you did know a certain amount about my business. Which means you also must know something about the woman he's vanished with."

"This is very awkward . . ."

"I just have to make contact with him. What he's doing is so unfair."

"I'm sorry, Sally. But I just can't help you here."

I phoned Tony's deputy, Simon Pinnock. He was similarly evasive (and just a little mortified) to be cornered like this by the shunned wife of his ex-boss.

"I really don't have a clue why he did what he did," he said, the nervousness showing.

"Come on, Simon," I said. "I think you do."

"If you'll excuse me, I'm being called into conference . . ."

I even tried ringing Tony's long-estranged sister—whom I'd never met (they'd had a falling-out over something he wouldn't discuss with me), and who now lived in East Sussex. It took some dogged online digging in the phone book to find her number. She didn't particularly want to talk with me either.

"Haven't spoken to Tony in years—so why should he call me now?" she said.

"It was just a long shot."

"How long have you two been married now?"

"Around a year."

"And he's already abandoned you? That's fast work, right enough. Mind you, I'm not surprised. He's the abandoning sort."

"You mean, he's done this before?"

"Maybe."

"That's not an answer."

"*Maybe* I feel I don't need to give you an answer. Especially having adopted that tone with me . . ."

"I didn't adopt a tone."

"Yes, you did. And it's not like I know you or anything . . ."

"Well, if I've offended you, I'm very sorry. And . . ."

"Don't feel like talking to you anymore."

And the line went dead.

I hit my hand against my forehead, congratulating myself on another tactical diplomatic victory. My inborn American inability to couch things in coded language caused me to strike out every time. Hadn't I learned anything in my months here?

I vowed to be on my absolute best behavior when I met Virginia Ricks the next day. I took the tube to Chancery Lane well in advance of our appointed time, and loitered for an hour in a Starbucks until three-thirty arrived.

The offices of Lawrence and Lambert were in a narrow-terraced town house, sleekly renovated inside. There was a security man on the door—who made me sign in and checked that I did have an appointment upstairs. Then I headed up in the elevator to the third floor and stepped out into a pleasant, modern reception area, with chrome furniture and copies of all the daily papers on the coffee table. While the receptionist phoned Virginia Ricks, I sat down and absently glanced through them, deliberately shunning the *Chronicle*.

Around five minutes later, a young woman in her early twenties came out. Blond. Big hair. Slutty suit.

"You Sally?" she asked. "I'm Trudy. We spoke yesterday. Doing all right?"

"Uh fine, yes."

"Great. But listen, Ginny's still tied up in court. Now we could re-schedule the whole thing for Monday . . ."

"I really need to see her today."

"Understood. And the good news is, she should be back at around four-thirty. So . . ."

I killed an hour in a branch of Books Etc on Fleet Street, then picked up another coffee and sat on a bench in Lincoln's Inn, shivering with the chill, chasing another two antidepressants with my latte, thinking that there is always something strangely comforting about a square like this one in the midst of a city—how it gives you a sense of enclosure and shelter.

Virginia Ricks was in her late twenties. As I expected, she was blond, slightly horsey in the face, but immaculately polished: the sort of woman who spent a good hour putting herself together in the morning before showing her face to the world. But what immediately struck me about her was a certain noblesse oblige manner—a slightly flippant superiority, no doubt taught to her at a young age by the kind of upscale parents who masked their own doubts behind an overweening public face.

"Ginny Ricks," she said, hurrying into the conference room into which I had been ushered, proffering her hand. It was now almost five o'clock. As she settled herself into the chair opposite mine, she kept up a steady, nonstop line of chat.

"So sorry to be so late. Ghastly day in court. It's Sally, right? Trudy fix you up with some tea, I hope? Hope she didn't take you aback, our Trude. A bit Estuary for some of my clients' taste—but she's brilliant with all the soccer players' wives we always seem to be representing. Puts them right at their ease, for some curious reason. So now, you have my complete, uninterrupted attention . . . though we will have to curtail things in about a half hour. Ghastly Friday night traffic again. Know the Sussex Downs, do you? Perfect romantic weekend spot, if you're . . ."

But she stopped herself.

"Oh, dear," she said, half-laughing to herself. "Can you believe such rubbish? So sorry. Well now, let's make a start. You were recommended to us by . . . ?"

"Alexander Campbell."

"Sorry, never heard of him."

"He ran Sullivan and Cromwell's London office for three years."

"But he never had business with our firm?"

"No—he just told me, through his wife, that you were the best divorce lawyers in London."

"Quite right too," she said. "And I presume that, because you're here, you want to get divorced."

"Not precisely," I said. And then I quickly took her through the entire story, right up to the bombshell court order. Ginny Ricks asked to see the order. I handed it over. She speed-read it.

"Evidently your husband got his barrister to convince a sympathetic judge that you were an unfit mother, and to grant this temporary order. Which, in turn, raises the unpleasant, but most necessary question: were you, in your opinion, an unfit mother?"

I shifted uneasily in my chair because I was aware that Ginny Ricks was now studying me with care.

"I don't know," I said.

"Well, let me ask you this: did you ever physically abuse your child? Shake it when it was crying, toss it across the room, that sort of thing?"

"No. I did get angry once or twice . . ."

"Nothing unusual there. Parents often get angry at children and say angry things. But words *is* cheap, as you Americans love to say."

Actually, we don't love to say that.

"As long as you didn't physically harm your child, we're on strong ground here. And during your stay at St. Martin's . . . you were never committed, were you?"

"No—it was a voluntary stay."

"No problem then. Postnatal depression is so common these days. Though we will naturally investigate what evidence they used against you, the way I see it, your husband really doesn't have much of a case."

"Then how did he get this court order?"

"You were out of the country, and his legal team obviously put together a case against you, in which it was argued that the safety of your child was at risk . . . oh, by the way, is it a boy or a girl?"

"His name's Jack."

"Well, they probably chose a judge who was known for his misogynist credentials—and as you were not represented at the hearing, he heard just what they wanted him to hear . . ."

"But could he rule against me like that without listening to my side of the story?"

"With the alleged safety of the child in question . . . absolutely."

"But does this mean that, for the moment, I'm barred from seeing Jack?"

"I'm afraid so. The good news, however, is that this *ex parte* order can come to an end at the next hearing, which is fixed for ten days' time—which means that we have just five working days, not counting both weekends, to build our case."

"Is that enough time?"

"It has to be."

"And do you also think you might be able to find out who this Dexter woman is?"

"Ah yes, the *femme fatale*." Another of her giggles. "Sorry—bad joke. But yes, that shouldn't take much effort. Now—just a little spot of housekeeping. My fees are £200 an hour, I'll need to put an assistant

242 • DOUGLAS KENNEDY

onto this immediately to help me with the research, and she'll cost around £50 an hour. Then we will also have to instruct a barrister, though that'll only be for the hearing itself. So, say a £2500 retainer to get us started . . ."

I was prepared for such an initial sum, but I still blanched.

"Is that a problem?" she asked.

"No, I have it. However . . ."

I then explained about him stopping the bank accounts, and what the guy at NatWest told me.

"But if you never insisted on a proper joint account . . ." she said, with a little supercilious shrug.

"I *thought* it was a joint account."

"You're obviously a very trusting person."

"What about him trying to sell the house?"

"You are joint owners, right?"

"So I thought."

"We'll search the land registry and check who owns the house. Anyway, if you put money into the house you'll get it back on divorce. And if you get to keep Jack, you'll probably get to keep the house . . . or, at least, while he's still at school."

"And when it comes to getting some sort of support from my husband . . . ?"

"That's Monday's job," she said, glancing at her watch. "So, Monday morning—we'll need the retainer and a list of assorted health care professionals and people who know you who can vouch for your good character and, most tellingly, your relationship with your son. That's critical . . ."

She pulled over a calendar, opened it, and glanced down a page.

"Now Monday's rather ghastly . . . but shall we say four forty-five?"

"Isn't that late in the day, if we only have this week to build the case?"

"Sally . . . I am trying to fit you in at a time when I really shouldn't be taking on any more clients. Now if you feel you can do better elsewhere . . ."

"No, no, Monday afternoon is fine."

She stood up and proffered her hand. I took it.

"Excellent. Until Monday then."

Later that night, while talking with Sandy, I said, "She strikes me as a bit young, but ultra-arrogant . . . which might be a good thing under the circumstances. She certainly seems to know what she's doing."

"Good, because you need a bitch in your corner. And she sounds like she fits the bill."

The weekend was endless. On Monday morning, I went to the bank. The American money had arrived. I bought a sterling bank check for £2,500. This left me with just under $6,000—or around £4,000 . . . which I could certainly live on for a bit, as long as my legal bills didn't spiral beyond the initial retainer fee.

I brought this concern up with Ginny Ricks later that afternoon. Once again, I was kept waiting more than a half hour, as she was "tied up" with another client.

"So sorry about that," she said, breezing in.

I showed her the list of contacts I'd drawn up. There were only four names: Dr. Rodale, Ellen the therapist, my GP, and Jane Sanjay, the health visitor. I mentioned that Ellen was out of town. "Don't worry— we'll track her down," Ginny Ricks said. She also wondered out loud if there was a friend in town—preferably English ("It will play better in front of the judge, show you've found a footing here, that sort of thing")—who could vouch for my good character.

"You see, Sally, before the next interim hearing next week, we will already have submitted witness statements to the judge. So the more people who have positive things to say about you as a mother . . ."

"I've only been a mother for a few weeks," I said.

"Yes, but surely there are some chums here . . ."

"I've only been in the country a few months. And I haven't really met many people . . ."

"I see," Ginny Ricks said. "Well . . . I'll have one of our researchers get cracking on the witness statements today. One last thing: you did bring the retainer, I hope?"

I handed over the bank check and said, "If there's any way we could keep costs within that £2,500, I would greatly appreciate it. My resources are fairly limited."

"We'll do our best," she said, "but if we do need to track people down and the like, it will run up things."

"Right now, I have exactly £4,000 to my name, no job, no bank account."

"I understand your position," she said, standing up. "And, no doubt, we'll be speaking in the next few days."

But the next person I ended up speaking with from Lawrence and Lambert was one of their assistants. Her name was Deirdre Pepinster. She also spoke in the same horsey voice affected by Ginny Ricks—yet with a "this is so *boring*" inflection that made me uneasy.

"Now I've been trying to reach this Ellen Cartwright for the past two days . . ."

"But I told Ginny Ricks that she was out of town."

"Oh, right. Anyway, turns out she's on some hiking trip in Morocco—and is completely out of contact until the week after next. And Jane Sanjay, your health visitor, is on extended leave of absence. Canada, I think. Won't be back for four months at least."

"Any chance of tracking her down?"

"It might run up the bill a little more."

"I could take care of it. Especially as she liked me. And I think she'd say nice things . . ."

"Leave it with me."

"And I'm sure I could also find out lots about the woman who's now with my husband . . ."

"Let us handle that as well. We too need her background information."

"But it's more hours on the clock, isn't it?"

"We want to do the most thorough job possible."

I didn't hear from her again until the end of the week.

"Right," she said. "The woman in question is named Diane Dexter. Home address: 42 Albert Bridge Road, London SW11. She also owns a house in Litlington, East Sussex, and an apartment on the Rue du Bac in Paris . . . which is a pretty nice part of Paris, not that Litlington is shabby either. Very handy for Glyndebourne . . . on whose board she sits."

"So, she's rich."

"Quite. Founder and chairman of Dexter Communications—a midsized, but highly successful marketing company. Privately owned. Very highly regarded. She's fifty, divorced, no children . . ."

Until now, that is.

"Any idea how or when she met my husband?"

"You'd have to hire a private detective for that. All I've been able to find out is the basic details about her."

"So you don't know where they are now?"

"That wasn't part of my brief either. But I did get a witness statement from your GP and from Dr. Rodale, who treated you at St. Martin's."

"What did she say?"

"That you had been suffering from 'pronounced postpartum depression,' but responded well to the antidepressants. That was about it, actually. Oh, and I found out what happened at the *ex parte* hearing. Seems you threatened the life of your son one evening . . ."

"But that was sheer exhausted anger."

"The problem is, you said it to your husband's secretary. Which means that a third party heard it. Which, in turn, means that there's third-party evidence. The other problem is that they essentially demanded a hearing by telephone on a Saturday night in front of a judge named Thompson who notoriously sides with the father in cases involving the mental health of the mother, and was presented with this evidence in conjunction with your extended stay in the psychiatric wing of St. Martin's. And you were also out of the country at the time, which, no doubt, they used to make you appear frivolous . . ."

"But I was at a funeral . . ."

"The judge didn't know that. All he knew was that you were a clinically depressed woman who had threatened to kill your baby, and then left the country at the first possibility. And as it was only a two-week order, I'm certain he had no problem signing it. Sorry . . .

"Now, back to the witness statements. On the health visitor front . . . it seems that Ms. Sanjay just left the place she was staying in Vancouver and has hit the road, traveling around Canada, but won't be back in the UK for around four months."

"Maybe she has an internet address?"

"You don't have it by any chance?"

I stopped myself from letting out an exasperated sigh.

"No—but if you call the local health authority . . ."

"Fine, fine, I'll follow it up," she said, sounding bored.

"And could you ask Ginny to call me, please. The hearing's next Tuesday, isn't it?"

"That's right. All our witness statements have to be with the court by close of business on Monday."

Which meant that she only had the weekend to track down Jane Sanjay by email . . . if, that is, Jane stopped in some internet café to check her email this weekend, and if the less-than-engaged Ms. Pepinster bothered to even find her address.

I waited by the phone all day Friday for a call from Ginny Ricks. None came—even though I did leave two messages with Trudy.

"Sorry, but she's left for the weekend," Trudy said when I called the second time. "But I know she'll be calling you as soon as she gets back from the country on Monday."

Ah yes, another weekend in the country—no doubt with her "chap," who was undoubtedly named Simon, and probably was an old Harrovian who now "did something in the City," and spoke in the same honk as his beloved, and favored Jermyn Street tailoring, and weekend casual by Hackett's, and no doubt had a lovely cottage on the Sussex Downs, so handy for those summer evenings at the opera at Glyndebourne, where Diane Dexter was on the board, and would be showing off her new acquisition(s) when this year's season . . .

I got up and went into the kitchen—to a small shelf in a cabinet where we kept assorted cookbooks and a London A-to-Z, and a UK road atlas. Litlington in East Sussex was around seventy miles from London—and an easy run from Putney. Before I could stop myself, I phoned information and asked if there was a listing for a Dexter, D., in Litlington, East Sussex. Sure enough, there was such a listing. I wrote it down. For around a half hour, I resisted the temptation to pick up the phone. Then I went back to the kitchen bookshelf and dug out a British Telecom guide to their digital phone services, discovering that if you wanted to make a call and not have your number traced (or appear on the other person's digital display), all you had to do was dial 141.

But it took another hour—and that evening's dosage of antidepressants—to screw up the courage to make the call. Finally, I grabbed the phone, punched in 141, then the number, covered the mouthpiece with my hand, and felt my heart play timpani as it began to ring. On the fifth ring—just as I was about to hang up—it was answered.

"Yes?"

Tony.

I hung up, then sat down in a chair, wishing that I was allowed to mix alcohol with my antidepressants. A belt of vodka would have been most welcomed right now.

Hearing his voice was . . .

No, not heartbreaking. Hardly that. In the week or so since this nightmare began, the one thing I felt toward my husband was rage . . . especially as it became increasingly clear that he had been hatching this plot for a considerable amount of time. I kept reviewing the last few months in my mind, wondering when his liaison with this Dexter woman began. Trying to fathom where he met her, whether it was a *coup de foudre*, or was she the predatory type who swept down on a man who (as I well knew) was fantastically weak and easily flattered. I thought back to all of Tony's late evenings at the paper, his occasional overnight trips to Paris and the Hague, and that wonderfully extended window of opportunity when I was doing time in the psychiatric unit: all those weeks when his wife and child were conveniently being looked after elsewhere, and he could do whatever he wanted, wherever he wanted.

The shit. That was the only word for him. And in the midst of my insane distress about being separated from Jack, my clear, ferocious fury at my husband provided a strange sort of equilibrium, a balance to the guilt and anguish that were otherwise eating away at me like the most virulent form of cancer.

But hearing his voice on the phone was also like one of those out-of-nowhere slaps across the face that shake you out of a stupor and force you to confront the grim reality of your situation. Before this call, there was a part of my brain that was still trying to carry on as if this were really not happening. It wasn't exactly denial (to use that hateful term), more something like extreme disbelief, underscored by a fairyland need to convince yourself that, any moment now, this entire sick black farce will end and your former life will be restored to you.

Now, however, there was no sidestepping the hard, cold facts of the matter: he was living in her house, with our son. And he had put into motion the legal machinery to separate me from Jack.

I had another bad, sleepless night. At seven the next morning, I rang Budget Rent-A-Car and discovered that they had a branch in the parade of shops near the East Putney tube station. When they opened at eight, I was their first customer, renting a little Nissan for the day—£32.00 total, as long as I had it back by eight the next morning. "Mind if I pay cash?" I asked. The clerk looked wary—but, after checking with a superior, he said that cash would be acceptable as long as they could make an imprint of my credit card, just in case there were any additional charges. I handed over my maxed-out Bank of America Visa card and hoped I was well on the road when—and if—they ran a credit check on it.

My luck held. He simply ran the card through his old manual machine, then had me sign several rental forms, and handed me the keys.

Traffic was light all the way south. I made the market town of Lewes in around ninety minutes—and stopped to ask directions to Litlington. It was another fifteen minutes southeast—past gently rolling fields and the occasional farm shop. Then I turned right at a sign marked Alfriston/Litlington, and found myself entering a picture postcardy image of Elysian England. I had driven into a well-heeled fantasy, of the sort that only serious money could buy. I knew I was looking for a house called Forest Cottage. I got lucky—driving down a particularly winding road, my eyes glancing at every small house sign, I noticed the plain painted marker half buried in some undergrowth. I braked and started to negotiate the steep, narrow drive.

Halfway up this avenue, the thought struck me: *what am I going to do when I get to her house? What am I going to say?* I had no planned speech, no strategy or game plan. I just wanted to see Jack.

When I reached the top of the drive, I came to a gate. I parked the car. I got out. I walked to the gate and looked up at the pleasant, two-story farmhouse around a hundred yards away. It appeared as well maintained as the manicured grounds surrounding it. There was a newish Land Rover parked by the front door. I decided that I would simply open the gate, walk up the drive, knock on the door, and see what would happen. There was a delusional part of me that thought: *all I need to do is show my face, and Tony and this woman will be so ashamed of what they've done, they'll hand over Jack to me on the spot . . .*

Suddenly, the front door opened and there she was. A tall woman. Very elegant. Good cheekbones. Short black hair, lightly flecked with gray. Dressed in expensive casual clothes: black jeans, a black leather jacket, a designer variation on walking boots, a gray turtleneck sweater . . . all of which, even from a distance, radiated money. And strapped around her neck was one of those baby slings, in which sat . . .

I nearly shouted his name. I caught myself. Perhaps because I was just so stunned by the sight of this woman—this *stranger*—with my son slung across her chest, acting as if he were her own child.

She was heading toward her Land Rover. Then she saw me. I didn't know if she'd ever been shown a photograph of me—but as soon as she caught sight of me at the gate, she knew. She stopped. She looked genuinely startled. There was a long, endless moment where we simply looked at each other, not knowing what to say next. Instinctively, she put her arms around Jack, then suddenly pulled them away, realizing . . .

What? That she had committed the ultimate theft, the most despicable form of larceny imaginable?

My hands gripped the gate. I wanted to run up to her and seize my son and dash back to the car and . . .

But I simply couldn't move. Maybe it was the wallop of what I was seeing, the absolute horror of watching that woman cradle my son. Or maybe it was a paralytic sort of fear, coupled with the disquieting realization that if I overstepped the boundaries here—and created a scene— I would simply be giving them further ammunition against me. Even being here, I knew, was an insane tactic . . . and one that might rebound on me big time. But . . . *but* . . . I had to know. I had to see for myself. And I had to see Jack. And now . . .

She suddenly turned away from me, heading back to the house, her gait anxious, her arms clutching Jack again.

"Tony . . ." I heard her shout. And I was gone. Hurrying back to the car, throwing it into reverse, making a fast U-turn, and shooting back down the drive. When I glanced in the rearview mirror, I could see Tony standing beside her, watching my car disappear.

I drove nonstop out of Litlington and back to the main road, pulling over into a rest stop, cutting the engine, placing my head against the steering wheel, and not being able to move for a very long time.

After around ten minutes, I forced myself to sit back up in the seat, turn the ignition key, put the car into gear, and head back toward London. I don't remember exactly how I got there. Some basic autopilot took over. I made it back to Putney. I dropped the car back at Budget, garnering a quizzical look from the clerk behind the desk when I handed in the keys so early. An hour later, I was lying on my bed at home, having taken double the recommended dose of antidepressants, feeling it deaden all pain, rendering me inert, inoperative for the rest of the day. That night, I also took double the dose of sleeping pills. It did the trick—comatose for eight hours, up in a fog until dawn. At which point, I started the double-dosing of antidepressants again.

And then it was Monday, and the phone was ringing.

"It's Ginny Ricks here," my lawyer said, sounding terse, preoccupied. "Sorry we couldn't chat on Friday—another ghastly day in court. But just to bring you up to speed on everything—Deirdre has finished all the witness statements, which we are lodging at court this afternoon. I'll be instructing the barrister today, and the hearing's at the high court tomorrow morning at ten-thirty. You know where that is, don't you?"

"Well . . . uh . . . I'm not . . ."

"The Strand. Can't miss it. Ask anyone. And I'll have Deirdre positioned just outside the main entrance to spot you coming in. We'll be outside the courtroom somewhere within the building. And I presume you have something smart but simple to wear. A suit would be best. Black even better."

"I'll see what . . . sorry, I . . ."

I lost track of the sentence.

"Are you all right, Sally?" she asked, sounding a little impatient with my vagueness.

"Bad night . . ." I managed to say.

"Sounds like a desperately bad night. And I hope you'll ensure that you have a far better night tonight—because, though you will not be called upon to testify tomorrow, the judge will be looking you over, and should you seem somewhat out of it, that will definitely raise concerns. And additional concerns are about the last thing we need right now."

"I promise to be . . . there," I said.

"Well, I should certainly hope so," she said.

Sandy had been away all weekend with her kids at a friend's house on the Cape—so we hadn't spoken. Immediately she could hear the fog in my voice. Immediately she guessed that tranquilizers were being taken in excessive amounts. I tried to reassure her. I failed. She pressed to know if something further had happened to tip me into this Valley of the Dolls state. I couldn't tell her about the weekend visit to East Sussex—and the sight of Jack in the woman's arms. Part of it was due to the fact that, beneath my druggy haze, I felt so ashamed and humiliated about having gone down there in the first place. But I also knew that Sandy herself was still in a desperately fragile state. Her sadness and regret—the sense of loss for a man whom she had so clearly adored, even after he discarded her like a broken-down armchair—were both poignant and unnerving. And I knew that she would obsessively worry for the next twenty-four hours if I revealed the reality of my current mental state. Not, of course, that she wasn't terrified about the outcome of tomorrow's hearing.

"You must call me the moment you've heard the judge's decision. What did your lawyer tell you today?"

"Not much. Just . . . well, we'll see, I guess."

"Sally—how many antidepressants are you taking right now?"

"The recommended dose."

"I don't believe you."

"Why would I . . ."

I shut my eyes as yet another sentence lost its way somewhere between my brain and my mouth.

"Now you're really scaring me," she said.

"Think, I dunno, maybe one too many earlier."

"Well, don't take any more for the rest of the night."

"Fine."

"You promise me?"

"You have my word."

Of course, I popped one shortly thereafter. I didn't need sleeping pills that night—because the extra dosage of antidepressants packed a sucker punch. But then, at five that morning, I snapped back into consciousness, feeling toxic, feverish, ill. Like someone who had just crashed out of an extended flight in the druggy stratosphere . . . which, indeed, I had.

I sat in a hot bath for an hour, a steaming washcloth over my face for most of the time. I dried my hair, I ignored the haggard face in the mirror, I went into the kitchen and made a pot of coffee. I drank it all. Then I made another pot and drained it too. When I returned to the bathroom and attempted damage control with the use of pancake base and heavy applications of eyeliner, my hands were shaking. Toxicity, caffeine overload, terror. The most oppressive terror imaginable. Because I was about to be judged—and though I kept telling myself that Ginny Ricks knew what she was doing, I still feared the worst.

I dressed in my best black suit, and touched up my face with a bit more pancake to mask the dark rings beneath my eyes. Then I walked to the tube. On the District line to Temple, I fit right in with the morning rush-hour crowd—I was just another suit, avoiding eye contact with my fellow passengers in true London fashion, stoically dealing with the overcrowded train, the cloying humidity, the deep indifferent silence of the citizenry en route to work. Only, unlike them, I was en route to discover whether or not I'd get to see my baby son again.

I left the tube at Temple and walked up to the Strand. I was an hour early (I certainly couldn't afford to be late for this event), so I sat in a coffee bar, trying to quell my nerves. I didn't succeed. I had been warned by Ginny Ricks that my husband might not show up at the hearing ("he's not bound by law to be there—and can let his legal team handle everything for him") but even the outside chance that he might make an appearance terrified me. Because I didn't know how I'd react if brought face to face with him.

At ten-fifteen, I approached the high court and walked up the steps. A young woman—plain, bespectacled, in a black raincoat over a simple gray suit—was waiting by the entrance doors. She looked at me questioningly. I nodded.

"Deirdre Pepinster," she said with a nod. "We're this way."

She led us through security to a large vaulted marble hall. It was like being in a church—with high vaulted ceilings, shadowy lighting, the echo of voices, and a constant parade of human traffic. We said nothing as we walked through the hall and then down assorted corridors. This was fine by me as I was becoming increasingly nervous. After several turns, we came to a door, outside which were several benches. Ginny Ricks was already seated on one of them, in conversation with an anemic looking man in his forties, dressed in a very gray suit.

"This is Paul Halliwell, your barrister," Ginny Ricks said.

He proffered his hand.

"I've just received the witness statements this morning," he said, "but everything seems to be in order."

Alarm bells went off in my head.

"What do you mean, you just received the statements?" I said.

"I meant to call you about this late last night," Ginny Ricks said. "The barrister I'd instructed fell ill . . . so I had to find a substitute. But really, not to worry. Paul is very experienced—"

"But he's just looking at the statements now—"

We were interrupted by the arrival of the other side. At first sight, they were like an identikit version of my team: a thin, gray man; a big-boned blond woman, exuding high maintenance—a few years older than Ginny Ricks, but very much graduates from the same noblesse oblige school. They all seemed to know each other—though, as I quickly realized, the gray man was Tony's solicitor, whereas the "to the manor born" blonde was his barrister. I watched her watching me as she spoke with the others—the occasional cool sideways glance, during which she was sizing me up, taking the measure of me, putting a face to all that she had been told about me.

Paul Halliwell came out and pulled me aside.

"You know that this is merely an interim hearing, which you are not obliged to sit through, as it can be a bit stressful."

"I have to be there," I said, wanting to add, *Unlike my husband, who's sent others to do his dirty work for him.*

"Fine, fine, it's obviously better, because the judge knows you really care about the outcome. Now, I'm just going to have a quick read of all this," he said, brandishing the witness statements, "but it does seem very straightforward. The report from the doctor at hospital is the key here. Very encouraged by your progress, and so forth. About the fact that you threatened your baby . . . I presume you were tired, yes?"

"I hadn't slept in days."

"And you never in any way physically harmed your son?"

"Absolutely not."

"That's fine then. The key here is that there was nothing violently aberrant in your behavior toward your baby that would convince the court you pose a risk to the child . . ."

"As I told Ginny Ricks . . ."

On cue, she poked her head into our conversation and said, "I've just been told we're starting in five minutes."

"Fear not," Paul Halliwell said. "It will all be fine."

The courtroom was a paneled Victorian room with leaded windows. The judge had a large chair at the front. Facing him were six rows of benches. Tony's team sat on one side of the courtroom, his barrister in the first bench, the solicitors behind him. My barrister sat in the same bench as Tony's, but on the opposing side of the court. I sat in the second row with Ginny Ricks and Deirdre. They informed me that, at this sort of hearing, the barristers didn't have to wear wigs and the judge wouldn't be in robes.

"Nice suit, by the way," Ginny Ricks whispered to me as we waited for the judge to arrive. "He'll immediately see that you're here—which speaks volumes about the fact that you so want your son back. And he'll also see that you're not some harridan, but eminently respectable and—"

The court clerk asked us to stand as the judge was due to arrive. A side door opened. He walked in. We all stood up. His name was Merton and he was noted for taking care of business in a brisk, no-nonsense manner.

"In the great scheme of things, he's not the worst," Ginny Ricks told me before he came in. "I mean, considering the number of genuine misogynists who could be hearing the case, we're rather lucky. He's old school but fair."

He certainly looked old school. A seriously tailored black suit, silver hair, a patrician bearing. He asked Tony's barrister to "open" the case, which she did in about two minutes, telling the judge who the parties were and explaining the background to the first *ex parte* hearing. The judge then said that he'd read the statements and that he just wanted to hear submissions.

Paul Halliwell stood up first, his diminutive height and off-the-peg grayness suddenly making him look a little shabby in front of the thoroughbred on the bench. But he spoke in a clear, moderately thoughtful voice, and from the moment he kicked off his submission with the words "My Lord" he narrated my side of the story with straightforward clarity and no lapses of concentration. The terrifying thing was, he was essentially winging it (how could he do otherwise?)—like one of those rent-a-chaplains at the local crematorium who insert the name of the deceased into the preordained service. At least here, he managed to sound reasonably convincing, but the argument he presented wasn't really an argument, merely a repetition of the facts.

"As Ms. Goodchild's attending psychiatrist, Dr. Rodale, states in her deposition, Ms. Goodchild responded well to treatment and rebonded well with her child. As to the claim that she informed her husband's secretary that she would kill her son . . . uh . . ."

He had to glance at one of the statements.

". . . her son Jack . . . the fact is that at no time did Ms. Goodchild ever actually physically harm her son. And though her comment may have been somewhat extreme—and one which Ms. Goodchild deeply regretted from the moment she uttered it—it is important to take into account the fact that, like any new mother coping with an infant, Ms. Goodchild had been suffering from extreme sleep deprivation which, in turn, can cause anyone to say excessive, unfortunate things in exhausted anger . . . which have no bearing whatsoever on the loving relationship that she has with her son. I would hope as well, My Lord, that the court will take into account the fact that this comment was made when my client was suffering from postpartum depression, which is a most common and fiendish medical condition, and which can make an individual temporarily behave in a manner completely out of character. Once again, I refer My Lord to the statement of Dr. Rodale . . ."

A few sentences later, he wrapped it up with the comment that it struck him as cruel and unusual punishment that my son be taken away from such an eminently respectable woman as myself—"a former distinguished journalist"—because of one angry comment spoken while "trapped within the horrendous mental labyrinth that is depression," a labyrinth from which I had now emerged back to "completely functional normality." And surely, how could the court keep a child from its mother, given the lack of any violent behavior on my part?

I judged it a rather good performance, considering the fact that he had been handed the role only minutes before curtain up. And I was pleased that he underlined the cruel extremity of the order against me— surely a sensible, no-nonsense judge like Merton would have to see the truth in such an observation.

But then Tony's barrister stood up. Ginny Ricks had told me that her name was Lucinda Fforde, and little more. Perhaps because she already knew something that I didn't . . . but was certainly about to find out. Fforde had the predatory instincts of a pit bull.

And yet, her voice—like her demeanor—was the apogee of culti-vated reasonableness. She sounded so calm, so concerned, so certain. And devastatingly precise when it came to undermining everything about me.

"My Lord, my client, Mr. Anthony Hobbs, would be the last to dis-pute the fact that his wife was once a distinguished journalist with the *Boston Post* newspaper. Nor would he dispute the fact that she has been through a serious psychological illness, through which he supported her with great sympathy and understanding . . ."

Oh, please.

"But the issue here is not about Ms. Goodchild's one-time profes-sional standing or the fact—clearly documented by her psychiatrist— that she is gradually responding to pharmacological treatment for her postpartum depression. No, the issue here is about the welfare of her son Jack—and the fact that, through her actions of the last few weeks, Ms. Goodchild has raised severe doubts about both her ongoing mental stability and her ability to cope with a young infant without endanger-ing its safety."

And then she brought out the heavy artillery.

"Now, My Lord, you will note from the witness statement by Ms. Judith Crandall—who was Mr. Hobbs's secretary at the *Chronicle*—that Ms. Goodchild rang her husband at the newspaper several weeks ago and said—and this is a direct quote—'Tell him if he's not home in the next sixty minutes, I'm going to kill our son.' Thankfully, Ms. Goodchild did not make good on this threat, and though her counsel can certainly argue that this heinous comment was made under duress, the fact, My Lord, is that all women dealing with newborn children suffer from sleep deprivation and its attendant lassitudes, but the vast majority of women do not threaten to kill their children, no matter how fatigued they might be. More tellingly, though one might be able to forgive one such outburst made in exhausted anger, the fact that Ms. Goodchild made such a comment twice . . ."

I heard myself saying, *"What?"* Immediately, every eye in the court was upon me, most tellingly that of the judge, who looked at me with care.

Ginny Ricks jumped in before he could say anything.

"Apologies, My Lord. That will not happen again."

"I should certainly hope not," he said. Then turning back to Lucinda Fforde, he said, "You may continue."

"Thank you, My Lord," she said, calmness personified, especially as she now knew that she had me. "As I was saying, Ms. Goodchild's threat to kill her child was not simply a one-off event. Following the delivery of her son, Ms. Goodchild was hospitalized in the Mattingly, during which time her postpartum behavior became increasingly erratic, to the point where, when her son was in the pediatric intensive care unit of that hospital, she was overheard by one of the nurses telling her husband—and this is another direct quote from one of the witness statements that My Lord has before him: 'He *is* dying—and I don't care. You get that? I *don't* care.'"

Ginny Ricks looked at me, appalled. I hung my head.

"However, not only did she publicly proclaim her lack of interest in whether her son lived or died, she also was seen by one of the nurses in the hospital to physically yank her infant son off her breast while feeding him so that the nurse was genuinely concerned about whether or not she might hurl the child onto the floor. Once again, My Lord, this is documented in the witness statements, taken by the nurse in question—a Miss Sheila McGuire, who was worked in the Mattingly for the past five years.

"You will also note a witness statement from the eminent obstetrics consultant, Mr. Thomas Hughes, who states, very clearly, that he became increasingly concerned by Ms. Goodchild's repeated emotional outbursts in hospital. As Mr. Hughes clearly notes in his witness statement: 'From the outset, it was clear to me that Miss Goodchild's mental condition was quickly deteriorating, to the point where myself and my colleagues at the hospital voiced private concerns about her ability to cope with the ebb and flow of postpartum care for her son.'"

The ebb and flow of postpartum care . . . I was being eviscerated with lethal ease.

"Sadly, the concerns of Mr. Hughes and his colleagues proved justified, as shortly after her release from hospital with her son, she was prescribed sedatives by her general practitioner to help combat the insomnia she had been recently suffering. Her GP had specifically warned her *not* to breast-feed her child while taking these sedatives. Shortly thereafter, however, her son was rushed to hospital in an unconscious state, having ingested tranquilizers from his mother's breast milk. And upon arrival at St. Martin's Hospital, the staff were so concerned about Ms. Goodchild's mental state that they admitted her to the psychiatric unit, where she remained for nearly six weeks—as she spoke not a word and refused all food for the first few days of her stay."

I found myself putting my hands over the top of my already lowered head, like someone protecting themselves from a series of repeated incoming blows.

She now moved in for the *coup de grâce*—talking about how Mr. Hobbs was the distinguished foreign correspondent for the *Chronicle*, who had just resigned his position as foreign editor to look after his son full-time . . .

Once again, I wanted to scream, *"What?"* but restrained myself. I was in enough trouble right now.

She then explained that Ms. Dexter was the founder and chairman of one of the most influential marketing companies in Britain, soon to be floated on the London Stock Exchange. She listed her real estate holdings, her chairmanships of assorted well-known companies, and the fact that she was planning to marry Mr. Hobbs as soon as his divorce was finalized.

"Most tellingly, from the outset of this familial crisis, Ms. Dexter has taken it upon herself to ensure Jack's safety and his well-being. To this effect, she has hired a full-time nanny to look after him—in adjunct to his father who, as I mentioned before, has demonstrated his deep commitment to fatherhood by giving up his position at the *Chronicle* to be with his son at the start of his life.

"There is no doubt that Mr. Hobbs and Ms. Dexter will provide the sort of loving, secure environment in which Jack will flourish. There is also no doubt that, though Ms. Goodchild may be responding well to pharmacological treatment, there are still large question marks over her ongoing stability, as proven by the fact that just two days ago, she arrived unannounced and uninvited at the gates of Ms. Dexter's weekend home in East Sussex—a most disturbing visitation, and one which contravened the *ex parte* order issued against her a fortnight ago.

"In conclusion, may I emphasize that neither Mr. Hobbs nor Ms. Dexter wish Ms. Goodchild ill. On the contrary, her estranged husband is deeply distressed by her current debilitated state. Nor was there any malicious or vengeful agenda behind his decision to seek an *ex parte* order against his wife . . . which was done *solely* to protect their child from further harm. His relationship with Ms. Dexter had already been well established before this decision was made. He simply felt that, unless he moved their son out of direct physical contact with Ms. Goodchild, he could be subject to further jeopardy. Ms. Dexter not only provided shelter for Jack, but also round-the-clock nursing care. Considering that she is not the child's mother, her behavior at this critical time can only be regarded as exemplary."

And then, suddenly, it was all over. Or, at least, Lucinda Fforde had thanked His Lordship and sat down. The judge then said he would retire to consider his decision and asked us all to return within twenty minutes when he would give judgment. Deirdre Pepinster nudged me to stand up as he himself rose and left. But I could barely make it to my feet.

Lucinda Fforde and the solicitor came down the right-hand side of the court, avoiding me as they walked by. Paul Halliwell followed.

"I'm sorry," he said. "But I can only play the hand I'm dealt."

Then he too left.

I sank down in the seat again. There was a very long pause. Then Ginny Ricks said, "You actually went to that woman's country house this weekend?"

I said nothing.

"And why didn't you tell us about the sleeping pills incident? Or the threats you made against your child? I mean," I heard Ginny Ricks say, "if you had been direct with us, we could have—"

I stood up.

"I need to go to the ladies' room."

I headed out, but my knees started buckling. Deirdre Pepinster was there to catch me.

"Steady on," she said.

"Stay with her," Ginny Ricks said in a voice so dismissive it was clear that they now considered me to be completely damaged goods—to be jettisoned from their lives twenty minutes from now, when this entire embarrassing episode was behind them.

I wanted to tell her what an incompetent Sloaney little bitch she was. Remind her how she failed to garner all the necessary facts from me, how she treated my case like an addendum to her ultra-busy life, how she failed to instruct my barrister until ten minutes before the hearing (and I don't care if he was a last-minute substitute—she could have found a replacement last night), and how she was now trying to blame me for her complete slipshodness.

But I said nothing and allowed Deirdre Pepinster to help me into the restroom, whereupon I locked myself in a cubicle, fell to my knees, and spent five long minutes divesting my stomach of its entire contents.

When I emerged from the stall, Deirdre Pepinster regarded me with nervous distaste, looked at her watch, and said, "We'd best be getting back."

I managed to swill some tap water around my mouth before we left. When we reached the court, I saw a look pass between Deirdre and Ginny Ricks.

Then the court clerk announced the entry of the judge. We all stood up. The side door opened, the judge walked in. He sat down. So did we. After clearing his throat, he began to speak. He spoke nonstop for just five minutes. When he was finished and the courtroom was empty, Ginny Ricks leaned over to me and said, "Well, that's about as bad as it gets."

TEN

THE JUDGE DIDN'T look at me as he talked. He seemed to be speaking to some nether place, located on the floor just beyond his desk. But his crisp voice was aimed directly at me.

His "judgment" was brief and to the point. After due consideration, he saw no reason to change the initial *ex parte* order—and therefore he was allowing this custody order to stand for the next six months, until the final hearing regarding residence could take place. However, he was adding a few provisos to the original order. Though he concurred that the safety of the child was paramount, he also ordered that "the mother be allowed weekly supervised contact at a contact center within the borough of her residence." He also commissioned a CAF-CASS report, to be filed five weeks before the final hearing, which he fixed for six months' time, "at which time the matter will be decided once and for all."

Then he stood up and left.

Lucinda Fforde leaned over and proffered her hand to Paul Halliwell. From the brevity of the handshake and the lack of conversation between them, I could sense that this was a mere end-of-hearing formality. Then she and her attorney hurried off, a quick nod to Ginny Ricks, hearing finished, job done, on to the next human mess. My barrister had a similar approach. He packed up his briefcase, picked up his raincoat, and left hurriedly, muttering "We'll be in touch" to my solicitor. Even though he had only been parachuted into the case today, he too looked decidedly embarrassed by the outcome. Nobody likes to lose.

Deirdre Pepinster also stood up and excused herself, leaving me and my lawyer alone in the court. That's when she sighed a heavy theatrical sigh and said, "Well, that's about as bad as it gets."

Then she added, "Like Paul Halliwell, I've always said about cases like these: I can only play the hand I'm dealt. And I'm afraid you've dealt me a busted flush. Had I only known . . ."

I wanted to respond to her—to tell her exactly what I thought of her. But I kept myself in check.

"I just need," I said, my voice shaky, "a translation of what the judge just said."

Another weary sigh. "A residence order is exactly what it sounds like. The court decides with whom the child should reside—and in this instance, the judge has decided to maintain the status quo of the last order. Which means that your husband and his new partner will have custody of your son for six months—which is when there will be what the judge called 'a final hearing,' at which time you will be able to argue your case again and hopefully work out a more favorable custody arrangement. For the moment, however, as he said, you will be granted supervised contact at a contact center—which essentially means a room in some social services office in Wandsworth . . . where you will have an hour to be with your child once a week, under the supervision of a social worker, who will be there to ensure that the child comes to no harm. CAFCASS stands for Child and Family Court Advisory and Support Service. And the CAFCASS report which he commissioned means that, in the ensuing six months, the court reporter will be investigating your background, and that of your husband and his new partner. And to be absolutely direct about it, given the case they have compiled against you, I honestly don't see how you will be able to change the court's opinion. Especially as, by that time, the child will be overwhelmingly settled with his father and his new partner. Of course, should you wish to instruct us to take the case . . ."

I raised my head and stared directly at her.

"There is absolutely no chance of that," I said.

She stood up, gave me another of her supercilious shrugs, and said, "That is your prerogative, Ms. Goodchild. Good day."

I was now alone in the courtroom. I didn't want to move from this spot. A court had declared me an unfit mother. For the next six months, my sole contact with my child would be a weekly sixty minutes, with some social worker standing by in case I went psycho. And Ginny Ricks was right: given the evidence stacked against me—and given the wealth and hyper-social standing of Ms. Dexter—the chances that I would be granted custody of Jack, or even permitted to see him on a regular, unsupervised basis, were around nil.

I had just lost my son.

I tried to fathom that—to reason it out in my head.

I had just lost my son.

I kept playing that phrase over and over again in my head. The enormity of its meaning was still impossible to grasp.

After ten minutes, the court usher came in and told me I would have to leave. I stood up and walked out into the street.

I made it to the Temple underground station. When the train came hurling down the platform, I forced myself against a wall and clutched onto a waste bin—to ensure that I didn't pitch myself under it. I don't remember the journey south, or how I got back to the house. What I do remember is getting to the bedroom, closing all the blinds, unplugging the phone, stripping off my clothes, getting under the covers, and then realizing that, though I could try to block out the world, the world was still there, beyond the bedroom window, indifferent to my catastrophe.

Not having a clue what to do next, I stayed in bed for hours, the covers pulled up over my head, wanting the escape of oblivion, yet being denied it. This time, however, I didn't find myself hanging onto the mattress as if it were the sole ballast that was keeping me from going over the edge. This time, though I felt an intense, desperate grief, it wasn't overshadowed by a feeling of imminent collapse or a downward plunge. I didn't know if it was the cumulative effect of the antidepressants or some chink in the armorlike depressive veil. All I realized was that I wasn't sinking any longer. My feet were on terra firma. My head was no longer fogged in. The view ahead was clear—and thoroughly dismal.

So I forced myself out of bed, and forced myself to take a hot-and-cold shower, and forced myself to tidy the bedroom, which had become something of an uncharacteristic dump over the last few days. When I broke down—a wave of sobbing that hit me shortly after I finished hanging up the last pair of cast-aside jeans—I didn't find myself falling into oblivion. I was simply convulsed by sadness.

I plugged the phone back in around four. Immediately it rang. It was Sandy. From the sound of my voice, she knew the outcome. But when I detailed the findings of the judge—and the supervised access I would have to Jack—she was horrified.

"Jesus Christ, it's not like you're an axe murderer."

"True—but they certainly gave their barrister enough ammunition to depict me as someone who was on the verge of catastrophe. And I certainly didn't make life easier for myself by . . ."

"Yeah?"

And then I told her about my weekend trip to the country, apologizing for not informing her before now.

"Don't worry about that," she said, "though you should know you can tell me anything . . . like *anything*, and I won't freak. The thing is, surely the court must have been sympathetic to the idea that you just *had* to see your son—which isn't exactly an abnormal instinct, now is it? And, like, it's not as if you pounded on their door at three in the morning, wielding a twelve-gauge shotgun. You just stood at the gate and looked, right?"

"Yes—but also the barrister representing me hadn't been properly briefed."

"What the fuck do you mean by that?"

I explained about the slapdash approach of my solicitor. Sandy went ballistic.

"Who recommended this bitch to you?"

"The husband of my friend Margaret Campbell . . ."

"She was that American friend living in London, now back in the States, right?"

Sandy certainly had a terrifying memory.

"Yes, that's her."

"Some friend."

"It's not her fault, nor her husband's. I should have researched things a little bit . . ."

"Will you stop that," she said. "How the hell were you to know about divorce lawyers in London?"

"Well, I certainly know a thing or two about them now."

Later that evening, the telephone rang and I found myself talking to Alexander Campbell.

"Hope this isn't a bad time," he said. "But your sister called Margaret at home today, and told her what happened, and how this woman—Virginia Ricks, right?—behaved. And I just want to say I am horrified. Truly horrified. And I plan to call Lawrence and Lambert myself tomorrow—"

"I think the damage has been largely done, Alexander."

"Damage for which I feel responsible."

"How were you to know?"

"I should have checked with other London colleagues about the best divorce firms."

"And I shouldn't have accepted the first lawyer I spoke with. But . . . there it is."

"And now?"

"Now . . . I think I've lost my son."

Margaret also called that night to commiserate, and to say how bad she felt.

"Did they fleece you, those lawyers?"

"Hey, you're married to a lawyer—you know they always fleece you."

"How much?"

"It's irrelevant now."

"How much?"

"A retainer of twenty-five hundred sterling. But I'm sure the final bill will come to more than that."

"And how will you cover it?"

With my ever-diminishing funds, that's how.

In fact, the Lawrence and Lambert bill arrived the next morning. I was right about it running beyond the original retainer—a cool £1,730 above the initial £2,500—every expense and charge laid out in fine detail. I also received a phone call from Deirdre Pepinster. She was as laconic as ever.

"One thing I wanted to raise with you yesterday—but didn't think you needed more bad news . . ."

Oh, God, what fresh hell now?

"I checked the land registry. The house is in both your names . . ."

Well, that's something, I guess.

"But before the hearing yesterday, we heard from your husband's solicitors. Seems he wants to sell it straightaway."

"Can he do that?"

"According to the law, each party who co-owns a house can force a sale. But it takes time and the divorce courts can stop it. Now, if you'd had custody of your child, that would be a different matter altogether. No court would allow the house to be sold under you. But in this situation . . ."

"I get it," I said.

"They have made an offer—a settlement offer, I should say."

"What is it?"

"Uh . . . Ginny Ricks said we won't be representing you from now on."

"That's absolutely correct."

"Well, I'll just fax it to you then."

It showed up a few minutes later—a lengthy letter from Tony's solicitors, informing me that their client wanted to expedite the divorce, and to be as generous as possible under the circumstances. As their client "would be retaining custody of his son," there were no child support issues to deal with. As I'd had an extensive journalistic career before moving to London, his client would argue that alimony was also not an issue here—as I was perfectly capable of earning a living for myself. And as their client had put 80 percent of the equity into the house, he could also expect to receive 80 percent of whatever profit the sale yielded (but given that we only owned the house for seven months, that profit wouldn't be enormous). However, wanting to be generous in this instance, he was offering the following deal: as long as I didn't contest custody, I would, upon the sale of the house, receive not just the £20,000 equity I had invested in it, but the £7,000 for the loft conversion (as I had paid for this myself), plus an additional £10,000 sweetener, plus 50 percent of whatever profit the sale yielded. If, however, I didn't accept this offer, they would have no choice but to take this matter to court, whereupon . . .

I got the point. Settle fast or be prepared for shelling out even more money in legal fees. Money that I simply didn't have right now.

There was one small respite in this otherwise politely couched, but completely threatening letter: I had twenty-eight days to reply to this offer before legal action ensued. Which meant that I could dodge deal-

ing with it for a bit. Especially as I had more pressing concerns to confront right now. Like my severe lack of money. Though I was expecting
an increased bill, there was a part of me that hoped that, given the negative outcome of the case, Lawrence and Lambert might have reduced
their costs. What an absurd idea—and just to pour battery acid into the
wound, their invoice for the additional £1,730 was marked: *To Be Settled
Within Fourteen Days.*

Of course, I wanted to crumple up this invoice and dispatch it to the
nearest circular file. Or find another lawyer and sue Ginny Ricks for complete professional incompetence. But I also knew that if I dodged this
bill, Lawrence and Lambert would not only come after me, but might let
word get around that, not only was I an unfit mother, but a deadbeat to
boot. So I went to the bank that afternoon and bought a £1,730 sterling
draft, and posted it to Lawrence and Lambert, and sat in a coffee bar
on Putney High Street, pondering the fact that my net worth was now
around £2,500—enough to see me through the next few months, as long
as I didn't employ another lawyer to fight the custody case.

I had to admire Tony's solicitors: their offer was ferociously strategic.
Accept our terms and you come out with a little money to get your life
restarted again. Turn us down—and we will embroil you in a legal battle
that you cannot afford, which will end up having the same result: Jack
stays with Tony and that woman.

Of course, there was a significant part of me that wanted to simply
agree to their shitty terms and be done with it—to take the money, and
try to find a new place to live and a job, and attempt to negotiate, over
time, a shared custody agreement. But that would mean Jack growing
up, looking upon that woman as his mother—whereas I would be some
damaged parental adjunct, whom he would eventually come to regard
as the person who had failed him by being unable to cope with motherhood. Judging from their behavior so far, I had no doubt that Tony and
that woman would do their best to poison him against me. But even if,
in due time, they became equitable and fair-minded, I would still have
been legally blocked by them from raising my son. And that was something I simply couldn't accept.

"You don't sound as shaky as I'd expect," Sandy said that night when
she phoned me.

"Oh, I'm shaky all right," I said. "And I find myself crying spontaneously. But this time I'm also angry."

Sandy laughed.

"Glad to hear it," she said.

But my anger was also tempered by the realpolitik of the situation. Legally and financially, I'd been trumped. For the moment, there wasn't a great deal I could do about it . . . except attempt to present an exemplary face to the world.

Which meant, from the outset, adopting a certain mind-set when it came to the social workers at the contact center who were now dealing with me. I could not come across as arrogant or enraged, or someone who believed it was her inalienable right to raise her child. In their eyes, the interim hearing order said it all: I had been declared dangerous to my child's well-being. It didn't matter that facts had been manipulated against me by a very clever barrister, or that I had been suffering from a clinical condition. I couldn't play the blame game here. Like it or not, I had to somehow accept that I was at their mercy.

So when a woman named Clarice Chambers phoned me from Wandsworth Social Services to suggest that my first supervised visit start in two days' time, I agreed immediately to the time she suggested and showed up fifteen minutes ahead of schedule.

The contact center was located in a grim, modern, cinder block building, just off Garratt Lane in Wandsworth. It was situated near a squat ugly tower block called the Arndale Center—which was known locally as one of the easiest places in the borough to score a vial of crack.

Certainly, my fellow unfit mothers at the contact center looked like they had all borne witness to assorted domestic horrors, not to mention the trauma of being legally cut off from their children. There were four of us waiting on a bench in a hallway with scuffed linoleum and dirty concrete walls. My three bench mates were all young. One of them looked like she was no more than fifteen. Another had the sort of zombie eyes and shell-shocked demeanor that made me wonder what controlled substance she was on. The third woman was vastly overweight, and was about to burst into tears at any moment. We said nothing while waiting for our names to be called.

After ten minutes, a woman appeared from a reception area, and said

"Sally Goodchild," then directed me to room 4, straight down the corridor, second door on my right. Walking down toward the room, I felt fear. Because I didn't know how I'd react to the sight of my son.

But he wasn't there when I went in. Rather, I found myself face to face with Clarice Chambers—a large, imposing Afro-Caribbean woman with a firm handshake and a firm smile. I noticed immediately that this room was set up as a nursery—with soft toys, and a playpen, and animal wallpaper that looked forlornly incongruous under the harsh fluorescent lighting and broken ceiling tiles.

"Where's Jack?" I said, my nervousness showing.

"He'll be with us in just a minute," she said, motioning for me to sit down in a plastic chair opposite her own. "I just want to chat with you for a bit before you have your visit with your son, and to explain how this all works."

"Fine, fine," I said, trying to steady myself. Clarice Chambers gave me another sympathetic smile, and then said that I should now consider this day and hour—Wednesday, eleven AM—as my time with Jack. His father had been informed of this fact—and Jack's nanny would be bringing him here every week. She would not be present during these visits—only myself and Clarice. However, if I wished, I could nominate a friend or family member as the supervisor for these visits—but, of course, this individual would first have to be vetted by Wandsworth Social Services to assess their suitability for this role.

"I'm still new in London, so I don't really know anybody who could . . ."

I broke off, unable to continue.

Clarice touched my hand. "That's fine then. I'll be your supervisor."

She continued, explaining how I could bring any toys or clothes I liked for Jack. I could play with him. I could hold him. I could simply watch him sleeping. I could also bottle-feed him, and Clarice would act as liaison between the nanny and myself to find out what sort of formula he was drinking and what his feeding routine was right now.

"The only thing you cannot do is leave the room with him unaccompanied. Nor, I'm afraid, can you be left alone with him at any time. Supervised contact means just that."

Another firm *we're going to get along just fine, aren't we?* smile.

"I know that this is all rather artificial and difficult for you. But we can try to make the best of it. All right?"

I nodded.

"Right then," she said, standing up. "I'll be back in a moment."

She disappeared into an adjoining room and returned a moment later, holding a familiar carrier.

"Here he is," she said quietly, handing him over to me.

I looked down. Jack was fast asleep. But what struck me immediately was just how much he'd grown in three weeks. He'd filled out a bit, his face had more definition, more character. Even his fingers seemed longer.

"You can pick him up if you want," she said.

"I don't want to disturb him," I said. So I placed the chair on the floor beside me, reached down and, using my right index finger, stroked his clenched fist. His hand unclenched, his fingers wrapped around mine, and he held on to me, still sleeping soundly.

That's when I lost the battle I'd been waging ever since I arrived here. I started to cry, putting a hand across my mouth to muffle the sobs and not wake him up. Once I glanced up at Clarice Chambers and saw her watching me with a cool professional eye.

"I'm sorry," I whispered. "This is all a bit . . ."

"You don't have to apologize," she said. "I know this is hard."

"It's just so good to see him."

He didn't wake for the entire hour . . . though his fist did unclutch after around ten minutes, so I simply sat by him, rocking him in his chair, stroking his face, thinking just how serene he was, and how desperate I was to be with him all the time.

Clarice said nothing for the entire hour, though I was conscious of her watching me—seeing how I related to Jack, how I was handling the highly charged emotionalism of this situation, and whether I seemed like a stable, balanced individual. But I didn't try to play to the gallery, or put on a big maternal show. I just sat by him, happy for the temporary contact.

Then, before I knew it, Clarice quietly said, "It's time, I'm afraid."

I gulped and felt tears sting my face.

"All right," I said.

She gave me another minute, then walked over to us. I touched his face with my hand, then leaned over and kissed his head, breathing in his baby powder aroma. I stood up and walked to another corner of the room, staring out a grimy window at a trash-strewn courtyard as she picked up the carrier and left. When she came back, she approached me and asked, "Are you all right?"

"I'm trying to be."

"The first time is always the hardest."

No, I thought. *Every time will be hard.*

"Remember—you can bring clothes and toys for him next week," she said.

As if he's a doll I can dress up and play with for an hour.

I shut my eyes. I nodded. She touched my arm with her hand.

"It will get easier."

I went home. I sat down on the bed and cried. This time, however, the crying wasn't underscored by that physical sensation of plummeting which I so associated with the start of an extended depressive jag. This was simply another ferocious expression of grief—and one over which I had no control.

They say there's nothing like a good cry to expunge all the pent-up sorrow you carry with you. But when I finally brought myself under control, and faltered into the bathroom to splash some water on my face, I found myself thinking: *that did me no good whatsoever.*

I thought: *if I am permanently kept from him, will this ever stop? Will I ever come to terms with it?*

The next six days were bleak. My sleep was broken—despite the on-going use of knockout pills. I had little appetite. I left the house for the occasional foray to the corner shop or Marks and Spencer. I found myself devoid of energy—so much so that when I did go down to St. Martin's Hospital for a consultation with Dr. Rodale, she immediately commented on my wan appearance.

"Well, it's not been an easy few weeks," I said.

"Yes," she said, "I did hear about the court order. I'm very sorry."

"Thank you," I said—though I was silently angry at her for her professional reserve, her refusal to tell me I had been so desperately wronged, especially when she knew that I was incapable of physically harming my child, and that I had been in the grip of a monstrous ailment over which . . .

No, no. I wasn't going to play the *don't blame me* card again. I was simply going to face the reality of the situation and . . .

. . . but why the hell couldn't Dr. Rodale tell me what she must know: that the court decision was so manifestly unfair?

"And how do you feel in yourself right now?"

She had quickly moved us back into the realm of pharmacological questioning. *All right then: you want straight answers, you'll get straight answers.* So I met her gaze and said, "I cry a lot. I find myself angry a great deal of the time. I think what's happened to me is completely unjust and underhanded."

"And those 'downward spirals' you used to describe?"

"They're not so frequent. It's not that I don't get low—I do all the time—it's just that I seem to be able to dodge the black swamp. But that doesn't mean I'm exactly happy . . ."

Dr. Rodale's lips contorted into a dry smile.

"Who is?" she said quietly.

At the end of our interview, she announced herself once again pleased with my progress, and appeared even more gratified by the knowledge that the antidepressants had proved so effective.

"As I told you from the outset, these sorts of drugs take time to build up in the system—and to demonstrate their efficacy. But the fact that you seem to be avoiding the 'black swamp' shows that they have made considerable positive impact. You may not be happy, but at least you're functioning again. Which is good news. So I see no need to alter the dosage for the time being. But on the unhappiness front . . . have you been in touch with Ellen Cartwright?"

Actually, she called me the day after I saw Dr. Rodale, apologizing profusely for being incommunicado when my solicitor's assistant came chasing her for a witness statement.

"The message on my machine was a bit garbled," she said, "so I didn't exactly understand why she needed this statement from me. Something about a court proceeding . . ."

I informed her about that proceeding, and its outcome. She sounded appalled.

"But that's scandalous," she said. "Especially as I could have told them . . . Oh God, now I feel dreadful. But how are you feeling?"

"Horrible."

"Would you like to start our sessions again?"

"I think that would be a good idea."

"Fine then. One thing, though—you know that I just do NHS locums at St. Martin's—and only for anyone who's resident in the unit. So if you want to see me, it will have to be on a private basis."

"And what's the charge?"

"It's £70 per hour, I'm afraid. But if you have private health care . . ."

"We were with BUPA, but I'm pretty sure I've been taken off the policy."

"Well, you should still give them a call, and if you're still covered they will tell you how many weekly sessions they're willing to cover— and for how long. You'll also need a reference from Dr. Rodale—but that will be no problem."

I did call BUPA, the private health insurance company, as soon as I finished speaking to Ellen. The "customer service representative" on the other end of the line asked me for my name, my address, and my policy number. Then, after a moment, she confirmed what I already suspected: "I'm afraid your policy has been canceled. You were insured under your husband's policy—which, in turn, is part of a group company policy. However, he left his job and the policy was canceled. Sorry."

I did some math. Even if I restricted myself to a session a week between now and the full hearing in six months' time, I would still end up paying £1,680 for Ellen's therapeutic service—an impossible sum, given that I didn't have a job. So it looked like I would simply have to make do with my antidepressants and my extended transatlantic phone calls with Sandy.

"You have to find a new lawyer," she said the night I discovered I had been dropped from our private health scheme. "Especially as you're going to have to deal with the house thing very soon."

"Maybe I should just accept his offer."

"No way . . ."

"But it's a no-win situation, no matter what I do. Tony knows this too. And he's got that woman behind him—with all the money they need to break me. Which is what they're certainly trying to do. As much as I'd like to say *climb-every-mountain* stuff like, 'They won't bring me down,' the fact is they can, and they will."

"Whatever you do, don't agree to anything until you get yourself another attorney."

"I can't afford another attorney right now."

"You're going to have to go back to work, aren't you?"

"I *want* to go back to work. I *need* to go back to work. Before I go completely crazy."

I articulated the same sentiment to a Ms. Jessica Law, the CAFCASS reporter, who visited me at home for what she described as a preliminary interview. She was around my age, wearing subdued clothes, wire-rimmed glasses, and a sensibly direct manner. From the moment I opened the door, I could see that she was sizing me up, trying to work me out and see whether all the reports she had undoubtedly read about me tallied with how she herself perceived me. Her early enforced pleasantness—a tone of voice that said, "*Let's try to get through this uncomfortable business as reasonably as possible*"—hinted that she was expecting a harridan, still in the throes of a major psychological rupture. I could also tell that she was taking in everything about my bearing, my manners, my dress sense (well-pressed jeans, a black turtleneck, black loafers), and my material circumstances. She noticed my collection of books and classical CDs, and the fact that I served her real French press coffee.

She then quickly let it be known that this was business.

"Now I know this can't be the easiest of situations for you . . ." she said, sugaring her coffee.

"No, it isn't," I said, thinking: *just about everyone I've met in the social services has used that expression—"this can't be easy for you." Is that an acknowledgment of my so-called "pain," or their way of informing me: but there's even more discomfort to come?*

"I plan to see you two or three times in all before I submit my report. I would normally see you on the first occasion with your husband, but given the sensitivity of the situation, I decided against that in your case. I will see him separately. What I would like to point out is that in no way should our conversations be considered as cross-examinations. You're not on trial here. My goal is simply to give the court an overall picture of your circumstances."

You're not on trial here . . . it's just a little chat. How wonderfully English. I was, without question, on trial here—and we both knew it.

"I understand," I said.

"Very good," she said. She bit into a stem ginger biscuit, contemplated it for a moment before swallowing, then asked, "Marks and Spencer?"

"That's right," I said.

"I thought so. Delicious. Now then . . . I note from your file that you moved to London just under a year ago. So I suppose a reasonable first question might be: how are you finding life in England?"

When I recounted this question to Sandy later that night, she said, "You've got to be kidding me? She actually asked you that?"

"And they say Americans are deficient in the irony department."

"Well, did you furnish her with the appropriate *ironic* answer?"

"Hardly. I was very polite, and moderately truthful—saying that it hadn't been the easiest of adjustments, but that I had also been ill for the past few months and therefore couldn't really judge the place from the standpoint of someone who wasn't yet a functioning part of it. Which is when she asked me if it was my intention to become 'a functioning part of England,' to which I said, 'Absolutely'—reminding her that I had been a journalist before coming to England, and had also been a correspondent here until my high blood pressure bumped me out of my job.

"'I should be able to find work here,' I said. 'Because there's so much journalistic work in London.'

"'So, should you regain custody of your son,' she asked, 'or should the court agree to shared custody, you would plan to raise him in England?'

"'Yes,' I said, 'that would be the plan—because he would then have access to both parents.'"

"Smart answer," Sandy said. "Did your interrogator approve?"

"I think so. Just as I also think she doesn't disapprove of me. Which is something of a start. Still, the critical thing now is to find work—and show that I can once again be a *functioning* member of society."

"But do you think you're actually ready for work? I mean—"

"I know what you're about to say. And the answer is: I have no choice. I need the money, and I also need to show the powers-that-be that I *can* work."

But finding a job proved to be a complex task. To begin with, my professional contacts in London were nominal—two or three newspaper editors whom I'd met during my short stint as correspondent here, and a CNN producer guy named Jason Farrelly, with whom I had become moderately friendly when he did a four-month stint in Cairo around two years ago. He had since been downgraded to the business news ghetto in the London bureau. But he was *the* senior producer of CNN Business News Europe—which meant that making telephone contact with him wasn't easy, as all senior news producers in big bureaus make it a point to be too busy to return your calls. So after leaving five messages, I decided to try my luck with one of the newspaper editors I'd met a few months earlier. Her name was Isobel Walcott. She was the deputy features editor of the *Daily Mail*. I'd taken her out to lunch when I was working on a piece about the decline and fall of London manners, as she had written a jokey little book on the subject. I remembered her as someone who combined a cut-glass accent with a propensity for dropping the word "fuck" into casual conversation; who drank about five glasses of sauvignon blanc too many, but who also told me toward the end of the lunch, "If you ever have a feature idea that might work for the *Mail*, do give me a bell."

Which is what I decided to do now. I even managed to dig out the business card she'd given me, and found her direct number. But when she answered and heard my name, she asked curtly, "Have we met?"

"I was the *Boston Post* correspondent who took you out to lunch a couple of months ago, remember?"

Suddenly, her tone went from abrupt to dismissive.

"Oh, yes, right. Can't really talk now . . ."

"Well, could I call you later? I have an idea or two for a feature, and as you did say that if I ever wanted to write for the *Mail* . . ."

"I'm afraid we're rather top-heavy with features right now. But tell you what . . . email me the ideas and we'll see. All right? Must dash now. Bye."

I did email her the two ideas, not expecting to hear from her.

I expected right.

I also tried phoning someone who worked on the *Sunday Telegraph* magazine—a guy named Edward Jensen, whom I remembered as friendly—and had known Tony when they were both doing journalistic stints in Frankfurt. Once again, I had his direct number. Once again, I wasn't received well. Only, unlike Walcott, he wasn't curt—rather, somewhat nervous.

"You've caught me at a bad time, I'm afraid," he said. "How's Tony?"

"Well . . ."

"Oh, God, how foolish of me. I had heard . . ."

"You'd heard what?"

"That the two of you . . . uh . . . dreadfully sorry. And I gather you've been unwell."

"I'm better now."

"Good, good. But, uh, I'm due in conference any moment. Could I call you back?"

I gave him the number, knowing he wouldn't call me back.

And he didn't.

Judging from his embarrassed tone, it was clear that word had spread through Media London about our breakup. As Tony was the man with all the connections, the world was hearing his side of the story. Which meant that Edward Jensen had evidently been informed that I had gone ga-ga and threatened the life of my child . . . and should therefore be dodged at all costs.

At least, Jason Farrelly finally returned my calls. And, at least, he was outwardly friendly . . . though he made it known pretty damn fast that (a) he was super-busy, and (b) there was absolutely no hope of any work at CNN right now.

"You know the cutbacks we've suffered since the merger. Hell, I'm lucky to be still in a job . . . and, believe me, business news is not my idea of a good time. Still, so great to hear from you. Enjoying London?"

This was the American approach to the dissemination of bad news: be ultra-friendly, ultra-enthusiastic, ultra-positive . . . even though what you were actually communicating was ultra-negative. Whereas the English approach to giving inauspicious tidings was either bumbling mortification or sheer rudeness. Somehow I preferred the latter approach. At least you knew what you were getting—and your expectations weren't raised by a surfeit of false bonhomie . . . like the sort that Jason Farrelly practiced.

"But hey, it would be great to see you, Sally. And you never know, maybe, I don't know, maybe we can find something for you here."

I was suspicious about this last comment, but as it was about the first halfway positive thing that anyone had said to me for a while, I wanted to believe that, perhaps, he could help me out.

"Well, that would be just terrific, Jason."

"One problem," he said. "I'm being dispatched to run the Paris bureau for the next three weeks . . . our head guy there had to rush back to the States after a death in the family . . . so I'm only here for another two days. And my schedule's completely full."

"Well, mine's pretty empty—so if you could just find a half hour . . ."

"Would nine-fifteen tomorrow morning work?"

"Whereabouts?"

"You know a restaurant in the Aldwych called Bank? They do breakfast. I won't have much time. Half an hour max."

I got my one decent black suit dry-cleaned, and dropped £30 I couldn't really afford to spend on a cut and a wash at a hairdresser's on Putney High Street, and showed up fifteen minutes early at Bank. It was one of those ultrachic food emporiums—all chrome and glass and sleek lines and braying well-dressed clients, talking loudly over the din of the action, even at breakfast time. Jason had reserved a table in his name. I was shown to it, and ordered a cappuccino, and read the *Independent*, and waited.

Nine-fifteen came and went. Nine-thirty came and went . . . by which point I was genuinely anxious as I had to be back in Wandsworth at eleven for my weekly supervised visit with Jack. Which meant I simply had to leave the restaurant by nine forty-five. I kept asking the waitress if she'd received a message from him. Sorry, nothing at all.

And then, just as I was calling for the bill, he showed up. It was nine-forty-three. He looked a little frazzled, explaining that the Hang Seng had done this fantastic out-of-nowhere rally first thing this morning, it was a big-deal story, and, well, you know how it is, don't you?

I did—but I also knew that I couldn't stay. At the same time, though, I didn't want to explain to him why I was leaving—and how I was now only allowed supervised contact with my son. I knew this was the one chance I'd have to pitch myself to him, and hopefully garner some sort of employment which, in turn, was crucial in terms of both earning a living and proving to the Wandsworth Social Services that I was a responsible person who could be trusted to bring up her son and attend to his needs.

So I decided to take a risk and splurge on a fast taxi directly to Garratt Lane after the meeting. And I explained to Jason that I really had to leave by ten-fifteen, no later. He ordered coffee, I joined him for a second cappuccino. For the first twenty minutes of our time together, he talked nonstop, telling me about the horrendous internal politics of CNN since the merger, and the number of layoffs, and how nobody who had been made redundant in Atlanta was finding jobs in the "news information sector," and how his ex-boss was now selling books at a local branch of Borders, work was so tight. The situation at CNN Europe, however, was a little better—because all their bureaus were streamlined operations, giving them room to hire freelancers on a short-contract basis.

I breathed a sigh of relief, thinking: *he's going to offer me something.* But then, suddenly, he changed the subject and said, "You know, Janie and I are separating."

Janie was his wife of four years. Like Jason, she was just thirty. Blond, pert, aggressive, and (when I met her in Cairo) already voicing frustration that journalists made such dismal money (she had been a Realtor in Atlanta before her marriage).

"When she met me, she was in her mid-twenties, a Georgia girl who thought it was dead glamorous to have an Ivy League boyfriend who was already a CNN journalist at twenty-five. But she hated the moving around—you remember how she complained all the time in Cairo and then she truly loathed the French when we were in Paris . . . but hey, I can say this now, she's the sort of American who always hates the French. And when London came up, I figured getting her back into the Anglophone world might help the marriage. Boy, was I wrong. The French were like fellow Confederates compared to the Brits. 'The most depressing, ill-mannered, stenchful people I have ever had the misfortune to meet' and please excuse the Scarlett O'Hara accent."

"Did she actually say *stenchful?*" I asked, wanting to sound politely interested, but also becoming increasingly worried about the passage of time. I glanced at my watch. Ten-ten. I had to cut him off, and somehow make my pitch. But now he was going on about how, just three weeks earlier, she'd returned from a fortnight's visit to Atlanta to inform him that she'd fallen in love with her former high school boyfriend . . .

"And no, his name's not Bubba. But it is Brad. And he is one of the biggest property developers in Atlanta, and a keen golfer, and the sort of guy who probably drives a big white Merc, and—"

I cleared my throat.

"Oh, hell," he said, "listen to me running off at the mouth."

"It's just . . . I really have to go in about two minutes."

"How are things yourself?"

"My husband and I broke up."

"You're kidding me. But didn't you just have a kid?"

"That's right. Listen, Jason . . . you know I'm a very adaptable journalist. I've written copy, I've covered wars, I've run a bureau—"

"Sally, you don't have to convince me. Hell, you taught me so damn much those couple of months I was in Cairo. The problem here is lack of budget. I mean, I've been told to cut two staff—"

"But you just said that CNN Europe was hiring freelancers . . ."

"They are. But not, for the moment, in London. If you wanted to try for six months in Moscow or Frankfurt, I'm pretty sure you'd have a very good shot at it."

"I can't leave London," I said.

"Then there's really nothing I can do."

"All I'm asking for, Jason, is something even part-time. Two, three days a week. More if you can—but the thing is: I really need the work."

"I hear you, Sal. And God knows, I'd love to help. But Atlanta has tied my hands in this regard. Anyway, like I told you on the phone, I'm off tomorrow to run the Paris bureau for a month . . ."

I glanced at my watch. Ten-eighteen.

"Jason, I have to leave."

"Hey, no problem. And I'm really sorry. But let's keep in touch, eh? Like don't become a stranger on me, okay?"

"I won't," I said, and dashed for the door.

Outside, the traffic on the Aldwych was flowing freely. But there was a problem. I couldn't find a cab. At least a dozen of the black beasts drove by me—all with their lights off. I waved frantically in their direction, hoping one of them might have forgotten to turn his light on. Not a chance. At ten-twenty-five, I realized emergency action was required, so I started running toward the Embankment Station—a ten-minute stroll at the best of times. My hope was to find a taxi heading down the Strand, and tell him to step on it. Around ten cabs passed me by, all with passengers. My gait now turned into a canter. As I ran, I used my cell to call information, and get the number for the Wandsworth contact center. But the operator couldn't find a specific listing for a contact center under Wandsworth Council, so she gave me the general number for Wandsworth Council. But it rang around twelve times before someone answered and put me on hold, by which time I was at Embankment tube, my suit now drenched with sweat, my expensive hairstyle a shambles, and with only fifteen minutes to get to Garratt Lane. Even if a helicopter had been standing by, it's doubtful I would have made it in time. But I had no choice but to hop the District line and fret like a lunatic all the way to East Putney—cursing Jason for his tardiness, and wasting my time by not being able to tell me over the phone what he already knew: there were no jobs going at CNN London.

And now . . . *now* . . . I was going to be desperately late for my one weekly hour with Jack. All the way south on the tube, I kept trying to use my phone—and managed to get connected to Wandsworth Council for a moment when the train briefly appeared above ground at South Kensington. But then the line went dead.

The next time I had a signal was when I alighted at East Putney station. It was eleven-twenty. I dashed down the steps, turned right and ran directly to a grubby little minicab dispatch office located on a parade of shops on the next street. The dispatch guy seemed a little bemused by my franticness, but he did find me a cabbie (in a battered Vauxhall) who couldn't do much in the way of speed when faced with road works on the Upper Richmond Road, with the result that I finally reached Garratt Lane by eleven-forty.

The receptionist seemed to be expecting me.

"Wait here," she said, then picked up the phone and dialed a number. After a moment, Clarice Chambers came walking down the hall.

"I cannot tell you how sorry I am," I said as I followed her back down toward the contact room. "I was at a job interview in the West End, the guy was late, I couldn't get a cab . . ."

However, instead of turning into the contact room, we veered left and entered a small office.

"Please shut the door and sit down," she said. I did as requested, immediately feeling worried.

"Has something happened?" I asked.

"Yes, something's happened," she said. "You're forty minutes late."

"But I was trying to explain to you . . ."

"I know: a job interview. And judging from your clothes, I'm sure you're telling the truth. But this one-hour period is your sole chance to spend time with your son during the week. And the fact that you've missed the second visit . . ."

"I haven't missed it. I'm here."

"Yes, but I sent your son home with his nanny ten minutes ago."

"You shouldn't have done that."

"But you weren't here, and the child was having a touch of colic . . ."

"Bad colic?"

"Colic is colic. But he was kicking up a bit, and as you weren't here . . . well, it seemed best to send them home."

"But I tried calling."

"I never received a message. I am sorry."

"Not as sorry as me."

"Next week will be here very soon," she said.

"Couldn't we arrange another visit before then?"

She shook her head. "That would be contravening the court order. None of us here can do that."

I shut my eyes. I cursed myself for so botching this up.

"In the future," Clarice said quietly, "it's simply best to keep Wednesday morning completely free. You *have* to be here."

This point was emphasized to me again two days later when Jessica Law came calling on me at home—buzzing me a half hour before her arrival to ask me if I wouldn't mind her dropping by this afternoon. I knew what was coming—a verbal spanking, a "talking to." But Jessica Law didn't go all schoolmarmy on me.

On the contrary, she accepted a cup of coffee and several stem ginger biscuits, and then said, "Now I'm sure you realize why I decided to make this rather sudden visit."

"If I could just explain . . ."

"Clarice did fill me in. And do understand: I am in no way trying to berate you for what was quite evidently a mistake . . ."

"The thing was," I said, "I had this job interview, and it was the only time the man could do it, and he was so late and . . ."

"I have read Clarice's report."

This stopped me short.

"She wrote *a report* about this?" I asked.

"I'm afraid she had to. You didn't make a supervised visit with your son, as specified by a court order. Now you know, and I know, that this happened because of circumstances somewhat beyond your control. The problem is, it is still a black mark against you—and one that your husband's lawyers might try to use against you at the final hearing . . . but you didn't hear that from me, now did you?"

"No, I didn't. But what can I do to try to rectify the damage?"

"Never be late for a visit again. And I will write up a report of my own, stating that we've had this talk, and that you were delayed due to a job interview, and in my opinion, this one bit of tardiness shouldn't be classified as 'irresponsible behavior,' especially as you were seeking employment at the time. How did the interview go, by the way?"

I shook my head.

"Keep looking," she said, her way of telling me that without a job, my chances in the final hearing would be lessened. And given that there was enough going against me right now . . .

But my attempts to find work were fruitless ones. If you're an outsider with few contacts, a vast global city like New York or London becomes an impenetrable fortress when you try to force your way into its economic structure. This is especially true when you have spent your professional life to date breathing the rarefied air of print journalism, but suddenly find yourself outside of your circle of contacts, not to mention your own country. And the great rule of thumb among all would-be employers in the media is always: *when in doubt, discourage.*

Well, I spent the next few weeks being constantly discouraged. I tried all the major American newspapers and networks, using my few contacts at NBC, CBS, and ABC. No sale. I tried the *New York Times,* the *Wall Street Journal,* and even my old stomping ground, the *Boston Post.* Once again, they had their own staffers running their bureaus. And when I called Thomas Richardson, the editor-in-chief of the *Post,* his assistant informed me that he was otherwise engaged, but he would get back to me. This he did a few days later, with a polite, to-the-point email:

> *Dear Sally:*
>
> *As I haven't heard from you in a while, I presume that you will not be taking up our offer of a position back in Boston. Naturally, I am personally disappointed that you won't be returning to us—but wish you well in all future endeavors.*

As soon as I received this email, I wrote him a reply, explaining that, as before, my newborn son was keeping me in London, but would the paper be willing to offer me a freelance contract for a few stories a month from this part of the world? I also played up the years of loyalty I had given to the paper, that I wasn't asking for a staff position, and also intimated (in as subtle a way as possible) that I really needed the work.

Thomas Richardson was always efficient, and his response arrived on my computer a few hours later.

> *Dear Sally:*
>
> *If it was my call, you'd still be one of our correspondents in London. But my hands are tied by the money men—and they are adamant: no additional staff or freelancers at any of our ever-dwindling foreign bureaus.*
> *I'm truly sorry about this.*

So that was that. I had no choice but to start working the British papers again. Here, the problem was that nobody knew who I was (and I certainly wasn't going to play the "I'm Tony Hobbs's estranged wife" card, as it might just blow up in my face). Still, after about a week of nonstop phoning, the features editors I managed to get through to at the *Guardian* and the *Observer* asked for ideas by email and samples of my work. Well, I sent off the requisite clippings and a couple of ideas. A week went by. I made the requisite follow-up phone calls. The editors were otherwise engaged. I followed up with reminder emails. No response. Which is what I expected—as journalism works that way. Especially if—in the eyes of the people to whom you're trying to sell an idea—you're a nonentity.

Even Margaret's husband, Alexander, made a couple of transatlantic calls on my behalf, seeing if there was something for me at Sullivan and Cromwell in London. I sensed that guilt about steering me into the hands of Lawrence and Lambert was behind his efforts on my behalf (that—and Margaret probably screaming at him to redress the mess by helping me out). But as I told Alexander, I had no skills that would be of use in a law firm. His colleagues in London concurred. I was neither a legal secretary nor a legal writer, nor did I possess any qualification at all that allowed me to practice as an attorney. So all I could do was thank Alexander for his efforts on my behalf and tell him to stop feeling guilty about the incompetent Ginny Ricks. It wasn't his fault.

But if the job search was bearing nothing, at least I seemed to be in the good books of my handlers from the Wandsworth contact center. I showed up for my weekly visits fifteen minutes early. Clarice told me that I seemed to be bonding well (that verb again) with Jack, and he was happily awake for all our sessions, which meant that I could feed him, and change his diaper, and try to get him interested in assorted infant toys, and hold him close, and wish to God that I didn't have to hand him back at the end of the hour. I resolved not to cry anymore during these sessions, deciding that I needed to show a certain stability and equilibrium in front of Clarice, to prove that I was dealing with the enforced separation from my son, even though it was agony. But as soon as the session was over I would walk slowly out of the building, my head bowed, and stumble out into the gray, litter-strewn shabbiness of Garratt Lane, and find the nearest wall, and put my head against it, and cry like a fool for a minute or so, and then collect myself and try to get through the rest of the day.

At heart, all grief centers around the realization that you can never escape the bereavement that has stricken you. There may be moments when you can cope with its severity, when the harshness temporarily lessens. But the real problem with grief is its perpetuity. It doesn't go away. And though you are, on one level, always crying for the loss you've sustained, you're also crying because you realize you're now stuck with the loss, that—try as you might—it's become an intrinsic part of you, and will change the way you look at things forever.

I didn't mention these cry-like-a-fool postvisitation moments to Jessica Law. All I would tell her was, "I find this situation desperately hard."

She'd look at me with a mixture of professional coolness and personal compassion, and say, "I am aware of that."

What else could she say—that, like a massive migraine, it would eventually abate? It wouldn't. We both knew that. Just as we both knew that—given the evidence stacked against me—the best I could hope for at the time of the final hearing was some sort of shared visitation situation.

"I do hope that you keep your expectations about a future with Jack realistic," she said during our third "chat."

"In other words, I'm not going to get him back."

"I didn't say that, Sally. And a lot could happen in the four and a half months. But the truth is . . ."

She paused, trying to find the right neutral language. I decided to cut to the chase.

"I've been declared an unfit mother—and once that's on the record, it's hard to erase."

"Yes, I'm afraid that's exactly it. But that doesn't mean that an arrangement can't be worked out with the court. It may not be perfect. It may not give you the access you want. But it will be better than what you have now."

After this conversation, I sensed that, in her own circumspect way, she was hinting that she didn't consider me unsuited to motherhood. Just that she was gently compelling me to grasp the reality of my situation. Whereas Sandy kept telling me not to lose hope in order to move forward, Jessica Law was inverting that same sentence: in order to move forward, you have to lose hope.

As I made my way home from my fourth supervised visit with Jack, trudging through the rain down West Hill, the American in me didn't want to accept the pragmatic pessimism that Jessica Law espoused, which struck me as so desperately English. I wanted to embrace that old hoary American fighting spirit. No wonder the English were so privately attracted to the pastoral. It was an antidote to all that hardheaded realism—the recognition that the Elysian Fields were merely the stuff of folklore, undermined by the merciless reality of class, personal limitations, and the crushing purposelessness of life which you must still somehow confront to give order and shape to the day.

Whereas, like most Americans, I was brought up on that stale mythological idea that with hard work and boundless optimism, you could be what you wanted to be—that the world was infinite in its possibilities and there for the taking.

In order to move forward, you have to lose hope.

The entire abstract logic of that statement was anathema to me. But as I turned into Sefton Street—and looked at the tidy terraces of middle-class houses, and saw a nanny loading her infant charge into the baby seat of a Land Rover, and remembered how Jack nuzzled his head against my cheek just ten minutes earlier, and realized that, like it or not, I would have to confront the letter that currently resided in the back pocket of my jeans (a letter from Tony's solicitors, informing me that the twenty-eight-day grace period had passed, and they would now take legal steps within seven days to put our house on the market unless I accepted their financial offer)—I stopped moving. And I suddenly lost all hope.

I sat down on the hood of a car parked outside my house and started to cry again—fully cognizant that I was weeping on the street where I lived, and unable to get myself through the doorway and into the home that would soon be taken away from me.

"Sally?"

It took me a moment to realize that someone had just called my name. Because I wasn't used to being called by my name on Sefton Street. I knew no one there. Except . . .

"Sally?"

I looked up. There was my neighbor, Julia Frank—the woman whom I'd met in Mr. Noor's shop all those months ago. Now standing by me, her hand on my arm.

"Sally . . . are you all right?"

I took a deep breath, and wiped my eyes. "Just a bad morning, that's all."

"Can I help?"

I shook my head.

"I'll be okay. But thank you."

I stood up to leave.

"Cup of tea?"

"Please."

She led me into her house, and down a corridor to her kitchen. She put the kettle on. I asked for a glass of water. I saw her watching me as I pulled my bottle of antidepressants out of my jacket pocket, removed a pill, and washed it down with the water. She said nothing. She didn't try to make conversation. She just made the tea. And arranged cups and saucers, and milk and sugar, and a plate of cookies. She poured me a cup and said, "I don't want to pry, but . . . has something happened?"

"Yes—something's happened."

Pause.

"If you want to talk about it . . ."

I shook my head.

"Fine," she said. "Milk? Sugar?"

"Both, please."

She poured in a dash of milk and one sugar. She handed me the cup. I stirred it. I put my spoon down. I said, "They took my son away from me seven weeks ago."

She looked at me with care. And then I told her everything. She said nothing. She just sat there and listened. When I finished, the tea was cold. There was a long silence. Then Julia asked, "Are you going to let them get away with it?"

"I don't know what to do next."

She thought about this for a moment, then said, "Well, let's find you someone who does know what to do next."

ELEVEN

FROM THE MOMENT I walked into his office, I didn't like the look of Nigel Clapp. Not that he appeared strange or threatening or abnormal. Actually, what first struck me about him was his absolute ordinariness—the sort of guy you would pass on the street and never register. He came across as a truly gray man who seemed like he was born at the age of forty, and had spent his entire life cultivating a gray functionary look, right down to the cheap gray suit he was wearing over a polyester white shirt and a grubby maroon knit tie.

I could have handled the bad clothes, the sallow countenance, the thinning black hair, the light, sleety accumulations of dandruff on both shoulders, and the way he never seemed to be looking at you while talking. *"Don't judge a book by its cover,"* as my wonderful mom (who had a thing about needlepoint mottos) used to say.

No, what really bothered me about Nigel Clapp was his handshake. It was virtually nonexistent—a brief placement of four damp, limp fingers into your right palm. It not only made you feel like you'd been given a dead mullet, but also that the purveyor of this hand had no personality whatsoever.

This perception was exacerbated by his voice. Low, monotonic, with a slightly hesitant cadence. It was the sort of voice that almost forced me to cup my ear to discern what he was saying. Coupled with the permanently stunned expression on his face (one that made him look like he'd just tumbled into an empty elevator shaft), he certainly didn't inspire confidence.

Which was something of a worry—considering that Nigel Clapp was my new solicitor, and my one hope of ever getting my son back.

Why did I end up with Nigel Clapp? Once again, I must recite another of my mother's preferred platitudes:

"Beggars can't be choosers."

Actually, the way I found myself in the offices of Nigel Clapp was courtesy of a process that started in Julia Frank's kitchen. After hearing my story, she called a friend who worked as a deputy editor at the *Guardian*, handling (among other duties) a couple of weekly law pages, which often dealt with family law cases. She outlined my situation, mentioning that I was married to a well-known journalist, but then playing coy about his name. The deputy editor told her that, as I had no income at present, I should qualify for legal aid—and gave her the number of a barrister named Jane Arnold, who specialized in family law cases. Julia called Jane. Who put her in touch with a friend named Rose Truman who happened to be an information officer at the Law Society (the registrar of all solicitors and barristers in England). Rose Truman in turn promised to post me out today a list of solicitors in my area who handled legal aid.

The speed at which Julia negotiated all this was dazzling. It also made me realize how little I understood about the way things worked here.

"Well, that's sorted then," she said, "though I know my friend at the *Guardian* would love me to drop the name of your husband to her."

"I don't want to spread gossip about Tony. I just want my son back. Anyway, as I told you, he's no longer at the *Chronicle*. He's a full-time father who's also probably trying to finish his novel."

"And the smart bastard found a wealthy patroness to subsidize his literary endeavors. I'd put serious money on your little boy being part of the Faustian pact they made."

I stared into my teacup. "That thought had crossed my mind, yes."

"You know what I also think?" she said.

"What?" I said, looking up.

"I think you need a very large drink."

"So do I. But I'm on these pills . . ."

"Are they antidepressants?"

"Well . . . yes."

"What kind?"

I told her.

"Then a large vodka won't kill you."

"How do you know that?"

"Because I was on them during my divorce . . . and also because my sister's a chemist. And she gave me the all-clear for a shot of Absolut every so often. You do like vodka, I hope?"

"Yes, that would be very welcome indeed."

She opened the freezer compartment of her fridge, retrieved the bottle of vodka, then found two glasses and poured out two small shots.

"You sure about this?" I asked.

"It never did me any harm. But, then again, I am from Glasgow."

"You don't sound Scottish."

"Glaswegian parents. Spent my first seven years there, then my father brought us south. Never went back—which probably means I'm completely deracinated."

We clinked glasses. I took a tiny sip. I had forgotten how anesthetizing frozen vodka can be. I allowed the liquid to loll about my mouth for a few moments, before letting it delightfully burn the back of my throat. After it slipped down, I let out a little sigh.

"Do I take that as a sign of approval?" Julia asked.

"You have good taste in vodka."

"It makes up for the bad taste in men," she said, lighting up a cigarette. "You don't mind if I indulge my filthy habit?"

"It's your house."

"Good answer. You can stay."

She downed her vodka and poured herself another small finger.

"May I ask you a direct question?" I said.

"Try me."

"Did you like antidepressants?"

"Enormously. And you?"

"I'd recommend them to anyone having their child taken away from them . . ."

I shook my head, took another small sip of the vodka, and said, "Sorry, that was crude."

"But accurate."

"How long were you on them for?"

"Nearly a year."

"Good God."

"Don't worry. It's not impossible to kick, especially if you're taken off them slowly. But, I must say, anytime these days that I find myself fighting off the black dog, I do think fondly back to my extended anti-depressant interlude."

"What do you use instead nowadays?"

"Marlboro Lights and Absolut—neither of which really has the same efficacy as antidepressants when it comes to dealing with what you're going through, which makes my ghastly divorce seem like a paper cut."

"Paper cuts can be painful. Was your divorce really ghastly?"

"Anyone who says that they had an amiable divorce is a liar. But yes, it wasn't a pleasant experience."

"Had you been married long?"

"Nine years. And though it went through the usual ups and downs during that time, I was just a little surprised when Jeffrey announced he was moving in with this French cutie he'd been seeing on the sly. I think that's the worst thing about discovering a long-term infidelity—being made to feel like such a slow-witted fool."

"Never underestimate the male propensity for the clandestine . . . especially when it comes to sex. Were you devastated?"

"Yes, I was shattered. 'The death of love' and all that. I read some-where—I think it was in some Irish novel—that a divorce is worse than a death. Because you can't bury the bastard—and you know that he's off somewhere else, having a life without you."

"And have you had a life without him?"

"Good God, yes."

"Anyone now?"

She took a deep drag on her cigarette.

"That's a rather direct question."

"I'm a bloody Yank," I said, imitating her accent. "Direct's my thing."

"Well then to be bloody direct about it: yes, there was somebody. But it ended about six months ago."

"I'm sorry."

"I'm not."

She then explained that around the time of her divorce, the small publishers for whom she worked as an editor were gobbled up by a major conglomerate, and she was one of the casualties of this merger-and-acquisition ("They blamed it all on 'economies of scale,' whatever that means"). At the time, she was living with her husband and her son Charlie in a large terraced house in Barnes. As part of the divorce settlement, Charlie resided with her, and she received just enough money to buy this cottage outright in Putney ("which puts me ahead of ninety-eight percent of the population of the planet, so I'm not complaining . . . even if the bastard only gives me £500 a month in child support"). But she had been able to find enough steady work as a freelance editor to pay the bills.

"I make enough to give Charlie and myself a good life. And though I might not have a chap on hand right now, the fact that I still have Charlie for the next few years makes everything . . ."

She stopped and said, "I'm sorry. That was thoughtless of me."

"Don't be sorry. What you said is true. Which is why this is so fucking hard."

"Once that list arrives tomorrow from the Law Society, find yourself a solicitor who's willing to fight in your corner."

"Against a rich woman with a lot of money and a big fat dossier of evidence against me? I doubt any solicitor is going to want to take me on," I said.

But the list arrived, and I discovered two things. Legal aid wasn't entirely free. If you were destitute, with no assets, you could obtain legal representation without charge. But if, like me, you had no income, but did have part ownership of a house, then the system operated more like a loan—in which all the costs you ran up eventually had to be repaid (with low interest, but interest nonetheless) from the eventual sale of said property. In other words, I'd be running up another debt—and one that would probably have to be settled once the house was sold from under me. At least, the legal aid rates were nothing compared with those charged by a private incompetent like Ginny Ricks.

The second thing I found out was that there were more than two dozen solicitors within the borough of Wandsworth who handled legal aid cases. I didn't really know which one to choose, or where to start—so I just began to ring up every name alphabetically.

The first four solicitors on the list were otherwise engaged that morning—and, judging from what their secretaries told me, tied up for most of the week. But when I reached name number five on the list—Nigel Clapp—his secretary said that, yes, he could see me tomorrow at ten-thirty.

But as soon as *I* saw Nigel Clapp, I thought: *no way*. It wasn't just his spiritless appearance that I found disheartening. It was also his office. It was located in another sector of Wandsworth called Balham. As I was car-less and very conscious of costs, I decided to eschew a £10 minicab ride to this eastern corner of the borough, so I walked to the Putney rail station, changed trains at Clapham Junction, then rode two stops south to Balham. The trains were strewn with rubbish. The seats were stained. The carriages themselves were covered with graffiti. And the thing was, even though I still glanced with momentary distaste on such shabbiness, another part of me had come to be inured to such public squalor, to almost expect it as part of the territory. Is that what living in London did to you—make you accept the dilapidated, the shabby, as commonplace?

Balham High Road was the usual mixture of chain stores, and curi-ous commercial left-behinds from the nineteen-sixties (a shop that sold used professional hairdressing equipment), and the occasional signs of encroaching gentrification (designer cappuccino bars, designer modern apartment buildings). Nigel Clapp's office was located above a dry clean-er's in an archetypal redbrick Victorian house. I entered his premises by a door on a side street, a door with old-style frosted glass, on which had been painted the name *Clapp & Co—Solicitors*. I negotiated a con-stricted, ill-lit stairwell, reached another door, and rang the bell. It was opened by a plumpish, matronly woman in her fifties, with what I had come to recognize as a pronounced South London accent.

"You the one here for the death cert?" she asked.

"I'm Sally Goodchild."

"Who?" she said loudly, as if I was a little deaf. I repeated my name again. "Oh, yeah, right," she said. "The legal aid case. Come in. He's busy right now, but shouldn't be too long."

Clapp & Co. comprised two rooms and a small waiting area, which was actually a narrow corridor, with a cheap sofa, two plastic potted plants, and a magazine rack, filled with six-month-old copies of *Hello!* and assorted real estate magazines. The walls were painted a dirty shade of cream, the floors were covered in yellowing linoleum, the lighting was provided by two fluorescent tubes overhead. The sole decoration was a calendar on the wall from a local Indian takeout: *With the Compliments of Bengal House, Balham High Road.* The plumpish woman—Clapp's secretary and general dogsbody—worked in a small cramped office without a door. As I waited in the hallway—idly browsing through a magazine for the local branch of Foxton's Estate Agents, noticing with amazement that you could easily spend £750,000 on a family house around here—she answered a steady stream of phone calls with that brutish voice of hers, while working her way through an open packet of bourbon creams on her desk. After a few minutes, she got up and said to me, "See if he's finally off the phone now."

She walked over to the adjoining door, opened it without knocking, put her head inside it, and said, "Your client is here."

Then I was ushered in to meet Nigel Clapp.

He did stand up when I entered. Then he offered me his dead mullet hand and motioned me into the cheap orange plastic chair opposite his steel desk, and started shuffling through papers, and avoided my gaze. I noticed a couple of framed family photos on his desk, as well as a framed law degree. He must have spent a good two minutes going through my file, saying absolutely nothing, the only noise in the office coming from the traffic on Balham High Road and the stentorian voice of his secretary next door. Clapp seemed oblivious to this high-decibel distraction—the way, I imagined, that people next to a railway track somehow became immune to the constant sound of rattling trains. My file was laid out across his desk. When he finally spoke, he didn't look up from the documents.

"So your former solicitor," he said in a voice so low and hesitant that I had to bend forward to hear him, "she never sought leave to appeal the order of the interim hearing?"

"We parted company immediately after the hearing," I said.

"I see," he said, his voice noncommittal, his eyes still focusing on the papers. "And this business with the house . . . can you remember the names of the solicitors who handled the sale?"

I told him. He wrote it down. Then he closed my file, and reluctantly looked at me for a moment.

"Maybe you'd like to tell me the entire story now."

"When you say 'entire'?"

"From . . . uh . . . I suppose . . . when you first met your husband to . . . uh . . . this morning, I suppose. The pertinent details only, of course. But . . . uh . . . I would just like an overall picture. So I can . . . uh . . . just have an overview, I suppose."

I could feel my spirits tumble even further into despair. This man had the personality of a paper cup.

But still I took him through the complete tale of my marriage—from Cairo to London, to the early problems with the pregnancy, to the postpartum depression, to my extended stay in the hospital, and the nightmare that I had walked into upon returning from Boston. I was absolutely frank with him—telling him exactly how I made angry verbal threats against my son, and my difficult behavior in the hospital after his birth, the sleeping pills incident, my absurd decision to seek out Diane Dexter's country home—in short, everything that Tony's solicitors could use against me.

It took around twenty minutes to get through the entire story. As I spoke, Clapp pivoted his chair in such a way that he was staring at a spot on the wall behind his computer screen. He showed no emotion as I spoke, he didn't interrupt, he didn't react to any of the more dire aspects of the tale. His presence didn't register at all. I might as well have been talking to a goldfish in an aquarium, considering the lack of reaction I was getting.

When I finally finished, there was another considerable pause—as if he didn't get the fact that my narrative was finished. Then, when this dawned on him, he turned back to my file, shuffled the papers together, closed it, and said, "Uhm . . . right then. We have your address and phone number here, don't we?"

"It's on the first page of the forms."

He opened the file again, peered inside, shut it.

"So it is," he said. Then he stood up and said, "Well, uhm, emergency legal aid will be available right now, although a final certificate won't be authorized until the forms have been processed. Anyway . . . uhm . . . we'll be in touch."

This threw me. Surely he was going to answer some questions, give me his legal point of view, speak about my chances in court, hint about the strategy he might adopt, *anything*. But instead, I was offered his dead mullet hand. And I was so flummoxed by this that I briefly squeezed his damp, flaccid fingers and left.

An hour later, I was in Julia's kitchen, accepting another shot of Absolut. I needed one.

"This guy isn't just diffident; he's one of those people who seem to be missing in action while still sitting in the same room as you."

"Maybe that's just his manner," she said.

"Damn right it's his manner—and it's a completely hopeless one. I mean, at first I thought: he's just boring. Or to be more specific about it: he's about the most boring person I've ever met in my life. But then— after taking him through every damn thing that's happened to me for the last six months—what's his reaction? 'We'll be in touch.' And you should have seen this guy during my extended monologue. I'm positive he was doing Transcendental Meditation with his eyes open."

"Are you certain he's not just a little shy?"

"A *little* shy? He came across as *pathologically* shy . . . to the point where I can't see how the hell he's going to make any inroads for me."

"Don't you think you should give him a little time?"

"I don't have much in the way of time," I said. "Less than four months, to be exact. And they don't call that final hearing *final* for nothing. I need someone who can, at the very least, attempt a little damage control here. I don't expect miracles. But he's like one of those freebie attorneys you read about in the States who get appointed to a capital murder case and end up sleeping through the prosecution's summation."

I paused. Julia just smiled at me.

"All right," I said. "Maybe that's just a little melodramatic. But—"

"I know what the stakes are, Sally. I really do. And even though Nigel is your lawyer, I gather that you can get permission from the legal aid authority to change your solicitor if you put forward a good enough reason. So if you have absolutely no confidence in this solicitor, then call up the other solicitors on the list and find out when they can see you."

I did just that the next morning, leaving three messages for three different solicitors. One of them, Helen Sanders, rang back. She didn't have time to see me face to face this week, but would be pleased to speak to me now. So, once again, I spent fifteen minutes telling this woman the entire saga—from beginning to end. Her verdict was stark and uncompromising.

"Whatever about the inherent unfairness of what happened to you," she said, "the sad fact of the matter is: they do have a strong case against you. More to the point, as perhaps other solicitors have informed you, once a child is settled with one parent, the court is loath to relocate him again."

This is exactly what the dreadful Ginny Ricks told me in the wake of the interim hearing disaster. So I asked Helen Sanders, "Are you saying that my case is hopeless?"

"I couldn't make a judgment like that without studying all the relevant documents and court orders. But from what you've told me so far . . . well, I'm not going to lie to you: I can't see how you'll have any chance of winning custody of your son."

She did offer to see me at her office next week, if I wanted to discuss matters further. But I simply thanked her for her time and hung up. What was there to discuss? Mine was a hopeless case.

"You mustn't think that," Julia said after I related this conversation to her.

"Isn't it better to face up to the truth?"

"I'm sure the right solicitor could dig up the right dirt on your husband's relationship with that Dexter woman, and how they set this whole thing up."

"Maybe," I said. "But I really need someone out there now, tracking stuff down, trying to look into Dexter's background to see if there's any dirt worth digging. And three months isn't really much time to pull all that together."

"Don't you have any mega-rich friends who could help you hire a private detective or someone like that to snoop around on your behalf?"

The only people I knew with any substantial money were Margaret and Alexander Campbell. But I felt that if I approached them now, it would seem as if I was demanding something back for referring me to Lawrence and Lambert. Like it or not, that would end things with Margaret. Once you've asked for money from a friend, the friendship is doomed.

"As I told you before, my only family is my sister. She's broke. My parents were schoolteachers. Their only asset was their house—and thanks to what lawyers like to call 'bad estate planning' and the suddenness of their death, their one asset, their house, was largely consumed by the government. Then there was the lawsuit after their death."

"What lawsuit . . . ?"

I paused for a moment, staring into my drink. Then I said, "The one against my dad. The autopsy report found that he was about two glasses of wine over the legal limit. Not a vast amount, but he still shouldn't have been driving on it. And the fact that he hit a station wagon with a family of five in it . . ."

Julia looked at me, wide-eyed.

"Was anyone killed?"

"The mother, who was all of thirty-two years old, and her fourteen-month-old son. Her husband and their two other kids somehow managed to walk away."

Silence. Then I said, "The thing was—the husband of the woman killed . . . he turned out to be an Episcopal minister, and one of those very principled types who really believed in Christian axioms like turning the other cheek and not seeking vengeance. So, when it came out that, technically speaking, my father was driving while intoxicated, he insisted that the whole thing be kept out of the papers, not just for the sake of Sandy and me, but also—he told me later—for his own sake as well. 'There's been enough tragedy already. I don't want public pity, any more than I want to see you and your sister vilified because your father made a mistake.'

"I think he might have been the most extraordinary man I've ever encountered . . . though, at the time, I wondered if his goodness was some sort of posttraumatic disorder. Isn't that an awful thing to think?"

"It's honest."

"Anyway, Sandy and I agreed that we should settle for whatever their insurers demanded. Which was essentially all our parents' insurance policies, the house, and just about everything else. So we both came out of it with virtually nothing. Our own lawyers kept telling us we should fight—that giving them the insurance policies was enough. But we felt so desperately guilty, we handed it all over to the minister and his children . . . even though he actually called me once and said we didn't have to go so far. Can you imagine someone saying that . . . not seeking revenge or retribution? But it convinced us even more that we had to give him everything. It wasn't just penance. It was an act of contrition."

"But you didn't drive the car," Julia said. "Your father did."

I fell silent for a while, wanting not to say any more. But then: "You're right, he drove the car. But before he got into the car, he was with my mom at a college graduation party for me. He was having a great time, talking with all my friends, being the usual nice guy that he was. Late in the evening, I handed him a glass of shitty Almaden wine, and he said he really couldn't handle anything more, and I said—and I remember this so damn clearly—'You going middle-aged on me, Dad?' And he laughed and said 'Hell no,' and downed it in one go. And—"

I stopped. I looked down into the vodka glass. I shoved it away.

"I still can't get over it. All these years later. It's there, every hour of every day. And it's now been with me so long that I just consider it part of my weather system—something that encircles me all the time."

"What did your sister say when she found out?"

"That's the thing—she never did find out. Because I couldn't bring myself to tell her . . ."

"Whom did you tell?"

I didn't answer. Finally she asked, "You never told anyone?"

"I spoke with a therapist about it. But—"

"You never said a word to your husband?"

"I considered telling him around the time I got pregnant. But I thought . . . I don't know . . . I thought Tony would have belittled me for holding on to such guilt. He would have said I was being pathetic. Now I realize that, had I told him, he would have turned this admission against me in a court of law. Not just a misfit mother, but an accessory after the fact to a vehicular manslaughter."

"But hang on—you don't really believe that you *were* responsible for the death of that woman and child?"

"I gave my dad the glass of wine that sent him over the limit."

"No—you just *handed* him the glass and then gently teased him about being middle-aged. He knew he had to drive after the party. He knew how much he'd drunk before you showed up with that last glass of wine."

"Try telling my conscience that. Sometimes I think that the real reason I eventually fled overseas was that I was trying to put as much geography as possible between myself and all that lingering guilt."

"The French Foreign Legion approach."

"Exactly—and it kind of worked for a while. Or, at least, I learned how to cohabit with it."

"Until they took Jack away from you?"

"I guess I'm that obvious. And yes, once this all happened, I was certain that this was some sort of cosmic retribution for causing that accident; that Jack had been taken away from me because I had given my father the drink that made him crash the car that killed a little boy."

Julia reached over the table and put her hand on my arm.

"You know that's not true."

"I don't know anything anymore. During the last few months, all logic's been turned on its head. Nothing makes sense."

"Well, one thing *must* make sense. You are not receiving some sort of divine punishment for your father's accident—because you had absolutely no role in that accident, and because it just doesn't work that way . . . and I speak as a semi-practicing Catholic."

I managed a small, bleak laugh.

"God knows, I wish I'd confessed all this to my sister years ago."

"But what good would that have done?"

"Recently, I've had this enormous need to confess all to her."

"Promise me you'll never do that. And not just because I truly believe that you have nothing to confess. It would just drop all the guilt you've been feeling for all these years right into her lap. And—this is the real Catholic in me talking now—there are many things in life that are far better left unsaid. We all want to confess. It's the most human of needs imaginable. To ask for some sort of absolution for making a mess of things—which everyone before us has done, and everyone afterward will continue to do as well. Sometimes I think it's the one great constant in all human history: the ability to screw it up for ourselves and others. Maybe that's the most terrible—and the most reassuring—thing about life: the fact that everyone's messed up like this before. We're all so desperately repetitive, aren't we?"

I thought about that later, as I sat at home staring at the list of alternative legal aid solicitors, supplied to me by the Law Society. There was an entire section of lawyers dedicated to family law—and all I could think was how, for these specialists in domestic dissolution, all stories must start to overlap or, at the very least, come down to a few basic plot points: *He met somebody else . . . We fight about everything . . . He just doesn't listen to me . . . She feels she doesn't have a life beyond the house and the kids . . . He resents the fact I make more money than him.* And all this dissatisfaction and disgruntlement and disappointment may, in part, be rooted in the usual bad matchups, the usual inability to cohabit. But Julia was right: it also stems from a need for turmoil, for change . . . all of which might be linked to that very human fear of mortality, and the realization that everything is finite. It is this knowledge that makes us scramble even harder for some sort of meaning or import to the minor lives that we lead . . . even if it means pulling everything apart in the process.

I narrowed my new solicitor possibilities down to four names—all of whom I chose because they were located within walking distance of my house. No doubt, they'd all tell me the same thing: *you're in a no-win situation.* But I still had to find someone to represent me during the final hearing. I was about to start phoning up these four candidates, but it was now around five PM on Friday afternoon, which meant that I would either be talking to answering machines or secretaries who were itching to get home, and certainly didn't want to be speaking to a legal aid case so late in the day. So I decided to start working the phones first thing Monday morning—and would now treat myself to an extended walk by the river. I was still reeling a bit from the disclosure I'd made to Julia. But I didn't feel relieved or unburdened. Nor did I take great consolation in what she said. Though others can advise you to divest yourself of all guilt, the ability to do so is always impossibly difficult. The hardest thing in the world is forgiving yourself.

I found my jacket, put on a pair of shoes, and was heading toward the kitchen bowl where I always tossed my house keys when the phone rang. *Damn. Damn. Damn.* A part of me wanted to let the machine take it—because there was a break in the weather, and I really needed an extended stroll in the open air. But being a glutton for punishment, I reached for the receiver.

"Uh . . . I'd like to speak with Ms. . . . uh . . . Goodchild."

Wonderful. Just wonderful. Exactly the man I wanted to hear from late on a Friday afternoon. But I maintained a polite tone.

"Mr. Clapp?"

"Oh, it is you, Ms. Goodchild. Is this a good time?"

"Sure, I guess."

"Uhm . . . well . . ."

Another of his awkward pauses.

"Are you still there, Mr. Clapp?" I asked, trying not to voice my impatience.

"Uhm, yes . . . Ms. Goodchild. And I just want to say that the court hearing went fine."

Pause. I was genuinely confused.

"What court hearing?"

"Oh, didn't I tell you?"

"Tell me what?"

"Tell you that I applied for a court order this morning, insisting that your husband pay the mortgage on your house until the divorce settlement is finalized."

This was news to me.

"You did?"

"I hope you don't mind . . ."

"Hardly. I just didn't know."

"Well . . . uh . . . I just thought, considering that you were being threatened with eviction . . ."

"No need to apologize," I said. "Thank you."

"Uh, sure. Anyway, uh, it seems . . . well, the court decided to preserve the status quo."

"I don't understand?"

"I obtained the order this afternoon at three. And the judge presiding over the hearing . . . well, over the strong objections of your husband's solicitor, the judge decreed that your husband must continue to pay the mortgage until you have worked out a mutually agreed financial settlement."

I couldn't believe what I was hearing.

"Does this mean that the house can't be sold out from under me?"

"Uh . . . that's right. And if your husband doesn't make the mortgage payments, he will be considered in contempt of court. Which means that he could actually be imprisoned for failing to meet his commitments to you."

"Good God," I said.

"One other thing," he said. "His solicitor said that he wants to make an offer vis-à-vis interim financial support for you."

"He *did*? Really?"

"I think he was rather nervous about the idea that, under the circumstances, the judge might instruct his client to pay you a substantial sum a month. So they offered you £1,000 a month in interim maintenance."

"You're kidding me?"

"Is that too low?"

"Hardly. I don't want a penny of it."

"Oh, right. But how about the mortgage?"

"That's different—because the house is a shared investment. But I certainly don't want to be supported by *her* money."

"Well, uh, that's your choice. And if, uh, you want me to continue handling this matter, I will inform them of your decision."

Was he always so self-denigrating? I paused for a nanosecond's worth of reflection, then said, "I'm very pleased to have you in my corner, Mr. Clapp."

"Oh . . ." he said, sounding somewhat bemused. And then added, "Uhm . . . thanks."

TWELVE

I DIDN'T HEAR FROM Nigel Clapp for another week. But he did send me a copy of the court order he obtained against Tony, along with a follow-up letter from Tony's solicitor confirming that his client would continue to pay the mortgage payments on our jointly owned house until such time as a legally binding agreement was reached on the disbursement of mutually owned assets. The letter also confirmed that I had turned down an offer of £1,000 per month in maintenance, and let it be known that, in light of this refusal to accept said offer, his side would enter into no subsequent negotiations in regard to interim maintenance payments until such time as the final financial settlement blah, blah, blah, blah . . .

"You should have taken the money," Sandy said after I read her this letter on the phone. "I mean, he's got his sugar mama covering everything. An extra grand to you a month would have bought you a reduction in financial pressure, and the ability to hire better legal counsel . . ."

"Like I told Clapp: there's no way I'm going to live on her money."

"You and your dumb pride. I mean, welcome to divorce—where the object of the exercise is to stick it to the other party. Which is precisely what the wonderful Tony and his rich bitch are doing to you. Which is why I think you were insane to turn down the dough. You have hardly anything left to live on, and also because, from what you've told me, the legal eagle representing you isn't exactly Mr. High Powered, Mr. Perry Mason. The other side will eat him alive once this goes to trial. And just think of the nonevent he'll entice to be your barrister. I mean, all courtroom lawyers are actors, right? So no big-shot 'actor' is going to work with a cipher like him."

"I think you're being a little hard on the guy."

"Hey, I'm just repeating what you told me."

"True—but that was before he won the mortgage payment thing . . . which, let's face it, has saved me from the street and kept me in the house. And yeah, you're right: he's like dealing with the world's greatest wallflower, which does worry me. But given how that upscale ineptitude at Lawrence and Lambert messed me over, I'm just a little suspicious of high-flying law firms right now."

"But that was just one up-her-ass limey bimbo. Surely there are some excellent divorce lawyers in London."

"Yeah, but I can't afford one now. And you're right—it's my own damn fault for turning down Tony's money. But the thing is: for the first time since this extended bad dream started, I've actually won an argument. And that's due to my very peculiar solicitor. So why turn my back on a guy who's trumped Tony?"

Still, Sandy was right about one point: dealing with Nigel Clapp was like dealing with the number zero. It was impossible to fathom him, or to work out his legal methodology. After his success on the mortgage front, he vanished for seven days. Then, out of nowhere, he made contact with me again.

"Uhm . . . ," he said after I answered the phone.

"Mr. Clapp?"

"I'd like to speak with Ms. Goodchild."

"That's me."

"Really?"

"I'm pretty sure of that, yeah."

"Oh, right. Well . . . uhm . . . names."

"Names?"

"Yes, names."

"I really don't follow you."

"I need the name of everyone who's dealt with you from the social services."

He paused—as if the effort of getting that one sentence out without an *uhm* had been overwhelming. Then he continued. "I also need the names of any nannies or nurses whom you might have used."

"Fine, no problem. Shall I email you them today?"

"Yes, uhm, email is all right."

"You know that my first lawyer took witness statements from just about everybody—with the exception of my health visitor who was in Canada at the time."

"Yes. I know that. Because I have the statements."

"You do?"

"Uhm, yes."

"How'd you get them?"

"I obtained copies of all court documents."

"Sure, sure. But if you've got all the witness statements, why do you need the names of everyone again?"

"Because, uhm . . . well, I would just like to speak with them all again."

"I see," I said. "Is that necessary?"

"Well . . . uhm . . . *yes*, in fact."

Later that day, while reporting this conversation to Julia over coffee in her kitchen, I said, "You know, I think that was the first assertive thing he's ever said to me."

"You shouldn't worry about him so much. He seems to know what he's doing."

Four days later, I was woken up by a phone call around one in the morning. At that hour, the sound of a phone ringing can only mean two things—(1) a drunken wrong number, or (2) very bad news. In this case, however, it was a youngish-sounding woman with a London accent who—judging from the static on the line—was calling from far away.

"Hello, Ms. Goodchild . . . Sally?"

"Who's this?" I asked, half-awake.

"Jane Sanjay."

"Who?"

"Your health visitor, remember?"

"Oh, yes, of course. Hello, Jane. Aren't you supposed to be out of the country?"

"I *am* out of the country," she said. "In Canada. Ever heard of Jasper National Park? Way up in Alberta. Amazing place—and a long way from South London. But listen, your solicitor, Mr. Clapp, tracked me down."

"Mr. Clapp found you?"

"That's right. And he explained what you've been going through—and asked me if I'd be prepared to testify on your behalf. Which, of course, I'm most willing to do, especially as I'll be back working for Wandsworth Council in just over two months' time. But the reason I'm calling—and I can't talk for much longer, as my phone card's about to run out—is just to tell you that I am so shocked that they took Jack away from you. From what he explained to me, they've done a complete stitch-up job on you. He also told me about the postpartum depression—which, in itself, should have got you off the hook. I mean, so what if you said something threatening when you were exhausted and suffering from a clinical condition? So what if you accidentally breast-fed your son while taking sleeping pills? We've had far worse cases in the borough—and I'm talking about genuine child abuse, where the mother still didn't have the child taken away from her. So as far as I'm concerned, this is outrageous. And I just wanted to let you know that I'm completely behind you, and will help in any way I can . . ."

I was so pleasantly stunned—and touched—by this out-of-nowhere transatlantic call that I mumbled a huge thank-you, and asked her to come over for lunch as soon as she was back. Then I called Sandy in Boston and told her the news.

"That is amazing," she said, genuinely excited. "I mean, the fact that she saw you at home with Jack is going to count for an enormous amount. And since it is her job to see how mothers are coping with their newborns, her opinion is going to carry a lot of professional weight. By the way, how did it go with Jack yesterday?"

Leave it to my sister to remember exactly when I had my supervised visit with Jack.

"He seems to recognize me now," I said. "Or maybe I'm deluding myself."

"No—babies do get a sense of who's around them."

"Which means that Jack most certainly thinks of that woman as his mom."

"He's only a few months old," Sandy said. "He doesn't know who's who yet."

"You're trying to humor me."

"Yes. I am," she said. "But the fact that he seems to know who you are . . . well, isn't that a great sign that you're bonding . . . ?"

Bonding. That word again.

"Yes, we're bonding all right . . . considering that we only have an hour a week to bond. Still, Clarice—the woman who supervises the visits—seems pleased. So does Jessica Law—who's doing . . ."

"I know: the CAFCASS report for the court . . ."

"You do impress me."

"Hey, I hang on to every detail you give me. But here's a question you should ask Ms. Law the next time you see her: why hasn't Tony once contacted you?"

"That's a simple one," I said. "Because he's a total coward."

"Without question. But why you should ask Ms. Law about it is because, as she's interviewing both parties in this case, she's probably in pretty regular contact with Tony. And if you sense she thinks you're all right . . . well, why not tell her that you're a little surprised not to have received any sort of communication from your husband? In the future you will have to be in close consultation about Jack's upbringing, no matter which one of you ends up getting custody. You see what I'm getting at here?"

I did—and so did Nigel Clapp. Without prompting from me, he raised exactly the same point the next day, when I called him to congratulate him on tracking down Jane Sanjay.

"Oh, right," he said.

"But you must have spent so much time trying to figure out where she was. I mean, the legal assistant at Lawrence and Lambert didn't seem to have any luck whatsoever, since Jane was moving around Canada all the time."

"Moving around? Really?" He sounded even more bemused. "Because what she told me was that she had been working at the Jasper Park Lodge for the past four months. And, uhm, finding her was . . . well, it took two phone calls. The first to the council. I explained who I was, and why I needed to speak with her. And although they didn't know where to find her, they said they'd call her mother on my behalf—since mothers usually know where to find their daughters. Which, uhm, turned out to be the case here. The council gave Mrs. Sanjay my number. She called me. We talked. She gave me her daughter's number in Canada. I called her. We talked. And she agreed to be a witness on your behalf at the final hearing. Oh, and . . . uhm . . . just in case she gets delayed in Canada or can't make it to the hearing on the day in question, I contacted the Law Society of Canada, and found the name of a solicitor in the town of Jasper, and spoke with him yesterday. He'll be taking a sworn affidavit from Ms. Sanjay later in the week—which he'll also have notarized, to make certain it's admissible in an English court of law. But that's just a precautionary measure on my part."

Then, with what almost seemed like a slight laugh, he said, "I am just a bit on the cautious side."

He also informed me that almost all the other people I had listed in my email had been interviewed by Mrs. Keating.

"Who's Mrs. Keating?" I asked.

"Oh, you don't know Mrs. Keating?"

"Uh, no . . . ," I said, stopping myself from adding: *"surely if I knew her, I wouldn't be asking you."*

"Maybe I didn't introduce you?"

"But where would I have met her?"

"At my office. You were here how many times?"

"Once."

"Is that all?"

"Absolutely."

"Rose Keating is my secretary."

Well, that took some effort to get out of him.

"And she interviewed all the social services people?"

"Uh, yes. She's very good at that sort of thing."

"I'm sure she is," I said. "Are you happy with the new statements?"

"Happy?" he asked, as if he didn't understand the meaning of the word. "I think they're fine, yes. But happy . . . ?"

There was a long existential pause on the telephone line as he pondered the semantic implications of "happy." God, this man was work. From our brief association to date, I could see that I would probably never understand him, let alone get to know him. After our initial meeting, all business was conducted by phone—and on the one or two occasions when I suggested I stop by and see him for a chat, he sounded almost horrified, telling me, "No need to trouble yourself coming all the way to Balham." I sensed he was very aware of his profound social awkwardness, his verbal hesitancy, his almost autistic inability to make even the most minor emotional connection with a client. But I now knew that he was very good at what he did—exceptionally thorough and considered. I was certain that behind all the awkwardness, there was a private man of some emotional complexity and feeling—he did have a wife and kids, after all. But he would never let me (or probably any other client) be privy to that side of him. It wasn't as if he was one of those much doted-upon English eccentrics who played to the gallery when it came to their idiosyncrasies. No, Nigel Clapp wasn't quaint or quirky—he was downright strange. Unnervingly so . . . given that he was my one hope out of this nightmare.

And yet, little by little, I was beginning to trust him.

"Mr. Clapp, are you still there?" I asked.

"I suppose so," he said. "So there was something else to discuss, wasn't there?"

"I don't know, Mr. Clapp," I said respectfully. "You called me."

"That's right, I did. Now . . . uhm . . . I think you should write a letter. You don't mind me saying that, do you?"

"No, if it is your professional opinion that I should write a letter that would be beneficial to my case, I'll write the letter. I just need to know *to whom* I should write the letter."

"To your husband. I'd like to establish . . . uhm . . . that you want contact with him as regards your son's well-being in his new home . . . as regards how this Ms. Dexter is treating him, and what his plans are for the future. I'd also like to suggest that you propose a face-to-face meeting . . . just the two of you . . . to discuss Jack's future."

"But I really don't want to meet him right now, Mr. Clapp. I don't think I could face him."

"I can appreciate that. But . . . uhm . . . unless I am mistaken . . . and I could be mistaken, I have been mistaken in the past, I do make mistakes . . . uhm . . . I don't think he'll want to see you. Guilt, you see. He'll feel guilty. Unless I am wrong . . ."

"No," I said. "I don't think you're wrong. In fact, my sister had a similar idea."

"About what?" he asked. And I dropped the subject before things got more confused.

But that evening I did write the letter.

Dear Tony,

I cannot begin to articulate the grief you have caused me. Nor can I fathom how you could have betrayed me and your son in such a ferocious, self-serving way. You used my illness—a temporary clinical condition, from which I am now largely recovered—as a means by which to snatch my son from me, and reinvent your life with a woman whom you were obviously seeing while I was pregnant with your son. The fact that you then manipulated the facts of my postpartum depression to claim that I was a danger to Jack is unspeakable in both its cunning and its cruelty.

But it is another, more pressing matter that compels me to write you. I am troubled by the fact that, as Jack's mother, I have been deliberately kept in the dark as to who is looking after him, whether he is being properly cared for, and if he is getting the proper maternal attention that an infant needs.

There are also questions about his upbringing—no matter what the final custody arrangements turn out to be— which we must decide together.

That is what I want to most emphasize now—the fact that, despite the desperate anguish I feel by being unfairly separated from my son, and despite my anger at your terrible betrayal, my primary concern is Jack's welfare and his future happiness. For this reason, I am willing to put aside my anguish to sit down with you for the first of what must be an ongoing series of conversations about our son and his future. For his sake, we should put all our animosities to one side and talk.

*I look forward to hearing from you shortly, proposing a
time and place when we should meet.
Yours*

"My, you are clever," Julia said after I showed her the final draft.

"You can thank Mr. Clapp for that. He made me write three different drafts before he was happy with the letter."

"Are you serious? Mr. Clapp—the original Mr. Tentative—actually *edited* you?"

"Not only that—but he kept emailing me back with assorted suggestions as to how we could push the knife in deeper . . . though, of course, he would never be so crude as to suggest that we were attempting to trip up my estranged husband, even though that was precisely the object of this exercise."

"Well, I must say that it is a most cunning letter. Because it points up your victimization without falling into self-pity. At the same time, it sticks it to him about two-timing you, and also raises all sorts of questions about his real motivations behind all this. And you then show tremendous graciousness about putting your anger to one side in order to do what's best for your son . . ."

Three days later, I received a letter from Tony.

Dear Sally,

*Considering the threats you made against the life of our
son—and considering your complete lack of maternal
interest in him following his birth—I find it rather
extraordinary that you write me now, speaking about how
I betrayed you. Especially when it is you who so betrayed an
innocent baby.*

*As to your accusation that I was betraying you while
pregnant, you should know that Diane Dexter has been
a close friend of mine for years. And I turned to her as a
friend for support when your mental health began to decline
during your pregnancy. Our friendship only turned into*

something else after your breakdown and your irresponsible,
endangering behavior against our son.

She could not be a better surrogate mother to my
son—and has provided Jack the safe, calm environment
he needs in these early days of his life. I am most certainly
aware of the fact that you—as Jack's mother—should have
an important input into decisions about his future. But
until I am certain that you are no longer a danger to him, I
cannot sit down with you to "talk things out." I do hope that
you are on the road to mental recovery—and have begun
to face up to your injurious behavior against our son. Do
understand: I hold no grudge against you whatsoever. And I
only wish you the best for the future.
Yours sincerely
Tony
c.c. Jessica Law, Wandsworth DHSS

The letter shook in my hands as I read it. I immediately faxed a copy to Nigel Clapp, and then knocked on Julia's door. She offered coffee and commiseration.

"You know a lawyer worked with him on this," she said.

"Just like my letter."

"Only yours was, at least, in your own voice. This missive . . . it sounds downright Victorian in places. *'Your injurious behavior against our son.'* Who uses language like that nowadays?"

"It's certainly not Tony's prose style—which is tight and clipped. And he never goes in for touchy-feely stuff, like: *'I hold no ill will against you whatsoever. And I only wish you the best for the future.'* He holds complete ill will against me, and hopes I'll walk under a bus at the earliest possible convenience."

"It's a divorce. And in a divorce, it always turns ugly. Especially when the stakes are so high."

Late that afternoon, Mr. Clapp rang me.

"Uhm . . . about your husband's letter . . ."

"It has me worried," I said.

"Oh, really?"

"Because it's allowed that bastard to refute everything I said in the first letter. And because it also allowed him to put on the record his contention that she 'saved' my son . . . which besides being a total lie is also totally offensive."

"I could see how . . . uhm . . . you might be upset by such a comment. But as regards the damage the letter might do . . . it's what I expected."

"Seriously?"

"Oh yes, I am being quite serious. It's what I expected and wanted."

"You *wanted* this sort of reply?"

"Uh, yes."

Then there was another of his signature pauses, hinting that he wanted to move on to another topic of conversation.

"May I ask you if you've had any further success finding work?"

"I've been trying, but I just don't seem to be having much luck."

"I spoke with Dr. Rodale, your . . . uhm . . ."

He cleared his throat, obviously not wanting to say the embarrassing word. So I helped him out.

"Psychiatrist."

"Yes, your psychiatrist. She told me that she will write a report, stating that, in light of your . . . uhm . . ."

"Depression."

"Yes, your depression, she considers you still unfit for full-time employment. That will, at the very least, cover us in case your husband's barrister raises the issue of your lack of work at the hearing. But if you could find some sort of job, it would reflect favorably on your recovery from the . . . uhm . . ."

"Depression."

"That's the word."

A couple of days later, I received a phone call from Julia. She explained that she was in the office of an editor friend. I'd mentioned to her in one of our early chats that I had spent my summer holidays during college working as a proofreader at a Boston publishing house.

"And when my editor friend here said he urgently needed a proofreader for a big job—and his two usual proofreaders were otherwise engaged—I immediately thought of you. If, that is, you're interested . . ."

"Oh, I'm interested . . ."

The next day, I took the tube to Kensington High Street and spent an hour in the office of an editor named Stanley Shaw—a thin, quiet, rather courtly man in his mid-fifties. He worked in the nonfiction division of a major publisher and largely handled big reference volumes, including their *Guide to Classical CDs,* which was published every other year and was a vast door-stopping paperback of some fifteen hundred pages.

"Are you at all knowledgeable about classical music?" he asked me.

"I can tell the difference between Mozart and Mahler," I said.

"Well, that's a start," he said with a smile, then quizzed me about my proofreading background—and whether I could adjust to Anglicisms, and technical musical terminology, and an extensive number of abbreviations that were a component part of the guide. I assured him that I was a fast learner.

"That's good—because we're going to need the entire guide proofread within the next two months. It is going to be technically demanding—as it is a critical compendium of the best recordings available of works by just about every major and minor composer imaginable. Put badly, it's a huge job—and, to be honest about it, not one which I would hand over to someone who's been out of practice as a proofreader as long as you have been. But I am desperate—and if Julia Frank believes you can do it, then I believe you can. That is, if you believe you can do it, and can have it all to me within two months."

"I can do it."

We shook hands on it. The next day, a motorcycle messenger arrived at my house with a large, deep cardboard box—and over fifteen hundred pages of proofs. I had cleared the kitchen table for this task—already installing an Anglepoise lamp and a jam jar filled with newly sharpened pencils. There was a contract along with the page proofs. Before signing it, I faxed it over to Nigel Clapp. He called me back within an hour.

"You've got a job," he said, sounding surprised.

"It looks that way. But I'm worried about something—whether my fee will invalidate me for legal aid."

"Well . . . uhm . . . you could always have them redraft the contract, guaranteeing you full payment upon publication, which is . . . according to the contract . . . eight months from now. So we could show the court that you have been working, but that you'll be remunerated after the final hearing, which would keep you qualified for legal aid. That is, if you can manage to afford not to draw a salary right now."

The hearing was in ten weeks' time, and I was down to the equivalent of £1,500. It would be insanely tight.

"Say I asked Stanley for a third of the fee up-front?"

"Yes—that would still put you well within the legal aid threshold."

Stanley Shaw was only too willing to redraft the contract, pointing out that, "In the thirty years I've been a publisher, this is the first time that a writer or an editor has asked for a delayed payment . . . which, of course, I'm most happy to facilitate."

That evening, I did a bit more simple mathematics. I had a total of sixty-one days to do the job. Fifteen hundred by sixty-one equals 24.5 pages per day, which divided by eight made three.

Three pages per hour. Doable. As long as I stuck to the task at hand. Didn't allow my mind to wander. Didn't dwell on the ongoing agony of missing Jack. Didn't succumb to the perpetual fear that the judge at the final hearing would side with Tony, and limit me to an hour a week's visit until . . .

No, no . . . don't contemplate that. Just go to work.

It took me four days to cross the threshold of the A composers (Albinoni, Alkan, Arnold, Adams) into the Bs—and gradually move through the Bach family. And, my God, there was an enormous amount of works under review. Then there was the critical pros and cons—the way the editors of the guide discussed whether, in the recording of the *B Minor Mass*, you should opt for the traditional *kappelmeister* approach of Karl Richter, or the leaner, reduced period forces of John Eliot Gardiner, or the interpretive brilliance of Masaki Suzuki, or . . .

That was the most intriguing thing about working on this guide (especially to someone with as little musical knowledge as myself)—the discovery that, in musical performance, interpretation changes with every conductor, every instrumentalist, every singer. But though you can play games with metronomic markings and tempi, you can't really deviate too much from the score. Whereas all stories are always open to speculation, conjecture, even reinvention . . . to the point where, in the retelling, you begin to wonder where the original narrative has gone, and how the plot line has been hijacked by the two principal protagonists, both of whom are now presenting diametrically different versions of the same tale.

"You must be going crazy, reading all that musicological stuff, word by word," Sandy said one evening during our daily phone call.

"Actually, I'm rather enjoying it. Not just because I'm finding it interesting, but also because it's given me something I've been craving for months: a structure to the day."

Three pages an hour, eight hours per day—the work broken up into four two-hour sessions, with a half-hour break between each period. Of course, I had to work this schedule around my weekly visit with Jack, my biweekly talk with Jessica Law, my biweekly consultations with Dr. Rodale. Otherwise, the work defined my time. Just as it helped me mark time, and accelerate the agonizing wait for the final hearing. Yes, I did find such intensive proofreading to be frequently exhausting. I was also simultaneously bored and overwhelmed by the enormity of the task. But there was also a certain pleasure in pushing my way deeper and deeper into the alphabet. After three weeks, Berlioz was a distant memory, as I'd just polished off Hindemith and Roy Harris. Getting through the entire recorded corpus of Mozart was a bit like a drive I once took across Canada—during which I kept thinking: *this has got to end sometime.* Then, in the middle of week five, I began to panic. I was just entering the big S section, with wildly prolific composers like Schubert and Shostakovich to work through. Stanley Shaw (another S!) checked in with me once, reminding me that the deadline was just two and a half weeks off. "Don't worry—I'll make it," I told him, even though I myself was beginning to wonder how I'd do it. I increased my workday time from eight to twelve hours. This paid off—as midway through the sixth week, I had managed to finish off Telemann and was dealing with Tippett. And during my subsequent session with Dr. Rodale, she informed me that I was now appearing so much more balanced and in control that she was going to begin the gradual reduction of my dose of antidepressants. A week later, while reading the section covering all complete sets of Vaughan Williams symphonies (the Boult was the favored recording),

I received word from Nigel Clapp that we had an exact date for the final hearing—June 18.

"Uhm . . . the barrister I want to instruct . . . and who does this sort of case very well . . . and . . . uhm . . . is also on the Legal Aid register . . . well, her name is . . ."

"Her?" I said.

"Yes, she is a woman. But perfect for your situation . . . sorry, sorry, that sounds all wrong."

"I know what you're saying. What's her name?"

"Maeve Doherty."

"Irish?"

"Uhm . . . yes. Born and raised there, educated at Oxford, then she was part of a rather radical practice for a while . . ."

"I see . . ."

"Did a lot of . . . uhm . . . substantial work. Especially in the family law area. She's available. She does legal aid. She will respond to the predicament you are in."

"And say she ends up facing a traditional judge who can't stand her politics?"

"Well . . . uhm . . . one can't have everything."

I didn't have time yet to dwell on this potential problem, as Vaughan Williams gave way to Verdi and Victoria and Vivaldi and Walton and Weber and Weekes and—twenty-four hours to go—I was still working on Wesley, and drinking nonstop cups of coffee, and assuring Stanley Shaw that he could have a courier at my door at nine tomorrow morning, and I was negotiating the complete organ works of Widor, and somewhere around midnight, I reached the last listing (Zwillich), and suddenly the sun was rising, and I tossed the final page on top of the pile, and smiled that tired smile that comes with having finished a job, and ran a bath, and was dressed and awaiting the courier when he showed up at nine, and received a phone call an hour later from Stanley Shaw congratulating me on making the deadline. An hour after that, I was holding my baby son under the increasingly less watchful eye of Clarice Chambers, who told me that she was going to leave us alone this morning, but would be down the corridor in the tea room if we needed her.

"How about that, Jack?" I said after she headed off. "We're on our own at last."

But Jack was too busy sucking down a bottle to respond.

I crashed out that night at seven, and slept twelve straight hours without interruption. I woke the next morning, feeling less burdened than I had felt in months. This lightening of mood carried on into the next week—when Stanley Shaw rang me and asked, "I don't suppose you're free to do another job?"

"As a matter of fact, I am."

"Tremendous. Because it is another doorstopper of a book. Our film guide. Currently clocking in at fifteen hundred thirty-eight pages. It needs to be fully proofed in nine weeks. Same terms as before?"

"Sounds good to me."

"Well, come by the office tomorrow around noon—and I'll take you through the basic parameters of it, and then I can buy us both lunch somewhere pleasant, if that's agreeable."

"You're on," I said.

Two days later, I was back at work, slowly inching my way through this fat critical compendium. And when Sandy asked me how I could mentally handle long stretches of such detailed work, I said, "I just fall into it—and black everything else out for the next couple of hours. So it's a bit like novocaine—a temporary, fast-acting anesthetic, which keeps everything else numb for a short amount of time. The pay's not bad either."

Around three weeks into this job, I received a phone call from Maeve Doherty. Whatever about her childhood in Dublin, her accent was Oxbridge, tempered by a pleasant phone manner. She explained that Nigel Clapp had given her the brief. As she liked to be instructed well before the date of the hearing and always met the individuals she would be representing, she would also like to meet me as soon as our mutual schedules permitted.

Four days later, I took an afternoon off. I hopped the underground to Temple, walked up to Fleet Street, and entered a passageway called Inner Temple, which brought me into what seemed to be a miniature Oxbridge college, of mixed Tudor and Gothic design: a small, calm enclave of the law, hidden away from London's continuous din. I came to a door, outside of which was a wooden board, upon which had been painted, in immaculate black letters, the names of fifteen barristers who made up this practice. *Miss M. Doherty* was near the top of the list.

Her office was tiny. So was she, with petite features to mirror her small stature. She wasn't pretty—in fact, she almost could be described as plain—but there was an attractive studiousness about her, and the hint of a deeply strong resolve that she had latched on to as a way of countering her diminutive size. Her handshake was firm, she looked me directly in the eye when talking to me, and though she was all business, she was likably all business.

"Let me say from the start that I do think you've been unfairly vilified. And I gather from Mr. Clapp that the barrister who acted for you during the interim hearing was only briefed on the case around a half hour before the actual hearing. What was his name again?" she asked, rummaging through the file. "Ah yes, Mr. Paul Halliwell . . ."

"You know him?" I asked, picking up the hint of contempt in her voice.

"It's a small world, the law. So, yes, I do know Mr. Halliwell."

"Well, the culpable party really was my solicitor, Virginia Ricks, of Lawrence and Lambert . . ."

"No, *formerly* of Lawrence and Lambert. She was let go last month after fouling up a very big divorce proceeding involving a very substantial Dubai client. She's now considered an untouchable."

She then talked strategy for the better part of a half hour, quizzing me intensely about my marriage to Tony, about his personal history, focusing on the way he shut himself away in his study all the time after the baby was born, the late nights out on the town, the fact that he was so evidently involved with Diane Dexter during my pregnancy.

"I saw that letter you wrote your husband just a few weeks ago, as well as his reply. Very adroit strategy—especially as it got him to state, in writing, that theirs was just a platonic relationship. And if Nigel Clapp's investigations into her background yield what we hope they'll yield, then we really should have an interesting case to present against them."

"Nigel Clapp is having the Dexter woman investigated?"

"That's what he told me."

"By whom?"

"He didn't say. Then again, as you've probably gathered by now, Mr. Clapp is someone who, at the best of times, has difficulty with compound sentences. But, whatever about his interpersonal skills, he just might be the best solicitor I've ever worked with—utterly thorough, conscientious, and engaged. Especially in a case like this one—where he feels, as I do, that our client has been seriously wronged."

"He told you that?"

"Hardly," she said with a smile. "But we've worked together often enough that I know there are times when he's passionately committed to seeing things set right. This is definitely one of those instances. Just don't expect him to admit that to you."

I certainly didn't expect such an admission—though when I did ask him, during our next phone call, if he had hired a private investigator on my behalf, he suddenly turned all different and defensive, saying, "It's . . . uhm . . . just someone who looks into things for me, that's all."

His anxious tone persuaded me to ask no further questions.

In the coming weeks, I concentrated on what *I* had to do: get this damn manuscript finished. Long days of work, the weekly visit with Jack, the twice-monthly consultations with Dr. Rodale and Jessica Law, the occasional phone call from Nigel Clapp, in which he would give me an update of how the case was proceeding—and also informing me that, as things stood now (and after consultation with Tony's legal team), it looked as if the final hearing would last around two days. I had two further telephone conversations with Maeve Doherty, in which she cleared up a few points with me, and also assured me not to worry about whatever judge would be hearing the case—we wouldn't know his name until the afternoon before the hearing.

Then, just two weeks before the date of this final hearing, I received a call from Nigel Clapp. It was nearly eight at night—an unusually late time for him to be calling me.

"Uhm . . . sorry to be phoning so late."

"No problem. I was just working."

"How's work?" he said, in an awkward attempt to make conversation.

"Fine, fine. Stanley is actually talking about another proofing job to follow this one. It looks like I might have a steady income soon."

"Good, good," he said, sounding even more distracted then ever. This was followed by another telltale Clapp pause. Then, "If you were . . . uhm . . . free tomorrow afternoon . . ."

"You want to see me?"

"Well, I don't *have* to see you. But . . . I think . . ."

He broke off. And I knew something was very wrong.

"You need to tell me something face to face?" I asked.

"It would be better . . ."

"Because it's bad news?"

An anxious silence. "It's not good news."

"Tell me now."

"If you could come to my office in Balham . . ."

"Tell me now, Mr. Clapp."

Another anxious silence. "Well . . . if you insist . . ."

"I do."

"Uhm . . . it's twofold difficult news, I'm afraid. And the first part of it has to do with Ms. Law's CAFCASS report . . ."

I felt a cold hand seize the back of my neck.

"Oh, my God, don't tell me she ruled against me?"

"Not precisely. She actually reported herself very impressed with you, very impressed with the way you have handled yourself in the wake of being separated from your son, very impressed as well with your recovery from your depression. But . . . uhm . . . I'm afraid she was also very impressed with your husband and Ms. Dexter. And although it isn't her business to make a recommendation, she has let it be known that the child is in very good hands with his father and surrogate mother."

I felt the phone trembling in my hand.

"Do . . . uhm . . . understand that this doesn't mean she's advised that the child stay with Ms. Dexter—"

"And the second piece of bad news?"

"Well, this only arrived around an hour ago and . . . uhm . . . I'm still trying to digest it. It's a letter to me from your husband's solicitor, informing me that your husband and Ms. Dexter are professionally relocating to Sydney for the next five years, where Ms. Dexter has been engaged to start up a major new marketing concern."

"Oh, God . . ."

"Yes . . . and their solicitor informs me they're planning to take Jack with them."

I was now rigid with shock.

"Can they legally do that?" I managed to say.

"If the hearing goes their way and they make an application . . ."

He broke off. I said, "Finish the sentence, Mr. Clapp."

"I'd really rather . . ."

"Finish the sentence."

On the other end of the line, I could hear him take a deep steadying breath before saying, "If the hearing goes their way—if they convince the judge that you are an unfit mother and an ongoing danger to your son—then you will have no say in the matter. They can take your son wherever they want to take him."

THIRTEEN

T HE ISSUE HERE," Maeve Doherty said, "comes down to one central question: where does the child best belong? That's what the court will be deciding—and because there have already been two legal decisions made in favor of the child's father, it's going to be our job to convince the judge that, at the very least, the child's best interests are served by joint custody between his mother and father, preferably with him spending more time with his mother."

"But if Tony wins custody?" I asked.

"Then you'll have no say about where the child lives with his father," Maeve said. "So if—as your husband's solicitors have indicated—he and his new partner are planning to settle in Sydney for several years, then they can most certainly take him there, even if you do object to being so geographically separated from your son. Naturally, should this happen, we can argue, and probably win you, visiting rights—but that will hardly be satisfactory. Unless, of course, you're willing to move to Australia."

"Without a visa or a job? Sure."

"Well, hopefully that won't come to pass. The problem here, however, is that two court orders have indicated that you could be considered an unfit mother, and that your alleged behavior after the child's birth indicated that the child could potentially be harmed by you. Which is what they are going to argue again. Now we can certainly call a variety of professional witnesses who can vouch for your mental stability, your fitness as a mother, and the fact that you were suffering from clinical depression at the time. How many statements do we have now, Nigel?"

"Eight altogether," he said. "And . . . uhm . . . they're all very favorably disposed toward Ms. Goodchild."

"Which means we can count on eight favorable witnesses. The big sticking point, however, is the CAFCASS report. The court *always* pays attention to this report. It inevitably wields a considerable amount of influence on the final decision—as it can only be commissioned by the court, and it's also looked upon as the definitive statement on the case from the social services. Which is why I'm rather worried about this report. Because it doesn't come down firmly on your side, Sally. You concur with my worries, don't you, Nigel?"

We were sitting in Nigel's office. It was two days after the bombshell letter had arrived from Tony's solicitors, announcing his intentions to move to Australia. Though she was trying to juggle around four briefs at the same time, Maeve Doherty considered the situation serious enough to find a free hour to get down to Balham for a meeting with the three of us. Which is how I found myself making only my second visit to Nigel Clapp's office since he had started representing me.

"Uhm . . . in my experience," Nigel said, "if the CAFCASS report doesn't challenge the status quo, the court will usually allow the status quo to be maintained. Which . . . uhm . . . I'm afraid to say might mean that custody will be granted to your husband, but with more generous and unsupervised visiting privileges. Which still means that they can take him to Australia. So, uhm, I'm in agreement with Ms. Doherty . . . we need to strive for some sort of joint residence arrangement . . ."

"But Nigel," Maeve said, "the problem here is not having any real ammunition against either Tony or his partner. Unless your 'detective' has turned up something."

Nigel almost managed a small embarrassed smile at the mention of his "detective."

"Shall I bring her in here to see what she's managed to uncover?" he said.

"Your detective's a *she*?" I asked.

Nigel started to blush.

"It's . . . uhm . . . Mrs. Keating."

"You're kidding me?" I said, then suddenly saw that this comment made him anxious.

"She's really rather good at it," he said.

"I can confirm that," Maeve said.

"Sorry, sorry," I said. "I didn't mean to imply . . ."

"Why don't you get her in here?" Maeve said.

Nigel reached for the phone and dialed a number. From next door, we could hear Mrs. Keating answer her phone with a loud, "Yeah?"

"Would you mind coming in here for a moment, Rose—and could you please bring the Goodchild file with you."

"Oh, yeah, right."

She showed up a moment later. As she came in, I noticed brownish crumbs on her large floral dress. The remnants of bourbon creams, no doubt. Nigel reintroduced us. Though she had let me into the office only ten minutes earlier, she still looked at me as if I was some stranger whom she had never laid eyes on before. Nigel said, "Ms. Goodchild and Ms. Doherty would like to hear the results of your investigation into Ms. Dexter."

"You want to read the report, or you want me to give you the condensed version?" she asked.

"Let's . . . uhm . . . hear the condensed version, then we can make photocopies for both of them of your report."

"Fine by me," she said, parking herself in a chair, and opening the file. "Got all her specs here. Diane Dexter, born Leeds, 15 January 1953. Father worked for the local gas board, Mum was a housewife. She went to the local grammar school, a state primary. Bright girl—won a place at Leeds University in economics. Went to London after getting her degree. Ten years in advertising. Worked for some big firms—including Dean Delaney, and John Hegarty. Then got headhunted by Apple UK to run their marketing division. Five years with them. Branched into market research. Cofounded a company—Market Force Ltd.—in 1987 with a partner named Simon Chandler, with whom she was romantically linked for a time. When they broke up in 1990, he bought out her share of the firm, which she used to set up Dexter Communications, which has become super-successful over the last ten years, to the point where she's now worth around ten million pounds, with houses in . . . well, you know all that from the earlier Lawrence and Lambert report in the file.

"Now, here's what little dirt I could find on her. Two months' hospitalization in 1990 at the Priory for 'psychotropic dependence'—better known as cocaine misuse. The bad news is that there were no arrests for drug possession, in fact nothing criminal whatsoever, bar a couple of points on her driving license for speeding. And she's been totally clean since the Priory stint in '90. In fact, she's actually given talks to youth groups about her past addiction, and has also raised money for a charity that sponsored drug education programs in and around Leeds."

Great, I thought. *A reformed druggie who's remained clean for thirteen years—and now does good charitable work as a way of making amends for her wayward past. Oh, and she's wildly successful and rich to boot.*

"The cocaine angle is an interesting one," Maeve Doherty said. "There might be something there. Anything else?"

"Besides the relationship with Simon Chandler, there have been two failed marriages: a two-year quickie to a chap she married out of university, and whom she divorced in '75. He's now a schoolteacher somewhere in Yorkshire. Then there was a six-year stint with a television director named Trevor Harriman, which ended when she met Simon Chandler in '85. In fact, Chandler was named as corespondent in the divorce petition by her erstwhile husband. Since she and Chandler parted company in 1990, there have been a few affairs—including one with that thriller writer fellow, Philip Kimball, but nothing solid. Until she met Tony Hobbs in 1999."

I interrupted here. "Now Tony insisted that, from the outset, they were just friends."

"Well," Rose Keating said, "they may have been 'just friends,' but she took him on a South African holiday in '99, then scuba-diving on the Great Barrier Reef the following year, then spent a month with him in Cairo in 2001."

"What month in 2001?" I asked.

"September."

"That makes sense. We first hooked up in October of that year."

"Hate to tell you this, but it was she who dropped him in September—on account of the fact that he wouldn't come back to London to live with her."

Maeve Doherty came in here.

"Did you manage to find out when they started seeing each other again?"

She nodded. "About twelve months ago—shortly after Mr. Hobb's return from Cairo."

I sucked in my breath. And asked, "How do you know that?"

"Ms. Dexter's ex-housekeeper told me. He came over one afternoon to see her."

Maeve Doherty asked, "But did the ex-housekeeper state whether he was just visiting her or actually *visiting* her?"

"Oh, it was definitely the latter. He stayed with her until about one in the morning . . . and they didn't emerge from her bedroom until it was time for him to leave."

. . . and to go home and tell me he'd been out boozing late with his chums.

Now I asked, "And according to the housekeeper, was he regularly at her place thereafter?"

"According to the housekeeper, yeah," Rose Keating said. "He was over there all the time."

Maeve Doherty asked, "I suppose Mr. Hobbs's barrister could question the validity of the housekeeper's testimony . . . especially as she was an ex-employee."

"That's right," Rose Keating said. "Fired for alleged stealing."

"Oh, great," I said.

"Yeah, but the housekeeper got legal advice and forced Ms. Dexter's hand. Turns out not only did she receive a written apology from her, saying the whole charge was false, but she also got a check for a year's wages as a way of saying sorry."

"And will this housekeeper be willing to testify?" Maeve Doherty asked.

"Oh, yes. She don't think much of Ms. Dexter, that's for sure. And she also told me where and when the two of them slipped out of town for a little romantic rendezvous over the past six months. Twice in Brussels, once in Paris. Got the names of the hotels, called them up, they confirm that Mr. Hobbs had company on both occasions. In fact, the concierge at the Hotel Montgomery in Brussels told me it was the same woman both times.

"Oh . . . one final important thing. Seems Ms. Dexter miscarried a child when she was big into cocaine. The year afterward, she tried IVF. Didn't take. Tried it again in '92 and '93, by which time she was forty, and the game was kind of over. The thing is—according to the ex-housekeeper—having a kid has become something of an obsession with her, to the point where, in the mid-nineties, she considered adopting for a while until business stuff superseded . . . seems she ran into a little corporate financial problem for a while . . ."

I looked at Rose Keating, amazed. "How the hell did you find all this stuff out?"

She gave me a coy smile. "I've got my ways, dear."

Maeve Doherty said, "The fact that they were carrying on while he was also married to you is good stuff. The fact that he has written that theirs was a friendship until your illness—and we have proof otherwise—is also good stuff. And the fact that she's been desperate for a baby all these years . . . well, we can certainly put two plus two together on that one."

But then she looked at me directly and said, "However, I have to be honest with you here, Sally. In my opinion, while all this evidence is useful, it still doesn't contradict, or undermine, the dirt they have against you."

I suddenly felt in need of an extra dose of antidepressants. Just as I suddenly saw myself down at the Aldwych, lining up with other would-be emigrants at Australia House, explaining to some bored consular official how my ex-husband and his new wife won custody of my child, and I wanted a visa for the Land of Oz so I'd be able to have my weekly visit with my little boy. To which the consular official would undoubtedly ask, "And why did your husband receive custody of your little boy?"

"Uhm . . . Ms. Goodchild?"

I snapped back to terra firma.

"You all right, dear?" Rose Keating asked me.

"I'm trying to be."

"The problem is," Maeve Doherty said, "the final hearing is in twelve days. And unless . . ."

Nigel Clapp came in here. "Uhm . . . I think what Ms. Doherty is getting at is . . . uhm . . . well, to be completely direct about it, we need to find something else on either your husband or Ms. Dexter. As Ms. Keating has done such a thorough job sifting through Ms. Dexter's life—"

"Can you think of anything about your husband that might be useful?" Maeve asked me.

"You mean, besides the fact that he dodged marriage for years and told me he never wanted kids?"

"But he still brought you with him to London when you became pregnant," Maeve said.

"I don't know," I said. "His life was pretty much work and the occasional girlfriend before I came along. I can't say he told me much about all that. In fact, the only time I found out anything about his old private life was when some journo in Cairo told me . . ."

At that moment, I heard a tiny little ping in the back of my brain, a single line of conversation that had been spoken to me around seven months ago. Something which, in my confusion at the time, I hadn't even picked up on. Until now. When, out of nowhere, it was yanked up from the dustbin of my brain and placed in front of me.

"Are you all right, dear?" Rose Keating asked me.

"Could I use your phone, please?"

I called information for Seaford. The number I wanted was listed, but the person I needed to speak with wasn't there. I left a message, asking her to call me at home in London urgently. Then I went back to Nigel's office and explained whom I was trying to contact, what she said to me some months earlier, and why it might prove useful.

"It's a bit of a long shot," I explained, "because what she said was pretty damn vague. But it's worth finding out what she meant by it."

"Uhm . . . do you think you could track her down and talk to her?" Nigel Clapp asked. "We have just twelve days."

Twelve days. That deadline kept looming in my mind. As did the realization that Maeve Doherty had been speaking the truth: without some new evidence, the court would probably find for Tony. The record spoke for itself.

Twelve days. I rushed home to Putney and checked my messages. Just one—from Jane Sanjay, informing me she was back in the country, but was down visiting friends in Brighton for a week before starting work again. "We'll do that lunch sometime in the future . . . and, of course, I'll see you at the high court for the hearing. Hope you're somehow keeping calm . . ."

Hardly. I redialed the Seaford number. Once again, I was connected to the answering machine. Once again, I left a message. Then I went back to work on the *Film Guide*. But unlike my previous proofreading stints, this time I was unable to fall into the rabbit hole of work and cut off from the outside world for a two-hour stretch. This time, I kept glancing at the phone, willing it to ring. Which it didn't.

So I called back and left another message. Then I started calling at three-hour intervals.

At the end of the day, the phone did ring. I jumped. But it was Rose Keating.

"Just called to see if there was any news?" she asked.

"She hasn't rung me back yet."

"Keep trying, dear," she said, though I also grasped the subtext of what she was saying: *we need something new.*

By midnight, I must have called another eight times. I slept fitfully and eventually found myself at the kitchen table around five that morning, proofing some more pages. At seven, I tried the Seaford number. No answer. I tried again at ten, at three, at six. Then, when I phoned at eight-thirty, the unexpected happened. It was actually answered. When Pat Hobbs heard my voice, she became indignant.

"Was that you calling me all the time yesterday?"

"Ms. Hobbs . . . Pat . . . please hear me out . . ."

"Don't you go calling me by my name. I don't know you."

"I'm Tony's wife . . ."

"I bloody well remember. You bothered me all those months ago . . ."

"It's an urgent situation."

"Is he dead or dying?"

"No, but . . ."

"Then it's not urgent."

"If you'd just let me explain . . ."

"Don't think I will."

"It's just one simple question."

"Which I'm not going to answer, no matter what it is. And I don't want you disturbing me again."

She hung up. I rang back. The line was busy. I called back again ten minutes later. Still busy. Half an hour later. Still busy. She'd taken it off the hook. I paced the kitchen with worry. I glanced at the clock on the wall. Then I found myself reaching for the phone and calling National

Rail information, and finding out that if I caught the 9:32 from Putney
to Clapham Junction, and changed for the 9:51 to Eastbourne, I would
arrive in Seaford at 11:22.

I threw a few things into an overnight bag—thinking that, as it was a
seaside town, there must be a few bed-and-breakfasts down there. Then
I ran for the train.

As I walked out of Seaford station two hours later, I caught that
iodine smack to the air that hinted that the sea was near. There was one
lone cab outside. I showed him the address—garnered from information.

"It's just three minutes' walk from here," he said, pointing toward
a Safeway supermarket opposite the station. I thanked him and started
walking. The streets were empty. The lamplight was low, so all I could
discern was a small main street with a jumble of Edwardian and modern
buildings—including a very modern, boxy branch of Safeway. I turned
right before it, and found myself on a street of low-lying shops, at the
end of which were a handful of pebble-dashed bungalows. Number 26
was the second from the end. It was painted cream. It had lace curtains
in the windows. It also had a wooden sign above the door, informing the
world that this house had been named: Sea Crest. My plan had been to
seek out the house, then find a B&B nearby, and set the little travel alarm
I brought with me for six-thirty, in order to be at her door by seven. She
might hate the early morning wake-up call, but at least I'd have a chance
of catching her before she went off to work (if, that is, she did work). But
when I reached her front door, I saw that all the lights were on. So, figuring it was best to incur her wrath while she was still awake, I approached
the door and rang the bell.

After a moment, the door opened slightly. It was attached to a chain.
Behind the chain, I could see a woman with a very lined face and scared
eyes. But the voice was as angry as before.

"What do you want at this time of night?"

I quickly put my foot into the space created between the open door
and the door frame, saying, "I'm Tony's wife, Sally Good—"

"Get out of here," she said, trying to slam the door.

"I just need five minutes of your time, please."

"You don't leave right now, I'm calling the police."

334 · DOUGLAS KENNEDY

She tried slamming the door again.

"Just hear me out . . ."

"At bloody midnight? No way. Now get going or . . ."

"He's taken my child from me."

Silence. This obviously gave her pause, and it showed.

"Who's taken your child from you?"

"Your brother."

"You have a child with Tony?"

"A son—Jack. He's about nine months old now. And Tony has . . ."

I put my hand to my face. I felt myself starting to get shaky again. I didn't want to cry in front of this woman.

"He's what?" she asked, the voice not so hard now.

"He's run off with another woman. And they've taken my son . . ."

I could see a mixture of concern and ambivalence in her eyes.

"I haven't had anything to do with my brother for nearly twenty years."

"I understand. And I promise you I won't take up more than ten minutes of your time. But *please*—the situation is rather desperate. Believe me, I wouldn't be here at midnight if . . ."

I heard her undoing the chain.

"Ten minutes, no more," she said. And she opened the door.

I stepped onto a patterned, wall-to-wall carpet. It continued down a hallway papered in a brownish floral print. The living room was off this corridor. More Axminster carpet, a three-piece suite in beige vinyl, an elderly television and video recorder, an old mahogany sideboard, on which sat a half-drunk bottle of Bailey's Irish Cream, and a half liter of inexpensive-looking gin. There were no decorations on the walls—just a different patterned floral wallpaper, sepia-toned and fading. There was a distinctive whiff of damp in the air.

"So what do you want to tell me?" she asked.

Like so many times over the past months, I worked my way through the entire story again. Pat Hobbs sat there throughout the telling, impassive, smoking one Silk Cut after another. I knew she was around ten years older than Tony—and though she wasn't chunky, her deeply ridged face and sad eyes and the elderly floral bathrobe that loosely covered her frame made her seem almost geriatric. Somewhere halfway through the story, she interrupted me, asking, "You drink gin?"

I nodded. She got up and filled two glasses with gin, then added some flat tonic from a bottle on the sideboard. She handed me a glass. I took a sip. The flat tonic was pretty vile. Ditto the metallic taste of the cheap gin. But it was alcohol, and it helped.

It took about another ten minutes to bring her fully up to date. She smoked another two cigarettes during that time. And finally said, "I could have told you my brother was a bastard. A charming bastard, but a bastard nonetheless. So, besides saying sorry for your troubles, what can I do about this?"

I took another steadying sip of gin, knowing that if I didn't win her over now, this entire late-night visit would come to naught. Then I said, "Remember when we spoke sometime ago, and I mentioned that Tony had just left me, and you asked me . . ."

I encapsulated the conversation for her, even though I remembered it, word for word.

"*How long have you two been married now?*" she asked me.

"*Around a year.*"

"*And he's already abandoned you? That's fast work, right enough. Mind you, I'm not surprised. He's the abandoning sort.*"

"*You mean, he's done this before?*"

"*Maybe.*"

I looked at her directly now and asked, "What did you mean by 'maybe.'"

She lit up another cigarette. I could see that she was weighing this all up, wondering if she should involve herself at all in my story. I was asking her to betray her brother. And though she mightn't have spoken with him for twenty years, her brother was still her brother.

She took a deep drag of her Silk Cut, then exhaled.

"I'll tell you—on one condition. You never heard this from me. Understand?"

I nodded. Now it was her turn to tell a story. Two stories in fact, though they were all part of the same central narrative. Then, when she reached the end of her tales, she stood up and went out into the hallway, and returned with an address book, and a scrap of paper and a pen. She found two numbers. She wrote them down. She said, "Now you can deal with them. But understand: I'm to be kept out of the picture."

I assured her that I'd say nothing about her involvement, then thanked her profusely for helping me out, letting her know that I realized what a difficult thing she had just done.

"It wasn't difficult at all."

She stood up, indicating it was time for me to leave.

"Must get up for work in the morning," she said.

"What do you do?"

"Cashier for a building society here in town."

"You like it?"

"It's a job."

"I can't thank you enough . . ."

She waved me off. She didn't want gratitude.

"All right then," I said, picking up my overnight bag. "But I still appreciate everything."

She gave me a brusque nod, then opened the door. I was going to ask her where I could find the nearest B&B, but thought better of it. I didn't want to engage her further. Especially as she had already done so much.

I headed up the street in the direction of town, not particularly worried if all the B&Bs in Seaford were full or shuttered for the night. If I had to sleep on a bench in the station, so be it. The gamble had paid off. A sleepless night was well worth what I had come away with. But halfway down the street, I heard Pat Hobbs's voice calling, "Where are you going now?"

I turned around. She was standing in the doorway of her house.

"I don't know. Figure there must be a B&B or a hotel open now."

"At nearly one AM in Seaford? Everyone's in bed. Come on, I've got a spare bedroom."

The room was narrow and musty. So too was the bed. There was a small, sad collection of old children's dolls on a windowsill. She didn't say much to me, except that the bathroom was down the hall and there was a spare towel in the linen closet. Then she wished me good night.

I undressed and crawled between the sheets. I fell asleep within minutes.

Then it was morning and she was tapping on my door, telling me it was eight and she had to be at work in an hour. Pat was dressed for the building society in a navy-blue uniform with a blue blouse and a blue-

and-white scarf depicting the corporate logo of the conglomerate that employed her. An old-style brown teapot was on a metal warmer. There was a steel toast rack with two slices of white toast awaiting me, as well as a jar of marmalade and a tub of margarine.

"Thought you might like a little breakfast," she said.

"Thank you," I said.

"Tea all right? I don't drink coffee."

"Tea's fine."

I sat down at the table. I reached for a slice of toast and spread it with marmalade. Pat lit up a cigarette.

"Made those calls for you already," she said.

"Sorry?"

"Them two numbers I gave you last night. I called them both already. They're both willing to see you. What are you up to today?"

"I'm free," I said, genuinely pleased and just a little surprised by such a gesture.

"That's good, because the first person—the one who lives in Crawley—said she's around this morning. And I called the rail station—there's a train from here to Gatwick Airport at 9:03, but you have to change in Brighton. You get to Gatwick at 10:06, and then it's ten minutes in a cab to her house. The other woman can't see you today. But she's free tomorrow morning. However, she lives in Bristol. She's expecting you at eleven, which means you'll need to be on a train from London around nine. All right?"

"I don't know what to say, except that I'm rather overwhelmed . . ."

"That's enough," she said, evidently wanting to avoid any more of my effusiveness. "Hope it goes well for you, and that's all I'm going to say about it."

We lapsed into silence. I tried to make conversation.

"Lived in Seaford long?"

"Twenty-three years."

"That's long. And before that?"

"Amersham. Lived with my parents until they both died. Then felt like a change. Didn't want to be rambling around their house without them. So I asked the building society to transfer me somewhere different. They offered Seaford. Kind of liked the idea of being near the water.

Came here in 1980. Bought this place with my share of the Amersham house. Never moved anywhere since."

"Were you married or—"

"No," she said, cutting me off. "Never did that."

She stubbed out her cigarette. I had crossed the frontier into the personal, and the conversation was now closed.

She walked me to the station. When we reached the entrance, I said, "Thanks for putting me up again. Hope I wasn't too much trouble."

"First time I've had anyone to stay in about seven years."

I touched her arm. "Can I call you, tell you how things worked out?"

"Rather you didn't," she said. And with another curt nod of the head, she quickly said "Good-bye" and headed off.

While waiting to board the train to Gatwick, I found myself studying a map of East Sussex on the wall of the station. As my eye moved slightly northeast of Seaford, I noticed the town of Litlington—scene of my infamous arrival at Diane Dexter's gate. Using my index finger, I gauged the distance between the two towns, then held my finger up against the mileage indicator at the bottom of the map. Tony was now spending weekends just three miles from where his sister lived.

I changed trains at Brighton. At Gatwick I took a cab to a modern house on a modest estate in Crawley. The woman there granted me thirty minutes of her time, told me everything I wanted to hear, and said that, yes, she would agree to an additional interview by one of my legal team. Then I took a cab back to the railway station. While waiting for the train, I called Nigel Clapp, excitedly blurting out everything that had happened in the last twelve hours. He said nothing while I rambled on. And when I finally concluded with the comment "Not bad, eh?" he said, "Yes, that is rather good news."

Which, from Nigel Clapp, ranked as something approaching high optimism.

He also said he'd make arrangements to dispatch Rose Keating down to Crawley to take a witness statement.

Around noon the next day, I called him from Bristol with more good news: I had heard exactly what I wanted to hear from my second Pat Hobbs contact, and she too was ready to make a witness statement. Once again, he was enthusiasm itself: "You've done very well, Ms. Goodchild."

Maeve Doherty concurred, ringing me two days later to say how pleased she was with my detective work.

"It is certainly very interesting testimony," she said, sounding cautious and guarded. "And if carefully positioned in the hearing, it might have an impact. I'm not saying it's the smoking gun I'd like—but it is, without question, most compelling."

Then she asked me if I was free to drop by her office for an hour, so we could go through how she was planning to examine me when I gave evidence at the hearing, and what I should expect from Tony's barrister.

Though she only needed to see me for sixty minutes, the round-trip journey to Chancery Lane ate up two hours. Time was something of which I was in short supply right now—as I had lost more than a full working day on my assorted expeditions to Sussex and Bristol, and as the *Film Guide* proofs had to be in before the hearing began. Once inside her office, I found myself kneading a piece of paper in my hands as we did a run-through of my testimony. She told me that kneading a piece of paper was something I must definitely *avoid* doing while being questioned, as it made me look hyper and terrified. Then she did a practice run of a potential cross-examination, terrorizing me completely, coldly haranguing me, attacking all my weaknesses, and undermining all my defenses.

"Now you have me scared to death," I said after she finished.

"Don't be," she said. "Because you actually did very well indeed. The thing to remember is that she will do more than her level best to trip you up, and to make you seem like a complete and utter liar. She will also try to make you angry. The one trick here is: *do not take the bait*. Keep your answers brief and concise. Avoid eye contact with her. Keep repeating the same thing, again and again. Do not deviate from your story and you'll be just fine."

I doubted that—but, thankfully, the terror of the hearing was briefly superseded by the more immediate terror of not making the deadline. I was actually grateful for the pressure, as it did block out the fear I had. It also forced me to work fourteen-hour days for the last week. Bar the occasional trip to the supermarket for food—and a fast thirty-minute canter along the towpath by the river—I didn't leave the house . . . except, of course, for my weekly visit with Jack. He was crawling now, and making a wide variety of sounds, and liked being tickled, and especially enjoyed a routine I did which involved holding him above me while I lay on the floor, and then going, "One, two, three, *boom*," and pulling him straight down on top of me. In fact, he thought this hilarious, and in his own monosyllabic way, kept indicating that he wanted me to repeat it, over and over again. Which, of course, I was only too willing to do. Until Clarice walked in and informed me that our hour was up.

As always, this was the hardest moment. The hand-over. There were days when I clutched Jack to me and fought tears. There were other days when he would look a little disconcerted and perturbed by having to end our fun together, and I fought tears. There were days when he'd fallen asleep or was having a crying jag or just generally feeling out of sorts, and I fought tears. Today was no different. I picked us both up off the floor. I put his head against mine. I kissed him. I said, "Next week, big guy."

Then I handed him to Clarice. She disappeared into the next room. I sat down in one of the molded plastic chairs and—for the first time since our initial supervised visit—I broke down. Clarice came in. She sat down beside me, and put her arm around me, and allowed me to bury my head in her shoulder as I let go. To her infinite credit, she said nothing. I think she understood the pressure I had been under—both to behave correctly and calmly in her presence, and to withstand the enforced separation of the last months with a necessary equanimity, in order not to be judged a troublemaker. Just as she also understood what I was facing in just three days' time. And how, if it didn't go my way . . .

So she held me and let me cry. And when I finally subsided, she said, "I hope that, by this time next week, these supervised visits will just be a bad memory for you, and you'll be back with your little boy."

Meanwhile, I had a job to finish—and I was determined to have it done before the start of the hearing, in order to allow me a decent night's sleep before heading to the high court.

A few days before the hearing Sandy called me.

"So, Tuesday morning's the big day, right?"

"That's right."

"I wish I was a Catholic. I'd have Mass said for you."

"Divine intervention isn't going to help me now."

"You never know. Anyway, promise you'll call me Tuesday evening."

"You'll definitely be hearing from me."

I hung up. And worked that night until three, then fell into bed, and got up again at seven, and worked straight through (with an hour's nap somewhere in the middle of the day) until seven next morning. At which time, I sat in a bath, and congratulated myself on finishing this endless proofreading job.

The manuscript went off by motorcycle courier at nine. I headed off to the public pool in Putney shortly thereafter and spent an hour doing laps. Then I went off and had my hair done, and took myself to lunch, then crossed the road to the local cinema and sat through some romantic drivel starring Meg Ryan, then collected my one suit from the dry cleaner's, and was home by five, and received a phone call from Maeve Doherty—telling me that she had just been informed of the judge who would be hearing the case.

"His name is Charles Traynor."

"Is he a reasonable judge?" I asked her.

"Well . . ."

"In other words, he's not reasonable."

"I would have preferred someone else besides him. Very old school. Very play-it-by-the-book. Very traditional . . ."

He sounded exactly like the last guy I faced. I asked, "Are you saying that he hates women?"

"Now to call him a misogynist might be just a tad extreme. But he does have a rather orthodox viewpoint on family matters."

"Wonderful. Did you ever argue a case in front of this Traynor guy?"

"Oh, yes. And I have to say that, when I came up against him five years ago, Charles Traynor struck me as the worst sort of Old Etonian: stuffy, conceited, and someone who clearly couldn't stand everything I stood for. Yet, by the end of the hearing, I completely respected him. Because—whatever about his High Tory demeanor and his questionable attitudes toward women, especially those who work for a living, he's also scrupulously fair when it comes to the application of the law. So I certainly wouldn't fear him."

I decided to put all such fears on hold for the night—because I knew they would all come rushing in at daybreak. So I forced myself into bed by nine and slept straight through until the alarm went off at seven the next morning.

As I snapped into consciousness, there was a moment or two of delicious befuddlement until the realization hit:

This is it.

I was at the high court just after ten-fifteen. I didn't want to get there too early as I knew I'd just loiter with intent outside the main Gothic archway, getting myself into an advanced stage of fear. As it was, I was clutching the *Independent* so tensely on the underground journey to Temple that it had started to fray. The court was already in full swing by the time I arrived, with bewigged barristers walking by, accompanied by solicitors lugging hefty document cases and anxious-looking civilians, who were either the plaintiffs or defendants in the legal dramas taking place within this vast edifice. Nigel Clapp appeared, pulling one of those airline pilot cases on wheels. Maeve Doherty was with him, dressed in a very conservative black suit—having explained to me during our meeting the previous week that, like the interim hearing, there would be no wigs, no robes. Just dark suits and (as she dryly noted) "the usual dour formalities."

"Uhm . . . good morning, Ms. Goodchild," Nigel said.

I attempted a smile and tried to appear calm. Maeve immediately detected my anxiousness.

"Just remember that it will be all over in a few days—and we stand a very good chance now of changing the situation. Especially as I spoke with those two witnesses yesterday on the phone. You did very well, Sally."

A black cab pulled up in front of us. The door opened—and for the first time in more than eight months, I found myself looking at the man who was still, legally speaking, my husband. Tony had put on a little weight in the interim, but he still looked damnably handsome, and had dressed well for the occasion in a black suit, a dark blue shirt, and a tie which I'd bought on impulse for him at Selfridges around a year ago. When he caught sight of me, his hand covered his tie for a moment, before he gave me the smallest of nods, then turned away. I couldn't look at him either and also deflected his glance. But in that moment, an image jumped into my brain: climbing aboard that Red Cross chopper in Somalia, and catching sight of Tony Hobbs seated opposite me on the floor, giving me the slightest of flirtatious smiles—one that I met in turn. That's how our story started—and this is where it had now brought us: to the steps of a court of law, surrounded by our respective legal teams, unable to look each other in the eye.

Tony's barrister, Lucinda Fforde, followed him, along with the same solicitor she used for the interim hearing. And then Diane Dexter emerged from the cab. Viewed up close, she did not contradict the image I had of her: tall, sleek, elegantly dressed in a smart business suit, tight black hair, a face that was wearing its fifty years with relative ease. I wouldn't have described her as a beautiful woman, or even pretty. She was handsome in a quietly formidable way. Having caught sight of me on the steps of the high court, she looked right through me. Then, en masse, the four of them walked by us into the building, the two barristers exchanging pleasantly formal greetings with each other. It then struck me that with the exception of Nigel Clapp, who was in his usual shade of mid-gray, all the other participants in this little drama were dressed in black, as if we were all attending a funeral.

"Well," Maeve said, "it looks like we're all here. So . . ."

She nodded toward the door and we all walked in. Maeve led us through the high court's vast foyer. We turned left, crossed a courtyard, and entered the Thomas More Building, which, according to Maeve, was largely used for family law cases. Then, it was up two flights of stairs until we reached Court 43, a large chapel-like courtroom in bleached wood, much like the one in which the interim hearing was held. There were six rows of benches. The judge's bench was positioned on a raised platform. The witness stand was to its immediate left. Beyond this was a doorway, which (I presumed) led to the judge's chambers. As before, we were on the left side of the court, Tony and company to the right. There was a court stenographer and a court clerk positioned at the front. Maeve had already explained to me that, as Tony was making "application" to retain custody of Jack, he had been (legally speaking) cast in the role of *applicant* . . . and since I was being forced to "respond" to this application, I would be known in court as the *respondent*. Tony's team would be opening the case and presenting their evidence first. His barrister would have already submitted her skeleton argument to the judge (as Maeve had submitted hers). Witnesses would be called, largely to corroborate the statements they had made. After each "examination in chief" Maeve would be permitted to cross-examine the witnesses, then Lucinda Fforde could reexamine, if she desired.

"We've largely gone over to the French inquisitorial model when it comes to family law," Maeve explained to me when we met in her office, "which means that, unlike the States, neither side can interrupt the other's examination of a witness unless it is absolutely crucial." After the applicant's case had been presented, we would give our evidence. Then after our case was presented, there would be closing arguments. We'd go first, with Tony's barrister to follow. Then Maeve would be allowed to make a response, after which Tony's barrister would have the final word.

"And I know what you're going to say: that is completely unfair if you happen to be the respondent. Which is, I'm afraid, absolutely right. But that's how the system works—and there's precious little any of us can do about it. Except to make absolutely certain that they won't be able to pick apart anything we've presented to the court—which is my job."

Whereas my job was to sit there and wonder if I'd ever live with my son again.

Maeve Doherty positioned herself in the front row of the courtroom. I sat with Nigel Clapp directly behind her. Tony's side had exactly the same seating arrangements. I glanced at my watch. 10:31 AM. The judge had yet to arrive. I knew already from Maeve that the hearing would be closed to members of the public, so the visitors' pews at the back of the court would remain empty. But then, suddenly, the main door opened and I heard a very familiar voice say my name.

The voice was that of my sister, Sandy. I turned around. There she was, looking tired and disorientated, and dragging a roll-on suitcase behind her. I stood up, stunned. I said, "What are you doing here?"

My tone wasn't wildly enthusiastic—and she picked up on this immediately.

"I just thought I should be here."

Tony craned his neck, and appeared stunned to see her in court.

"What are you looking at?" she snapped at him, and he instantly turned away. Then she turned to me and whispered, "Aren't you pleased I'm here?"

I gave her a quick hug and whispered, "Of course, of course. It's just a shock, that's all. Did you just arrive?"

"Yep. Just took the subway in from Heathrow. I suppose you can find a bed for me for a couple of nights."

I managed a small smile. "I think that can be arranged. Who's looking after the kids?"

"You know my neighbors, the Fultons? Their two are away at summer camp, so it was no sweat for them to . . ."

But we were interrupted by the court clerk announcing: "Please stand." I motioned Sandy to find a seat, and I went racing back to my spot next to Nigel Clapp. He was already standing.

"My sister," I whispered to him.

"Oh . . . uhm . . . right," he said.

The rear door opened, and Mr. Justice Charles Traynor walked in. He was in his early sixties. Large. Imposing. Well-upholstered. With a full head of steel hair and an imperial bearing that immediately let it be known he thought a great deal of himself. His three-piece black suit was immaculate. So too were his white shirt and a school tie, which I guessed to be Eton (and which Maeve later confirmed to be correct). He took his place on the bench. He bowed to us, we bowed to him. He nodded for us to sit down. He removed a pair of half-moon spectacles from the breast pocket of his suit and placed them on his nose. He cleared his throat. The clerk called the court to order. Traynor peered out at us. I could see him catch sight of the lone visitor in the back row.

"And who might you be?"

Nigel quickly whispered an explanation to Maeve Doherty, who rose and said, "My Lord, that is the sister of the respondent, who has just arrived from the States to be with Ms. Goodchild for the hearing. We ask the court's permission to allow her to stay."

Traynor looked toward Lucinda Fforde.

"Does the applicant's counsel wish to raise any objections to this visitor?"

"One moment, please, My Lord," she said, then leaned back and had a quick *sotto voce* conversation with Tony and his solicitor. After a moment, she stood and said, "We have no objections, My Lord."

"Very well then—the visitor may stay."

I avoided turning around and looking at Sandy right then—for fear she'd do something mildly triumphalist and well-meaning, like giving me the thumbs-up.

Traynor cleared his throat. Then, without any fancy preamble or explanatory comments, he asked the applicant's barrister to begin presenting her client's case.

Lucinda Fforde stood up with a little bow of the head toward the bench, and began to speak.

"My Lord, having been in receipt of my statement, you are in no doubt aware that this is, without question, a desperately sad and tragic case . . ."

With that, off she went, painting a picture of an intensely successful professional man—Anthony Hobbs, "one of the outstanding journalists of his generation"—who had found himself involved with a woman about whom he knew very little, and who became pregnant only a few short weeks into their liaison. Of course, Mr. Hobbs could have played the cad and turned his back on this woman. Instead, upon learning of his transfer back to London, he asked if she would like to accompany him—and, in fact, regularize their situation through marriage. Now, though there's no doubt that Ms. Goodchild had a most difficult pregnancy, and also had to cope with a most severe postpartum depression, her behavior became exceptionally erratic, to the point where . . .

And then—as in her opening at the interim hearing—she listed and embellished everything they had against me. My initial anguished statement in hospital that I didn't care if Jack lived or died. My increasingly erratic behavior while at the Mattingly. My threat to kill him. The sleeping pill poisoning incident. My incarceration in the psycho ward. The wondrous steadfastness of my husband through all of this . . .

At which point, in the back of the court, there was a loud angry exhalation of breath. Sandy. Lucinda Fforde stopped in mid-speech, and craned her neck to see who caused this interruption. So did Maeve and Nigel Clapp, while Mr. Justice Traynor simply peered over his bifocals and asked, "Did somebody say something?"

Sandy hung her head, avoiding all those accusatory eyes.

"See that it doesn't happen again," the judge said crisply, in a tone that indicated the next time he would not be polite about it. Then he asked Lucinda Fforde to continue.

She picked up from where she left off, outlining Tony's decency, and how he stood by me even after I spoke of murdering our son, and how he turned, in despair, to his old friend, Diane Dexter, who offered shelter from the maniacal . . .

And so forth. And so on. I had to hand it to her: she was brisk. She was concise. She was tough. She left the listener in no doubt that I had turned infanticidal—and that, as horrible as it was to separate a mother from her child, there was no choice in this instance. To allow the child back with its mother now, she argued, would only put him back in re-newed jeopardy—something, she was certain, the court didn't want to facilitate. Especially as the child was so happily settled with his father and Ms. Dexter.

Now I had heard most of these arguments before. But it still didn't lessen the impact of hearing them again. Like all good barristers, Lu-cinda Fforde was a brilliant persuader—and one who, in clear, precise, rational language, turned me into a terrifying wretch who so didn't know what she was doing that she seriously considered killing her son.

It was now Maeve's turn to outline our case, and she did so with impressive lucidity and compactness—brevity (she told me) being one of the virtues that Traynor preferred. She began by quickly reminding the judge of my journalistic background, my long-standing work as a foreign correspondent with the *Boston Post*, my ability to cope admirably as a journalist and a woman in the Middle East. She then detailed, in about three sentences, my whirlwind romance with Mr. Hobbs, becom-ing pregnant at the age of thirty-seven, reaching that "now or never" juncture that a woman approaching forty reaches on the question of motherhood, deciding to come with him to London, and then being hit with a nightmare pregnancy.

She took him through my decline and fall—her language economic, rigorous, and devoid of melodramatic pity for what had befallen me. She was a first-rate storyteller—and she had Traynor's full attention as she pressed forward to the end of her opening statement.

"Though Ms. Goodchild has never denied that—while in the throes of a clinical depression—she once expressed lack of concern about the child's survival, and once uttered a threat against her son, she never carried out this threat or committed any violent action against him. She also openly admits that, while suffering from sleep deprivation and her ongoing post-partum depression, she did accidentally breast-feed her son while taking sedatives—an incident for which she still feels ongoing remorse.

"But those three incidents I've just outlined are the entire sum total of the 'crimes and misdemeanors' that my client has been accused of committing by the applicant. And out of these three incidents, the applicant manipulated the facts to initially obtain an emergency *ex parte* order against Ms. Goodchild—a hearing that conveniently took place while she was out of the country at a family funeral. The applicant has since further exploited these incidents to win the interim order, granting him custody of the child, essentially condemning Ms. Goodchild as an unfit mother, and, with the exception of one pitiful hour a week, separating my client from her infant son for the past six months. I say that the applicant has acted in a ruthless, opportunistic fashion against his wife—and all for his own gain."

She sat down. There was a moment's pause. Then Lucinda Fforde stood up and called her first witness: Mr. Thomas Hughes.

In he marched, dressed in an excellent suit, his demeanor every bit the arrogant Harley Street specialist. He stepped into the witness box, took the oath, and then nodded with a certain old-boy politeness to Mr. Justice Traynor. It was at that moment that I noticed they were wearing the same school tie.

"Mr. Hughes, you are considered, are you not, one of the leading obstetrics specialists in the country," Ms. Fforde began, and then reminded the court that his witness statement had been submitted earlier. But just to verify the details of this statement, was it his opinion that Ms. Goodchild's behavior was abnormally extreme while under his care at the Mattingly Hospital?

He launched into this subject with reasoned relish, explaining how, in all his years as a consultant, I was one of the most aggressive and extreme patients he had encountered. He then went on to explain how, shortly after the birth of my son, the nurses on the ward had reported to him about my dangerously "capricious and volatile behavior."

"Desperate stretches of crying," he said, "followed by immoderate bouts of anger, and an absolute lack of interest in the welfare of her child—who, at that moment, was resident in the pediatric intensive care unit."

"Now, in your witness statement," Lucinda Fforde said, "you emphasize this latter point, noting how one of the nurses reported to you that Ms. Goodchild said—and this is a direct quote: 'He *is* dying—and I don't care. You get that? I *don't* care.'"

"I'm afraid that is correct. After her son was recovering from jaundice, she became extremely unsettled in front of the entire maternity ward, to the point where I had to verbally calm her down and inform her that her behavior was most unacceptable."

"Now it has been clinically argued that Ms. Goodchild was in the throes of a postpartum depression during this time. Surely, you have dealt before with other patients suffering from this sort of condition?"

"Of course. It is certainly not an atypical condition. However, I have yet to deal with a patient who reacted in such a profoundly aggressive and dangerous manner—to the point where, when I heard that her husband had sought a court order to remove the child from her, I was not at all surprised."

"Thank you very much, Mr. Hughes. No further questions at this juncture."

Maeve Doherty now stood. Her voice was cool, level.

"Mr. Hughes . . . I'd like to ask you when you had Ms. Goodchild bound to her hospital bed."

He looked startled. "I never ordered that at all," he said, his tone indignant.

"And when did you have her heavily tranquilized?"

"She was never heavily tranquilized. She was on a modest antidepressant to deal with the postoperative shock she suffered from her emergency caesarean . . ."

"And when you had her committed to the psychiatric wing of the Mattingly . . ."

"She was never committed, she was never heavily tranquilized, she was never bound to her bed."

Maeve Doherty looked at him and smiled.

"Well sir, having stated that, how can you then say that she was a dangerous patient? Surely if she had been a dangerous patient, you would have ordered her to be bound . . ."

"It is true that she did not commit acts of physical violence, but her verbal behavior . . ."

"But, as you just said, she was suffering from postoperative shock, not to mention trying to cope with the fact that her son was in intensive care. And there was an initial worry about whether the child had suffered brain damage during the delivery. Now, surely, under such circumstances, one might expect the patient to be rather agitated."

"There is a large difference between agitation and . . ."

"Rudeness?"

Traynor came in here.

"Please refrain from putting words in the witness's mouth."

"Apologies, My Lord," Maeve Doherty said, then turned back to Hughes.

"Let me put it to you this way: if we have agreed that Ms. Goodchild wasn't violent or so extreme in her behavior, then how can you justify your claim that she was one of the most extreme patients you have ever dealt with?"

"Because, as I was trying to say earlier, before you interrupted me, her verbal abusiveness was so immoderate."

"In what way immoderate?"

"She was thoroughly rude and disrespectful . . ."

"Ah," Maeve said loudly. "She was *disrespectful*. Toward you, I presume?"

"Toward me and other members of the staff, yes."

"But specifically, toward you, yes?"

"She did act in an angry manner toward me."

"Did she use obscene language, did she hurl insults at you, or call you names . . . ?"

"No, not exactly . . . But she did challenge my medical judgment."

"And that is extreme verbal abuse, in your book?"

Hughes glanced at Lucinda Fforde, like an actor asking for a prompt.

"Please answer my question," Maeve Doherty said.

"My patients usually don't question me like that," he said.

"But this *American* one did—and you didn't like it, did you?"

But before he could reply, she said, "No further questions, My Lord."

The judge turned to Lucinda Fforde and asked if she'd like to re-examine.

"Please, My Lord," she said, standing up. "Mr. Hughes, please repeat for me the comment which one of your nurses reported as being said by Ms. Goodchild when told about her son."

Hughes's lips twitched into a relaxed smile. Then he wiped that off his face and stared at me with cold ire.

"She informed me that Ms. Goodchild said: 'He *is* dying—and I don't care. You get that? I *don't* care.'"

"Thank you, Mr. Hughes. No further questions."

He looked to the judge, who informed him that he could step down. Then, glowering at Maeve Doherty, he left the court.

Next up was Sheila McGuire—the ward nurse who had reported me to Hughes about the breast-feeding incident. She seemed desperately nervous and ill at ease on the stand, and had a handkerchief between her hands, which she continued to knead. Maeve knew she was going to be the second witness, and told me that a useful passive-aggressive tactic against someone who would be testifying against me was to catch her eye, and simply stare at her throughout her testimony. I did just that—and it did have the desired effect, as her discomfort level increased proportionately. But she still managed to recount the entire story about how I yanked Jack off my breast in anger while feeding him, and had to be restrained from throwing him across the room.

During cross-examination, Maeve Doherty cornered her on her use of the word "yanking."

"Now, explain this to me clearly," Maeve said. "Ms. Goodchild just suddenly yanked the child off her breast in fury at having been bitten . . ."

"Well, it wasn't exactly a *yank*."

"By which you mean what?"

"Well, she yanked, but she didn't intentionally *yank* . . ."

"I'm sorry, I don't follow."

"Well . . . Ms. Goodchild had been suffering from acute mastitis . . ."

"Otherwise known as inflammation of the breast which can calcify the milk flow, yes?"

"It doesn't always calcify, but it can cause a terrible blockage which can be deeply painful."

"So her breasts were profoundly swollen and painful, and then her son clamped down on her swollen nipple, and she reacted the way anyone would react if suddenly subjected to sudden pain."

"Do please desist from leading the witness," Traynor said.

"Apologies, My Lord. I will rephrase. Nurse McGuire, would you say that Ms. Goodchild jumped in pain after her son bit down on her nipple, yes?"

"Yes, that's true."

"So the yank you speak about—it wasn't a deliberate, premeditated movement, was it? It was, in fact, nothing more than a shocked reaction?"

"That's right."

"So if we agree that she had a shocked, instinctive reaction to pull her son off her breast, then can we also agree that, for a moment, it seemed like she was about to hurl the child."

"Absolutely."

"But she stopped herself, didn't she?"

"Well, we were there to . . ."

"Did you make a grab for the baby?"

"Uh . . . no."

"So Ms. Goodchild stopped herself. No further questions."

There was a short ten-minute adjournment after McGuire stepped down, during which Sandy came hurrying up to where I was conferring with Nigel and Maeve.

"I'm so sorry," she said, sounding deeply contrite. "It's just, when that woman started painting that bastard as some sort of noble knight . . ."

I put my hand on her arm, signaling her to stop. Then, turning back to Nigel and Maeve, I said, "I'd like you to meet my sister, Sandy, in London on a surprise visit from Boston."

Nigel stood up and gave her his usual dead mullet handshake. Maeve smiled tightly and said, "I can understand why you reacted the way you did. But if you want to help your sister, please take heed what the judge said, and don't do that again."

The second half of the morning was taken up with testimony from two other nurses from the Mattingly, both of whom confirmed Mr. Hughes's opinion that I had been trouble incarnate while on the ward. Maeve managed to puncture some of their criticisms—but the point was still made that, in the eyes of the hospital nurses and my consultant, I had been seriously bad news.

Then, just before lunchtime, came my great friend, Jessica Law, author of the CAFCASS report which essentially let it be known that, though I was on the road to recovery, Tony Hobbs and Diane Dexter had provided an exemplary environment for Jack.

"I have no doubt in my mind," she said under questioning from Lucinda Fforde, "that Sally Goodchild is conscious of the fact that she went through a desperately traumatic period, which made her do and say things that she regretted saying. I also have no doubt that when she recovers fully from her condition, she will be a most conscientious and caring mother. The reports I have received from Clarice Chambers— who has supervised all of her visits with her son—have been nothing short of exemplary. Ms. Goodchild has also managed to find work as a freelance proofreader, and is beginning to find her way in this new endeavor. In short, I am most impressed by the courage and the tenacity she has shown under exceptionally difficult circumstances."

But then she began to wax lyrical about Chez Dexter. How the Divine Ms. D. stepped into the breach and "magnificently" provided for Jack's needs. How Mr. Hobbs appeared to her as a most caring and devoted father who was also clearly most happy in his relationship with Ms. Dexter, and had put his career on hold to care for his son on a full-time basis. How there was also a full-time nanny to supplement Mr. Hobbs's child care. How she could not find fault with this arrangement, and how she was certain that Jack was—and this was the killer comment—"in the best place he could be right now."

I expected Maeve Doherty to take her apart, to make her reiterate her positive assessment of my condition, and then question her about the real workings of the Hobbs-Dexter household.

But instead, she just posed one question.

"Ms. Law, in your considered opinion, doesn't Jack Hobbs deserve to be raised by both his parents?"

"Of course he does. But . . ."

"No further questions."

I was stunned by the brevity of this cross-examination, and by the way Maeve didn't look at me on the way back to her place. Then Lucinda Fforde rose to reexamine.

"And I too just have one question for you, Ms. Law. Would you mind confirming that the last sentence you spoke during my examination-in-chief was: 'I am certain Jack is in the best place he could be right now.'"

"Yes, that is what I said."

"No further questions, My Lord."

And we broke for lunch.

Once Mr. Justice Traynor was out of the room and Tony and Co. swept out, looking most pleased with themselves, I turned to Maeve and said, "May I ask you why—?"

She cut me off.

"Why I didn't try to pull Jessica Law apart? Because Traynor immediately gets his back up if anyone attacks a CAFCASS report or the author behind it. Though he may be an Old Tory, he does have a strong respect for professional opinion. And yes, what she said just now was harmful to us. But it would have been more harmful if I began to question her judgment, or insinuate that she had been entranced by the other side . . . which is obviously the case. Trust me here—Traynor would have turned against us on the spot."

"But what about the damage she's done?" I asked.

"Let's see what this afternoon brings," she said. Then she said that she and Nigel needed to go over a few things during lunch.

So Sandy and I retreated to a nearby Starbucks.

"Just like home," she said, looking around. "Except for the prices. Jeez, how do you afford it?"

"I don't," I said wearily.

"Please don't tell me how heavy I look," she said, wolfing a fudge brownie, washed down with sips of a mocha latte with whipped cream. "I know how heavy I am—and I am going to be addressing that issue just as soon as the summer is over."

"That's good, Sandy," I said, staring into my paper espresso cup.

"You should eat something," she said.

"I'm not hungry."

"You know, I think your barrister did a great job with that awful doctor and that Irish idiot of a nurse. But I still don't understand why she just let that social worker woman off with just—"

"Sandy, *please* . . ."

She looked at me with a mixture of jet lag, confusion, and hurt.

"I shouldn't have come, should I?"

"I'm not saying that."

"No, you're right. I'm just shooting my fat old mouth off . . ."

"Stop that," I said, taking her by the hand. "I am very pleased you're here."

"You're just saying that."

"No, *really*. Because you could not have been a better sister to me during this entire horrible business. Without you, I would have gone under. But . . ."

"I know, I know. The tension's unbearable now."

I nodded.

"That's why I decided I had to come over here," she said. "Because I would have found it absolutely unbearable to be sitting in Boston, wondering how the hell this was going."

"Not good, is what I'm thinking right now."

"All right, maybe she didn't score with the social worker, but look how she dismembered Mr. Big Shot Consultant . . ."

"The 'social worker,' as you call her, counts for everything in this case. Her report is like the alpha and the omega to the court—because it is court commissioned. You heard what Maeve said—the judge takes her word more seriously than anyone else's. Which is why this is looking so bad. Not that I didn't know that from the moment I read the CAFCASS report. But I really thought Maeve would stick it to her."

"Especially since, I bet you anything, Ms. Social Worker walked around Ms. Rich Bitch's designer house, saw the photos of her with Tony and the Missus at Downing Street, was probably flattered to death to be taken so seriously by such a *player*, that she turned all *starfucky* . . . excuse my American."

"You're excused," I said. "And I think you're right."

"Who's up next this afternoon?"

"My wonderful husband."

"I can't wait."

I had to hand it to Tony, his testimony was masterful—a true performance, of the convincing sort I used to see him trot out in front of some heavyweight Arab foreign minister, from whom he wanted something. Tony in the witness box became Anthony Hobbs of the *Chronicle*: erudite, serious, a man of gravitas, yet also one of great compassion, especially when it came to dealing with his tragically wayward wife. Encouraged to wax humanitarian by Lucinda Fforde, he took her through the entire story of my breakdown, how he tried so hard to help me through it, how I rejected his support, and how he still stuck by me even after I threatened the life of our son.

Then he went into his "friendship" with Diane Dexter—that, yes, it had always been a flirtatious friendship, but it had never been anything other than that until his marriage began to disintegrate and he began to fear for the safety of his son. And then he made an impassioned "new man" spiel about how fatherhood had been the best thing that had ever happened to him, how he had never really understood the remarkable joy and pleasure that having a child could bring to your life, just as he could not ask for a more remarkable (yes, he used that word twice) partner than Diane Dexter (and he looked directly at her as he sang her praises), and he was desperately, *desperately* distressed by the fact that he had no choice but to take Jack away from my "self-destructive rampage," but he did hope that—once I found my equilibrium again—I could perhaps play a role in his life. For the moment, however, he was fully committed to being Jack's "principal carer," which is why he had decided to give up his job on the *Chronicle*, and how—when they moved to Australia next month—he would also not be seeking full-time employment for at least another year or so, in order "to be there for Jack."

As Tony went on with this *at one with his inner child* routine, my growing sense of rage was only mitigated by the fear that Sandy might start making nauseated sounds in the back row.

Then Maeve Doherty stepped up to the plate. She looked at him with cool detachment.

"Now then, Mr. Hobbs," she began. "We've just heard your appreciation of the joys of fatherhood. Which, of course, is most commendable. Just out of interest, sir, why did you wait so long before having children?"

"My Lord," Lucinda Fforde said, sounding truly annoyed. "I really must object to this line of questioning. What on earth does this have to do with the matter at hand?"

"Let the witness answer the question," Traynor said.

"And I'm happy to answer it," Tony said. "The reason I didn't have children until I met Sally was because of the nature of my profession, and the fact that, because I was a nomadic journalist—wandering from war to war, foreign capital to foreign capital—I simply never had the chance to meet someone, settle down. But then I met Sally—and her pregnancy coincided with my return to London and the foreign editorship of the *Chronicle*. So this seemed like the ideal moment to make a commitment both to her and to fatherhood."

"And before this, you simply had no experience of fatherhood?"

"No, none whatsoever."

"You're obviously making up for lost time."

"Ms. Doherty . . . ," Traynor said witheringly.

"I withdraw the comment. Now Mr. Hobbs, let's turn to another pertinent issue here . . . your decision to leave the *Chronicle*. You worked for the *Chronicle* for over twenty years. Is that correct?"

"Yes, that's right."

"One of their most distinguished foreign correspondents, covering, as you mentioned, a goodly number of wars, not to mention being the *Chronicle*'s man in Washington, Tokyo, Frankfurt, Paris, Cairo. And then, just over a year ago, you were recalled to London to become the foreign editor. Were you pleased about this recall?"

"My Lord, I must object again," Lucinda Fforde said. "This is deviating from the . . ."

"Do let us complete this witness's cross-examination," Traynor said. "Please answer the question, Mr. Hobbs."

"It was . . . yes, I'll admit it . . . it was rather difficult to adjust at first to office life again. But I did settle in . . ."

"Even though, some months later, you not only quit the foreign editorship, but also resigned from the paper. And during this same week, you also decided to end your marriage to Ms. Goodchild, to seek an emergency court order in order to gain custody of your son, and move in with Ms. Dexter. Quite a number of life-changing decisions in just a matter of days, wouldn't you agree?"

"The decisions I made were all predicated on the danger I perceived my son to be in."

"All right, let's say you did decide it was important that you be at home with Jack for a while. Surely the *Chronicle* has a reasonably enlightened management, and surely, had you gone to them and said you wanted a leave of absence for personal matters, they would have been sympathetic. But to quit your job just like that, after over two decades with the paper? Why did you do that?"

"It wasn't 'just like that,' it was a decision that had been building for some time."

"Ah then, so you really didn't readjust to life behind a desk at Wapping . . . ?"

"Not precisely. It was just time to move on . . ."

"Because?"

"Because I had discovered other ambitions."

"Literary ambitions, perhaps?"

"That's right. I was writing a novel."

"Ah yes, your novel. In her witness statement—which you have undoubtedly read—Ms. Goodchild reports that after your son came home from hospital, you became increasingly preoccupied with your novel, locking yourself up in your study, sleeping up there as well, making your wife deal with the broken nights, the four AM feeds, and all the other messy bits of child care."

Tony had anticipated this question and was completely prepared for it.

"I think that is a profoundly unfair interpretation of the situation. After Sally lost her job . . ."

"Didn't your wife have no choice but to give up work because of a medical condition that threatened her pregnancy?"

"All right. After my wife was forced to give up work, I was the family's only source of income. I was putting in nine- to ten-hour days at the *Chronicle*, a newspaper at which I was no longer happy, and I was also attempting to fulfill a long-standing ambition to write fiction. On top of that, I was also coping with my highly unstable wife who was in the throes of a major depression . . ."

"But who was still coping with all the difficult business of child care. You didn't have a nanny at home, did you, Mr. Hobbs?"

"No—but that's because finances were a little tight."

"So your wife had to handle all that herself. And for someone in the throes of a major postpartum depression, she handled all that rather remarkably, wouldn't you agree?"

"She spent nearly two months in a psychiatric ward."

"Where your son was looked after as well. Leaving you plenty of time to develop your friendship with Ms. Dexter into something else . . ."

Traynor let out one of his exasperated sighs.

"Miss Doherty, please resist the temptation to conjecture."

"Apologies, My Lord. Now when your wife did leave the hospital— and it should be pointed out that, recognizing that she did have a problem, she remained in that psychiatric unit of her own accord—did you not find her a calmer, more rational person?"

"From time to time, yes. But she was also prone to terrible mood swings."

"As befitting anyone battling with clinical depression."

"She worried me constantly."

"Even though there wasn't a specific incident in which you thought that the child's life was in danger?"

"You don't think that breast-feeding a child while on an extremely high dosage of sedatives is endangering a child?"

"Mr. Hobbs," the judge said, "you are not asking the questions here."

"Nevertheless I will answer it, My Lord," Maeve said. "Though it is true that your son ended up in the hospital after this incident, it's also very clear that a mistake had been made on the part of your wife. A mistake made when she was suffering from both depression and extreme sleep deprivation. A mistake she made while you were getting your eight hours, fast asleep on the sofa in your study."

She paused for emphasis. Then her voice lost its steely chill and she became dangerously pleasant again.

"A very simple question, sir: did Ms. Goodchild do anything after her return from hospital to make you fear that the child's life was in danger?"

"As I said before, she suffered from severe mood swings which made me fear that she might lash out."

"But she didn't lash out, did she?"

"No, but . . ."

"And on the subject of her earlier outbursts, let me ask you this: have you never said something foolish in anger? An anger fueled by post-operative shock and clinical depression?"

"I've never suffered from either of those conditions."

"That is fortunate. But you've never said something in anger?"

"Of course I have. But I've never threatened a child's life . . ."

"Returning to your book . . ."

This sudden veering away from the subject immediately worried me. It showed that Maeve had conceded a point to him and was trying to cover her tracks by moving on as quickly as possible.

"Now, I gather you have received an advance for your novel?"

Tony looked surprised that she knew this information.

"Yes, I've recently signed a contract with a publisher."

"Recently—as in four months ago?"

"That's right."

"So, up until that point, what did you do for income?"

"I had very little income."

"But you did have Ms. Dexter . . ."

"When she knew that Jack was in danger, Ms. Dexter . . . Diane . . . did offer to take us in. Then when I decided to look after Jack full-time, she offered to take care of our day-to-day running expenses."

"Now you say you're looking after Jack 'full-time.' But isn't it true that Ms. Dexter has hired a full-time nanny to look after Jack?"

"Well, I do need time to work on my book."

"But you said the nanny is full-time. So how many hours a day do you write?"

"Four to five."

"And what does the nanny do the rest of the time?"

"All the other duties associated with child care."

"And so, after the four to five hours of writing time, you're with your son."

"That's right."

"So you really didn't leave the *Chronicle* to look after your son full-time. You left the *Chronicle* to write your novel. And Ms. Dexter was there to conveniently subsidize that endeavor. Now, Mr. Hobbs, your advance for this novel of yours. It was twenty thousand pounds, if I'm not mistaken?"

Again, Tony looked thrown by the fact that she knew this sum.

"That's right," he said.

"Not a vast sum—but about average for a first novel. And if I'm not mistaken, Ms. Dexter hired Jack's nanny from a firm called Annie's Nannies, just down the road from you in Battersea."

"I think that was the name of the firm, yes."

"You *think*? Surely a committed father like yourself would have been in on this nannying decision from the start. Now I checked with Annie's Nannies—and it seems that the average cost of a full-time nanny is, before tax, around twenty thousand pounds per annum. Which means your advance just about covers the cost of your son's child care, but nothing else. Ms. Dexter does all that, doesn't she?"

Tony looked at Lucinda Fforde for guidance. She indicated that he had to answer.

"Well . . . I suppose Diane does cover the bulk of the costs."

"But you yourself bought your wife's air ticket to the States when she had to rush back after her brother-in-law's death."

"*Ex*-brother-in-law," Tony said.

"Indeed. But your wife rushed back to comfort her sister, is that not right?"

"Yes, that's true."

"Did you encourage her to return to the States?"

"I thought her sister needed her, yes."

"Did you encourage her. Mr. Hobbs?"

"Like I said, it was a family emergency, so I thought that Sally should be there."

"Even though she was very worried about being away from her son for several days?"

"We had child care . . . our housekeeper."

"Answer the question, please. Was she concerned about being away from her son for several days?"

Another nervous glance toward Lucinda Fforde.

"Yes, she was."

"But you encouraged her to go. You bought her ticket. And while she was out of the country, you went to court and obtained the *ex parte* court order that temporarily granted you custody of your son. Is that the correct sequence of events, Mr. Hobbs?"

Tony looked deeply uncomfortable.

"Please answer the question," Traynor said.

"Yes," Tony said, in a low voice, "that's the correct sequence of events."

"One final question. Did you buy your wife an economy class ticket to Boston?"

"I don't remember."

"Really? Because I have the ticket here, and it's a higher-priced business class ticket. You don't remember buying her this more comfortable class of travel?"

"I let my travel agent handle the details."

"But surely you instructed him about which class she should travel in? I mean, the difference between an economy and a business class ticket is over three hundred pounds."

"He might have offered me the business class ticket as an option, and—"

"Because you wanted her to be comfortable on her flight to and from Boston, you approved the extra expenditure?"

"Yes, I suppose so."

"And having flown her business class to the States, you then went to court to obtain the order effectively barring her from seeing her son . . . ?"

Lucinda Fforde was on her feet. But before she could say anything, Maeve cut her off.

"No further questions," she said.

Tony did not look happy. Though he'd managed to deflect a few of her attacks, he was also someone who hated to be wrong-footed. And I thought she'd done a rather good job of that.

"Reexamination?" Traynor asked in that slightly bored voice of his.

"Yes, My Lord," Lucinda Fforde said. "And it is just one question, Mr. Hobbs. Please remind us again why you felt it necessary to seek an emergency order, taking custody of your son."

"Because I feared that she might fall into one of her dangerous moods again and, this time, actually carry out her threat to kill him."

I gripped my hands tightly together, trying to force myself to stay silent. I had to admire Lucinda Fforde's supremely clever tactical logic: after all the palaver of a cross-examination, return to just one central point and undermine all the other points scored earlier against her client by one reiteration of an absolute fucking lie.

When Tony was told he could step down, he returned to his seat next to the Dexter woman. She gave him a little hug and whispered something into his ear. Then her name was called to enter the witness box.

She looked very impressive, standing up there. Poised, assured, just a little regal. I could understand what Tony saw in her. She possessed a certain glamour quotient that I knew he always craved. Just as I also knew that he probably took one look at her property portfolio—and her taste in interior decor—and realized that she was a great catch. Just as she—a woman who had recently edged into fifty—would have admired his professional accomplishments, his worldliness, his sardonic wit, and his need to flee the entrapments of home and office. And then there was the little fact that he came accompanied by a child . . .

But as Lucinda Fforde took her through a review of her witness statement, it was clear how she was playing this game: the great friend who found herself falling in love with her great friend, but knew she couldn't break up his marriage (especially right after he-and-his had just had a baby). But then, his wife had her "mental crisis," Tony was desperately worried about little Jack's safety, she offered a room in her house, one thing led to another, and . . .

"I must emphasize," she said, "that this wasn't a *coup de foudre*. I think I can speak for Tony when I say that we both had these feelings for each other for quite a number of years. Only we never had the opportunity for involvement before now."

Then Lucinda Fforde took her through these newfound maternal feelings: how she felt completely committed to Jack, how she only wanted the best for him, and how she was taking a considerable amount of time off work to be with him.

"This is possibly the central reason I decided to relocate to Sydney for several years. My company is opening a new office there. I could have farmed out the job of getting it up and running to one of several colleagues. But I felt that it would be good to take myself out of the London rat race for a few years, and also give Jack the opportunity of being raised in Sydney."

She would also be working her schedule to make sure that she would have ample time with him. And she went on to describe the house she had rented in Point Piper—right on the water and near excellent schools (when that time came). As she went on in this real estate agent vein, I found myself clutching my hands together again in an attempt to keep myself under control. Because I wanted to tell her just what a lying bitch I thought she was.

But then, finally, she came around to the subject of me.

"I've never met Sally Goodchild. I certainly hold nothing against her. On the contrary, I feel so desperately sorry for her, and can only imagine what the horror of the past few months must have been like. I'm certain that she regrets her actions. And God knows, I do believe in rehabilitation and forgiveness. Which is why I would never bar her from Jack, and would welcome an open visiting arrangement in the future."

As soon as she said that, I had a picture of myself, jet-lagged out of my brains after a twenty-six-hour flight to the bottom of the world, staying in some fleabag motel, then taking a bus out to her palatial harborside house, to be greeted by a little boy with a thick Aussie accent, turning to the Dexter woman and saying, "But, Mum, I don't want to go off with her for the day."

Diane Dexter finished off her testimony for Lucinda Fforde with the statement: "I do hope that Ms. Goodchild will make a full recovery— and that, one day in the future, perhaps we can be friends."

Absolutely. In fact I'll tell you exactly when we can be friends. On the twelfth of never.

Maeve Doherty stood up and smiled evenly at the woman in the witness stand.

"You've been married twice in the past, haven't you, Ms. Dexter?"

She didn't like that question and it showed.

"Yes, that's right," she said.

"And did you try to have children during these marriages?"

"Yes, of course I tried to have children during these marriages."

"And you did have a miscarriage around 1990?"

"Yes—I did. And I know what your next question will be and I'd like to answer it . . ."

The judge came in here. "But you must first let Ms. Doherty *pose* the question."

"I'm sorry, My Lord."

"But yes, I would be very pleased to know what you thought my next question would be?" Maeve said.

Dexter looked at her with calm, steely anger: "'Did you, Ms. Dexter, miscarry the baby because of drug abuse?' To which my answer would be: Yes. I was seriously abusing cocaine at the time, and it provoked a miscarriage. I sought professional help after this tragedy. I spent two months at the Priory Clinic. I have not used or abused drugs since then. If I now drink a glass of wine in the course of an evening, it's an event. And my charitable work on drug education in schools is well known."

"And you also attempted several IVF treatments in 1992 and 1993, both of which failed?"

Again, Dexter was taken aback by the revelation of this information. "I don't know how you found out those facts, but they are correct."

"Just as it's also correct that the Harley Street specialist you were seeing at the time then told you there was no chance of you conceiving again?"

She looked downward. "Yes, he did tell me that."

"And since then, you did try to adopt in . . . when was it? . . . 1996, but were turned down because of your age and your single status?"

"Yes," she said, her voice barely a whisper.

"And then Tony Hobbs appeared in your life again, now back in London, now a new father with an infant child, and a wife who was suffering from profound clinical depression . . ."

Dexter looked at Maeve with barely contained rage.

"As I made clear earlier . . ."

"Now let me ask you this, Ms. Dexter: if an acquaintance was to run into you on the street where you live, and saw you pushing Jack along in his pram, and ask, 'Is he your child?' how would you respond?"

"I'd say yes, I'm his mother."

Maeve folded her hands across her chest and said nothing, letting that comment fill the silence in the courtroom. A silence that the judge broke.

"But you are *not* his mother, Ms. Dexter," he said.

"Of course, I'm not his biological mother. But I have become his surrogate mother."

The judge peered at her over his half-moon spectacles and spoke in that half-weary voice he so preferred.

"No, you haven't. Because it has yet to be legally determined whether or not you will be assuming the role of surrogate mother. The child in question has a mother and a father. You happen to live with the father. But that does not give you the right to state that you are the child's mother, surrogate or otherwise.

"Any further questions, Ms. Doherty?"

"No, My Lord."

"Reexamination, Ms. Fforde?"

She looked seriously disconcerted. "No, My Lord."

"Then we'll reconvene after a ten-minute adjournment."

Once he was out of the court, Maeve sat down next to Nigel and myself and said, "Well, that wasn't bad at all."

"Why did the judge so jump on her comment about considering herself his mother?" I asked.

"Because if there's one thing Charles Traynor hates more than barristers who try to attack a CAFCASS report, it's the new partner of someone in a divorce dispute, going on as if she's the newfound parent. It goes completely against his sense of propriety or familial fair play, and he always jumps on anyone who tries to play that card."

"Which is why you walked her into it?"

"Precisely."

Sandy came down and joined us.

"You were brilliant," she said to Maeve. "You really shoved it in the face of that nasty little—"

"That's fine, Sandy," I said, cutting her off.

"Sorry, sorry," she said. "I think I'm suffering from Tourette's today."

"Otherwise known as jet lag," I said.

Maeve turned to Nigel and said, "Hobbs did score one off me, didn't he?"

"I think you actually . . . uhm . . . did rather well there, considering . . ."

"That he won the point with that 'I've never threatened a child's life' comment."

"I don't think it was a hugely damaging blow," he said. "Especially after what you did to Ms. Dexter."

"What now?" I asked.

"I . . . uhm . . . think that's it for the witnesses. So I presume the judge will reconvene just to formally end the proceedings and tell us all to be here at nine tomorrow morning."

But when the judge returned, Lucinda Fforde had a little surprise for us.

"My Lord, we have a last-minute witness we would like to call."

Traynor didn't looked pleased—as he probably pictured himself at home an hour from now. Instead . . .

"And why has this witness been called at the last minute?"

"Because he's resident in the United States—in Boston, to be specific about it—"

I turned around and looked at Sandy, wondering if she had any idea whom they were planning to call. She shook her head, looking as nervous as I now felt.

"—and we were only able to obtain his statement the day before yesterday and fly him in last night. We apologize to the court for the lateness of his arrival. But he is crucial to our case and—"

"May I see his statement, please?" the judge asked, cutting her off. "And please give a copy as well to Ms. Doherty."

She handed the statement to Traynor and to Maeve. My barrister scanned the document and didn't look pleased. In fact, she noticeably stiffened. The judge looked up from his copy of the statement and asked, "And is Mr. . . ." He peered down at the document again. ". . . Mr. Grant Ogilvy here now?"

Grant Ogilvy. The name rang a distant bell somewhere.

"Yes, My Lord," Lucinda Fforde said. "He can testify immediately."

"Well, what say you, Ms. Doherty? You can raise all sorts of objections to this, should you wish to . . . and I would be obliged to back you up."

I watched Maeve—and could see her thinking fast. She said, "My Lord, with your permission, I'd like a five-minute consultation with my client before I make a decision."

"Five minutes is fine, Ms. Doherty. Court will stand in recess."

Maeve motioned for me and Nigel to follow her outside. She found a bench. We grouped around it. She spoke in a low voice.

"Did you ever see a therapist named Grant Ogilvy?" she asked.

I put my hand to my mouth. *Him*? They found *him*?

I suddenly felt ill. Now I was certain to lose Jack.

"Ms. Goodchild," Nigel said, his voice filled with anxious concern, "are you all right?"

I shook my head and sat down on the bench.

"Can I read what he told them?" I asked.

"Read it fast," Maeve said, "because we need to make a decision in about four minutes."

I read the statement. It was what I expected. Then I handed it to Nigel. He lifted his glasses and glanced right through it.

"Uhm . . . isn't there some sort of patient-doctor confidentiality agreement about this sort of thing?" he asked.

"Yes, there is," Maeve said, "except when—as in this case—there is a child protection issue. Then the cloak of confidentiality can be breached. But I'm sure we could challenge it, and hold things up for weeks, and incite Traynor's ire in the process. And the other thing is: from what I've read here, this all happened so damn long ago that I can't imagine Traynor will consider it substantive evidence against your character. You look skeptical, Nigel."

"In . . . uhm . . . all honesty, it is a risk. And I'm sorry to say this, Ms. Goodchild, but it could call into question aspects about your character. Even though, personally speaking, I don't find that it changes my perception of you whatsoever."

"The problem here," Maeve said, "is that tomorrow, we want to spring two surprise witnesses on them—which I always thought was going to be a tricky maneuver, but which Traynor will more readily allow if we've already accepted their surprise witness. It is a gamble—but one which I think is worth taking, as our witnesses will have far more bearing on the case than theirs will have. But, ultimately, it has to be your decision, Sally. And, I'm afraid, you need to make it right now."

I took a deep breath. I exhaled. I said, "All right. Let him testify . . ."

"Good decision," Maeve said. "Now you have exactly three minutes to tell me everything I need to know about what happened back then."

When we returned to the courtroom, Maeve explained our position to Mr. Justice Traynor.

"In the interests of expediting the hearing, and not causing any further delays, we will accept this last-minute witness."

"Very well," Traynor said. "Please call Mr. Ogilvy."

As he walked in, I thought: *fifteen years on and he still looks almost the same*. He was in his mid-fifties now. A little heavier around the middle, somewhat grayer, but still wearing that same sort of tan gabardine suit that he was sporting in 1982. The same blue Oxford button-down shirt and striped tie. The same horn-rimmed glasses and brown penny loafers. He kept his line of vision aloft as he walked to the witness stand, so as not to see me. But once he was on the stand, I stared directly at him. He turned away and focused his attention on Lucinda Fforde.

"Now Mr. Ogilvy—to confirm your statement, you have been a practicing psychotherapist in the Boston area for the past twenty-five years."

"That's right."

"And after the death of her parents in a car accident in 1988, Ms. Goodchild was referred to you as a patient?"

He confirmed this fact.

"Well then, could you also please confirm what Ms. Goodchild told you in the course of one of her sessions."

For the next ten minutes, he did just that—recounting the story in just about the same way that I recounted it to Julia. He didn't try to embellish or exaggerate anything. What he said was a reasonable, accurate rendering of what I told him. But—as my eyes bored into him—all I could think was: *you haven't just betrayed me, you have also betrayed yourself.*

When he finished, Lucinda Fforde looked at me and said, "So, put rather baldly, Ms. Goodchild gave her father the drink that sent him over the limit and caused him to crash the car—"

"I thoroughly object to this line of questioning, My Lord," Maeve said, genuinely angry. "Counsel isn't simply surmising, she is also writing fiction."

"I concur. Please rephrase, Miss Fforde."

"With pleasure, My Lord. Though Mr. Goodchild informed his daughter that he was over the limit, she still gave him the glass of wine. Is that correct?"

"Yes, that's correct."

"And later that night, he crashed his car into another vehicle, killing himself, his wife, a young woman in her thirties, and her fourteen-month-old son?"

"Yes, that's correct."

"And did Ms. Goodchild share this information with anyone else but you?"

"Not to my knowledge."

"Not with her one sibling, her sister?"

"Unless she did so in the last two decades, no. Because, at the time, one of the central themes of her conversations with me was the fact that she couldn't confess this fact to her sister. She couldn't confess it to anyone."

Suddenly, I heard a long choked sob behind me. Then Sandy stood and ran out the back door of the court. As soon as she was outside, her crying reverberated in the hallway. I started to stand up, but Nigel Clapp did something very un–Nigel Clapp. He grabbed my arm and caught me before I could give pursuit, whispering quickly, "You mustn't leave."

Back up front, Lucinda Fforde continued on.

"What therapeutic advice did you give Ms. Goodchild at the time, sir?"

"I told her she would be better off making a clean breast of things with her sister."

Lucinda Fforde turned toward the back of the courtroom. "Wasn't that Ms. Goodchild's sister leaving the court just now?"

Then, after the requisite dramatic pause, she said, "No further questions, My Lord."

Maeve Doherty stood up and simply stared at Grant Ogilvy. She held this glare for a good thirty seconds. He tried to meet her contemptuous gaze, but eventually turned away. Mr. Justice Traynor cleared his throat.

"You won't be kept here much longer, Mr. Ogilvy," Maeve said. "Because I really don't want to spend much time talking to you."

She too paused for effect before commencing her cross-examination. "How old was Ms. Goodchild when she saw you as a patient?"

"Twenty-one."

"How old was her father when he died?"

"Around fifty, I think."

"Ms. Goodchild handed him a drink at that party, yes?"

"Yes."

"He refused."

"Yes."

"She said, 'How middle-aged.' And he drank the drink. Is that right?"

"Yes."

"And you believe, because of that, she should be held culpable for the fatal accident he had several hours later?"

"I have never been asked to comment on her culpability."

"But you've been brought all this way across the Atlantic to sully her character, haven't you?"

"I was brought here simply to relate the information she told me."

"While she was a patient of yours, yes?"

"That's right."

"Aren't there laws in the United States about patient-doctor confidentiality?"

"I'm not a doctor. I'm a therapist. And yes, there are laws. But they mainly have to do with criminal malfeasance."

"Now if Ms. Goodchild didn't speak with anyone else about this, how on earth did Mr. Hobbs's people find you after all these years, and why did you agree to be brought over here?"

"Because they asked me to testify, that's why."

"And what are they paying you for your trouble?"

"My Lord, I do hate to interrupt yet again," Lucinda Fforde said, "but this is improper."

"Oh, *please*," Maeve hissed. "He's obviously not over here for altruistic reasons . . ."

"We are running out of time, Ms. Doherty," Traynor said. "Is this line of questioning likely to take matters further?"

"I have no further questions for this . . . *gentleman*."

Traynor heaved a huge sigh of relief. He could go home now.

"The witness is dismissed. Court is adjourned until nine tomorrow morning."

As soon as Traynor had left the court, I was on my feet, racing out the back door in search of Sandy. I found her on a bench in the hallway, her eyes red, her face wet. I tried to touch her shoulder. She shrugged me off.

"Sandy . . ."

The door of the courtroom opened, and out came Grant Ogilvy, accompanied by Tony's solicitor. Before I could stop her, Sandy was in his face.

"I'm going back to Boston in two days," she yelled, "and the first thing I'm going to do is make certain everyone who counts in your profession knows what you did here today. You understand? I am going to fucking ruin you. Because you fucking deserve it."

A court usher, hearing her raised voice, came running toward the scene. But Tony's solicitor shooed him away.

"It's over now," he whispered, and hustled a wide-eyed and deeply distressed Grant Ogilvy out of the building.

I turned toward Sandy, but she walked away from me. Maeve and Nigel were at the door of the courtroom, looking on.

"Is she going to be all right?" Maeve asked.

"She just needs to calm down. It's a dreadful shock for her."

"And for you too," Nigel added. "Are you all right?"

I ignored the question and asked Maeve, "How much damage do you think he did?"

"The truth is, I don't know," she said. "But the important thing now is: go deal with your sister, try to stay calm, and—most of all—get a good night's sleep. Tomorrow will be a very long day."

I noticed Nigel had Sandy's roll-on bag beside him.

"She left this behind," he said. "Anything I can do?"

I shook my head. He awkwardly reached over and touched my arm.

"Ms. Goodchild . . . Sally . . . what you were just put through was so dreadfully wrong."

Then, almost shocked by this show of emotion, he nodded good-bye to me.

As I went off to find Sandy, I realized that that was the one time Nigel Clapp had ever called me by my first name.

FOURTEEN

SANDY WAS WAITING outside the court, leaning against a pillar. "Let's get a cab," I said.

"Whatever."

In the ride back to Putney, she didn't say a word to me. She just leaned against one side of the taxi, exhausted, spent, in one of those dark states that I got to know during childhood. I didn't blame her for being in such a black place. As far as she was concerned, I had betrayed her. And she was right. And now I didn't have a clue about how I should (or could) make amends for such a huge error of judgment.

But I also knew enough about Sandy to realize that the best strategy right now was to let her get through the big monstrous anger phase of this freeze-out. So I said nothing to her on the way out to Putney. When we reached the house, I made up the guest bed and showed her where the bathroom was, and let her know that there was plenty of microwavable food in the fridge. But if she wanted to eat with me . . .

"What I want is a bath, a snack, and bed. We'll talk tomorrow."

"Well, I'm going to take a walk then."

What I wanted to do was knock on Julia's door and ask her to pour me a vodka and allow me to scream on her shoulder for a bit. But as I approached my front door, I saw a note that had landed on the inside mat. It was from her, saying:

> *Desperate to know how it went today . . . but had to go out*
> *to a last-minute business thing. I should be home by eleven.*
> *If you're still up then and want company, do feel free to*
> *knock on the door.*
>
> *Hope you got through it all.*
> *Love, Julia*

God, how I needed to talk to her, to anyone. But instead, I took what solace I could from a walk along the river. When I got back I found that Sandy had indeed eaten a chicken madras and had taken her jet lag and her anger to bed early.

I picked at a microwaved spaghetti carbonara. I stared blankly at the television. I ran myself a bath. I took the necessary dose of anti-depressants and sleeping pills. I crawled into bed. The chemicals did their job for around five hours. When I woke, the clock read 4:30 AM—and all I could feel was dread. Dread about my testimony today. Dread about yesterday's debacle with Sandy. Dread about the influence that Grant Ogilvy would have on the judge's decision. Dread, most of all, that I was now destined to lose Jack.

I went down to the kitchen to make myself a cup of herbal tea. As I walked by the living room, I saw that the light was on. Sandy was stretched out on the sofa, awake, lost in middle-of-the-night thought.

"Hi," I said. "Can I get you anything?"

"You know what really kills me?" she said. "It's not that you gave Dad that last drink. No, what so fucking upsets me is that you couldn't tell me."

"I wanted to, but . . ."

"I know, I know. And I understand all your reasons. But to keep that to yourself for all these years . . . Jesus Christ, Sally . . . didn't you think I'd understand? Didn't you?"

"I just couldn't bring myself to admit . . ."

"What? That you've been carrying fifteen years' worth of guilt for no damn reason? I could have talked you out of your guilt in a heartbeat. But you chose not to let me. You chose to keep stagnating in the fucking guilt, and that's what really staggers me."

"You're right."

"I know I'm right. I may just be a fat little suburbanite . . ."

"Now who's trading in self-hate?"

She laughed a cheerless laugh. And said, "I don't know about you, but I've always hated my last name. *Goodchild*. Too much to live up to."

She pushed herself up off the sofa. "I think I'll try to get two more hours of sleep."

"Good idea."

But I couldn't sleep. I just took up her place on the sofa, and stared at the empty grate in the fireplace, and tried to fathom why I couldn't bring myself to tell her what I should have told her, why I dodged the absolution I so craved. And why every child wants to be a good child—and never can really live up to the expectations of others, let alone themselves.

Somewhere over the next few hours, I did nod off—and then found myself being nudged by Sandy, who had a mug of coffee in one hand.

"It's eight AM," she said, "and this is your wake-up call."

I slurped down the coffee. I took a fast shower. I put on my good suit again. I did a little damage control with foundation and blusher. We were out the door and on the tube by nine-fifteen. It was a brilliantly bright, sundappled day.

"Sleep all right?" Maeve asked me as we settled down in the front left-hand row of the court.

"Not bad."

"And how is your sister?"

"A bit better, I think."

Just then Nigel showed up, accompanied by Rose Keating. She gave me a little hug.

"You didn't think I was going to miss this, did you?" she asked. "Who's the woman in the back row?"

"My sister," I said.

"All the way over here from the States to support you? Good on her. I'll sit with her."

"How are our last-minute witnesses?" Maeve asked.

"Due here this afternoon, as requested," she said.

"They know how to get to the high court?" Maeve asked.

"It's all arranged. Nigel's meeting one of them at Paddington during the lunch break, and I'm going to Victoria for the other one."

Tony and Co. then arrived—his lawyers nodding at their counterparts on this side of the court, their client and his new partner avoiding my gaze as before. Just as I also didn't want to make eye contact with either of them.

Then the court clerk stood up and asked us to do so as well. Mr. Justice Traynor entered, sat down, greeted us with a brief "Good morning," and called the hearing to order.

It was now Maeve's turn to present our case. And so she called her first witness: Dr. Rodale.

She didn't smile at me from the witness stand. She seemed to be deliberately ignoring my presence—perhaps because that would give her testimony more weight.

Maeve got her to recite her professional qualifications, her long-standing association with St. Martin's, the fact that she'd had two decades' experience of treating women with postpartum depression, and had written several medical papers on the subject. She then had her outline, briefly, the emotional and physiological roller-coaster ride that was this condition, how it sneaked up on its victims unaware, how it often caused those in its vortex to do uncharacteristic things like uttering threats, becoming suicidal, refusing to eat or wash, committing violent acts . . . and how, with rare exceptions, it was always treatable.

Then she detailed my clinical case.

When she had finished Maeve asked her, "In your opinion, is Ms. Goodchild fully capable of resuming the role of full-time mother?"

She looked straight at Tony and said, "In my opinion, she was fully capable of that role when she was discharged from hospital nearly ten months ago."

"No further questions, My Lord."

Lucinda Fforde stood up.

"Dr. Rodale, during the course of your twenty-five-year career, how many women have you treated for postpartum depression?"

"Around five hundred, I'd guess."

"And, of these, how many documented cases can you remember of a mother threatening to kill her child?"

Dr. Rodale looked most uncomfortable with this question.

"When you say 'threatening to kill a child . . . '?"

"I mean, just that: someone threatening to kill a child."

"Well . . . to be honest about it, I only remember three other *reported* instances . . ."

"Only *three* other instances, out of five hundred cases. It's obviously a pretty rare threat to make then. And let me ask you this: of those three cases . . . actually four, if you include Ms. Goodchild, how many of those actually went on to murder their child?"

Dr. Rodale turned to the judge.

"My Lord, I really find this line of questioning . . ."

"Doctor, you must answer the question."

She looked straight at Lucinda Fforde.

"Only one of those women went on to kill her child."

A triumphant smile crossed the lips of Lucinda Fforde.

"So, given that, one of those four women actually killed her child, there was a twenty-five percent chance that Ms. Goodchild would have killed her child."

"My Lord—"

But before Maeve could utter anything more, Lucinda Fforde said, "No further questions."

"Reexamination?"

"Absolutely, My Lord," Maeve said, sounding furious. "Dr. Rodale, please tell us about the patient who killed her child."

"She was suffering from extreme schizophrenia, and one of the worst cases of manic depression I've ever treated. She had been committed— and the murder happened on a supervised visit with her child, when the supervisor became physically ill and had to leave the room for no more than a minute to seek help. When she returned, the mother had snapped her child's neck."

There was a long silence.

"How rare is this sort of case in postpartum depression?" Maeve asked.

"Rarer than rare. As I said, it's the one instance in five hundred or so cases I've treated. And I must emphasize again that, unlike all the other cases, this was one where the patient was essentially psychotic."

"So there is absolutely no relation whatsoever between the condition suffered by the woman who killed her child and that of Ms. Goodchild?"

"Absolutely none whatsoever. And anyone who attempts to make that sort of comparison is guilty of a monstrous manipulation of the truth."

"Thank you, doctor. No further questions."

Next up was Clarice Chambers. She did smile at me from the witness box and, under gentle, brief questioning from Maeve, told her how well I had "bonded" with Jack, the grief I had displayed at our first supervised visit, and the way I had been able to establish a genuine rapport with him during our hourly visits each week. And then Maeve asked her virtually the same question she had posed to Dr. Rodale.

"As you have been the one and only person to have watched the interaction of Ms. Goodchild and her son over the past months, is it your professional opinion that she is a caring mother?"

"A *completely* caring mother, in whom I have the greatest confidence."

"Thank you. No further questions."

Once again, Lucinda Fforde played the "I have just one question for you" game. And the question was, "In your experience, don't all mothers who have been legally prevented from unsupervised contact with their child—due to worries about the child's safety—don't they always express terrible grief in front of you?"

"Of course they do. Because—"

"No further questions."

"Reexamination?"

"Ms. Chambers, is it true that, for the past six weeks, you have allowed Ms. Goodchild to have unsupervised contact with her child?"

"That is completely correct."

"And why have you permitted this?"

"Because it's clear to me that she is a normally functioning person, who presents no danger whatsoever to her child. In fact, I've actually felt that way about her since the beginning."

"Thank you very much, Ms. Chambers."

Moving right along, Jane Sanjay took the stand. She explained that she had been my health visitor—and had seen me several times after I had come out of hospital with Jack. And she reported that she had no doubts about my competence as a mother. Maeve asked, "However, this was before the full-scale effects of the postpartum depression had afflicted her, is that correct?"

"Yes, that's true—but she was, at the time, obviously suffering from exhaustion, postoperative stress, not to mention ferocious worry about her son's condition. The exhaustion was also exacerbated by sleep deprivation, and the fact that she had no help at home. So, under the circumstances, I thought she was coping brilliantly."

"So, there was nothing in her behavior to indicate a woman who could not deal with the day-to-day business of child care?"

"None at all."

"You know, of course, that she did accidentally breast-feed her son while taking a sedative. Is that, in your professional experience, a rare occurrence?"

"Hardly. We must have a dozen of those cases a year in Wandsworth. It's a common mistake. The mother isn't sleeping, so she's on sleeping pills. She's told, 'Don't breast-feed while taking the pills.' The child wakes up in the middle of the night. The mother is befuddled. She breast-feeds the child. And though the child goes floppy for a bit, he or she simply sleeps it off. And in the case of Sally . . . sorry, Ms. Goodchild . . . the fact that this happened didn't have any bearing whatsoever on my opinion that she was a thoroughly competent mother."

"No further questions."

Up came Lucinda Fforde.

"Now, Ms. Sanjay, didn't the breast-feeding incident of which you speak happen *after* your dealings with Ms. Goodchild?"

"That's right. She entered hospital for a time thereafter."

"She *entered* a psychiatric unit thereafter . . . the breast-feeding incident being the event that brought her to hospital. So how can you say that you *know* that this incident was just a common mistake if you weren't there?"

"Because I've dealt with these sorts of cases before."

"But you didn't specifically deal with this one . . ."

"I dealt with Ms. Goodchild . . ."

"But *before* the incident, is that not right?"

Pause. Jane was cornered, and she knew it.

"Yes, I suppose that's right."

"As for your claim that 'though the child goes floppy for a bit, he or she just sleeps off the drugs,' I have a clipping here from the *Scotsman*, dated 28 March of this year—a short news item, detailing a death of a two-week-old boy in a Glasgow hospital after his mother breast-fed him while taking a similar sedative. No more questions."

"Reexamination, Ms. Doherty?"

"Yes, My Lord. Ms. Sanjay, have you ever dealt with a death like the one just described?"

"Never—but I am certain it could happen. But only if the mother had ingested far beyond the normal dose of sedatives. I'd be interested to know if that mother in Scotland had been a drug addict—because many addicts mainline high doses of the drug. And if you then breast-fed a baby after mainlining an overdose of sedatives, well . . . a tragedy like that can happen."

The judge came in here.

"Just out of interest, was the Glaswegian mother a drug addict, Ms. Fforde?"

Ms. Fforde looked profoundly uncomfortable.

"She was, My Lord."

After Jane was dismissed, the moment I was dreading had arrived. Maeve Doherty called my name. I walked down the aisle, entered the witness box, took the oath. I looked out at the courtroom and had that same sensation I had the one and only time I appeared onstage in a school play: the sheer terror of having all eyes upon you, even if the audience (in this case) was such a small one.

Maeve was brilliant. She stuck to the script. She didn't ooze sympathy ("That won't play with Traynor"), nor did she lead me by the nose. But, point by point, she got me to explain the whirlwind nature of my relationship with Tony, my feelings about being pregnant in my late thirties, my difficult pregnancy, the horror of discovering that Jack was in intensive care after his birth, and the fact that I began to feel myself mentally slipping into a black swamp.

"You know the expression 'In a dark wood'?" I said.

"Dante," Mr. Justice Traynor interjected.

"Yes, Dante. And an apt description of where I found myself."

"And in those moments of lucidity when you reemerged from this 'dark wood,'" Maeve asked, "how did you feel about shouting at doctors, or making those two unfortunate comments about your son, or accidentally breast-feeding him while on sleeping pills?"

"Horrible. Beyond horrible. And I still feel horrible about it. I know I was ill at the time, but that doesn't lessen my guilt or my shame."

"Do you feel anger toward your husband about how he has behaved?"

"Yes, I do. I also feel that what's happened to me has been so desperately unfair, not to mention the most painful experience in my life . . . even more so than the deaths of my parents. Because Jack is my son. The center of my life. And because he's been effectively taken away from me—and for reasons that haven't just struck me as unjust, but also trumped up."

I gripped the rail of the witness stand as tightly as I could during this final statement. Because I knew that if I let go, the entire court would see my hands shaking.

"No further questions, My Lord," Maeve said.

Lucinda Fforde now looked at me and smiled. The smile of someone who wants to unnerve you, wants you to know they've got you in their sights and are about to pull the trigger.

"Ms. Goodchild, after being told of your son's critical condition while at the Mattingly Hospital, did you say: 'He *is* dying—and I don't care. You get that? I *don't* care'?"

I gripped the rail tighter.

"Yes, I did."

"Did you, a few weeks later, call your husband's secretary at work and say: 'Tell him if he's not home in the next sixty minutes, I'm going to kill our son'?"

"Yes, I did."

"Did you breast-feed your son while taking sedatives after being specifically told *not* to do so by your GP?"

"Yes, I did."

"Did your son end up in hospital after this incident?"

"Yes, he did."

"Were you hospitalized for nearly two months in a psychiatric unit after this incident?"

"Yes, I was."

"In 1988, did your father attend your commencement party at Mount Holyoke College in Massachusetts?"

"Yes, he did."

"Did you give him a glass of wine at that party?"

"Yes, I did."

"Did he tell you that he didn't want that glass of wine?"

"Yes, he did."

"But you made the comment, 'How middle aged,' and he downed the wine. Was that the correct sequence of events?"

"Yes."

"Did he then drive off later that evening, killing himself, your mother, and two innocent passengers in another car?"

"Yes, he did."

"I thank you, Ms. Goodchild, for confirming that all the major accusations against you are correct ones. No more questions, My Lord."

"Reexamination, Ms. Doherty?"

"Yes, My Lord. But before I begin, I would like to take issue with the fact that counsel used the word 'accusations' in the context of my client. It should be noted that Ms. Goodchild is *not* on trial here."

"Noted," Traynor said, with a bored sigh.

"Ms. Goodchild, did you mean what you said when you said: 'He *is* dying—and I don't care. You get that? I *don't* care'?"

"No, I didn't mean it at all. I was suffering from postoperative shock."

"Did you mean what you said when you threatened the life of your child?"

"No—I was suffering from clinical depression."

"Did you ever commit any violent act against your child?"

"Never."

"Did you ever breast-feed him again while taking sedatives?"

"Never."

"Are you now over your postpartum depression?"

"I am."

"Did you give a glass of wine to your father on the fateful June night in 1988?"

"Yes, I did."

"Now even though you didn't force it down his throat—and, in fact, made nothing more than a flippant comment—do you still feel guilty about giving him that glass of wine?"

"Yes, I do. I've always felt guilty about it. And I've lived with that guilt, day in, day out, for the last fifteen years."

"But do you think you deserve that guilt?"

"Whether or not I deserve it, it is there."

"I think that's called having a conscience. Thank you, Ms. Good-child, for so clearly stating the *real* facts of this case. No more questions."

I stepped down from the bench. I walked down the aisle. I sat down next to Nigel Clapp. He touched my shoulder and said, "Well done."

High praise from Mr. Clapp. But I still thought that Fforde had scored serious points against me—and had pointed up, for Traynor, the fact that I had validated all the accusations against me.

There was one more witness before lunch. Diane Dexter's former housekeeper—the Hispanic woman I had met on that day I had rushed to Dexter's house. Her name was Isabella Paz. A Mexican, resident in the United Kingdom for ten years. In Ms. Dexter's employ until four months ago. And she confirmed that Mr. Hobbs had been a regular guest to her residence since 1998 . . . and no, they did not sleep in separate rooms during these occasional visits that occurred when he was back in London from assorted overseas postings. She confirmed that Ms. Dexter had gone on holiday with him in 1999 and 2000, and that she had spent a month with him in Cairo in 2001. And yes, he had been regularly visiting Ms. Dexter since then—and, in fact, all but moved into her house for around eight weeks this past year . . . which, as Maeve Doherty helpfully added, was the eight weeks when Jack and I were resident in the psychiatric unit of St. Martin's.

"In other words, Mr. Hobbs and Ms. Dexter had been carrying on an occasional romance since 1999, and a rather steady romance since his return to London in 2002?"

"That was how I saw it, yes," she said.

During her cross-examination, Lucinda Fforde said, "Weren't you fired by Ms. Dexter for theft?"

"Yes—but then she took back what she said and paid me money."

"And before Ms. Dexter, didn't you work for a Mr. and Mrs. Robert Reynolds of London SW5?"

"Yes, I did."

"And weren't you fired from that job as well? For theft again?"

"Yes, but—"

"No further questions."

"Reexamination?"

"A very fast question, Ms. Paz," Maeve said. "Were you ever charged with theft by Mr. and Mrs. Reynolds? Officially charged, that is?"

"No."

"So you don't have a criminal record?"

"No."

"And if the court wanted proof of the dates of, say, the holidays Ms. Dexter took with Mr. Hobbs, how could they obtain proof?"

"She keeps a diary by the phone, writes everything in it. Where she's going, who with. Once the year is finished, she puts the diary in a cabinet under the phone. She must have ten years of diaries down there."

"Thank you, Ms. Paz."

When we broke for lunch, I leaned forward and asked Maeve, "Did she really get fired for stealing in her first job?"

"Oh, yes," she whispered. "A diamond necklace, which was fortunately recovered from the pawnbrokers where she sold it. And I think it was her mad plea for mercy that made her employers decide not to involve the police. And I'm pretty certain she did steal from Dexter—but, knowing that she was involved in this case, Paz decided to scream false accusation and raise the roof. Which is why Dexter paid up. So, if you're looking for a housekeeper, don't hire her. She's completely larcenous . . . but she certainly served our purpose."

Then she gave me a little shrug of the shoulders, as if to say: *I know it's not pleasant, but if you want to win, you have to engage in a little suspect play, just like the other side.*

"You did well in the witness box," Maeve said.

Rose and Nigel shot off to retrieve our two last-minute witnesses. Maeve excused herself to prepare for her final two examinations in full. So Sandy and I took a walk by the Thames. We didn't say much—the pressure of the hearing and yesterday's revelations stifling any serious conversation. But my sister did suggest that the morning went well for me.

"But how well?"

"Tony and his rich bitch were caught out lying about the newness of their relationship, and about only being just friends until after he snatched Jack. And I thought you were impressive."

"I hear a *but* coming on."

"*But* . . . I did think that Tony's barrister nailed you in her cross-examination. Not that you did anything wrong. Just that all the question marks hanging over you were confirmed by you. But maybe I'm just being overly pessimistic."

"No, you're completely spot-on. Maeve thought so too. I'm worried. Because I can't read the judge, and I don't know what line he's taking on the case . . . except wanting to get it over with as fast as possible."

When we returned to the court after the two-hour recess, Maeve was sitting alone on our side of the court and told me that—in order to ensure that Tony and company didn't run into our surprise witnesses—Nigel and Rose were dawdling with them in two separate coffee bars nearby. And as soon as the other side was in place . . .

In they walked, Tony and I pretending that there was a Berlin Wall between us. Immediately, Maeve was dashing up the aisle, her cell phone in her hand. She was back within a minute, breathless, just as the clerk was calling the court to order. Traynor came in, just as Nigel came rushing down the aisle to slide in next to me. Traynor didn't like this at all.

"A little late, are we, sir?" he asked.

Poor Nigel looked mortified. "I'm . . . uhm . . . terribly sorry, My Lord."

"So, Ms. Doherty," Traynor said. "We *are* going to finish up this afternoon, I hope?"

"Without question, My Lord. But I must inform the court that, like the applicant, we also have last-minute witnesses."

Traynor's lips tightened. He didn't like this news at all.

"You said 'witnesses,' Ms. Doherty," Traynor said. "By which you mean how many?"

"Just two, My Lord."

"And why are they so last-minute?" Traynor asked.

"We were only able to obtain their statements in the past day—and these were still being proofed this morning."

"Are the witnesses here now?"

"They are, My Lord."

"May we know their names, please?"

Maeve turned herself slightly to aim her statement in the direction of Tony.

"Of course, My Lord. Their names are Elaine Kendall and Brenda Griffiths."

Tony immediately started whispering into the ear of Lucinda Fforde. His instantaneous panic was evident.

"And do you have the statements from Ms. Kendall and Ms. Griffiths?" the judge asked.

Nigel opened his briefcase and handed a thick file to Maeve.

"We do, My Lord."

"Well, let us take a look at them."

She handed out copies of the two statements to the judge, to Lucinda Fforde, and to her accompanying solicitor. I watched as Tony immediately relieved the solicitor of his copies, and scanned them, becoming increasingly perturbed with each paragraph, then loudly saying, "This is outrageous."

Traynor peered at him over his half-moon specs and asked, "Please refrain from disturbing this courtroom, Mr. Hobbs."

Lucinda Fforde put a steadying hand on his shoulder and said, "My client apologizes for that small outburst, My Lord. Might I have a minute to consult with him?"

"A minute is fine," he said.

There was a very fast, agitated huddle in Tony's corner. Maeve stood throughout the minute, looking on, impassive, resisting the temptation to smile or look smug.

"Well then," Traynor said when the minute was up. "May we please proceed now, Ms. Fforde?"

"My Lord, we do have a serious problem with these statements."

"And what may that problem be, Ms. Fforde?"

"Well, whereas Mr. Ogilvy's statement only arrived here yesterday from the States, along with himself, we sense that the opposing counsel might have been sitting on these statements—from two UK residents— for a considerable amount of time."

"Ms. Doherty, how do you respond to this?"

"My Lord, I've already explained why they are so last-minute."

"So, Ms. Fforde," Traynor said, "do you object to these two last-minute witnesses?"

"I do, My Lord."

"Well," he said, "given that the respondent's counsel accepted your last-minute witness yesterday—and given that none of us wants to have this case postponed—I am going to allow these witnesses to be examined."

"My Lord, I wish to speak with my client for a moment about whether he wishes me to lodge an objection, and also ask for a suspension of this hearing until such time as . . ."

"Yes, yes, we all know how that sentence finishes, Ms. Fforde," Traynor said. "And the ball is, as they say, firmly in your court. Either you accept counsel's last-minute witnesses—as she accepted yours yesterday—or we all say good-bye until four months from now, as I am going on circuit after the summer recess. So, if you want proper time to study the statements of the respondent's new witnesses, then the case will be postponed, and we'll all be called back here in the autumn time to agree what could have been agreed here and now. But the choice, of course, is entirely between yourself and your client. Perhaps you would like a moment to speak with him?"

"Thank you, My Lord."

There was another frantic huddle on Tony's side of the court. Only this time, the Dexter woman was very much involved in this whispered debate—and from the vehement way she was gesturing, it was clear that she had a very forceful point of view on this subject. As they continued their hushed discussion, Maeve leaned over to me and whispered, "Australia."

Suddenly, I saw the brilliant stratagem behind Maeve's gamble. Knowing full well that Diane Dexter needed to be in Sydney as soon as possible to get her new office up and running, she wagered that Dexter would raise major objections when our side threatened a suspension of the hearing. Because that would mean Tony and Jack wouldn't be able to join her for at least four months—if, that is, Traynor ruled in their favor at that future time. Watching her now take charge of the discussion with Tony and their legal team, I guessed what she was telling them in her low but insistent voice: *How damaging can these witnesses be? We can't afford the delay . . . let's finish this now.*

Or, at least, that's what I hoped she was telling them.

Their debate continued for another minute, during which time Tony tried to raise an objection, but was hissed down by Dexter. He looked rather defeated.

"So, Ms. Fforde," Traynor said, interrupting this conclave. "Have you and your client reached a decision?"

Fforde looked directly at Dexter—who nodded affirmatively at her. Then she turned to Traynor and said, "With reluctance—but not wishing to delay the conclusion of these proceedings any further—we will accept the respondent's two new witnesses."

Traynor looked most relieved. So too did Maeve Doherty, who afforded herself the most momentary of smiles. Traynor said, "Please call your first witness, Ms. Doherty. Who will it be?"

"Elaine Kendall, My Lord."

Nigel went scurrying up the aisle and out the back door. A moment later, he returned, followed by Elaine Kendall. She was a small, rather tired-looking woman in her late forties, with a smoker's face and fatigued eyes. She entered the witness box and stared straight at Tony with a look of joyless disdain. She took the oath, she steadied herself, Maeve began.

"Ms. Kendall, would you please tell the court how you know Mr. Tony Hobbs?"

She started telling her story in a slow, hesitant voice. She had grown up in Amersham and at Christmas 1982, she was working at a local pub when in came "that gentleman sitting over there." They got chatting over the course of the evening ("I was serving him, you see"), and he explained he was back in Amersham visiting his parents, and that he was some big-deal foreign correspondent for the *Chronicle*.

"Anyway, he was very charming, very sophisticated, and once I was finished work, he asked me out for a drink. We went to a club. We drank far too much. One thing led to another, and we woke up next to each other the following morning.

"After that, he vanished—and a couple of weeks later, I discovered I was pregnant. Now I tried to contact him through the newspaper—but got nowhere. And my dad and mum being real Irish Catholic and all . . . well, there was no way I was not keeping the baby. But . . . that man . . . he was in Egypt or somewhere at the time, and though we kept trying to get in touch with him, there was just silence from his side.

"Eventually, we had to hire a solicitor, make a fuss with his paper. Way I heard it, his bosses told him he had to settle this somehow, so he agreed to finally pay me some sort of child support."

"What was that amount?"

"Fifty quid a month back in '83. We managed to get another solicitor on the job around '91. He got him up to one hundred and twenty-five pounds a month."

"And Mr. Hobbs never showed the slightest bit of interest in you or your son . . . ?"

"Jonathan. He was called Jonathan. And no, that man didn't want to know. Every year, I'd send him a picture of his boy, care of the *Chronicle*. Never a reply."

"And—although I know the answer to this question already, and must apologize to you for raising such a painful subject—where is your son now?"

"He died in 1995. Leukemia."

"That must have been terrible."

"It was," she said—but her voice was hard, and her gaze remained on Tony.

"Did you write to Mr. Hobbs, informing him of his son's death?"

"I did. And I called the paper too, asking them to contact him. Never a word. I thought, at the very least, he could have called me then. It would have been such a small, decent gesture."

Maeve Doherty said nothing for a moment, holding the silence. Then, "No more questions."

Lucinda Fforde had a frantic huddle with Tony. I looked over at Dexter. She was sitting there, cold, impassive.

"Ms. Fforde?" Traynor asked. "Do you wish to cross-examine?"

"Yes, My Lord," she said, but I could see that she was desperately trying to find an impromptu strategy, a damage control reaction. And God, was she fast on her feet. Because she said, "Ms. Kendall, as much as I appreciate the tragedy of your story . . . I must ask you this: do you really think a one-night fling constitutes a lifetime commitment?"

"When the result is a son, yes, I do."

"But didn't Mr. Hobbs make an ongoing financial commitment to you and your son?"

"A measly commitment, which my solicitor had to fight for."

"But hang on . . . I presume you were a sexually active woman at the time. After all, you did sleep with Mr. Hobbs after just one night. Surely he could have demanded a paternity test."

"I wasn't the local mattress. It was his baby. I'd slept with nobody before him for about a year."

"But did he demand a paternity test?"

"No . . . he didn't."

"You received a sum of money from the man who fathered your child. And surely fifty pounds meant something in 1983. Just as one hundred twenty-five pounds meant something in the early nineties. So he did meet his responsibilities to you. And in the matter of the death of your son . . . surely, you must recognize the fact that, as tragic as that death may have been for you, he had absolutely no connection with the boy. So . . ."

Suddenly, Elaine Kendall began to sob. She struggled to control it but couldn't. It took her nearly a minute to bring herself under control, during which time everyone in the court could do nothing but watch helplessly. And I felt appalling guilt. I'd talked her into this. Sat with her in her Crawley living room, she telling me how she moved to that godawful town after Jonathan died to get away from the place she so associated with him, how he was her only child, how she'd never married, worked bad jobs to keep them both afloat, but difficult as it was, Jonathan was the center of her life. And then . . . out of nowhere . . . leukemia. And . . .

The story was so painful to hear. Agony, in fact. Especially as I knew that this woman had lost the one thing in her life that mattered. Like any parent who had lost a child, she would never get over it. And yet—and this was a terrible admission—I also saw her story as a big opportunity for my case, a way of exposing Tony for the heartless shit that he was. I was direct with her about this. I told her—in very clear language—how her testimony might help me get my child back. I pleaded with her to help. And she agreed. And now . . . now she had been put through the most needless torment. And yes, I had gotten what I wanted from her. But watching her sob in the witness box, I felt nothing but shame.

392 · DOUGLAS KENNEDY

When she finally stopped crying, she turned to the judge and said, "I must apologize, My Lord. Jonathan was my only child. And even now, it's hard to talk about it. So I am sorry . . ."

"Ms. Kendall, you owe this court no apology. On the contrary, it is we who owe you an apology."

Then, sending a daggerlike look in the direction of Ms. Fforde, he asked, "Have you any further cross-examination, Ms. Fforde?"

"No, My Lord."

He gave Maeve a similar withering look and asked, "Reexamination, Ms. Doherty?"

"No, My Lord."

"Ms. Kendall, you are free to leave."

It took her a little effort to leave the witness stand. As she passed me by, I whispered, "I'm so sorry . . ." But she moved on without saying a word.

Traynor said nothing for a few moments. It was clear that he had been affected by the sight of that poor woman sobbing in the witness box. And he too needed a moment to collect himself before returning to business.

"And now to your final witness, Ms. Doherty."

"Yes, My Lord. Ms. Brenda Griffiths."

Unlike Elaine Kendall, the woman who walked down the aisle of the court exuded assurance . . . indeed, the same sort of self-confidence as Diane Dexter. Though her clothes weren't designer—she wore a simple green suit—she carried herself with great elegance, a forty-year-old woman who wasn't bothered about being a forty-year-old woman. And when she got into the witness box, she favored Tony with a little wry nod.

Maeve Doherty asked her to explain how she met Tony Hobbs.

"In 1990, when I was a journalist on the *Chronicle,* I was dispatched for three months to cover the Frankfurt financial scene. Tony was the head of the bureau there. We were a two-person office. We were both unattached. We had a fling. We also had a less-than-sober evening toward the end of my stay there, when contraception was not considered. Upon my return to London, I discovered I was pregnant. Naturally I contacted Tony. He was most unhappy about the news, and he certainly didn't offer to 'make me an honest woman' or anything like that . . . not that I wanted or expected that from him. Instead, he begged me to have an abortion . . . which, I told him, straightaway, was not going to happen. 'Well then,' he said, 'don't count on anything from me except financial support.' Not a pleasant comment—and yes, I was very upset about it at the time. But, at the same time, I did strangely admire his honesty. He let me know, from the outset, that he wanted nothing to do with this child.

"Anyway, I'm originally from Avon—and I never really liked London, so after finding out I was pregnant, I started asking around about jobs in the Bristol area. Found an opening in BBC Bristol News. Took the job. Moved. Had the baby. Was fortunate enough to meet the most wonderful man around a year later. We married. Catherine, my daughter by Tony, considers Geoffrey to be her father. Geoff and I also have a child together—another daughter, Margaret. And that's about all there is to tell, really."

"Except that Tony Hobbs has never met his daughter, Catherine—who is now nearly twelve years old?" Maeve asked.

"That's right. I have dropped him the very occasional note over the years, offering him the opportunity to meet her. But eventually, his lack of response said it all. So I haven't bothered contacting him for . . . God, it must be six years."

"No further questions, My Lord."

"Cross-examination, Ms. Fforde?"

"Yes, My Lord. Ms. Griffiths, why did you agree to testify today?"

"Because Ms. Goodchild came to me, explained what Tony had done vis-à-vis their baby, and asked if I would inform the court about Mr. Hobb's lack of interest in his daughter. Given the extremity of Ms. Goodchild's situation—and given that Tony was playing the 'caring father' card—I felt compelled to bear witness, so to speak, to Tony's previous lack of paternal interest."

"But could it be that in the twelve years that have elapsed since the birth of your daughter, Mr. Hobbs has changed his attitude about fatherhood? Especially when dealing with a woman who has physically threatened . . ."

"Ms. Fforde," Traynor said irritably, "this witness cannot answer that question."

"Apologies, My Lord. Did you bring your daughter here today, Ms. Griffiths?"

"God no. I wouldn't expose her to something like this, let alone put her on show."

"I congratulate you on your concern for the emotional concerns of others."

"What did I just say to you, Ms. Fforde?" Traynor asked.

"Apologies again, My Lord. And no further questions."

As soon as Brenda Griffiths was out of court, Traynor glanced at his watch and said, "As that was the last witness for the respondent, I would now like to hear closing submissions."

But I didn't hear those two arguments, let alone the responses, or Lucinda Fforde exercising her legal right (as counsel for the applicant) to have the final word. Though I didn't move from my seat and was in clear hearing range of both barristers, something in me shut off. Perhaps it was my continued sense of shame at what I had visited upon Elaine Kendall. Maybe it was emotional exhaustion. Maybe I had reached that saturation point where I just couldn't bear to hear the two sides of the story argued out again. Whatever it was, I just sat there, staring at the floor, willing myself not to hear—and succeeding.

Then Nigel Clapp was nudging me. Traynor was speaking.

"As that concludes all evidence and submissions in this hearing, I am now going off to consider my judgment. And I shall return in two hours' time to deliver it."

This snapped me back to the here and now. After Traynor took his leave, I leaned forward to Maeve and urgently asked, "If he's giving his judgment in two hours, does it mean he's already written most of it?"

"Perhaps he has," she said, sounding deflated. "Then again, he might just want to avoid coming to work tomorrow. I know that sounds prosaic, but it's the truth. He's noted for getting things done quickly."

"Especially when he's already decided what the outcome will be."

"I'm afraid so."

Rose Keating had come down to us. She put a consoling hand on my shoulder.

"You all right, dear?"

"Just about. How's Elaine Kendall?"

"Bearing up. Just. I think I'll get her home to Crawley. Don't want to send her back on her own."

"Good idea," Nigel said. "And I'll get Ms. Griffiths to Paddington."

"You will be back for the decision?" I asked.

"Of course," he said. "Will you be all right for the next two hours?"

I glanced across the court. There, opposite us, sat Diane Dexter. Immobile. Rigid. Her face reflecting a mixture of emotional concussion, fury, and sadness. There, next to her, was Tony, frantically whispering to her, trying to bring her around, their relationship suddenly gone haywire after the revelations just disclosed. Revelations that only came out because they had tried to rob me of my child. Which gave me no option but to lash out and find something to undermine them. Just as Maeve and Lucinda Fforde had worked so hard on our respective behalf to decimate the other's case. And now, here we were—in thrall to the forthcoming judgment of a third party—exhausted, spent, equally decimated. No one wins in a case like this one. Everyone comes out looking shabby and squalid.

I put my hand on Maeve's shoulder.

"Whatever happens now, I cannot thank you enough."

She shook her head. "I'm going to be straight with you, Sally. I think it looks bad. I could tell that Traynor truly hated our final flourish. Especially poor Elaine Kendall."

"That was my fault. My great proactive move."

"No—it was the right move. And what she said needed to be said. I should have briefed her myself, gauged her emotional state. That was my job—and I didn't do it properly."

"What are you going to do for the next two hours?"

"Go back to my office. And you?"

I grabbed my sister from the back of the court. We walked across the bridge, and lined up for last-minute tickets to the London Eye. We managed to obtain two places. Up we went into the clouds, the city stretched out on all sides of us like one of those sixteenth-century maps of the world, where you can begin to believe that the world is flat, and can actually see where the city ends, the precipice begins. Sandy peered out west—past the Palace, the Albert Hall, the green lushness of Kensington Gardens, the high residential grandness of Holland Park, into the endless suburban beyond.

"You say this town has got its great moments," she said, "but I bet most of the time, it's just grim."

Which kind of sums up so much of life, doesn't it?

When we were released from that massive Ferris wheel, we bought ice cream like a pair of tourists temporarily freed from the day-to-day demands of life. Then we crossed Waterloo Bridge back to the Strand, and entered the high court for what I knew would be the last time.

En route back, we fell silent until we reached the court. At which point Sandy asked, "Can I sit next to you for the judgment?"

"I'd like that."

Tony and his team were already in place when we got back. But I noticed that Diane Dexter was now sitting next to their solicitor. Maeve was in the front row next to Nigel. No one greeted each other. No one said a thing. Sandy and I sat down. I took a few deep breaths, trying to stay calm. But no one in this room was calm. The aura of fear was everywhere.

Five minutes went by, then ten. Still, we all sat there in silence. Because what else could we do? Then the clerk entered. And we all stood up. Traynor walked slowly to the bench, a folder held between his long, elegant fingers. He bowed. He sat down. We bowed. We all sat down. He opened his file. He started reading. As he began his recitation, I remembered what Maeve told me some days earlier.

"In the course of his judgment, he may make what he refers to as 'findings.' These are considered to be, in legal terms, irrefutable facts—which essentially means that, once made, they cannot be challenged."

But from the outset, he let it be known that he wasn't pleased with the entire tone of the case.

"Let me say at the start that, in the two brief days of this final hearing, we have had much dirty linen washed in a most public way. We have learned that Mr. Hobbs has had two children by two different women, and that he forged no relationship with these children. We've learned that Mr. Hobbs's new partner, Ms. Dexter, had a drug addiction problem, which she courageously overcame after it caused her to miscarry a child. And I must say, I found Ms. Dexter's candor about her past addictions both courageous and exemplary. She was a most impressive witness . . ."

Oh, God . . .

"Since then, as we've also learned, Ms. Dexter has gone to extreme lengths to have children . . . to the point where, if the respondent's counsel is to be believed, she was willing to conspire with her partner to snatch his son away from her mother, on allegedly trumped-up charges of threatened child abuse."

Sandy glanced at me. Traynor had just hinted that he hadn't bought our case.

"We have learned that, over twenty years ago, Ms. Goodchild handed her father a drink which may—or may not—have put him over the legal limit, and may, or may not, have contributed to the fatal accident in which he was killed along with his wife and two innocent people.

"And we've also learned that Ms. Dexter and Mr. Hobbs weren't particularly honest about the actual duration of their relationship . . . though, in truth, the court can't really see the importance of whether they were first intimate three years ago or just three months ago."

Another nervous glance between Sandy and myself. I glanced around the court. Everyone had their heads lowered, as if we were at church.

"And I say that because, amid all the evidence of the last two days, the central issue has been obscured: what is best for the child? That is the one and *only* issue here. Everything else, in the opinion of the court, is extraneous.

"Now, without question, the relationship between a mother and her child is the most pivotal one in life. One might go as far as to use the word 'primordial' to describe this immense bond. The mother brings us into life, she suckles us, she nurtures us in the most critical early stages of our existence. For this reason, the law is most reluctant to disturb, let alone rupture, this primordial relationship—unless the trust that society places in a mother has been profoundly breached.

"Earlier today, counsel for the applicant outlined the 'accusations'—as she called them—against the respondent. And it must be acknowledged that these accusations are most grave and serious. Just as it must also be acknowledged that the respondent was suffering from a severe clinical disorder that impaired her judgment, and also caused her to behave in a thoroughly irrational way.

"But while acknowledging said clinical condition, can the court risk jeopardizing the child's welfare? This is the central dilemma that the court has had to address. Just as it has also had to study whether the child's welfare will be better served by being placed in the care of its father and his new partner—a woman who may claim to be his surrogate mother, but who will never, in the eyes of this court, be considered so."

He paused. He looked up over his glasses in my direction.

"Threatening a child's life—even in delusional anger—is a most serious matter . . ."

Sandy reached over and clasped my hand, as if to say: *I'll be holding you as he sends you over the edge.*

"Doing so twice is profoundly worrying. So too is poisoning a child with sleeping tablets—even though it was the result of a befuddled accident.

"But are these actions enough to break that primordial bond between mother and child? Especially when questions must be raised about the ulterior motives of the child's father, and the real reasons for the legal action he took eight months ago to gain custody of the child?

"Ultimately, however, we turn, once again, to the heart of the matter: if the mother is granted sole or shared custody of the child, will she act on the threats she made earlier? Shouldn't we be prudent in this case, and thus breach that primordial maternal bond, in order to serve the best interests of the child?"

Traynor paused and sipped at a glass of water. In front of me, Nigel Clapp put his hand to his face. Because that last sentence had given the game away. We'd lost.

Traynor put the water down and continued to read.

"These are the questions that the court has had to ponder. Large, taxing questions. And yet, when all the evidence is carefully studied, there is a clear answer to all these questions."

I bowed my head. Here it was now. Finally. The judgment upon me.

"And so, after due consideration, I find that the mother, Ms. Goodchild, did *not* intend to harm her child, and was *not* responsible for her actions during this period, as she was suffering from a medically diagnosed depression.

"I also find that the father, Mr. Hobbs, has done everything he can to sever the bond between the mother and the child. As such, I find that the motivations of Mr. Hobbs—and of his partner, Ms. Dexter—in claiming that the child was at risk were not wholly altruistic ones. And I also find that they manipulated the truth for their own gain."

Sandy was now squeezing my hand so hard I was certain she was about to break several bones. But I didn't care.

"These are the reasons it is the *decision* of this court that this child must see and spend substantial time with both parents . . ."

He stopped for just a second or two, but it felt like a minute.

". . . but that I grant custody of the child to the mother."

There was a long, shocked silence, broken by Traynor.

"As I also find that there was malice directed against the respondent, I order that the applicant pay the respondent's costs."

Lucinda Fforde was instantly on her feet.

"I seek leave to appeal."

Traynor peered down at her. And said, "Leave refused."

He gathered up his papers. He removed his half-moon glasses. He looked out at our stunned faces. He said, "If there is no further business, I will rise."

FIFTEEN

S IX WEEKS LATER, London had a heat wave. It lasted nearly
a week. The mercury hovered in the early eighties, the sky was a
cloudless hard dome of blue, and the sun remained an incandes-
cent presence above the city.

"Isn't this extraordinary?" I said on the fifth day of high temperatures
and no rain.

"It'll break any moment," Julia said. "And then we'll be back to the
gray norm."

"True—but I'm not going to think about that right now."

We were in Wandsworth Park. It was late afternoon. Around a half
hour earlier, Julia had knocked on my door and asked me if I was up for
a walk. I pushed aside the new manuscript I was working on, moved Jack
from his playpen to his stroller, grabbed my sunglasses and my hat, and
headed off with her. By the time we reached the park, Jack had fallen
asleep. After we parked ourselves on a grassy knoll by the river, Julia
reached into her shoulder bag, and emerged with two wine glasses and a
chilled bottle of sauvignon blanc.

"Figured we should celebrate the heat with a drop of drinkable
wine . . . that is, if you can indulge just now?"

"I think I can get away with a glass," I said. "I'm down to two antidepressants a day now."

"That is impressive," she said. "It took me nearly a year to be weaned
off them."

"Well, Dr. Rodale hasn't pronounced me 'cured' yet."

"But you're certainly getting there."

She uncorked the wine. I lay back for a moment, and felt the sun
on my face, and let the sour lemon aroma of the grass block out all the
usual urban odors, and thought: *this is rather pleasant.*

"Here you go," Julia said, placing a glass beside me, then lighting a cigarette. I sat up. We clinked glasses.

"Here's to finished business," she said.

"Such as?"

"Finally wrapping up a fucking awful project."

"The East Anglian history thing?"

"Yes, that beast," she said, mentioning some tome she'd been editing which had bored her senseless (or so she had kept telling me). "Done and dusted last night. And anyone who's spent three months enveloped in East Anglian history deserves a few glasses of wine. You still working on the *Jazz Guide*?"

"Oh, yes—all eighteen hundred pages of it. And I still haven't gotten beyond Sidney Bechet."

"Watch out—Stanley will get worried."

"I've got seven weeks before it's due. And given that Stanley just asked me out, I doubt he'll be hectoring me about—"

Julia nearly coughed on her cigarette.

"Stanley asked you out?"

"That's what I said."

"My, my—I am surprised."

"Over the course of my adult life, men have occasionally asked me out."

"You know what I'm talking about. It's Stanley. Not exactly the most forward of men. And even since his divorce, he's maintained a pretty low profile on that front."

"He's quite charming, in his own avuncular way. Or, at least, that's the impression I got when we had that lunch all those months ago."

"And he's only in his early fifties. And he does look after himself. And he is a very good editor. And I hear he does have a rather nice maisonette in South Ken. And—"

"I'm certain he can hold a fork in his hand without drooling."

"Sorry," she said with a laugh. "I wasn't really trying to sell him to you."

"Sell him as hard as you like. Because I've already told him I'm too busy for dinner right now."

"But why? It's just dinner."

"I know—but he is my sole source of income at the moment. And I don't want to jeopardize that by veering into situations nonprofessional. I need the work."

"Have you reached a settlement with Tony's solicitors yet?"

"Yes, we've just got there."

Actually, it was Nigel Clapp who got us there, forcing their hand through his usual hesitant determination—a description that if applied to anyone else would sound oxymoronic, but made complete sense when portraying Nigel. A week after the hearing, the other side got in touch with him and made their first offer: continued shared ownership of the house, in return for 50 percent payment of the ongoing mortgage, and an alimony-child support payment of £500 a month. Tony's solicitors explained that, given that he was now no longer in full-time employment, asking him to pay the entire monthly mortgage, coupled with £500 for the upkeep of his son and ex-wife, was a tremendous stretch.

As Nigel explained to me at the time, "I . . . uhm . . . did remind them that he did have a wealthy patroness, and that we could dig our heels in and force him to hand over ownership of the house to you. Not that we would have had much chance of winning that argument, but . . . uhm . . . I sensed that they didn't have the appetite for much of a fight."

They settled rather quickly thereafter. We would still own the house jointly—and would split the proceeds when and if it was ever sold, but Tony would handle the full mortgage payment, in addition to £1000 maintenance per month—which would cover our basic expenses, but little more.

Still, I didn't want any more. In fact, in the immediate aftermath of the hearing, my one central thought (beyond the shock of winning the case and getting Jack back) was the idea that, with any luck, I would not have to spend any time in the company of Tony Hobbs again. True, we had agreed on joint custody terms: he'd have Jack every other weekend. Then again, the fact that he'd be spending all forthcoming weekends in Sydney ruled out much in the way of shared custody . . . though Nigel was assured, through Tony's solicitors, that their client would be returning to London on a regular basis to see his son.

Tony also assured me of this himself during our one conversation. This took place a week after the hearing—the day both our solicitors had agreed upon for Jack to be returned to me. "The hand-over," as Nigel Clapp called it—an expression that had a certain Cold War spy novel ring to it, but was completely apt. Because, on the morning before, I received a phone call from Pickford Movers, informing me that they would be arriving tomorrow at nine AM with a delivery of nursery furniture from an address on Albert Bridge Road. Later that day, Nigel rang to say he'd heard from Tony's solicitors, asking him if I'd be at home tomorrow around noon, "as that's when the hand-over will take place."

"Did they say who'll be bringing Jack over?" I asked.

"The nanny," he said.

Typical Tony, I thought. Leave it to a third party to do his dirty work for him.

"Tell them I'll be expecting Jack at noon," I said.

The next morning, the movers arrived an hour early ("Thought you wouldn't mind, luv," said the on-the-job foreman). Within sixty minutes, not only had they unloaded everything, but they'd also put Jack's crib, wardrobe, and chest of drawers back together in the nursery. Accompanying the furniture were several boxes of clothes and baby paraphernalia. I spent the morning putting everything away, rehanging the mobile that had been suspended above his crib, setting up a diaper-changing area on top of the chest of drawers, repositioning the bottle sterilizer in the kitchen, and setting up a playpen in the living room. In the process, I started erasing all memories of a house without a child.

Then, at noon, the front doorbell rang. Was I nervous? Of course I was. Not because I was worried about how I'd react, or whether the momentousness of the moment would overwhelm me. Rather, because I never believed this moment would happen. And when you are suddenly dealing with a longed-for reality—especially one that once seemed so far beyond the realm of possibility—well, who isn't nervous at a moment like that?

I went to the door, expecting some hired help to be standing there, holding my son. But when I swung it open, I found myself facing Tony. I blinked with shock—and then immediately looked down, making certain that he had Jack with him. He did. My son was comfortably ensconced in his baby carrier, a pacifier in his mouth, a foam duck clutched between his little hands.

"Hello," Tony said quietly.

I nodded back, noticing that he looked very tired. There was a long awkward moment where we stared at each other, and really didn't know what to say next.

"Well . . ." he finally said. "I thought I should do this myself."

"I see."

"I bet you didn't think I'd be the one to bring him."

"Tony," I said quietly, "I now try to think about you as little as possible. But thank you for bringing Jack home."

I held out my hand. He hesitated for just a moment, then slowly handed me the carrier. I took it. There was a brief moment when we both held on to him together. Then Tony let go. The shift in weight surprised me, but I didn't place the carrier on the ground. I didn't want to let go of Jack. I looked down at him. He was still sucking away on his pacifier, still hanging on to the bright yellow duck, oblivious to the fact that—with one simple act of exchange, one simple hand-over—the trajectory of his life had just changed. What that life would be—how it would turn out—was indeterminable. Just that it would now be different from the other life he might have had.

There was another moment of awkward silence.

"Well," I finally said, "I gather the one thing our solicitors have agreed upon is that you're to have contact with Jack every other weekend. So I suppose I'll expect you a week from Friday."

"Actually," he said, avoiding my gaze, "we're making the move to Australia next Wednesday."

He paused—as if he almost expected me to ask about whether he'd managed to work things out with Diane after all the courtroom revelations about his past bad behavior. Or where they'd be living in Sydney. Or how his damn novel was shaping up. But I wasn't going to ask him anything. I just wanted him to go away. So I said, "Then I suppose I won't expect you a week from Friday."

"No, I suppose not."

Another cumbersome silence. I said, "Well, when you're next in London, you know where to find us."

"Are you going to remain in England?" he asked.

"At the moment, I haven't decided anything. But as you and I have joint parental responsibility for our son, you will be among the first to know."

Tony looked down at Jack. He blinked hard several times, as if he was about to cry. But his eyes remained dry, his face impassive. I could see him eyeing my hand holding the carrier.

"I suppose I should go," he said without looking up at me.

"Yes," I said. "I suppose you should."

"Good-bye then."

"Good-bye."

He gazed at Jack, then back at me. And said, "I'm sorry."

His delivery was flat, toneless, almost strangely matter of fact. Was it an admission of guilt or remorse? A statement of regret at having done what he'd done? Or just the fatigued apology of a man who'd lost so much by trying to win? Damn him, it was such a classic Tony Hobbs moment. Enigmatic, obtuse, emotionally constipated, yet hinting at the wound within. An apology that wasn't an apology that *was* an apology. Just what I expected from a man I knew so well . . . and didn't know at all.

I turned and brought Jack inside. I closed the door behind us. As if on cue, my son began to cry. I leaned down. I undid the straps that held him in the carrier. I lifted him. But I didn't instantly clutch him to me and burst into tears of gratitude. Because as I elevated him out of the chair—lifting him higher—to the point where he was level with my nose, I smelled a telltale smell. A full load.

"Welcome back," I said, kissing him on the head. But he wasn't soothed by my maternal cuddle. He just wanted his diaper changed.

Half an hour later, as I was feeding him downstairs, the phone rang. It was Sandy in Boston, just checking in to make certain that the hand-over had happened. She was at a loss for words (something of a serious rarity for Sandy) when I told her that it was Tony who had shown up with Jack.

"And he actually said sorry?" she asked, sounding downright shocked.

"In his own awkward way."

"You don't think he was trying to wheedle his way back into your life, do you?"

"He's off to Sydney with his fancy lady in a couple of days, so no—I don't think that's in the cards. The fact is, I don't know what to think about why he was there, why he apologized, what his actual agenda was . . . if, that is, there was any agenda at all. All I know is: I won't be seeing him for a while, and that's a very good thing."

"He can't expect you to forgive him."

"No—but he can certainly *want* to be forgiven. Because we all want that, don't we?"

"Do I detect your absurd lingering guilt about Dad?"

"Yes, you most certainly do."

"Well, you don't have to ask for my forgiveness here. Because what I told you back in London still holds: I don't blame you. The big question here is can you forgive yourself? You didn't do anything wrong. But only you can decide that. Just as only Tony can decide that he did do something profoundly wrong. And once he decides that, maybe . . ."

"What? A Pauline conversion? An open confession of transgression? He's English, for God's sake."

And I could have added: like certain self-loathing Brits, he hates our American belief that, *with openness, honesty, and a song in our hearts*, we can reinvent ourselves and do good. Over here, life's a tragic muddle which you somehow negotiate. Back home, life's also a tragic muddle, but we want to convince ourselves that we're all still an unfinished project—and that, in time, we will make things right.

"Well, in just a little while, you won't have to deal with Englishness again," she said.

This was Sandy's great hope—and one that she had articulated to me five weeks earlier as we waited for her flight at Heathrow. The hearing had just ended. Tony and company had left hurriedly—Diane Dexter having all but dashed alone up the aisle of the court as soon as Traynor had finished reading his decision. Tony followed in close pursuit, with Lucinda Fforde and the solicitor finding a moment to shake hands with Maeve and Nigel before heading off themselves. Which left the four of us sitting by ourselves in the court, still in shock, still trying to absorb the fact that it had gone our way. Maeve eventually broke the silence. Gathering up her papers, she said, "I'm not much of a gambler—but I certainly wouldn't have put money on that outcome. My word . . ."

She shook her head and allowed herself a little smile.

Nigel was also suitably preoccupied and subdued as he repacked his roll-on case with thick files. I stood up and said, "I can't thank you both enough. You really saved me from . . ."

Nigel put up his hand, as if to say: *No emotionalism, please.* But then he spoke. "I am pleased for you, Sally. *Very* pleased."

Meanwhile, Sandy just sat there with tears running down her face—my large, wonderful, far too gushy sister, emoting for the rest of us. Nigel seemed both touched and embarrassed by such raw sentiment. Maeve touched my arm and said, "You're lucky in your sister."

"I know," I said, still too numb by the decision to know how to react. "And I think what we all need now is a celebratory drink."

"I'd love to," Maeve said, "but I'm back in court tomorrow, and I'm really behind in preparation. So . . ."

"Understood. Mr. Clapp?"

"I've got a house closing at five," he said.

So I simply shook hands with them both, thanked Maeve again, and told Nigel I'd wait for his call once Tony's people wanted to start negotiating terms and conditions for the divorce.

"So you want to keep using me?" he asked.

"Who else would I use?" I said. And for the first time ever in my presence, Nigel Clapp smiled.

When he left, Sandy said we should definitely down a celebratory drink . . . but at the airport, as she had a plane to catch. So we hopped the tube out to Heathrow, and got her checked in, and then drank a foul glass of cheap red in some departure lounge bar. That's when she asked me, "So when are you and Jack moving to Boston?" One thing at a time, I told her then. And now—as she raised this question again on this first afternoon at home with my son—my answer was even more ambiguous. "I haven't decided anything yet."

"Surely, after all they did to you, you're not going to stay."

I felt like telling her that the "they" she spoke of wasn't England or the English. Just two people who caused damage by wanting something they couldn't have.

"Like I said, I'm making no big choices right now."

"But you belong back in the States," she said.

"I belong nowhere. Which—I've come to the conclusion—is no bad thing."

"You'll never survive another damp winter over there," she said.

"I've survived a little more than that recently."

"You know what I'm saying here—I want you back in Boston."

"And all I'm saying to you is: all options are open. But, for the moment, all I want to do is spend time with my son and experience something that's been eluding me for around a year: normal life."

After a moment she said, "There is no such thing as normal life."

That was several weeks ago. And though I do agree with Sandy that normal life doesn't exist, since then I have certainly been trying to lead something approaching a quiet, ordinary existence. I get up when Jack wakes me. I tend to his needs. We hang out. He sits in his baby seat or his playpen while I work. We go to the supermarket, the High Street. Twice since he's come home, I've entrusted him to a babysitter for the evening, allowing me to sneak off to a movie with Julia. Other than that, we've been in each other's company nonstop. And I like it that way—not just because it's making up for a lot of lost time over the past few months, but also because it locks us into a routine together. No doubt, there will come a point when such a routine needs to be altered. But that's the future. For the moment, however, the everydayness of our life strikes me as no bad thing.

Especially since the sun has come out.

"Five pounds says it won't rain tomorrow," I told Julia as she poured herself another glass of wine.

"You're on," she said. "But you will lose."

"You mean, you've heard the weather forecast for tomorrow?"

"No, I haven't."

"Then how can you be so sure it will rain?"

"Innate pessimism . . . as opposed to your all-American positive attitude."

"I'm just a moderately hopeful type, that's all."

"In England, that makes you an incurable optimist."

"Guilty as charged," I said. "You never really lose what you are."

And, of course, late that night, it did start to rain. I was up at the time with my sleep terrorist son, feeding him a bottle in the kitchen.

Suddenly, out of nowhere, a large heaving clap of summer thunder announced that the heavens were about to open. Then, around five minutes later, they did just that. A real tropical downpour, which hammered at the windows with such percussive force that Jack pushed away the bottle and looked wide-eyed at the wet, black panes of glass.

"It's all right, it's all right," I said, pulling him close to me. "It's just the rain. And we'd better get used to it."

ACKNOWLEDGMENTS

I OWE AN ENORMOUS debt of thanks to Frances Hughes of Hughes Fowler Carruthers, Chancery Lane, London WC2A. Not only did Frances give me a crash course in the complexities of the English legal system, but she also vetted two early versions of the manuscript. I hope I never need her professional services.

Dr. Alan Campion made certain that all the medical terminology and procedure in the novel was appropriate. And a remarkable woman I will simply refer to as "Kate" was invaluable to me when it came to detailing—with arresting honesty—her own nightmarish descent into the dark room that is postpartum depression.

Any errors of legal or medical fact are my own.

Two friends on opposite sides of the Atlantic—Christy Macintosh in Banff and Noeleen Dowling in Dublin—read different drafts of the book. They are my "constant readers"—and never pull punches when it comes to telling me whether the narrative is on- or off-track.

This novel was started in one of the Leighton Studios of the Banff Center for the Arts, amid the epic grandeur that is the Canadian Rockies. It is the best writing hideout imaginable.

My editor, Sue Freestone, is one tough operator—and I am very grateful to have her in my corner. Just as my agent, Antony Harwood, is about the best friend this novelist could have.

Finally, twenty years after we first met, I would like to thank Grace Carley for still being Grace Carley.

A SPECIAL RELATIONSHIP

DOUGLAS KENNEDY

A Readers Club Guide

INTRODUCTION

Sally Goodchild is a foreign correspondent living a life of action, independence, and intelligence. She has it all: a solid résumé, an active career, and a strong journalistic reputation. The one thing she has never encountered is a man who can match her intelligence, her wit, and her lifestyle. That is, until fellow foreign correspondent Tony Hobbs saves her life on the flooded plains of Somalia. His acerbic humor, confidence, and elite British charm quickly seduce her. But their journalistic love affair is threatened when Sally becomes pregnant with his child. Much to her surprise, Tony is pleased and asks for her hand in marriage and a life with him back in his hometown of London. This sets in motion a downward spiral of depression and deceit, as the man whom she thought she loved attempts to take from her what matters most, her own son. Sally must fight to rebuild her life against a rising tide of opposition as a stranger in a strange land.

QUESTIONS AND TOPICS FOR DISCUSSION

1. When we first meet Sally Goodchild, she is living the life of a foreign correspondent—rootless, brave, with a schedule in a constant state of flux. She must travel all around the world to dangerous and precarious locations. What types of individuals are drawn to this manic lifestyle? What are the payoffs? What are the sacrifices?

2. Sally is instantly attracted to Tony Hobbs, the charming journalist she meets in Africa. However, there are potential warning signs that Sally ignores. "He enjoyed repartee—not just for its verbal gamesmanship, but also because it allowed him to retreat from the serious, or anything that might be self-revealing" (p. 15). What clues does this give to Tony Hobbs's personality and his eventual betrayal?

3. Early in Sally's life, she suffers the death of her parents. She develops a philosophy to cope with this loss: "you come to realize pretty damn fast that everything is fragile that so-called security is nothing

more than a thin veneer that can fracture without warning" (p. 23). Is this particular cynicism and fear of instability what leads her to fall into Tony Hobbs's arms so quickly? Why would Sally jump into a risky situation with a man she hardly knows?

4. The novel discusses the differences between American and British culture. What are some of these intrinsic differences? How does Sally's use of language differ from that of the people who surround her in London? How does being a foreigner affect her life in England?

5. As Sally and Tony's love affair continues, she receives odd reports about Tony's recklessness, one from a colleague from the *Daily Telegraph*: "It's common enough knowledge back in London that Hobbs is something of a political disaster when it comes to the game of office politics" (pp. 25–26). This information from a fellow journalist does not dissuade Sally from falling head over heels in love with Hobbs. What causes her blindness? Does the fact that she is "crowding middle age" play a factor in her decisions?

6. When Sally learns she is pregnant with Tony's child, she immediately tells him, expecting this to complicate things between them. However, Tony agrees to keep the child, and furthermore, offers marriage as well. For two people bent on independence and freedom for all of their lives, why does Tony go along so easily into this new arrangement? More important, why does Sally?

7. Sally explains: "We can delude ourselves into believing that we're the master captain, steering the course of our destiny . . . but the randomness of everything inevitably pushes us into places and situations where we never expect to find ourselves" (p. 80). One of these "random" situations Sally finds herself in is married, pregnant, and living in a stable home in London, a far cry from her adventure-laden journalistic lifestyle. Sally blames her situation on this "randomness." Is this really accurate? How much of Sally's own free will, not randomness, is the cause of her current predicament? What could she have done differently to have avoided this fate?

8. As her pregnancy progresses, Sally begins to experience numerous health problems, which force her to leave her job and remain in the hospital until her child is born. This is the beginning of Sally's decline, mentally and physically. "I always had to be active, always had to be accomplishing something—my workaholism underscored by a fear of slowing down, of losing momentum" (p. 82). How does this "down time" begin to chip away at her mental health? What happens to a person so accustomed to action when they are suddenly confronted with no responsibilities or deadlines?

9. Soon after she recovers and is able to leave the hospital, Sally receives word that her job with the *Post*'s foreign bureau is no longer available. This is the beginning of the descent for Sally. Was it fair for Sally to be let go because of health conditions? Was there anything she could have done to prevent this?

10. The marital bliss between Tony and Sally starts to unravel sooner than expected. "But what I couldn't get out of my brain was the larger, implicit realization that I had married someone with whom I didn't share a common language" (p. 88). Despite some advice from her sister about marriage, this divide between Tony and Sally only grows deeper. How are they missing each other? What are some examples from their lives that show this breakdown in communication?

11. Once little Jack is born, he suffers from a serious case of jaundice. The first time Sally is allowed to see her son, she is shocked by her initial feelings of disconnection. "But another terrible thought hit me: *could that really be my son?* They say that you should be swamped by unconditional love the moment you first see your child . . . and that *the bonding process* should begin immediately. But how could I bond with this minuscule stranger, currently looking like a horrific medical experiment?" (p. 96). Can you identify with Sally here? Why does she feel this way?

12. As the months of banality pile up on one another, Sally finds herself caught in a nightmarish world of postpartum depression, which

this novel grimly confronts. The disconnection between her and Tony grows; their sex life is nonexistent; and her time is divided between sleeping (alone), feeding little Jack, and changing diapers. "The hopelessness of my situation took hold. I wasn't just a useless mother and wife, but someone who was also in a no-exit situation from which there was no escape. A life sentence of domestic and maternal drudgery, with a man who clearly didn't love me" (pp. 164–165). This is the point of view of a woman obviously suffering from postpartum depression, a serious condition of clinical depression. What are some of the ways Sally tries to reach out for help? Are these cries for help answered?

13. In therapy, Sally confesses to experiencing a "feeling of inadequacy— the perennial worry of the perennial B student . . . who never felt she was achieving her potential" (p. 199). What do you believe are some of the causes of Sally's feelings of inadequacy? Is there a link to the feeling of responsibility for her parents' death?

14. As Sally's life becomes more manageable, she begins to experience a sort of cathartic realization about pain. "At heart, all grief centers around the realization that you can never escape the bereavement that has stricken you. There may be moments when you can cope with its severity, when the harshness temporarily lessens. But the real problem with grief is its perpetuity. It doesn't go away. And though you are, on one level, always crying for the loss you've sustained, you're also crying because you realize you're now stuck with the loss, that—try as you might—it's become an intrinsic part of you, and will change the way you look at things forever" (pp. 285–286). What instances of grief is Sally referring to? What tragedies has she overcome, and still must overcome? Do you agree that these tragedies never leave us?

15. Sandy, Sally's sister, is angered when she hears in court about Sally's feelings of responsibility for her parents' death. She is offended, not because she actually believes Sally is responsible for their accident, but because Sally did not trust her sister and tell her she felt this way. Why did Sally keep this secret from her sister for so long?

ENHANCE YOUR BOOK CLUB

1. Read *Journalistas: 100 Years of the Best Writing and Reporting by Woman Journalists*, edited by Eleanor Mills, to get a taste for the exciting and often dangerous lifestyles of foreign correspondents like Sally Goodchild.

2. Postpartum depression, or postnatal depression, is a form of clinical depression that affects more than 25 percent of woman after childbirth. This condition is a debilitating and dangerous illness resulting in fatigue, irritability, sadness, reduced libido, anxiety, and crying episodes. All of these symptoms afflict Sally Goodchild after the birth of her son, Jack. Research the effects of postpartum depression with source materials such as Brooke Shields's memoir *Down Came the Rain* and Dr. Sandra L. Wheatley's *Coping with Postnatal Depression* to learn about this common and debilitating illness.

3. The distinct differences between British and American style of discourse, modes of expression, and cultures are noted numerous times in the novel. "That was the most intriguing thing about London—its aloofness. Perhaps it had something to do with the reticent temperament of the natives" (p. 44), Sally comments. In contrast, she finds considerable trouble caused by her "inborn American inability to couch things in coded language" (p. 239). Sally refused to "accept the pragmatic pessimism that . . . struck me as so desperately English. I wanted to embrace that old hoary American fighting spirit" (pp. 286–287). Compare and contrast the American and British worldviews as depicted in the novel. What do you find to be specific to each culture's social and personal philosophies?

A CONVERSATION WITH DOUGLAS KENNEDY

Common traits in your characters are the need for unrelenting independence and a yearning for freedom. However, this independence

and freedom are challenged by the act of falling in love. Is the act of love diametrically opposed to freedom and independence?

Romance is one thing, domesticity another. And do note that I choose to use the word "romance" rather than "love" in this context. All love stories begin as a romance. And speaking from personal experience, all romances begin (or, at least, *should* begin) with sexual and emotional headiness. Then, of course, the moment arrives when someone has forgotten to do the dishes for the first time—and the entire game changes. Love, of course, is a wholly different construct from romance. Love is about proper intimacy and true complicity. And that's why it is so damn difficult to sustain.

The novel opens with terse action and vivid portrayals of flooding in Somalia and the chaos ensuing on the ground. You have traveled extensively around the world. Have you been a witness to such chaos?

I have been chased by three brick-wielding youths down a backstreet in Algiers. I was arrested, temporarily, by the military police in the Egyptian oasis of Siwa for traveling into a "security zone" without proper authorization. I have woken up in a no-star hotel in the Moroccan town of Meknes to find a guy in my room, going through my suitcase—and I did catch him in the back of the head with my shortwave radio, which I grabbed off the bedside table . . . and which was smashed in the process. And I have ventured into a bikers' bar in Alabama and emerged with all my teeth intact (no easy trick that). So, yes, travel, especially travel in edgy places, has its attendant dangers, which is, after all, the point of venturing into edgy places.

Your work is reminiscent of the classic *Madame Bovary*, particularly with the theme of women trying their best to avoid the banality of a suburban life. What influence does Gustave Flaubert have on your work?

Flaubert did something absolutely epoch-changing in *Madame Bovary*. He was the first novelist ever to confront a key malaise: boredom. All those novels (mine included) that have grappled with marital discontent and the horrors of quotidian life owe a huge debt to Flaubert. He articulated for the first time the way the day-to-day can grind us down, and how we often turn to banal melodrama (like an affair) as a way of subverting the cul-de-sac in which we have imprisoned ourselves. More tellingly, Flaubert understood the fact that we are the architects of these cul-de-sacs . . . and that we frequently imprison ourselves in lives that we don't want.

Sally Goodchild's slow descent into the horror and the hopelessness of postpartum depression is expressed so harrowingly across the page. At what lengths did you research this terrible condition experienced by women after birth?

I met a woman in her mid-thirties at a dinner party in London, who, after around three large glasses of chardonnay, started telling me about the fact that, though she had so wanted a big family, after the birth of her son she had been hit with a postpartum depression so severe that she never had a second child. I explained my interest in such a story. I'd begun to think about a novel centering around motherhood-as-nightmare and asked her for her phone number (reassuring her that it was for professional reasons only). We met for coffee around a week later and she talked nonstop for three hours (no one had ever asked her about her descent into postpartum hell—and her stockbroker husband found the whole episode so distasteful that . . . well, you can complete the sentence). I took extensive notes while she spoke, then read two books on postpartum depression afterward, and also spoke at length with a doctor on the subject. After that, during the actual writing of the novel, it was essentially all about imagining my way into Sally's head as she plunged into this hellish vortex. Some years after the original UK publication, while giving a talk at the Edinburgh Book Festival, I was approached by two women from the British Society of Postnatal Depression. They told me that this novel had become, for them, a standard set text on the subject, and one that they gave to women in the throes of this nightmare. "How did you get it so right?" they asked me. It was the nicest compliment imaginable because, while working on the novel, I was so cognizant of the fact that (as a man) I was dealing with a great *terra incognito*.

Examples of the differences between American and British social mores and communication styles are rampant throughout the novel. As an American man who lives in London, what personal experiences informed these frequent philosophical quips about the differences between the two cultures?

I once told a rather shocked English journalist that the only way to live in London as an American was to become an Anglophobe. It's an

English perversity, but they prefer someone who is slightly contemptuous of them to someone who is desperate to fit into English life. I love London for its theaters, its museums, its concert halls, my great friends, its extraordinary ethnic diversity, its social tolerance and social democracy, its stealthy sense of irony, and the fact that it hates self-importance. But I have never considered myself residing in the UK, rather in the city-state that is London. And perhaps that tells you all you need to know about my relationship with the place!

The British legal system, something quite foreign to an American audience, is depicted quite extensively in this work. What were your research methods for getting it right?

I had the great counsel of a wonderful divorce lawyer named Frances Hughes, a very smart, canny woman who had seen it all when it came to the folly of marriages gone wrong, and who gave me a crash course in the British legal system, which, indeed, is so wildly different from our own in the U.S. Life is full of extraordinary ironies. And perhaps the biggest one in relationship to Frances, who was so clever and dry and perceptive when it came to the legal aspects of the novel, is that when my own marriage fell apart six years later she was the lawyer whom I engaged to handle my divorce. And she did a brilliant job, keeping me sane during the yearlong roller coaster ride that ensued.

The art of survival and facing challenges is a common theme in your works. Sally Goodchild is brought to the brink of madness before she begins to fight against powers that are trying to destroy her. Have you faced any challenges when you had to fight, much like your characters, for your own survival?

Put it this way: Like everyone I know I have had my share of personal upheavals and challenges in life. But I have also come to appreciate the fact that such crises are part of the price we pay for being alive. There are crises that you yourself spark. There are crises that others spark. And there is the happenstantial stuff that can send your life into a downward spiral. I think the trick is to understand that we all land in a very dark wood from time to time. Extricating oneself from this enclosed place is never a simple matter, but it usually teaches us enormously about ourselves and the people to whom we are (allegedly) closest.

There is an interesting passage in the novel regarding the breakdown of human relationships: "it also stems from a need for turmoil, for change . . . all of which might be linked to that very human fear of mortality, and the realization that everything is finite. It is this knowledge that makes us scramble even harder for some sort of meaning or import to the minor lives that we lead . . . even if it means pulling everything apart in the process" (p. 302). Do you believe this to be true? Is there something essential built into the human structure that desires to destroy itself?

We are all sold a bill of goods in life about the absolute need for stability. The fact is, nothing in life is truly stable, and to think otherwise is to engage in profound self-delusion. More tellingly, I do think there is a self-destructive aspect built into us all, and one that certain people (in my experience) foster more than others. "Things fall apart, the centre will not hold," Yeats noted in his great poem "The Second Coming." But the truth often is that things fall apart because we ourselves don't want the center to hold.

The passages about grief in this work are very powerful, especially about how grief becomes "an intrinsic part of you." Coupled with the ideas that "everything is fragile," the world you paint of modern life is riddled with fear and misfortune. As Sally whispers to her son at the close of the novel: "It's just the rain. And we'd better get used to it." Is this a perspective you share with your characters?

I sense one of the reasons my books have such a wide and diverse public in so many countries is precisely because they grapple with modern anxiety. And, let's face it, we all love reading about other people's nightmares, especially ones we know could easily happen to us.

When Sally Goodchild first sees Tony Hobbs after he tried to take her son away from her, she can't help but reminisce about their first meeting in the helicopter over a flooded Somalian valley: "That's how our story started—and this is where it had now brought us: to the steps of a court of law, surrounded by our respective legal teams, unable to look each other in the eye" (p. 343). This reflection on the path of one's life is an important one. It is amazing to see where the path one starts on can lead. Did you envision this kind of success when you left Manhattan for Europe in 1977?

Of course I find the way my life has progressed in the thirty-three years since leaving Manhattan nothing less than intriguing (please note the use here of understatement). And yes, I also frequently find myself wondering just what level of alcoholic I'd be right now if I had followed my father's advice and become a lawyer (and I say that as someone with many lawyer friends, but they wanted to enter the legal profession and, ergo, have a great passion for it). I started out running theaters, then wrote plays, then wrote narrative travel books and journalism, then wrote novels, and, in my early forties, finally worked out that my metier was indeed as a novelist. In the midst of all these different creative lives, I have lived in Dublin, London, Paris, and Berlin, learned how to speak fluent French, traveled everywhere from the Australian Outback to Patagonia to Western Samoa to Vietnam to Egypt to Indonesia to Newfoundland to the American Bible Belt to . . . well, I could go on, but it might get tedious. But I still think of so many places that I haven't seen and so many novels I still want to write. As I tell my children constantly, the key to an interesting life is twofold: openness and curiosity. Perhaps there's a third key: doing what you want, not what others expect of you. And you also need to be aware of the fact that life can change in an instant. It's just that we never know when or where that instant will come.

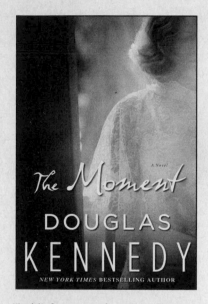
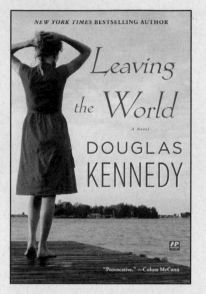